The Children of the Sea

Book Two of The Secrets of Achaea

By T.J. Vincent

Kindle Direct Publishing

Edited by: Francie Futterman

Cover design and maps by: Aven Jones

Printed in the United States of America

to my grandparents, GJ, Baba, and Paw Paw,

for your love and your stories

"There are people whose brilliance continues to light the world even though they are no longer among the living. These lights are particularly bright when the night is dark."

Hannah Senesh

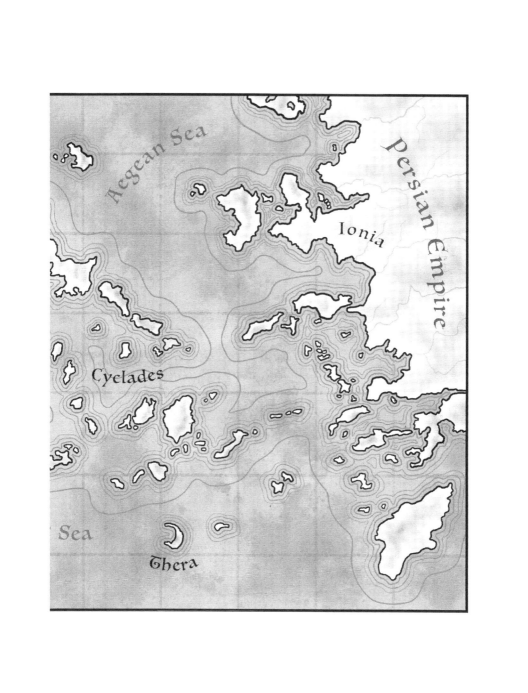

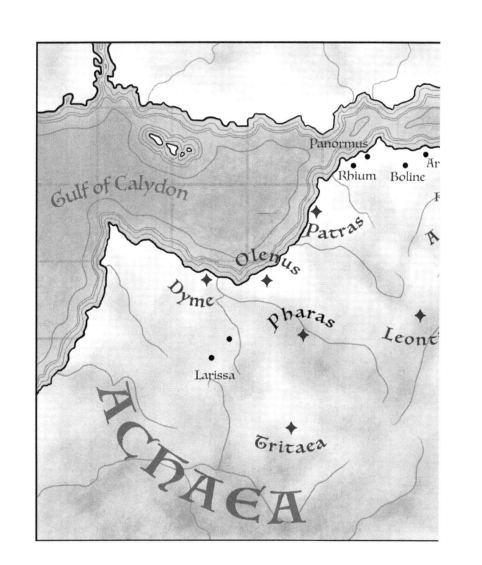

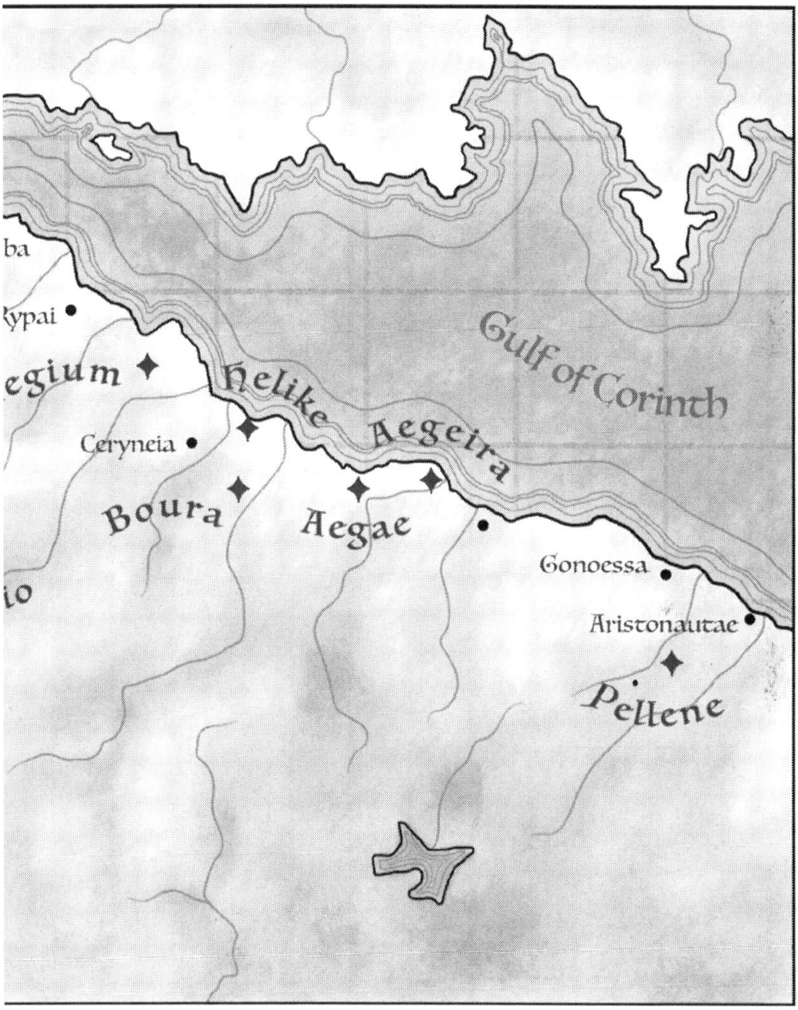

ba
Rypai
egium
Helike
Gulf of Corinth
Ceryneia
Aegeira
Boura
Aegae
Gonoessa
io
Aristonautae
Pellene

Helike

- ◊ Orrin, the Golden Spear: Councilor of Helike
- ◊ Simon, the Flat-Nose: Councilor of Helike
- ◊ Kyros: Councilor of Helike
- ◊ Gaios: Councilor of Helike
- ◊ Furel: Commander of Heliken Army
- ◊ Julan: Commander of Heliken Army
- ◊ Hira: Commander of Heliken Army
- ◊ Nicolaus: Attendant to Orrin
- ◊ Opi: Attendant to Simon
- ◊ Perl: Attendant to Gaios
- ◊ Krassen: Pub Owner
- ◊ Keoki: Farmer
- ◊ Felip: Farmer
- ◊ Agnes: Farmer
- ◊ Rosie: Daughter of Orrin
- ◊ Gerrian: Husband of Rosie
- ◊ Elfie: Wife of Orrin
- ◊ Philomena: Trader
- ◊ Mako: Smith

Boura

- ◊ King Ucalegon: King of Boura
- ◊ Wyrus Warren: Nobleman of Boura
- ◊ Parex the Hammer: Commander of Bouran Army
- ◊ Sir Farlen: Officer of Bouran Army
- ◊ Melani: Artist and Healer
- ◊ Xander Atsali: Smith
- ◊ Loren: Healer of Bouran School
- ◊ Loren's husband: Soldier of Bouran Army
- ◊ Marlo: Baker
- ◊ Aggio: Fisherman
- ◊ Mari: Fisherman
- ◊ Tarlen: Fur-Trader, Fisherman
- ◊ Rizon Atsali: Fisherman
- ◊ Asala: Sister of Melani
- ◊ Osanda: Mother of Melani
- ◊ Corvius: Father of Melani

The Children

◊ Teremos: First Child of the Sea

◊ Gerros: Senior Child of the Sea

◊ Sapphir: Daughter of Teremos

◊ Ivy: Daughter of Sapphir

◊ Cy: Son of Sapphir

◊ Egan: Son of Sapphir

◊ Maya: Daughter of Sapphir

◊ Celia: Daughter of Sapphir

Achaean Territories

Aegium

◊ Zaphan: Inkeep

Rhium

◊ Babs: Fishcook

Patras

◊ Patreus: Representative of Patras

◊ Patreus: First Son of Patreus

◊ Patreus: Second Son of Patreus

Olenus

◊ Basilius: King of Olenus

◊ Venedictos: Advisor to Basilius

◊ Eté: Advisor to Basilius

◊ Rolal: Baker

◊ Tati: Baker

Leontio

◊ Asklepia: Healer

Prologue

A gentle drizzle began to fall, causing Gaios' normally well-groomed hair to cling to his forehead. The loose tunic he wore had a black hood, but he left it draped over his shoulders. Gaios always chose to leave his head uncovered. For some reason, people kept a keen eye on men who tried to hide their faces. It was much easier for him to steal away on nights like these under the guise of total normality.

Gaios had left the Heliken castle shortly after darkness fell, using a cramped tunnel to exit unnoticed. The passageway led to a steep slope, which ended at the river.

He had met his Bouran visitor in secrecy thrice before, always on the damp riverbank. Gaios had little love for the man, but he never let antipathy get in the way of judging a person's value. Affection was the bane of progress; and progress was to be the subject of tonight's meeting.

THE CHILDREN OF THE SEA

Progress... tragic progress...

He still admired the late councilor. The Golden Spear had rarely agreed with Gaios, challenging him vocally on most every proposition. But he had respected this strength of will, knowing that Orrin's concerns were born from a love of their city.

However, Councilor Orrin had been fearfully clumsy with his grasp of the city's politics. Helike would never advance under such a ruler.

He saw too much good.

Gaios noticed the danger of Orrin's bungling positivity when ruthless magicians had plagued Helike. Orrin had viewed them as naught but outliers among more peaceable men and women.

The fool... knowing the power those magicians held?

Gaios had understood that dealing meekly with the Children of the Sea would allow their resentment the chance to fester. Yes, despite Orrin's disagreement, the Children had needed to be expunged. Thankfully, Gaios avoided becoming the face of such a bold endeavor.

Euripides was more than willing to take the hero's role.

While Orrin and Euripides had bickered over how to deal with the Children, Gaios focused on Helike's bright future – a future that would soon become reality. The war with Boura edged ever closer once the Children of the Sea were removed, but Orrin had suspected nothing until the soldiers were already sharpening their blades.

It is truly a shame. The Golden Spear became cleverer just as his days became numbered.

The thought of the great General Orrin swallowing his pride to spy behind the Council's back amused Gaios.

He must have felt so devious... so dishonorable.

And his efforts had been futile.

But the Egyptian... the boy is another story.

Simon had warned Gaios to keep a close eye on Orrin's little servant months before.

"That one listens, Gaios. More than he knows," he had said, fixing his thin eyes on Gaios as they stood in the palace courtyard, the fountain bubbling melodiously.

"Simon, what does it matter? He is naught but a boy. A foreign one, at that."

Simon's mouth had twitched at this. "Foreign boys become Achaean men after living in this city long enough."

The Flat-Nose, of course, had once been a foreign boy himself.

I should have listened, should have addressed the boy earlier.

Now, he was certain that Orrin's servant had released Helike's most prized prisoner. He must have struck a deal with the assassin in their brief conversation. The Golden Spear would not have known. Certainly, he could never condone anything so drastic.

Gaios was uncertain if the boy had survived the explosion. Perhaps he perished alongside his councilor. Informants had given mixed reports on the matter. If all were to be believed, the boy had been stabbed earlier in the battle, killed himself after seeing Orrin's lifeless form, and also ran away as other soldiers tried to save their leader.

It cannot be all three.

But Gaios had a strong suspicion that the servant was alive, somewhere in Helike. Gaios closed his eyes, listening to the river. The Bouran would arrive any minute. He brushed a drop of water from his brow.

Perhaps the Golden Spear had ordered the boy to release the prisoner. He might have thought it would end the war, somehow.

Gaios knew that Orrin was perplexed by the fact that Rizon Atsali was not a known Bouran soldier, nor a Child of the Sea. To Orrin, those had been the only options.

Perhaps he still believed Rizon Atsali to be one of Ucalegon's men. Releasing him could have been a... peace offering of sorts.

Gaios picked up a pebble, wiping away the grime with a long finger. He rotated it slowly, sliding his thumb along its rough edge before flicking it towards the river.

Only a fool would think a Bouran soldier would kill a councilor of Helike.

The rock splashed, indistinguishable from the falling rain.

A fool who refused to learn the most unsavory of Achaea's secrets... and Orrin never bothered to learn the true nature of the Fishermen.

This, of course, was what Rizon Atsali had been – a Fisherman who had lost sight of the catch, and nearly paid with his life. The Fishermen knew how to negotiate with desperate traitors.

When a man knows he has been caught, he becomes very

easy to use.

Perhaps, something about Rizon Atsali captivated Orrin's sympathy and attention – enough to send his little steward to finish the dirty work. More likely, Gaios figured, the boy acted of his own accord.

Gaios picked up another pebble. The rain fell harder. The mystery of Rizon Atsali's escape bothered him.

If the Egyptian boy was alive, surely, he would turn up.

Gaios skipped the pebble gracefully and picked up another. He would determine the truth when he had the boy.

Unless...

The Flat-Nose had left during the Battle at the Beach, assuring the Council he would only return with Rizon Atsali. Simon's eagerness to find the escaped prisoner would make even more sense if he were trying to cover his own treachery.

No... no, Simon knows Rizon Atsali's importance. He would have been a vital prisoner for me. Helike continues to love Euripides. The people long for justice.

Rizon's execution would have been a great triumph for Gaios and the Council.

No, it could not have been Simon.

Gaios' long, spindly fingers tapped lightly against his ever-dampening robe, as if laughing at him. Gaios took a deep breath, annoyed at himself for doubting that the servant boy was the culprit. He whipped the rock into the river; the splash was audible.

Or am I annoyed for ignoring what could be true?

Another light splash caused Gaios to refocus. He straightened as he noticed the skiff gliding down the river. Inside, a broad-shouldered man paddled as another sat huddled beneath a dark cloak. The paddler wore black chainmail, which reflected curiously under the moonlit rainclouds. Gaios could not see it in the darkness, but he knew a hammer was branded on his left bicep.

Parex the Hammer.

The Champion of Boura, general of their military, and one of the most impressive warriors in Achaea – Parex looked unnatural without his great Warhammer. As he approached, Gaios spoke first.

"I hear you're wielding a battle-axe these days, friend."

"W-What does it matter, C-Councilor?"

Parex spoke with a stutter, which Gaios always found humorous. It was at odds with his confidence and splendor.

"I worry that our friends might not recognize Parex the Hammer on the battlefield. That is, if he isn't wielding a hammer."

"M-My hammer isn't th-the thing that p-people recognize when th-the fighting begins."

He leapt off the boat, landing beside Gaios before tying it to a nearby tree.

"Careful there, Parex. The ground's slippery. We wouldn't want Boura's champion meeting an untimely death at the hand of a light rain."

Parex sneered, touching the dagger at his belt. The message was plain enough.

"I mean no threat. Wouldn't dare it, in fact. I fear my talents with a knife leave something to be desired."

Gaios could feel the cold steel of his own dagger beneath his cloak and hoped there would be no need to draw it. He was more able than he let on, but diplomacy would be easier than killing Parex the Hammer.

Parex's lips thinned, but he withdrew his hand. He strode back to the boat and reached for the man who had remained seated.

"Ah yes, and a good evening to you, my Lord," Gaios said, letting the politeness in his voice cover the small insult.

The man huffed and replied brusquely, "Greetings to you, as well, Gaios. I continue to wonder why you don't send messengers and letters. It would be easier than meeting on a rainy night."

"Yet, here we are. Messengers and letters leave too much out of my own, capable hands," Gaios said wiggling his spindly fingers.

The man snorted, removing his cloak to reveal a regal robe. He was short and thin, which must have factored into his ever-suspicious attitude.

Easy to be suspicious when a gentle breeze could be the death of you.

His head was balding, which Simon joked was the reason the man had crowned himself. Gaios knew he couldn't let these preconceived notions of the man affect his manner. He extended his hand.

"I do apologize for the weather; I'm sure you understand the need for us to be covert."

King Ucalegon of Boura accepted the gesture, then wiped his hands on his robes.

"Yes, of course, Lord Gaios. I believe we have much to discuss, and precious little time."

Chapter 1

Ivy

"Ivy! Ivyyyy! Wait!"

Grassy hillsides flashed in Ivy's peripheral vision as she sprinted away from her younger siblings. Cy was ten paces behind Celia, closing fast. His blonde hair gleamed in the mid-afternoon sun, bringing out the startling blue of his eyes. Even from this far away, Ivy could make them out.

"Ivy! He's going to get me!"

Celia stumbled, catching herself on the soft ground and shrieking. Cy skidded to a stop, tapping her roughly on the shoulder.

"Gotcha!"

Ivy grinned at her brother. Celia pounded her fist angrily into the dirt.

"Ivy! You said you'd wait for me! We were gonna hide! He wouldn't have found us! He wouldn't have EVER found us!"

"You're too slow, C!" Ivy exclaimed, bouncing on her feet out of Celia's reach.

Celia's hazel curls were frizzy and wild, making her look like some feral creature. Ivy felt bad that her sister seemed upset, but this was how the game was supposed to be played!

"Yeah, C, I would've caught you guys anyway," Cy added boastfully.

"No, you wouldn't have! Celia and I would've hid somewhere you'd never find us."

Celia frowned, looking puzzled, "Then why didn't you wait for me?"

"I told you, C! You're TOO. SLOW! Let's go, Cy."

Cy nodded, hopping over Celia's arm as she grabbed for him.

"See you at dinner, sister!" Cy called, laughing, as he and Ivy rushed away.

Celia's protests faded into the distance as Cy and Ivy raced through the fields. To her left, Ivy could see dozens of cattle grazing peacefully. She and Cy would hide behind the grapevines again. Just as they did yesterday. Celia never ventured that far away from Fil and Agnes' house, so they were sure to win the game.

Ivy always won.

They'd been at the farm for a few weeks now, spending most of the days playing outside and helping Keoki with the cows, or Fil with the grapes. It was nice to finally explore the mainland. Ivy missed being able to swim in the ocean every day, but it was exciting to see the area surrounding the big city, and she loved being with Fil and Agnes.

Kiki seems to like being back here, too.

Ivy remembered how excited she had been when Mother brought him back to the island that morning. Keoki had looked thinner than usual, and his beard was all scruffy. Ivy didn't like the beard, so she was happy when he shaved it off. He had looked a little angrier that day, too.

But Kiki's always angry.

Mother had picked Maya up and happily announced that they were going back to Agnes and Felip's farm. Ivy, Celia, and Cy couldn't contain their excitement, whooping aloud. They were finally going to see the Heliken countryside! Egan didn't seem to care much. Maya had looked nervous. Ivy could understand why Maya felt scared to be back on the mainland. The last time they had been there together...

I shouldn't have taken her with me. I knew I should've gone alone.

Well, part of her thought that way. But Ivy also knew she had needed Maya more than her little sister was aware.

The bandits... she saved me, and I...

"Ivy," Cy whispered sharply, "Come on, get behind the vines."

"Right, behind the vines."

Ivy dropped to the ground, rolling next to Cy. She picked a plump grape hanging eye-level and popped it into her mouth.

Sweet, sugary juice coated her taste buds, and Ivy chewed delightedly.

"I never knew they had grapes when I was here last time. Kiki only showed me some of the cows," Ivy said.

Cy looked away, pretending he hadn't heard.

He hates when I bring up the last time.

Ivy was certain that Cy was jealous of her adventures, wanting the glory and excitement for himself.

He wouldn't have been able to fight off those bandits like I did.

"Cy, do you want a grape?"

"I can reach them myself," he responded, still avoiding her gaze.

Ivy felt unsure how to proceed, not wanting to upset her brother any more than she already had. Cy plucked a grape and squished it in his palm. Before Ivy could say anything else, she heard gentle footsteps walking along the rows of grapevines.

Cy finally looked at her and nodded seriously. Celia must have found them at last, and they couldn't let her catch them.

What made her brave enough to come this far?

Cy and Ivy slunk back away from the noise, hoping to disappear into the plants. Suddenly, the leaves behind them moved.

"Gotcha!" Celia squealed in delight, grabbing both her siblings with elation.

"Ah, so the two great explorers have been discovered!" Felip said, his deep, mellow voice reverberating through the field.

"Yes! I found you guys! You said I wouldn't find you, but I did!"

"You cheated!" Cy said with indignation, "Fil isn't allowed to help!"

"Oh, I didn't have anything to do with this, son," Fil said, smiling innocently.

Celia lifted her arms in the air, revealing the tiny scratches on both her arms that came from her bird, Blackwing. Ivy knew they'd been beaten. It was revenge for double-crossing Celia, she supposed.

"Good job, C," Ivy said, patting her sister on the arm.

Cy looked at Ivy, betrayed, "No, Fil helped! We didn't even try to run away!"

Felip sauntered over, brushed the dirt off Cy's chest, and offered him some fresh grapes, "Now, son, be graceful in defeat. That is something we all must learn."

Cy maintained his pouty look but held his tongue. Something about Felip's gentle smile lines and wispy white hair made everyone feel calmer. The old man gestured to the sun, which was quickly approaching the horizon.

"Shall we walk back to the house, children? I'm getting quite hungry myself, you know. I believe your mother has made quite the feast."

Ivy smiled at that. She couldn't help herself. Most meals were good at the farm, but it seemed like years since Ivy had enjoyed one of her mother's specially cooked dinners. She was tiring of cheese, bread, and vegetables.

"What are we having tonight?" she asked.

"I believe a nice, big fish and some meaty sea crabs," Felip said.

Even Cy's spirits seem lifted at the mention of fish and crab. Ivy and Cy both shook the rest of the dirt off themselves as they prepared to enjoy a delicious meal. Ivy took Celia's hand. She was pleased at how tightly her little sister held on.

****

By the time Ivy finished bathing, the sky was orange and pink. Celia, Cy, Egan, and Maya were already sitting around the small table. The cramped space was meant for only three. The smell of seafood wafted through the room, and Ivy could feel her mouth begin to water.

"Ivy, sit by me!" Celia said, patting the empty chair by her side.

Ivy obliged, noticing how Cy looked at the floor with a mood resembling his older brother, Egan. Maya sat between the boys, running her finger along Egan's arm slowly.

She's the only one that can make him smile.

"Where's Mother?" Ivy asked, watching Fil and Agnes maneuver the kitchen busily.

"Your mother will be back with Keoki in just a few minutes,"

Agnes said, "Or a few hours. The two of them sneaking off... it's becoming far too regular!"

Agnes breathed hard and audibly through her nose as she imagined all the things that Keoki and Ivy's mother could be doing. Ivy loved Agnes, but sometimes preferred Fil's more calming presence.

And she doesn't like Mother all that much.

Ivy suspected this, at least. She could not see why anyone wouldn't love her mother.

"Well now, dear," Fil said, "We know they're planning this big journey of theirs."

"What journey?" Celia asked, swinging her legs beneath the table.

"Celia, they've told you every night for the past week!" Ivy interjected, annoyed at her sister's stupidity.

"Oh. They're going to Paters, that's right."

"Pa-tras," Ivy said, "P-A-T-R-A-S. They're going to Patras."

"Pa-tr-as," Celia repeated, sounding the word out with care, "Patras. Why are they going there again?"

Ivy sighed, looking at Celia's round face, which was lost in her mountain of bushy curls. She wished Mother were staying longer with them at the farm. She had missed her more than she thought possible when she'd run away with Maya.

I just wanted to see the big city. I didn't want to run away.

But now, she was finally here, on the mainland with her family. And Mother was leaving with Keoki.

At least I have everyone else with me this time.

"They're looking for Keoki's brother," Fil answered.

Agnes glanced at him out of the corner of her eye as she came to join them at the table, "That's right, children. Keoki thinks he knows where his baby brother is after all this time."

"And your mother will be a great help, of course," Fil added, "She's a resourceful woman, that one."

He gave Ivy a wink, as if the two of them were sharing a secret. *Does he know about Mother? And us?*

Mother always told Ivy and her siblings to control their powers carefully, especially around people without such gifts. It was crucial that no living person knew of their curious capabilities.

"I didn't know Keoki had a brother," Cy said, finally lifting his eyes from the floor at last.

Ivy pondered this. She also hadn't heard Keoki mention a brother. He sometimes spoke of his parents, who had died a long time ago, but he never referenced any living family.

"Ah, yes," Fil said, "He doesn't like to talk much about Keon. I fear it is a painful memory."

"Keon and Keoki," Celia said, "That's funny."

"No, it's not it's just their names," Cy retorted.

The two began to bicker, and Felip leaned back in his chair. The fish on the table was still warm, but steam had stopped rising from its pink flesh. She understood why Keoki wouldn't want to talk about his brother if they had not seen each other for a long time.

16

Suddenly, Ivy's head began to hurt. A face flashed in her mind – one she didn't recognize. But it was still somewhat familiar. The slender boy had black hair and green eyes. He looked remarkably similar to Ivy. Then, the boy became one of the bandits, holding a knife to her throat as Maya let out a blood-curdling scream. The bandit was dying now, his eyes frenzied with pain as the muscles of his neck spasmed.

The images vanished in an instant and Ivy gasped softly. Cy and Celia stopped their argument, and Cy resumed staring at the floor. Only Maya seemed to notice Ivy's flushed face from across the table. Her green eyes were filled with concern. She looked just like Ivy.

Of course, she's like me. We're sisters.

"Sorry we kept you," Keoki said, taking a chair next to Ivy quickly.

Ivy found herself distracted by his muscular arms and wild black hair, which curled like Celia's but fit his frame much better. Her mother followed him in, smiling warmly at her children and acknowledging Felip and Agnes with a polite nod.

"Yes, we are nearly ready to leave tomorrow morning. It all smells wonderful here, Agnes."

Agnes gave a tight smile that didn't reach her eyes.

"Thank you, dear. I hope it tastes as good as it smells! Shall we pray, children?"

As Ivy took her sister's soft hand and Keoki's rougher one, she tried to remember what had upset her so much moments earlier.

But when she fixed her eyes on Maya to focus, she saw only the face of her sister.

Chapter 2

Melani

Melani could scarcely recognize herself in the bronze plate. She looked down into the iron bowl, filled with black paste and locks of brown hair. The Flat-Nose had given her the dark hair dye and a sharp blade that morning.

"It may shock you to hear this, but few will recognize you without your hair. Even someone as pretty as you."

Melani hadn't complained. The Flat-Nose was correct, of course. If she and Rizon were going to flee the Fisherman, to truly disappear, she needed to commit to some drastic changes before docking in Patras. Her skin was flecked with sunspots and burns from being on the deck of the ship. Every day she tried retreating to the cabin but found that her stomach couldn't take the rocking. Whenever the ship bobbed up and down with the waves, she could feel her insides shifting. She vomited into the sea once or twice most mornings.

Is it the baby? Or just the ocean?

She was still not visibly larger, though she had been pregnant for over a moon's turn at least. Whether she was sick from the ocean or the baby, Melani could not wait to be back on dry land.

They had left Helike ten days prior, boarding the Heliken councilor's ship after leaving the gruesome scene on the beach. She spent the first few days in silence. She was furious at Rizon for making her leave, and furious with herself for giving in. Though he likely would have forced her onto the ship.

There was wisdom in fleeing; he is not entirely in the wrong.

Melani tried to convince herself of this, knowing that the Fishermen posed a very immediate threat, especially if she and Rizon remained in Helike. But she could not rid herself of the guilt of leaving Xander.

He would not have done that to me. He would have walked right into the palace and taken me back himself.

Of course, she could only hope to save him if he were alive.

He must be alive. He must... for me... for the child...

She had not spoken to her crewmates until the fourth day of their journey.

"The voyage to Patras shouldn't be this long, Rizon. And why can't I see the coast? Has Patras moved since I last visited?"

"Ah, the brooding lover broods no more," the Flat-Nose answered, stepping between Rizon and Melani, "Forgive me, dear.

I shouldn't trouble you for mourning."

Melani gave him a scathing look, trying to appear tougher than she felt, "You're right."

Simon clicked his tongue, "I am grievously sorry, Lady Melani. I fear my old habits are still lingering from my time on the Council."

"There is nothing old about those habits," Rizon cut in, stepping so the three were facing each other in a triangle, "I believe it was only a few days ago that I was your prisoner."

"Perhaps not *old* habits. But ones I hope not to use much longer. I have my doubts that Gaios will allow me to return to Helike once he puzzles together the nature of your escape."

He laughed. It was a strange hoarse sound that didn't agree with his voice or features. Melani tried not to stare at his nose. She closed her eyes as a particularly large wave hit the side of the ship, sea spray exploding onto the deck.

I mustn't be angry with Rizon; he is as sad as I am.

She wiped sea foam from her cheek, "And we thank you for that. I don't mean to be contentious, Lord Simon. You understand my grief though, I'm sure. As does Rizon."

She had wondered then, if the Flat-Nose loved as she did.

He can't love as I do.

"No need to call me lord, Lady Melani."

"No need to call me lady."

They had gone on like this, and afterwards Melani was much more amicable. In fact, she found herself taking quite a liking to

Simon, as well as the ship's captain, Lathor, and the deckhand, Col.

Lathor was a burly man with strong hands and a ship's wheel tattooed on his left shoulder. He was often shirtless, exposing his immense black torso. Xander was muscular too, though less bulky and more chiseled than Lathor. Lathor was a gregarious man, always cheerful despite his hard exterior. He hailed from Nok, far south and west from Achaea, across the sea and thousands of miles of desert. He and his brother, Col, had commandeered their vessel as their farming village warred with a neighboring state.

"Ship takes us all the way to the Spartans," Col had explained in his broken speech, "Then Ionia and Egypt. The Simon, he finds us in Egypt."

"Oh, we've got much to thank Simon for, don't we Col?" Lathor added.

"The Simon gives us jobs. Take me here, take friends there."

Melani wondered how the Flat-Nose had come across Lathor and Col but was thankful he had. Lathor had been the one to explain the reason for the extra-long journey to Patras.

"Well, Missus, you know how it is. The Fisherfolk..."

"Fishermen?"

"Yes, Fishermen. They've eyes everywhere. They see a ship fleeing Helike for Patras, you bet they'll follow by land. They see a ship headed to the open sea, and they either have to take ship to follow, or suppose it's just a trader, and let it go."

"And if they try to follow?" Melani had asked, glancing behind them as the ship drifted across the open ocean, fearing that Tarlen and other trained killers would be on their tail.

No, Tarlen is dead.

The memory of Rizon's blade piercing the supposed fur trader's neck made Melani shiver. She still flinched at the thought of his warm blood spattering her legs.

"Well, if'n they tried to follow, they'd have a tall task catchin' us. No ship moves like *Eagle*. She's fast, she is. So, we'll sail out five days, then turn to the West, and to Patras we go."

Melani still worried that she'd wake up one day surrounded by Fishermen, though it was encouraging to know that they weren't sailing aimlessly. She was unsure where they would go after Patras, but Melani hoped she could see her family one last time.

Rizon must have some plan... besides disguising ourselves and leaving Helike... there must be more.

The last of the paste was out of her hair now, leaving behind short, black hair. Melani almost laughed at the sight.

Xander loves my hair. It looks silly this dark.

Her smile faded as she thought of Xander again. She took a deep breath and ascended the stairs. The deck was easier on her stomach anyway, and her brief time below had already made the baby stir.

Melani stumbled when she exited the cabin, as the ship rocked against another wave. Col caught her. He was thinner than his brother but still a large man. His face was younger, and he smiled often.

"Oh, don't falls then!"

"Thank you, Col."

"Looks at your hair then! Black like mine!"

Melani laughed, "And shorter, too."

Col grinned, twisting a rope-like coil of his dark hair with a finger. He held her arm gently and helped her to her favorite spot, towards the bow of the ship. There was a pile of blankets so she could sit comfortably, and the mast kept it relatively shady. Clouds filled the sky today, thankfully.

"Sit then, Missus Melani. The Simon wants to talks with you."

Melani sat, sighing as she leaned against the rail. Her stomach settled a little as she gazed at the foggy horizon. Her eyes adjusted, and she realized that she could make out land. She turned her gaze to the other side and was surprised to see the same.

The Strait of Rhium. Melani could picture maps of Achaea. They were nearing Patras.

Thank the gods!

She hadn't been back to Patras in over a year. She longed to see her family.

Will they be in less danger if I stay far away? Or more?

Either way, the thought of being off the ship and back in her hometown warmed Melani's insides.

"Yes, we are close," Simon said, sitting next to Melani on the wood. "I saw you admiring our surroundings. It's a welcome sight, isn't it? I do enjoy the sea, especially with Col and Lathor. But I also despise it."

He coughed out his queer, hoarse laugh.

"Quite a welcome sight."

"How are you feeling, Melani?" Rizon asked.

Melani blinked. She hadn't heard Rizon approach. He leaned against the rail opposite Melani.

He never sits.

He was growing his beard out. It was well-groomed, and he looked much less wild than he had when she'd first seen him. Melani shuddered once more. She pictured Xander's brother, standing over the body of Tarlen with feral eyes, his blade dripping red.

He's much better like this.

"Better. Better now I can see land. We're only a few hours from Patras?"

"Indeed," Simon confirmed, "Two hours, maybe three. No ships behind us, and none in front. I'm sure we'll see plenty once we arrive, but we aren't being followed."

So far as we know...

"I was hoping we weren't being followed," she said.

Rizon crossed his legs, "Not being followed, but the Fishermen will be coming for us, Melani. I've been talking to the Flat... Simon. I've been talking to Simon, and we agree that the two of us need to die."

Simon nodded.

"I would prefer not to," Melani said, "If I have any voice in the matter."

"Oh, Melani. You're sharper than that," Simon said coyly.

She paused, "Oh."

"See, you caught on much more quickly than Rizon Atsali. I told you she's smarter than you," he added, smirking at Rizon.

"I never claimed otherwise."

Melani blushed, and Simon winked at her.

"Yes, the Fishermen will pursue you until they know their job is done. Right now, they've surely found their dead fur trader. They know you two are on the move. But if they are informed of your death – need I say more?"

"Right. So how do we plan on doing that?" Melani asked.

"I still have Fishermen. I mean, I have people I know. People who I know are Fishermen. One in Patras, well, he owes me," Rizon explained, "I'll go alone. You go home, to your parents. Tell them to leave the city or at least be cautious for the next few weeks."

"You think they're in danger?" Melani wondered.

"I am unsure how much the Fishermen know about you. But we should assume they know everything," Rizon said.

Melani heart contracted. She missed her family dearly. Her mother and sister would be so excited to see her. It would be worth it to see them one more time; she wasn't sure how many more chances she would get.

"You go home and warn your parents. I'll find my Fisherman, make him tell the rest that the job is done."

"That we've been dealt with?"

"Yes. I think... I think that will at least buy us time to get away for good."

"I'm not getting away, Rizon. I'm going back for him."

"Mel, he's… it's not safe."

Simon watched the exchange, riveted as though he were at the Olympic games.

"Will you have me go alone? Because I'm going," she declared.

"No," Rizon responded, looking flustered, "If you go, I go."

Melani glared at him. She wanted to make him ashamed. For giving up on Xander. Rizon's normally hawkish features seemed docile as he met her eyes.

"Are you sure you can trust this Fisherman?" Melani asked.

"Yes," he said firmly.

"Don't be stupid," Simon interjected.

"Okay, no. But it's our best chance of throwing them off our trail. The Fishermen are relentless. They're always watching. They have ears everywhere, I know."

"And do they listen with their eyes?" she quipped, trying to make light of the situation.

Rizon remained stony, but Simon clapped his hands and bobbed his head forward in amusement. Rizon glowered at him.

"Oh, cheer up, Rizon Atsali. You two are on the right path."

"Where will you go?" Melani said.

"I have business to attend to throughout Achaea," Simon said, the same answer he gave everyone.

The fog was beginning to clear, though the sky remained cloudy. The ship had passed through the strait, now banking left as it rounded the northernmost part of Achaea and began its course to Patras. To home.

"Private business. Won't you just tell me before I die?"

He chuckled, "But you won't die, will you? And I do hope I'll be seeing you again. Perhaps I'll tell you then, yes?"

She patted his hand gently, "I would like that."

Chapter 3

Nicolaus

The wine was the best Nicolaus had ever tasted, but he couldn't bring himself to enjoy it. He was lounging uncomfortably in one of the soft chairs that belonged to a man much larger than him. Orrin's wife, Elfie, had just retired for the evening, patting Nic lightly with her only arm as she left. She insisted that he sit in Orrin's old chair when they gathered for dinner every night.

"It's the nicest in the house dear, and I'd feel strange taking my husband's spot."

If it feels strange for you, imagine how it feels for me.

The Council had held Orrin's funeral three days prior, dressing The Golden Spear in a clean himation and laying an ornamental golden spear alongside him. Thousands attended. Nic had stayed home with the Bouran soldier; Elfie seemed to think it best that he continue to recover.

Nic knew his body had already healed in the week that had passed since the Battle at the Beach, but he was glad he had an excuse to stay out of sight.

I don't think I could have seen him.

Nic didn't want to break down in front of Orrin's family, though he knew they would understand more than most. It wasn't entirely from sadness either. Of course, he felt remorse for his fallen friend, but he didn't want to look at Orrin's body knowing what lay before him – knowing the task Orrin had left him with – and knowing that he would fail.

"Help them... all of them." How can I?

Elfie was remarkably at peace; at least, she seemed that way. Her eyes had welled with tears the moment he arrived after the battle, with the Bouran hero leaning heavily against him.

It was as if she knew without me saying a thing.

Elfie had waved him inside and given her hand to help support the wounded soldier. With their combined effort, they were able to lay him on the bed that had once belonged to Cerius, Orrin and Elfie's son. It was the very same bed that Nic had used after trying to help the baker girl.

The poor girl. That seems like years ago.

The Bouran had muttered thanks before losing consciousness. Elfie examined his leg, before leaving to retrieve a strange mixture from her room.

"Gods, what is that stuff?" Nic had asked, repulsed by the

smell.

"Strengthen your stomach, child. Wine to clean it, honey to ease the burns, and a few other choice ingredients..."

His skin was blackened, and it looked as if some sort of leather had melded to the flesh. Nic guessed that the Bouran would never walk again.

How will this disgusting concoction do him any good?

"...if it saves his leg, he won't mind the smell."

I wasn't worried about him *minding the smell.*

Nic had erased the smell with a cask of wine. That was it. Elfie asked no questions, shed no tears in front of Nic, and went on with her life. Elfie's daughter was not so stoic. When the news was delivered to her later in the day, Rosie had fallen to the ground and sobbed.

I should have comforted her. Said anything to help.

Instead, Nic had averted his gaze and tried not to weep himself. Gerrian had taken her outside to console her, though Nic could tell that Orrin's death distressed him greatly, too.

Rosie avoided Nic most of the time, engaging in brief conversations on occasion. He got the sense that she was mad that he had brought a Bouran soldier into their home after her father's death.

And she doesn't even know he may be the one who caused it.

A voice in the back of his mind seemed to whisper something, yet he couldn't figure out what it was. He looked at his wine and shuddered.

Or did he have nothing to do with it? Why did I even bring him here in the first place?

Nic still harbored no anger for the man, though he could not figure out why. He wanted to feel hatred. But the Bouran was quiet and polite, and amazingly, able to walk on his burned leg if he leaned most of his weight on a wooden crutch. Nic often found himself wondering how he could view the man as an enemy when he acted and talked so similarly to them.

He set down his cup of wine and closed his eyes.

How many cups have I had since coming here?

When he opened them again, the man was hobbling into the room.

"I couldn't sleep. Mind if I join you?" he asked, already pulling out the chair diagonal from Nic's.

"Be my guest. I suppose that's what we are."

"Is there any more wine left, Nicolaus?"

"Nic, please. I don't feel proper enough for Nicolaus."

"Ah. Well in that case, Nic. Is there any wine left?"

"Oh, yes. Sorry," he said, sliding a pitcher to the Bouran.

The soldier's name was Xander. He had sandy hair and tan skin, though not as dark as Nic's. He was perhaps three years older than Nic and looked three times more muscular. He had a sunspot on one of his hands, a unique imperfection that still made Nic jealous. Something in his eyes was vaguely familiar, though Nic could not place the feeling. Now that he was cleaned up, Nic wondered if Rosie noticed how handsome the man was.

That's stupid, she has Gerrian. And why should I care?

"So Xander," he asked, "What did you do in Boura?"

Before you started killing Helikens, that is.

Xander took a deep sip of his wine before responding, "I made weapons. Armor and swords and stuff. I was a smith."

"So, you armed your soldiers in addition to fighting with them? You're doubly dangerous to us."

Nic tried to keep his tone light, but the joke was rooted in truth. He could tell Xander felt uncomfortable.

"Well, I armed all sorts of people across Achaea. Probably armed some of the people that took a stab at me on the beach," he laughed then, "Makes me think I shouldn't make everything so perfect all the time."

"Would've made killing them that much easier."

Xander cocked his head, "I don't find killing of any type easy. Have I done something to offend you?"

Nic paused.

Orrin would've liked this one. He doesn't mince words.

Nic looked away from Xander, somewhat ashamed, "I'm sorry. I don't know if I'm supposed to despise you or not. It's... it's a strange feeling."

Xander considered this for a moment. He took another sip of his wine.

"It's good wine, Nic."

"Thanks. I mean, it's not mine, but I'm sure Elfie would appreciate that."

"This wine would be good if it were a Bouran vintage, too. Do you know what I mean?"

"I... no. I like the wine, but–"

"All I'm saying is that I don't particularly care where this wine came from. I'd like it if it were Heliken; I'd like it just the same in my home city."

"So, you think I shouldn't hate you."

"I don't care. But I don't hate you because you are of Helike. Nothing good can come from that."

An interesting metaphor.

"Then why join the Bouran army? Why kill men from Helike? Why... why go after Orrin?"

Nic could feel the blood rushing to his face. His anger was not directed towards Xander, though he wanted it to be. Xander remained calm, finishing his cup and refilling it immediately.

"I didn't fight because I wanted to kill, Nic. I joined for the same reason you did. You were on that beach, just as I was. If you were better with a spear, I could be asking you the very same questions."

This time, he finished his wine in one gulp. He refilled it again.

"I don't even know why I joined," Nic said, topping off his cup as well.

"Sure, you do. Honor. Pride for your city," Xander said, waving his hand, "all that horseshit you learn as a child."

Nic stayed silent, thinking this over, though his mind was beginning to slow as he drank more wine. Xander seemed as sharp as ever.

I didn't learn that as a child. Why do I care for this city?

"Would you do it again?" Nic asked.

"Fight?"

"Yeah."

"For the honor of my city? No, I suppose not." Xander seemed amused by his own answer.

Nor would I. Not after the beach.

"Then, what for? Is there something?"

A smile crept over his face and he took a deep breath, "Something? No."

Nic was confused. He looked at the wine in his cup. It was deep red.

If not something, then what?

The first image that came to him was his family. He thought of Gabbi and Ibbie, his little sisters whom he hadn't seen in years. Their faces became Orrin's, Krassen's, Elfie's. And Opi. He was surprised to think of Opi before he even thought of Rosie.

"Is there some*one*?"

Xander nodded sagely, his face reddening. The wine was settling in his larger frame. "Someone, yes. She... yes. Is there someone for you?"

Nic thought of this person who had softened a warrior like Xander. He wished there was someone for him.

"I don't know," Nic said, "I have friends and family. I love them."

They sat in silence with their wine for a few minutes.

"Do you have a family?" Nic asked.

"A brother. A brother and parents. But I haven't seen my brother in years."

"What does he do?"

Xander laughed, "I'm not quite sure, to be honest. He would've been a great soldier; he was always faster and better than me. Smarter, too. But I don't know."

Nic wondered if Xander's brother lived somewhere in Helike.

"I don't know what my family does either. I haven't seen my sisters since they were just young girls. I... I was taken before I got to see them grow up."

"From where?" Xander said, genuinely interested.

"Egypt. Memphis actually. You wouldn't know of it."

"I've heard of Egypt."

"No, I meant, never mind."

Xander laughed and Nic began to giggle.

"It's good wine, isn't it?" he said.

Xander nodded. "It's good wine."

✳✳✳✳

Nic woke the next morning to the sound of Elfie rustling in the kitchen. She was stirring a cup of ironwort tea with her only hand while a pot boiled over a fire nearby. A drop of honey clung to the side of the cup. He had fallen asleep in Orrin's chair.

Oh gods.

Nic's head pounded from the wine. His back ached from sleeping in a slumped position, and he envied Xander for somehow finding his way to bed. Nic wondered if Xander felt as terrible as he did.

He probably feels perfectly fine.

"Good morning, Nicolaus," Elfie said, green eyes fixed on the honey. She wiped it off and licked her finger.

"Hi," Nic croaked, and cringed at the sound of his voice. "How are you this morning?"

He tried to muster the energy to stand but was glued to the chair.

"Doing well. I see you finished off the wine."

"Yes, sorry. I had a cup or two with Xander after you retired. I can go buy a cask today from the market."

Gods, I hope it wasn't expensive.

"Oh, no worries, dear. I wouldn't have finished it without help. I'm afraid wine makes an old lady like me quite tired."

Every time Nic opened his mouth it felt as if he were peeling his tongue from the back of his teeth.

How can my throat be this dry after drinking so much?

If Nic had a chance to sit down and talk with the gods, or whatever had made him the way he was, he would be sure to ask that question.

"Are Rosie and Gerrian around?" Nic asked, trying to

revitalize the conversation.

"No, they went for a walk by the river. Then they'll be going to the market. Perhaps they can pick out more wine if they desire it. The Bouran is still fast asleep."

"He isn't the worst sort," Nic said.

He still felt guilty for bringing Xander to Orrin's family. The man had certainly played a part in Orrin's death. The hushed voice in his mind whispered again.

"Yes. Yes, I suppose he is not. He's nothing but a brave soldier. Orrin would have liked him," Elfie smiled sadly.

"Elfie, I... I never got to apologize. I–"

"Apologize? Don't be foolish, boy."

Nic slunk deeper into his chair. He knew she would be mad at him for being such a worthless steward on the day of battle. He'd let the Bourans get too close to Orrin.

I should've given my life for him.

Elfie sat beside him, setting down her tea and putting a hand on his shoulder. "Nicolaus, you don't owe an apology to anybody. My husband was a wonderful man, but I pleaded with him time and again to put down the spear. When Cerius left... and Rosie's children... I was sure he would lay that cursed golden thing to rest."

Nic couldn't put any words together.

"You should have heard the way he spoke about you," Elfie continued, taking a sip of her tea, "I hadn't heard him talk about anyone that highly since before our son joined the League's Guard. He wanted you to take his place, not just clean his room and bring his food."

"He... he did?"

"Of course, he did! He shared too much important information with you as far as I'm concerned," Elfie laughed. "I don't mean any offense, dear, but I wouldn't have told my steward nearly as much. Or my spouse. He knew you were smart and brave – I'll say, I believed him more after that night with the baker's girl."

"That wasn't brave."

"Oh hush, dear. Anyway, you don't need to apologize for being someone Orrin trusted. I should thank you for that; he needed someone in those damned Council chambers that he could trust."

Nic blushed.

He trusted me...

Elfie took a small sip of her tea and set the cup down. She took a deep breath, then wiped her mouth.

"So, tell me, Nicolaus. I've thought about asking for a few days now," Elfie met his eyes with a mixture of anger, sadness, and sympathy.

I'm too sick for this.

"How did my husband die?"

Chapter 4

Keoki

Keoki had never left Helike before. He'd lived with Felip and Agnes at the farm, had a brief stay in a cave on Sapphir's island, and been tied to a pole in the mountains overrun by wild clans. But he'd never *really* been to another Achaean city. Now that he stood atop a rocky hill looking down on the Selinus River and Aegium, he realized he wasn't missing much.

It's just a smaller Helike.

Aegium was the largest of all the fishing villages on the coastline northwest of Helike. In the middle of a mess of shacks and carts, there was a Homarium dedicated to Zeus. The stone platform with columns and a triangular roof was the only building with any clear connection to the gods.

Perhaps that isn't a bad thing.

Beside the Homarium was a wooden stage, prominent among the surrounding shacks. According to Sapphir, this was where the town convened to vote. A majority of men in the town had to agree for any decision to be made in Aegium.

No wonder it still looks like this.

"We're stopping here for the night?" Keoki asked, looking to Sapphir.

Sapphir's pale skin and red hair seemed to mix pink in the sunset, and Keoki tried to avoid staring. Her blue eyes and scar remained as prominent as ever.

"Yes. Yes, we can try to stay at an inn by the Homarium," she said. "We've covered over fifty stadia today; that's plenty. We can take a break."

Keoki agreed. Though his feet were hard and calloused from the farm, he was still relatively thin and weak after days in Sapphir's cave.

He and Sapphir avoided discussing Keoki's imprisonment. It hung over them like a stubborn raincloud. Time at the farm had eased the tension slightly, but she still seemed distant, despite his many efforts.

I shouldn't be the one seeking approval. I was her prisoner... not the other way around!

Keoki already missed Felip and Agnes. He'd cherished every warm smile from Fil and every scowl from Agnes, especially when it was directed at Sapphir. Agnes even went as far to admit that she was sad to see him leave a second time.

"It was harder to carry heavy things without you here," she said, fussing with Keoki's ragged shirt, "But now we have all these children to lighten the load and deal with the cattle, so don't worry about us. They won't eat any more than you would on your own, either."

"What she means is that we love you, son," Fil cut in, "Good luck finding your brother."

"Yes," Agnes said curtly, shooting a sideways glance at her husband before eyeing Sapphir darkly. "But don't bring Keon back here. One of you is enough."

Aegium was even less impressive from sea level than it had been from above. There was a very distinct fish smell, and every gentle breeze made Keoki less hungry.

"You in the mood for fish?" he asked Sapphir, who shook her head but didn't respond.

Perhaps we can find a nice family here and steal from them. Would she like that more?

The entire Homarium could have fit inside one room of Helike's Temple of Poseidon. Even the statue of Zeus looked cramped on his throne, holding his lightning bolt at arm's length as if he were trying to make the most of his tight space.

A few citizens of Aegium were kneeling or sitting at Zeus' feet. Most people were either buying fish or selling it. Finally, Sapphir stopped at a shack no different from any other. She knocked.

A flap on the door swung inwards, revealing a grizzled face, "We've got no rooms lef– oh. It's you."

Sapphir said nothing, and the flap closed. The door opened. Inside was a bar, two tables, and a hallway leading to four doors. The grizzled face belonged to a squat man with uneven legs.

"Welcome back, Helen. Same room as last time?"

Helen?

Sapphir flicked a trident at the man, "That would be great, Zaphan. Thank you."

"What about your friend?"

"He can stay in mine."

Zaphan gave Sapphir a knowing smile and she winked back at him, grinning. When he turned away, her grin disappeared, and the sincerity returned to her eyes.

I don't like the arrangement either.

Zaphan hobbled to a room behind the bar and Keoki heard keys jingle. Sapphir motioned for Keoki to follow her.

"Sorry about the mess," Zaphan said, gesturing to an unmade bed and a robe on the floor, "You're up there."

He pointed to a ladder, which Sapphir was already climbing. Before Keoki could follow, Zaphan stopped him. "I didn't catch your name, friend."

"Keon," Keoki responded.

"Ah, lovely. Well, please come down for soup once you're settled. We have a delightful fish broth with leeks and carrots.

Fish. What a surprise.

"Thank you, Zaphan. I'm sure we'll oblige in a minute."

Zaphan chuckled and shook his head as he left the room,

shutting the door behind him.

The room at the top of the ladder was a mirror of the one below, but the roof slanted towards the bed, cutting the space nearly in half. Sapphir set down her pack at the foot of the bed and removed her sandals. Keoki did the same, feeling self-conscious about the state of his feet.

"Zaphan says there's fish soup if we want it."

"Yes, I heard," Sapphir said, "You're welcome to eat, I'm not too hungry."

"Are you sure? All we had was some bread and figs after breakfast. I think we should both eat before—"

"I'm not hungry. I'll eat in the morning."

Sapphir was on the bed, her eyes closed, and hands folded on her stomach. She looked inhuman – postured as if she were made of ceramic.

Are they entirely human? Her kind? The Children.

"So, Helen, when did you first meet Zaphan?" he asked.

Sapphir kept her eyes closed, "I've been to the inn before."

"Yes... obviously. But he knew to give you this room? And, uh... Helen?"

"I was with my father the first time," she said, "He has a way of convincing people to be compliant."

"Oh. How many times have you been here, then?"

"Seven."

"And you don't think Zaphan will be able to tell your father that you're here?"

"He can't. Father can only contact others like us. There are none like that in Aegium. At least not right now. And Zaphan hasn't seen Father in years."

How would she know that?

Sapphir had explained how she could track other Children of the Sea and magicians when they began planning their journey to find her father. It was how she had tried to track Ivy and Maya. Keoki had spent much of his life hating magicians – wishing that all the Children were dead. Now, his purpose was to travel from town to town and seek out Children of the Sea. Sapphir was certain that if she could find one, they would give her the location of her father.

And if they refuse to provide assistance, Sapphir has her methods to make them... and me? She doesn't even need me.

Keoki *did* long for revenge. Killing Teremos would give him satisfaction of some kind.

But can I do it? Knowing I'm helping her? When she took them? Ivy and the others...

"Well, I'm going to get some soup. Are you sure you don't want anything?"

Sapphir nodded, eyes still closed. Keoki climbed back down the ladder, opened the door, and took a seat at one of the tables. The hair on his exposed arms stood up as a breeze wafted through an open window.

"I'll have some soup now. Thanks," Keoki said.

"It's no trouble. Helen isn't hungry, then?" he asked, ladling a thick soup into a wooden bowl.

""Hel–" Keoki paused, "Oh yes, Helen isn't hungry."

"I suppose you've satisfied her enough then, eh Keon?"

Keoki pretended not to hear as he accepted the soup. He couldn't meet Zaphan's eyes. The stout man hobbled back behind the bar, pouring himself a splash of clear liquid and downing it quickly.

The soup was surprisingly good, though Keoki's standards were low at that moment. A day of walking across the mountainous terrain had left him exhausted. Keoki knew that their quest for Teremos would have much more challenging days.

I need my strength more than I thought.

He and Sapphir had been planning and gathering supplies for almost a week, though there wasn't much they could anticipate. Mostly, Sapphir had tried to educate him on the history of the Achaea – the cities and towns they would visit, and the important people they might come across.

"Father was very... thorough in his instruction. He always said it was just as important to learn about the League as it was to practice magic."

My parents weren't quite as comprehensive.

Keoki knew plenty about the gods, and his years as a smith and farmer had given him insight into tradesmanship, but he was lacking in history.

Their trip would begin in Aegium. From there, Keoki and Sapphir would continue up the coast, staying a few miles inland, to Arba, Boline, Panormus, and Rhium. Keoki knew Panormus was the site of a great battle in the Peloponnesian Wars.

Or was it Rhium?

Either way, these towns were much smaller than Helike, a mix of fishing and farming. The grander cities of Patras, Dyme, and Olenus, which lay to the West, would be far more mysterious.

With Sapphir doing all the tracking, Keoki felt quite useless. She had taught him about the spells he might have to face and people to look out for, but he could do nothing to defend against those anyway.

As long as I get to avenge my parents. Then... then it will have been okay. I can deal with her children later.

Keoki continued eating the fish soup, glad for the sustenance. He felt bad lying to Ivy, Maya, and the others about the reason for their dangerous journey. They weren't too young to understand the risks – the attack from the mountain clans had made sure of that. But the chance that both Sapphir and Keoki would return were slim and divulging this to Sapphir's children would have been unwise.

Not her children. Not actually.

No, it was easier to leave the children with hope. They could believe Sapphir and Keoki would come back with Keon, the false brother.

I always wanted a brother.

Sapphir, believing Keon to be real, had insisted that Keoki tell this lie to Felip and Agnes as well. Ivy and Cy were excited to meet

Keon.

"We'll all be able to fish together when you get back! And there are so many more games we can play with four people," Cy exclaimed.

"Five!" Celia interjected.

"Yes, C," Ivy said, "Five."

She had rushed to hug Keoki then, and he felt genuine sadness to leave them all, though he knew they'd be happy with Felip and Agnes. Maya had shuffled towards him and hugged his leg gently before climbing into her mother's arms.

Not her mother.

Keoki stared at his unfinished soup. He wasn't hungry anymore, for some reason. He brought the bowl to Zaphan.

"Aw, you didn't like it, then?"

"No, no. It was delicious. Really," Keoki said, hoping Zaphan would take the compliment in earnest.

"Ah well, I'm glad. In a rush to get back to Helen, then. I understand. Here, take a mint leaf. Get that fish smell out of your mouth, eh."

Keoki blushed, and stammered, "I... we..."

He took the leaf anyway.

When Keoki got back to the room, Sapphir was in the same position as before. He had to lean to avoid hitting his head on the roof, but he could feel his curls pressed up against the angled side. He tried his best to stay quiet, assuming Sapphir was asleep.

"How was the soup?" she asked.

Keoki jumped, startled, and hit his head on the roof. He rubbed the sore spot for a moment, "It was good actually. Much better than I thought it would be."

"Zaphan is a good cook."

"Apparently," Keoki's mouth began to taste slightly bitter as the mint leaf lost its flavor. With nowhere to spit it out, he swallowed it instead. The leaf was scratchy.

He shifted the packs on the ground to make enough room to lie down and stood up to see Sapphir's eyes opened.

"You can have the bed if you want," she offered, "I'm used to sleeping on floors."

"No, it's fine, don't worry. The floor is a lot smoother than a rocky cave."

Sapphir's face flushed in embarrassment.

"But it was a lot more spacious than this. There was a nice view of the ocean, too."

Sapphir cracked a smile, the natural pale color returning to her face. Her hair was messy but somehow still looked nice.

"Glad to hear it. You're always welcome back – doesn't cost a trident, either."

He laughed, then lay down with his face pressed against his leather pack. It felt nice to joke, but the laughter was still stale.

Truthfully, the floor was no more comfortable than the cave had been. He could hear Sapphir shifting on the bed above him, and the cramped room was warm from their body heat.

He knew he wouldn't sleep well. Sleep had not been easy to

come by recently. Between the bandits, the cave, and the impending meeting with Teremos, he was growing used to the fatigue. However, the lying remained troubling to him.

They're not her children. But I told her I wouldn't tell anyone.

Sapphir wouldn't worry about Keoki sharing her secret now that they spent all their time together. As far as Sapphir knew, Fil, Agnes, and her children were at home, safely waiting for her and Keoki to return with Keon, his fictitious brother.

But Sapphir thinks he's real... I had to let her think Fil and Agnes would believe me.

"We'll have to find an excuse for where Keon is after all this is done. If we are able to go back, that is," she had said, "Perhaps he can settle down in Aegium. Perhaps we'll tell them that you'll stay with him for a while? Do you actually know where your brother might be?"

I know we'd never find him, no matter how hard we pretend to look.

Keoki turned over, trying to get comfortable, but his eyes stayed open. Sapphir was fast asleep.

They're not her children. And I told her that her secret was safe with me. I was just... so angry. I still am... angry.

Keoki stayed still for five minutes, seeing if that would help. It did not, and he was stuck looking at the slanted ceiling of their tight quarters.

And Fil and Agnes know I don't have a brother.

Chapter 5

Simon

Simon paced the deck of the beached ship, taking two steps towards the starboard side, then two steps to port.

I have spent too much time on ships these past weeks.

Simon did not mind the open ocean, but he was glad this ship would do no sailing. The Sunken Ship of Patras was a famed vessel, washed ashore during a battle long ago. The ship's back half had dug itself so deep into the sand, that it was now anchored to its spot, just at the edge of the water during high tide.

The vessel leaned at a shallow angle, making Simon feel slightly unbalanced, though he much preferred being in the open air to the Court of Helike.

How much longer does Patreus expect me to wait?

Patreus, Son of Patreus, Son of Patreus, *and so on,* was a direct descendant of the city's founder. Like his father before him, Patreus was well-regarded as a wise man and worthy representative of the city, though he was not its ruler. Patras was a democracy. All men in the city were afforded the chance to vote on every one of its issues.

A city with slow progress.

Simon had been waiting for his brief meeting with Patreus for three days. He had no qualms with democracy, but it seemed unnecessary to require a majority's consent to perform menial tasks. The lack of leadership also raised the concern that the city would be unprepared in the face of an emergency. Could the town even come to an agreement on how to respond?

Perhaps I do have a few qualms. Gaios would never allow it for Helike.

No, Gaios was far too confident in his abilities as a ruler to relinquish any power. Helike would never become the dominant force in Achaea, as Gaios desired, under democratic rule.

The man had enough trouble beginning the Heliken conquest already... and he only had the Council to contend with.

Simon suddenly became very aware of his pacing. He sat for a moment, tapping his knees rhythmically. He saw a child splash into the ocean, giggling as his mother chased him. Simon waved down from the grounded ship. The woman nodded her acknowledgement before turning away briskly, the boy gathered in her arms.

"Fetch Patreus on your way out."

Simon began pacing the deck again, frustrated by the standstill. His thoughts meandered back to Gaios.

Have I doomed the city? Leaving it alone in his hands?

The Golden Spear was a constant voice of reason against some of Gaios' more ambitious ideas, though Orrin lacked the intellect to develop policies of his own. Would that be enough?

If only we still had Euripides.

Euripides had always been the most competent leader.

And that was too much for Gaios.

Simon's worst fears about Euripides' demise had never been confirmed, but he was fairly sure they were accurate.

Gaios' hand was involved. In some way.

No matter how much time Simon spent with Gaios, he would never have a proper read on the man. The two were far more different than even the public realized; and they already saw quite a few differences. Gaios was the tall, brown-haired, and tan-skinned native Heliken. Simon was the Flat-Nose.

Simon ran a finger over the bridge of his nose unconsciously. His eyes roved the city of Patras, flitting past the Agyian Swamp, farmland, and scattered houses. He wondered where the young lady, Melani, was and if she had made it to her family safely. He hoped so.

A sweet girl. Clever, though lacking ambition.

To Simon, this wasn't a bad thing. Everyone he knew had too much ambition. The girl was refreshing.

She will keep an eye on Rizon Atsali.

Finally, his gaze rested on the beach, where the envoy was arriving at last. Two men supported a teetering, older one, as they picked their way slowly across the sand.

An old man... What will Patreus think of a foreign councilor?

Simon had been born east of Persia – further to the East than most maps showed. His earliest memory was of a ship being tossed like a rag in the middle of the ocean. He had cried for his mother and father. Today, he couldn't even picture their faces.

Patreus and his two companions stopped at the staircase leading up to the Sunken Ship's deck. The two younger men were muscular and towered over the hunched old man. Patreus leaned heavily against a cane, his beard and tufts of white hair frizzed in the wind. He waved to Simon.

"Come on... climb the stairs, old man," Simon muttered into the wind.

Simon brushed a damp hand across his forehead. It was always a strange thing, meeting important Achaeans.

He's just an old man... just one old man with a couple guards.

Simon's journey to Helike had been long and arduous. It consisted mostly of reading by himself and attending those more powerful than him. Occasionally, he missed those days when responsibilities were limited.

It made life... easier.

The old man rested halfway up the stairs. His two guards appeared quite bored. He smiled at Simon with chapped lips.

He's missing quite a few teeth.

Patreus looked harmless enough, but Simon knew appearances could be misleading. The first king Simon attended had *seemed* benign, with a warm face and easy smile.

King Pausanias had been many things. But kind was not one of them. Pausanias had ruled Sparta through the Peloponnesian War – the same war that gave the Golden Spear his name. The attendant preceding Simon had been executed.

For spilling a cup of wine...

When Simon replaced her, battles erupted once more. Thankfully, the Corinthian War, another territorial spat did not end as well for Pausanias. Simon received only a few weeks of torture before the king was exiled for poor leadership during Sparta's devastating loss in Haliartus.

Pausanias' son, Agesipolis, replaced him.

Even young, Agesipolis was a better leader.

The letter placing the rightful blame on Pausanias for the embarrassing defeat was one of Simon's best pieces of writing.

At some point in more recent years, Simon became an attendant for the strapping Councilor Euripides. Euripides was kinder than Pausanias, but still brash and self-assured. However, Simon would always be thankful for Euripides. After Councilor Tavorn died at the age of seventy-three, Simon replaced him.

Patreus looks to be at least that old. Perhaps closer to his eightieth year.

Simon did not know his own age and wondered if he was closer to death than he knew. Deterioration came naturally with age; Simon just hoped his mind would degrade slower than his body.

Finally, the three men summited the stairs. Patreus' cane clacked against the wooden ship as he shuffled closer to Simon.

"Councilor Simon," Patreus greeted cordially, eyes squinting.

"Patreus, Son of Patreus," Simon said, fearing he could not get the second "Son of Patreus" out without laughing.

"I was so pleased to receive your message when you arrived. It is not often we entertain visitors from the great city of Helike, let alone councilors."

Patreus' warbly voice was creaky with age. The men flanking him bore a striking resemblance to one another.

"The pleasure is all mine. I have been meaning to leave Court for quite some time. Explore Achaea a little more," he explained, before pointing to the younger accomplices, "And who might you two be?"

"Patreus, Son of Patreus," the taller of the two said simply, "Here with my brother, Patreus."

That must be confusing.

"Son of Patreus, I assume?" Simon quipped looking at the younger.

"Yes."

Not as sharp as their father, perhaps. Though Old Patreus can't be too clever if the only name he can come up with is his own.

"Any daughters, my friend?"

Patrius, maybe?

"Unfortunately, no. The gods only gifted me with these two boys. Men now, heehehe," he chuckled.

"Ah, praise the gods."

"Yes, indeed. Well, what can I do for you today, Councilor Simon? And please, let us sit."

Simon and Old Patreus sat down on a wooden bench fastened to the slanting ship.

"I am sure you are aware of the unrest between my city and Boura."

It was not a question. Old Patreus nodded.

"The state of affairs is unfortunate, and I worry that this is just the beginning. Councilor Gaios calls for war. And Helike will win."

"This seems... eh, positive for you, Councilor Simon, heehehe. Victory for Helike is in your best interest."

He's baiting me.

Old Patreus was much more comfortable on the wooden bench, and it seemed that his mind could move faster now that his legs were steady.

"War is never in my best interest. More importantly – what may follow this griping between Boura and Helike is much worse."

Simon was cautious with his wording. He did not want to reveal too much – it was always best to know pieces others did not. And he was reluctant to cast Gaios in too bad a light.

I must, though. This is the path I have chosen. To be apart from him.

"When Helike wins," Patreus warbled, "there is worse in store for Achaea?"

"Gaios will not stop at Boura."

Old Patreus let out his whistling cackle. "Heeehehehe! Patras will not war with your city. We are fishers and farmers; we are large but not strong. Many... but with little might, heehehe."

"He will conquer the East first," Simon said, "This much I know. But there is little I could do to help those cities by rushing to warn them."

Simon wondered then if he should divulge that Helike's victory over Eastern Achaea would be assured by an alliance with Ionia, now controlled by the even mightier Persian Empire.

An alliance I forged.

He continued, "Patras is one of the only cities with the numbers to stand against Gaios. Especially if you unite with the other western cities. Dyme, Olenus, Tritaea – you must all work together."

Old Patreus looked at his son and took a rattling breath. "We cannot fight, Councilor Simon. Let Gaios have his conquest."

For the first time, he did not laugh.

"But what of your democracy, Patreus. What of your people?"

"My people?" he looked at his sons, who remained emotionless. "The League will have one ruler sooner or later, councilor."

"What do you mean?"

"How much do you know of King Basilius of Olenus? Has word of this man reached Helike?"

Basilius. The King named King.

"We... we know little aside from his existence."

Old Patreus grinned widely and slapped his leg. "Heeehehe! Then you've lost! Fools in Helike, hehehe."

"What do you mean, Patreus? Help me understand."

"You think Gaios is a man of war? Heehehe... the King named King has much to teach him. We already belong to him; he simply hasn't claimed us. You see, hehe... he told all his neighbors, all the cities you speak of. Dyme, Pharae, and us," the old man coughed, "Surrender. Or war. Who are we to do battle with those mightier than ourselves?"

Simon felt foolish. Of course, the other Achaean cities were busying themselves the same as Helike and Boura. Why hadn't he bothered to learn more about King Basilius?

Gaios, I thought I understood. Need there be more threats to the League's peace?

"How did this come to be? Have relations with Olenus been strained before?"

Old Patreus laughed slowly. "Kings will always wish for more than they have, Councilor Simon. I thought this much would be obvious. I'm afraid Basilius wants war simply to have more. He tires of being seen as the King only within Olenus' walls."

"And you are just going to let him have his way with Patras. Him or Gaios?"

"It is not my choice! Heehehe, oh Simon. It is not my choice. The city of Patras has agreed. We have voted. Basilius, Gaios. What does it matter? Perhaps good men can make Gaios a fair leader. Or Basilius. I would be happier if the Golden Spear were still alive."

Patreus shook his head sadly, spitting a wisp of beard from his mouth and licking his chapped lips.

The Golden Spear? Still alive?

This time, Simon could not contain his surprise. "What?!"

Patreus rapped his cane against the ship deck.

"I suppose word does not reach the ocean. Yes, four became three in Helike. Councilors are dropping like eggs from a hen, heehehe. It is lucky perhaps, that you left before three became two."

Simon searched his emotions for the right one.

I should pity Orrin and his family. I should.

But did he? Simon and the Golden Spear were never friends; he had respected and liked the man well enough, but they had never been close confidants.

I had a chance to make him my ally... he could have been... he was good.

His mind wandered to the young boy, Nicolaus.

I wanted that one to survive. Right?

However, attendants, especially those serving in war, rarely outlived their councilors and kings.

And if I truly wanted him to survive, I would have told him to leave the Court – to get as far away from the Council chambers as he could.

He *had* said as much to his own attendant, Opi, warning her to seek shelter before he freed Rizon Atsali and fled to Patras. She was shrewd enough to heed his advice.

"Yes, I suppose I had a timely departure. I am saddened by this news of the Golden Spear. He was... an honorable man."

Simon had trouble meeting Old Patreus' eyes.

"Yes, quite honorable indeed. The best Helike had to offer."

Old Patreus struggled back to his feet, clutching one of the beefy arms of Young Patreus. He steadied himself with the cane and spoke once more. There was sincerity in the creaky voice.

"Thank you for coming today, Councilor Simon. I know you wished only to provide us a warning. For some, war would indeed be the right course... but the people of Patras will be safer surrendering as one."

Simon grimaced internally. "I understand, Patreus, Son of Patreus. Your city is wiser than most."

"It is the will of the people."

And the people will suffer.

"I do hope our paths cross again, my friends," Simon said, nodding at the three Patreuses, "Your city is quite beautiful."

"It is not *our* city. But yes. Beautiful. Patras is beautiful. There are plenty of men and women I can introduce you to if you wish. The innkeepers prepare wonderful fish. And the women? Heeehehe!"

Simon smiled tightly. "I'm sure this is true; unfortunately, I am not hungry."

It seems the hungrier men are already on the move. First

THE CHILDREN OF THE SEA

Gaios, now...

Simon watched Patreus and his sons descend the stairs cautiously. The city of Patras, with its huts and farmhouses seemed suddenly dreary to Simon.

It will be a shame when they lose this.

Simon began pacing the deck once more. Two steps to starboard, and two to port. He needed time to think. First Gaios, now Basilius. Simon surveyed the horizon. Somewhere, many stadia away, was the city of Olenus...

And their king... moving.

Chapter 6

Sapphir

At least it's in better shape than Panormus.

The township of Rhium was nestled into the foothills fifty stadia along the coastline from Patras. Its neighboring village, Panormus, had once been a mirror image of Rhium. After being ravaged by the Battle of Naupactus during the Peloponnesian War, however, it was a husk in comparison.

Neither had been large cities like Helike or Boura, but Rhium still resembled a cohesive town. Numerous huts and skiffs lined the shore – a series of beautiful beaches that reminded Sapphir of home. When she needed food for her children, she usually went to Aegium or Arba.

Perhaps I should come here instead.

Rhium numbered 500 at most – fishermen, fisherwomen, and

their families. Like Panormus, the city heeded the governance of Patras.

Father had always been venomous when speaking of Patras and their democratic rule.

It puts too much power in the hands of ungodly men. And of course, "Only those who speak directly to the gods should rule."

For most of her life, Sapphir had believed him. Now, she was unsure – though in truth, it no longer mattered much. Sapphir's troubles were different than most common folk.

"It's not so bad here, is it?" Keoki said, "Any Children here?"

Sapphir ignored him. She and Keoki were arriving in Rhium after five days of onerous travel. They had slogged from Aegium, through Arba, around Boline, and finally, across the ruin of Panormus. Sapphir's feet ached from constant walking, and there were cuts at the base of her ankles from her leather sandal straps.

We should have risked the boat.

Using her enchanted skiff would have been faster, less painful. But she'd been reluctant to do so, fearing that any Child of the Sea would sense her coming if she used magic. The fatigue was making her rethink this decision.

Keoki fought me on that... I should have listened.

Perhaps she would swallow her pride and conjure the boat after a night's rest in Rhium. She needed sleep.

And food.

Even though she had been thin before, Sapphir knew she was losing weight already. The last opportunity for a hearty meal had been in Aegium, and Sapphir had rejected it.

That was foolish of me. Keoki was right about that too.

The farm boy was in better shape than her. After days in the cave and their demanding expedition, he was still thinner than when she first met him. But his muscles were more toned than they had been, making him lean rather than bulky. His hair was still dark and scraggly, and his beard was growing back less patchy.

Focus.

"I'm getting hungry. Should we find a place to eat?"

He would talk to the birds if there was nobody around!

Sapphir did not regret holding Keoki captive. The more they traveled, however, the worse she felt about it.

It was for my children. Ivy, Cy, Maya, Celia, Egan. They must never know their true identity.

This was what worried Sapphir the most as they journeyed to find her father. She did not fear Teremos; she did not fear death. Perhaps she should have, but anger clouded those emotions. Certainly, there were frightening dangers on the path to ending her father's life, but she was far more terrified of losing her grip on her children.

Memory charms were complex enough when the caster and the subject were in close proximity, but they were nearly impossible to maintain from great distances. She'd always known this in theory.

And she still remembered the first day she left Egan and Ivy on the island years ago.

GHE CHILDREN OF GHE SEA

I just wanted to buy some fresh oranges for the children.

She had been handing the man at the fruit stand a couple mares when her breath began to quicken. She'd known right away. Ivy's mind was still adjusting to her new memories; they were slipping. And it was beginning to drive her mad.

The experience had shaken Sapphir, but she gradually became more adept at keeping her children safe. She still feared that those old memories were dormant. The ones where she was not their mother.

"Yeah, I'm definitely too hungry. We need food."

Sapphir glared at the back of Keoki's head.

Calm. I must remain calm. Nothing will happen; they've been mine long enough.

Still, the idea of a lengthy expedition concerned her. Keoki assured her that her children would be safe and happy on Felip and Agnes' farm; she had no choice but to place her trust in him. After a week with Felip and Agnes, she could tell they enjoyed the change in scenery.

If only it weren't so temporary. Though maybe we'll be free once the Children are gone.

She could only hope as much. Even in their old age, Felip and Agnes seemed spry enough to care for their new company. Felip certainly welcomed the help around the farm. Agnes may have as well, though she was more guarded.

That one has no love for me.

Sapphir was beginning to see Rhium in more detail as she and

Keoki approached. She tightened her hand around her pack. Her knuckles were cracked and white.

So far from home.

****

"It will be like I never left!"

Egan gave her a sad look that was conspicuous on his normally impassive features.

He suspects we're not just looking for Keoki's brother.

Ivy, Cy, and Celia were all shifting impatiently, their emotions frayed. A knot of stress balled in Sapphir's stomach; they believed the lie for now, but they were all too smart to remain ignorant. And they sensed that she was holding back information.

"Promise you'll be kind to Felip and Agnes. For these next few weeks. I'll be awfully embarrassed if I find out you've been troubling this lovely old couple!"

"We'll be good, Ma. Won't we C?" Ivy said.

Celia nodded dutifully, looking at her older sister with admiration.

"I'm looking at you two, especially!" she pointed at Ivy and Cy, "You *must* stay on the farm, and you *must* keep your gifts hidden from Fil and Agnes!"

"Yes, Mother!" Ivy and Cy assured.

Maya gave Sapphir a quizzical look, as if she were wondering why her mother would trust the two ruffians to follow her orders.

I trust them because I have to. As long as they stay on the farm... even within a couple stadia... no Child of the Sea will find them. The protections I cast will keep them hidden.

"I'll make sure they listen," Egan assured her, his voice softer than usual.

Maya patted his leg. Sapphir fought back the tears that threatened; she didn't want to give her children further cause for distress.

✳✳✳✳

"Sapphir," Keoki said, "Sapphir do you sense anything?"

"Huh?" she asked, nearly crashing into his immobile form.

"Distracted?"

"I... no. I was just admiring the beaches. What'd you say?"

Keoki chuckled lightly, "Yeah, you're distracted. I was asking if you sensed any of them here. And about the city. And food. You... uh... haven't been responding. So, is there any magic here?"

"Oh, yes. No."

"Those are the two options."

Sapphir glared at him. "No, there are no Children here."

Truthfully, she hadn't focused enough to check. She would need to wait until they sat down, and she could clear her head.

"Great, maybe we can get a meal then. It's easier when we...

uh pretend to be together. I mean, uh... innkeepers are much friendlier to couples."

He was right, of course, and it had been her idea the first time.

So why does it make me uncomfortable?

Keoki extended his hand to her. She rolled her eyes. He raised an eyebrow.

"Fine."

She took his hand reluctantly as they passed the first few huts. The entirety of Rhium smelled like saltwater.

All of these fishing villages have this same scent.

Saltwater and fish.

An old woman with thin legs and loose skin smiled at them as they passed. She was seated next to a wagon filled to the brim with trout. Behind her, two children played with a hoop in the space between two wooden shacks.

The sun was now a semicircle reflected on the ocean beneath a pink-orange sky. Sapphir slipped on a loose pebble, and Keoki caught her.

"We need to get you some dinner, don't we?" he said.

It wasn't a question. Outside a different wooden house, this one with a thatched roof, a large woman rocked in a proportionally large chair.

"Ma'am! My, uh, wife. Sa–Helen... do you have food?"

"Very eloquent," Sapphir muttered, and Keoki's face reddened.

"Me name's not Heln. But food? That I have."

The woman had a kind tone, but her eyes were fixed on Sapphir with something like curiosity.

"Oh, no. Sorry," Keoki sputtered, "This is Helen, my wife."

He held up her arm to provide more context to the woman. Sapphir rolled her eyes once more.

"Sorry to bother you, ma'am. My husband can be quite a bumbling oaf." She smiled sweetly. "We were just passing through from Arba to Patras and were wondering if you knew of a nice place to sit down for a meal."

The woman returned Sapphir's smile, her enormous breasts bouncing to her chin as she stood. "Look no further, dears! Yer welcome inside. I've cooked a trout in olive oil just now. Delicious, if I say so meself. Even took out the bones meself."

"We can pay you well for the meal," Sapphir offered, following the woman inside as she fussed with her bodice.

"Oh, dear, don't ya worry now. We in Rhium, well we don't get much company since the Spartans came."

Sapphir's instincts warned her to leave right away. Nobody, man, woman, or child, was this kind to strangers. She could sense Keoki's trepidation as well. If anything were to happen, she feared she didn't have the energy to resist. Keoki squeezed her hand tighter.

"You need the food," he muttered.

He's right.

"Oh, thank you! You're far too kind. As my husband mentioned, you may call me Helen. His name is Felip. And you?"

70

"Babs, dear. Ya can sit down there, if ya like."

There was a small table beside a cookfire where the trout was still warming. It smelled amazing. Babs set three separate plates out and loaded each with fish and onions. Keoki still looked bashful and mumbled a thank you when she set his portion down.

Babs took a seat, her chest smashed against the table. She was a homely woman but in a pleasant way. Sapphir wondered if she lived alone. She couldn't tell if Babs was younger or older than herself.

"Is it just you, here, Babs?" she asked.

"Well I got friends, yes. But only meself to live with. Ever since me mom and dad died, just a year or two ago."

"Oh, I'm sorry to hear that. Were they elderly?"

Sapphir spoke between bites. The fish tasted wonderful, and she found herself caring less whether or not Babs was secretly more villainous than she appeared.

"Perhaps twenty years older than yerself. I'm just nearin me thirtieth year. It's quiet in Rhium, but I do like it here."

Babs was cheerful as she spoke, even though Sapphir could find plenty of sadness in her story. "Do you work?"

"I'm a fishcook, aren't I!" she pointed at the tools she had on the stone counter behind them, "Every man around here is a fisherman, and their wives is cooks or with the children or fisherwoman. I have no fisherman meself, and no children. But I cook em nonetheless."

"And you're quite good at it," Keoki said sheepishly.

"Well thank ya, dear. And what do ya two loverlies do in Arba?"

Sapphir swallowed a particularly well-spiced piece of fish. "My dear Felip is a farmer, and I sell his goods around town. Closer to Helike, actually."

"Oh, how loverly," Babs said, then began to chatter about her favorite farmed vegetables.

This reinvigorated Keoki properly. He was able to explain how some of these were planted, which Babs was very excited to hear. The two conversed, and Sapphir closed her eyes momentarily, trying to savor every bite of fish. She could feel strength returning to her limbs, and magical energy beginning to spread through her veins as she ate and drank.

Perhaps Babs is just a kind lady after all.

Sapphir wanted to berate herself for being so quick to judge the jolly woman.

"And grapes? Do ya need rain to keep 'em? Are they thirsty fruit?"

Keoki nodded, "Well, yes. They need water, but not as much as you'd think. Fe... my uh, farmhand... he has these great barrels for when it rains."

"Oh, yer clever, then!" Babs chuckled, "So what brings you travelin' to Patras?"

Sapphir looked down at her fish. Keoki cleared his throat.

"Visiting my brother. Yeah, we like to pay him a visit or two every year."

"Isn't that loverly!"

Babs gushed about the prospect of having a brother. To her, it sounded like the most wonderful thing in the world. Keoki was smiling more than he had in days. As Babs ate her fish, she realized she had never seen onions grow.

"Do ya know how that happens, Felip? Onions? I love to cook me fish with an onion."

Sapphir wished she could stay with the warm lady forever.

It would be so simple.

Sapphir forced her eyes shut, focusing all of her mental energy on the town of Rhium.

Surely, there will be a Child in Patras… but I must check.

She pictured it all – the huts, the beaches, and the mountains that surrounded it. People began to appear in her mind – townsfolk she had never seen before and voices she had never heard.

Search for it… you know what to look for.

For a moment, nothing happened. Just as she was about to open her eyes, a flash of pain burned white-hot in her chest. And a broken-down shack, with a red stone at its doorstep engrained itself into her mind.

She gasped.

"Everthing okay, dear," Babs said, pausing her discussion with Keoki about growing onions.

"Sa–Helen?" Keoki said, looking at her with concern.

She looked back at him, eyes sharp with intensity. They

needed to leave. Now. They needed to find the red stone and the broken-down shack. If she could sense him, he could sense her. Keoki scrunched his eyebrows and his mouth tightened.

Come on, Keoki. You know what I'm trying to tell you.

They needed the Child; they needed him if they wanted to find her father. They needed him to ensure the safety of her children.

They had to act before he slipped through their fingers.

Come on!

His eyes widened, and he nodded.

"Uh, Babs, I'm really sorry," he began, "We have to be going. I'm afraid... well, I think Helen is feeling unwell."

"Oh," Babs said, looking crestfallen. Then her eyes lit back up, "Well, no need to be sorry. The gods've smiled at me today, bringin' ya here! Yer welcome to stay if ya don't feel good."

Sapphir was legitimately sorry to leave Babs alone, especially after she had been so welcoming. But there was no time to waste.

"I wish we could, Babs, honestly... But I think we should get going to Patras as soon as possible."

Babs opened her mouth, then closed it. She must have wondered why Helen and Felip would leave if Helen felt sick. But she was too nice to question them. She stood, extending her arms for a hug from Keoki and Sapphir. Sapphir knew Keoki did not care much for hugs, but they both obliged.

"I hope ya do feel better, Heln."

"Thank you, Babs. Thanks again."

Sapphir gave the woman's hand a squeeze, then yanked Keoki

back outside. It was dark, a moonless night.

"Did you?"

"Yes."

"But you said there weren't any."

"I was wrong."

The image of the run-down shack with the red stone popped into her head once more, and in the dim light of fires and candles scattered throughout the huts, it caught her eye. They needed to catch the Child. They needed to know where her father was hiding.

"So…" Keoki began.

"Yes. Steel your nerves, Keoki," Sapphir whispered, "There's a Child of the Sea in Rhium."

Chapter 7

Ivy

Ivy tossed one of the grapes aside. It was too squishy, and she hated squishy grapes. She popped the second into her mouth, letting the juices seep out as she crushed it slowly.

"Celia, look," she said through her teeth.

"What?" Celia asked, stretching a vine out with one hand as she followed Ivy's instructions.

Ivy spat the seeds at her. A few stuck to Celia's curls.

"Hey!!" Celia yelped, wiping away the juice and trying to pick seeds off her skin and hair. When she let go of the vine, it whipped back into place, startling her further.

Celia sniffled. She was far too trusting, and these small betrayals always took her by surprise. When she heard Ivy's gleeful laughter, however, she smiled.

In the seven days since Mother and Keoki had left, Ivy had spent most of her time with Celia and Felip. Many of Felip's grapes were ripening, and he needed the girls to pick as many as possible for his wine and jams before the fruit went rotten.

She would usually have preferred to play games and practice magic with Cy, but he was still being cold to her. She didn't want to bother with his grumpy attitude. Ivy wished he would get over it.

He's too sensitive! I just wanted to explore alone. I didn't even plan to bring Maya along.

Ivy wondered what it would take for Cy to forgive her. She couldn't change the fact that she'd left him behind! Until she figured this predicament out, Celia's company would have to suffice.

"Is this one good, Ivy?" Celia asked, holding a grape out for Ivy to inspect.

"Yes, that one looks good," Ivy confirmed confidently, though she didn't actually know what made one grape much better than another.

"How full are the buckets, C?"

"Maybe a hundred more grapes and then they'll be full," she responded thoughtfully.

100. Not too many left.

They picked for another quarter hour. The sun left its imprint on Ivy's neck and amplified the speckles on Celia's face. The two walked back to the farmhouse, carrying the bucket between them.

They passed Felip milking a heifer and patting its side gently.

"Hello girls!" he called, "Looks like another successful harvest out there! You two are natural farmers."

"The grapes are yummy!" Celia responded, perking up at the compliment.

Felip was so kind to Ivy and her siblings. It was hard not to smile in the warmth of his company. They continued inside, letting the bucket fall with a thud next to the table.

Egan was reading with Maya, pointing out harder words and speaking them aloud, though she remained quiet throughout. Maya bounced off his lap when she saw Celia and Ivy, waltzing over to examine the grapes.

She picked an extra-large one out for Egan, and one small grape for herself, then returned to her reading. Celia flopped into a chair after grabbing herself a cup of water. She drank noisily. Her face was flushed and sweaty.

"Has Agnes left for the town yet?" Ivy asked, letting excitement creep into her voice.

"Not yet," Egan said, continuing to read his book. "She won't take you though. Mother wouldn't like that, remember."

Ivy frowned, "Why can't we leave the farm?"

Egan looked up sternly, "Ivy, perhaps this time you should listen to Mother. She must have a good reason. There's plenty of dangers in the woods around here. You should know that by now."

"But if I'm with Agnes–"

Egan was about to retort when Agnes rushed into the room,

towing a small cart with casks of wine and cheese. Her onyx hair was orderly as always, framing her wrinkled face.

"No, child. I'm sorry. Your brother is right. Your mother told me to keep you here, so that's what must happen. Plenty to do today, though! There're grapes to crush! Cy has been looking forward to it. You can join him."

Before Ivy could respond, Agnes brushed past her, hurrying to reach the city before midday. People were surely out and about already, shopping for cheese and wine.

"Perhaps once your mother returns! I'll still be going to the market then!" Agnes called, letting the door shut behind her.

Ivy pretended not to care. Celia was now looking at Maya and Egan's scroll, trying to read along with them. Feeling out of place, Ivy slipped back out to the field. She spotted Cy milking alongside Felip.

"This heifer here is the best we have right now." Felip was saying, "I wish you could've met our old brown-spotted cow – mischievous as they come, always wandering off! But boy, did she make me a lot of coin."

Ivy kept her distance from the two, walking to the hill where she could see the city in the distance. Felip and Cy's voices were fading away.

"Did she die?"

"We never figured that out, Cy. One day, Keoki went out to tend to her, and she'd disappeared! Couldn't find her. Clever girl, though... I'm sure she's found somewhere else to cause mischief."

Ivy picked up her pace.

I didn't know it was their cow… I just wanted to show Maya a cool trick!

When she couldn't hear or see Felip and Cy anymore, she slowed down again. The grapevines were terraced in a hill that was rather high at its top. Ivy sat down when she reached it, concealed from the house by the grapevines. Between the leaves, she could see the city. Roads cut through the forest, radiating from Helike's center across the entire world.

So much out there. So much I haven't seen.

Ivy wished Mother and Keoki had taken her along. Something told her they weren't just going to Patras. And a brother? Keoki had never mentioned a brother. Ivy curled up under the vines, letting the leaves shade her from the ever-rising sun.

Why couldn't I go with them? Why do we have to stay on the farm? It's not dangerous in the city!

She felt strangely drained, though it was still early in the day.

I want to wrestle with Cy. I want to go to the city with Agnes, find Felip's bear in the forest, and turn her back into a cow…

Her thoughts became fuzzier and stranger as she closed her eyes, longing to be anywhere but her island or the farm.

****

The sun stopped rising and made its way towards the Western

horizon. Eventually, the grape leaves proved useless at sheltering Ivy in the cool shade. She blinked and rubbed her eyes. Her muscles stirred.

Did I fall asleep?

Ivy rolled out from the soil and clambered to her feet. She hadn't realized how exhausted she had been. As she slogged back to the farmhouse, Ivy wondered why nobody had woken her up.

It must have been hours!

She passed the field where cows grazed absentmindedly, noticing that Felip and Cy were no longer tending to them. She couldn't see the city but assumed the bustle would be dying down by now. Agnes would return soon with stories from the day and her usual complaints.

"There you are!" Celia skipped out to greet her, "We've just been playing with Felip's bows and arrows!"

"Not playing!" Felip called from inside the house. "Archery is no game, Celia!"

"Right," Celia said, stopping in front of Ivy, a huge smile on her face, "Felip was teaching us. But he said not to tell Agnes."

"Oh. That sounds fun, C. Can I try?"

"I'm afraid Agnes will be home any minute," Felip said, leaning against the doorframe. "She... well, I don't think she'd like me teaching you children to use weapons. Maybe tomorrow though, if we don't lose you again."

He winked. Ivy was disappointed.

"I wasn't lost. Just tired, that's all."

"Ah, I've had my fair share of surprise slumbers. Egan was certain you had run off to the woods, but I said you were much too clever to get yourself into trouble again, eh?"

Celia nodded emphatically. "That's right, Ivy wouldn't do that again, would you Ivy?"

Will they ever trust me the same?

Ivy repressed an exasperated frown and replied, "No. I just wanted to see the city from the hill."

Felip shrugged, then patted Celia's shoulder and went back inside. Celia and Ivy followed. Egan and Maya hadn't moved, though Maya was now drawing. Egan watched her proudly. As he glanced towards Ivy, his face transformed into an expression of disapproval. Cy sat in another corner, pretending to shoot at the wall with an imaginary bow and arrow. He didn't acknowledge Ivy.

Great. Both of my brothers hate me.

"Hey! Ivy, look! I see Agnes!"

Celia was pointing excitedly out the window at the woman approaching, pulling her cart of fresh bread and honey. She looked worn but still quite lively for her age.

"Agnes!" Celia greeted, giving her a delighted hug.

"Ah, hello again. Yes, I'm back." She brushed her clothes off when Celia extracted herself.

"Hello, my love," Felip said, kissing her cheek.

Agnes blushed and looked away, beginning to unpack the jars and loaves.

"It's honey and jam on bread tonight if you little ruffians want to eat. There is some cheese and olives, too. Over by the cupboard, I think."

In an attempt to ignore her frigid brothers, Ivy turned her attention to Agnes. "How was the city?" she asked.

"Not as exciting as you'd like it to be. Another day of listening to Philomena whine about this and that."

Philomena was one of Agnes' good friends, but the source of many of her gripes. Ivy wondered if the two even liked each other.

"Were there any funny people in the square?" Ivy asked, hoping for another story like the one she'd told the day before about a man in a lion's mask chasing rats.

"Hmmm... not that I can remember. Hate to be a disappointment, but some days it's just buying, selling, and chattering."

Ivy wished she could have joined, even if it was just buying, selling, and chattering. All of that sounded so interesting if it meant she could be in the big city for once.

"Oh, Felip," she whispered sharply, though the children could still hear, "Another child..."

Agnes made a grabbing motion, and Felip's face fell.

"Another?"

"What?" Ivy asked, "Another child what?"

Egan's eyes lifted from Maya's drawing. Cy and Celia were entirely disengaged from the conversation.

Another child...

Suddenly, she saw a fountain she'd never seen before, plain as

Agnes' face in front of her. Inside stood a massive statue of Poseidon, trident raised boldly. Around him, kids raced about, and men and women conversed indiscernibly.

"Oh nothing, dear. Just little kids trying to snatch my cheeses."

She's lying.

Ivy's head began to spin.

Where have I seen that statue? Was that...? I... I was in Helike...

She stumbled, bumping into Cy as he fired an imaginary arrow at Celia. Their little sister ran away, cackling, "You missed!!"

"Ivy!" Cy yelled and shoved her away from him.

She fell hard. Tears welled up, stinging her eyes.

He pushed me...

"Cy!" Egan's voice was deep and foreboding.

He grabbed his younger brother by the wrist, moving quickly for a boy of his size, and pulled him outside. Felip and Agnes watched wordlessly. Ivy clutched her knees tightly, closing her eyes as her mind steadied. She could hear Egan berating Cy outside but couldn't make out his words.

By the time she stood, Egan was back inside. He motioned for Ivy to approach.

"I think it's time you and your brother talked."

Ivy thanked him quietly and shuffled through the doorway sheepishly, averting her gaze. When she got outside, Cy was kicking a rock and staring at the ground. The door closed, leaving the two alone in the glow of the sunset.

"Cy..." she started.

"I'm s–"

"Let me finish."

"Sorry."

His voice was quieter and slower than usual.

"I'm sorry I left... I'm sorry I left the island with Maya. And didn't take you."

Cy finally looked at her, clasping and unclasping his hands. He kicked the rock as far away as he could.

"I'm sorry I pushed you."

"No, it's... I fell into you."

A minute passed. Ivy hoped Cy felt as uncomfortable with this as she did. This wasn't how they acted around each other. She just wanted to push him back, but playfully, and run as fast as she could to see if he could catch her.

Cy's blonde hair was growing long enough to cover his blue eyes. He let the inkling of a smile pass his lips.

"Bet you wished you'd brought me when you ran into those bandits."

Ivy scowled. "You would've slowed me down."

She could tell Cy's energy was returning. He was bouncing from one foot to another, itching to move. But he was still restrained.

"You know, there was something I wish I could have shown you," she said, hoping he would pursue further. "Maybe if you would've been there, I could've done it properly."

Cy took a few seconds before responding, "Okay, fine. Tell me."

Ivy smiled coyly.

"Are you going to tell me?"

"You know that cow... the one Felip was telling you about earlier?"

"His favorite one? The one that always ran off?"

He was legitimately interested now, leaning in and standing still.

"I know where to find her."

"What!?"

"Well... I know where I saw her last."

Cy took a step closer and lowered his voice to a whisper. "Can we find her?"

Ivy could see the wheels spinning in his head; he wanted to help Felip and Agnes, wanted to be the brave explorer this time.

I have him again. Like I have Celia and Maya.

"You and me," Ivy confirmed. "She's out there in the woods."

"But Mother told us to stay here..."

"The two of us, though? We'll be safe. And smart!"

Cy grinned in spite of himself, swinging his arm as if brandishing an invisible sword.

"There's just one thing... well, the last time I saw the cow... I kind of changed her."

"Changed her?"

"The cow, yeah. We can find it together. But she isn't a cow anymore."

Cy shook his head, his blonde hair flapping over his eyes.

"She's a bear."

Chapter 8

Nicolaus

The question hung in the air for a full minute as Nic tried to process it. There was a sheen of sweat between his leg and the huge chair that had once belonged to Orrin.

"How did my husband die?"

"Um," Nic whispered softly, his addled mind searching for any words.

Elfie said nothing. She knew he had heard her just fine. She sipped her ironwort tea, and Nic noticed a slight tremble in her hand as she set it down. The scarred stump where her second arm should have been was uncovered.

The beach flashed in Nic's memory – dead bodies, screams, and smells he never wanted to experience again; and Orrin. Nic remembered Orrin sparring with three men as Xander closed in.

He'd tried to stop the Bouran.

Then Xander knocked me down, and...

"There was an explosion."

"Yes, Nicolaus. This part, I know," Elfie said, her voice firm yet gentle, "I want to hear more. You know what I mean, I think."

Does she mean Xander? How would she know?

Nic felt oddly concerned about Elfie's opinion of the Bouran soldier. After all, he had been the one to drag him to their house.

I did it to save him!

"Help them... all of them..."

"Well... I mean, Counc– Orrin was fending off three soldiers at the time. I was fighting with one myself. Um, if you can call it that, I guess. He knocked me down in seconds. Then, it was just Orrin and the Bouran soldier who had beaten me."

Elfie nodded, "I'm sure they were all going after my husband. The great Golden Spear."

Her tone became bitter as she invoked his legendary title. Nic wondered why. Certainly, Elfie was not jealous of the good graces her husband held amongst the Achaean people.

It's what made him such a target. That's what she despises.

"Yes. So, there he was. At the end, that is. Fighting with a soldier." Nic shut his eyes, trying to picture the scene perfectly. "And he knocked the man away, but three more soldiers rushed in. Or was it four? Bouran soldiers. The first one knocked me down again... and he was standing over me..."

Nic's voice trailed off.

But he didn't kill me.

Elfie twisted her cup of tea around. "This was when the explosion happened?"

Nic was suddenly thrust back into the moment. He was covered in wet sand, looking up at the Bouran soldier, his hand extended. Xander. Then, everything went white; the light came before the noise – a deafening bang.

"I didn't see Orrin when it happened," Nic's voice was soft again. "I... he was..."

Elfie patted Nic's hand, "You did everything you could, I know. Nicolaus... was he in pain? Did the explosion end everything... at once?"

Nic was back on the beach. Red crawled across Orrin's linens, spreading radially from wounds in his neck, back, and stomach.

And his armor.

His incredible breastplate was twisted and warped, shimmering with the same oozing blood that had already found its way to Nic's hand.

Wet. Warm and wet.

"He was already gone when I saw him. Peacefully."

Elfie sighed.

Peacefully. Has there ever been a death in war that was peaceful?

She finished her tea. Hoping Orrin's wife had reached some sort of satisfactory closure, Nic leaned back in his chair and closed his eyes. He was pleased that he had not cried in his retelling. He hated weeping in front of others.

Nic heard the squeaking of a chair, followed by a rustle. When he opened his eyes again, Elfie was pouring herself a cup of water.

"I'm sure this hasn't been easy for you, Nicolaus. So, thank you. But I'm afraid there is more I must ask."

Nic's palms began to sweat.

"The Bouran soldier…"

"I–" the words were stuck in the back of Nic's throats.

She can't know it was Xander… can she?

"The soldiers may have been the ones fighting my husband. We can agree upon this. And they wanted to kill him. And I'm certain he killed many of them."

What?

Nic tried to dry his hands on his shirt.

Elfie sat down once again, "How many Heliken soldiers were killed in the blast?"

The haze of last night's wine was finally dissipating, enough that Nic thought he understood where Elfie was going. The nagging voice in his mind whispered once more. Clearer now.

"Not many. At first… well, at first I thought both sides would have suffered…"

"But they didn't. Not really. You brought me home a wounded Bouran soldier. From what I've heard, there were hundreds more like him. Burned. But our losses… ours were not as great."

I've been drinking too much.

Nic had forgotten how strange he'd found that the day of the battle. Everything had happened so fast since then. He'd been so distracted.

That's why *I took Xander back with me. He spared my life...*

"You don't think..."

...and the explosion. Something was wrong with it.

"You were there, Nicolaus. How many of our officers had retreated before the explosion?"

"All of them. All but Orrin."

"You've already thought about what this means; I can tell."

Nic's head wasn't spinning so much now. He took a sip of Elfie's water, apologized, then tried to stand.

When standing failed, Nic asked, "Why though? Why..."

"Oh, you know why! Helike wins the battle! Boura's forces were already outmatched, but this explosion ensured the victory. As if that weren't enough, *someone* removed my husband. What better way to commit a murder than in the middle of battle?"

Nic knew she was right. His first impulses after the battle had been correct; the drinking had repressed it. It must have. The small voice that had plagued his mind for days giggled.

I tried to remind myself. Did I simply not want it to be true?

"What should we do?" Nic had no idea.

"I'm sure you have a notion of who's behind this. Like I've said, my husband was many things, but he was not a politician. He shared far too much with both you and me; he saw us as confidants – people to whom he could gripe and complain. But it is more than that. You and I were his advisors."

"I wasn't..."

I was his steward. His attendant. Not an advisor.

"He trusted you like you were his own son. I truly believe he wanted you in his place."

"I'm only sixteen!"

And I don't want that. I don't want anything to do with the Council.

Elfie's voice began to rise, "Don't equate age with wisdom, Nicolaus. We must find out the truth of Orrin's death. You must know people in the castle. For his honor, find out all you can."

Nic closed his eyes. He took a deep breath.

Elfie stood, rubbing her forehead. "I'm sorry. I shouldn't ask all this of you. When you leave, you are welcome to go where you wish... but..."

She wiped away a tear. Nic stood, successfully this time, and walked to face the one-armed widow. He hugged her awkwardly, and when he pulled away, saw that she was smiling – a sad smile, but a smile, nonetheless.

"I want to help. I... I need to. For your husband. And for you."

And Rosie, and her lost children.

Elfie turned to hide her face, motioning towards her room and mumbling about needing to grab something. She disappeared, crying quietly.

"Great work, Nicolaus," Nic said under his breath

He sipped on his water, then set the cup down, stretching his arms and flexing his legs. Moments later, Elfie returned clutching a scroll in her one hand. The scroll was not large, perhaps the length of his forearm, and composed of thick papyrus. Elfie offered it to him. Nic took it. The package was somewhat weighty, and he realized there were actually several scrolls rolled up.

"What are these?"

"Maps and notes about the cities of Achaea. If you are going to help protect this territory, you need to familiarize yourself with it."

"Oh," Nic said, suddenly finding the scrolls heavier. "Thank you."

"Everything that you would need to know about the governances and natures of each city is in these scrolls. Of course, there is only so much that can be written about such things; you would need to travel there to truly understand."

The scroll on the outside unfurled to reveal a map of Achaea and its surrounding regions. He could see Dyme and the Dymean Wall, Olenus, Boura, Pharas, Helike, Pellene, Persia, Ionia... and in the southernmost corner, Egypt.

"So... you want me to read them?"

"Oh, use your wits, child! They aren't for kindling! Orrin said you were sharper than him; now sharpen even further! This information, and anything else you can find – this is your weapon. This is your Golden Spear. Use it. Protect and avenge the people you love. My husband..."

Nic looked down at the map. It certainly did not look like a golden spear.

"I must find out how he truly perished... and why."

****

Nic strapped the dark leather bag shut, making sure his belongings were secure before hoisting it over his shoulder. There wasn't much inside, just an extra robe and his scrolls. Elfie had also given him bread, salted meats, and a handful of silver crowns. It had been two days since he'd received the scrolls, and Nic had barely made it through any of the information.

His head was swimming with the names of kings, councilors, and diplomats from each city – Pharas was a democracy, or was Patras? Or perhaps both? Elfie was correct; he needed much, much more time to improve his understanding of the Achaean League.

Xander had already made for Boura, leaving early that morning to return to his beloved. His departure had been brief, though complete with expressions of gratitude to Elfie and Rosie. He had promised them anything they desired in return, and Nic wondered how he could fulfill such a lofty obligation.

Then, he had turned to Nic. "Nicolaus, I'm going to be forever grateful. You had no reason to bring me here. My-uh... my child can grow up with a father now."

Oh.

Nic hadn't known how to respond.

Xander is a father?

He hadn't known. He blushed fiercely. "Well, you didn't need to spare me on the beach. I suppose we're even."

Xander nodded, shaking his hand with a surprisingly gentle grip. Then, he turned his very handsome face to the door, and disappeared into the timid dawn.

With his few belongings in tow, it was Nic's turn to bid his farewells. Gerrian and Rosie were in the kitchen, along with a tired-looking Elfie. Nic noticed that Rosie looked at him with less interest than Xander, and much less adoration than Gerrian.

"Well…"

"Nicolaus, this has been a gift," Elfie said.

"No, I… thank you, Elfie. I don't know what to say; you all have been too good to me. I'm… well, I'm not sure how I could repay you."

Rosie gave a weak smile, and Gerrian nodded formally.

"Dear, you don't need to give us anything in return. You meant so much to my husband. He would be so happy to know you were here."

In Elfie's deep green eyes, Nic could see that there was one thing he could do to repay her – he could avenge her husband. But he could also tell that she expected no payment.

A truly good person. This is why Orrin married her.

Nic wished he knew more people like her. He hugged Rosie awkwardly, shook Gerrian's hand, and embraced Elfie.

"Thank you all, again. Sincerely. I hope this isn't the last we see of each other."

"It won't be," Elfie assured, opening the door for him.

"Be well, Nicolaus," Rosie called half-heartedly.

The afternoon sun was warm. Nic hadn't been in the fresh air for over ten days. He took a deep breath, seeing the city as if for the first time – the palace, nestled in the hillside. Seagulls soared above towards the open ocean. The place felt tranquil, as if thousands hadn't died in a battle ten days prior.

The town was strangely empty, especially with such beautiful weather. He set out for Krassen's bar. A cup of wine would accompany his studies well. He passed the bakery where the baker's girl worked, focusing intently on the road.

I can't see her right now.

He rounded a corner. Krassen's pub was straight ahead.

A cup of wine. Perhaps a game of senet.

Suddenly, Nic felt a sharp tug on his robe. He gasped, but before he could call out, he was yanked into the alleyway.

A hand covered his mouth.

"Wait!" Nic yelped, his voice muffled.

He twisted, hoping to get a look at his would-be killer. Then, he realized, the hand was smaller than his. It was rough, but not unkind.

"What in the name of Hades are you doing here?"

Nic looked into a familiar face, with brown eyes, caramel skin, and hair like his.

"Opi?" he muttered, his voice muffled.

She removed her hand, whispering sharply, "We can't be here. Follow me. Unless you wish to be executed."

Chapter 9

Keoki

Keoki didn't know whether to be afraid or excited as he and Sapphir approached the hut. It was completely dark outside, save for the candles that shone through neighboring windows and dim moonlight. Sapphir put a finger to her lip, raising her eyebrows at Keoki as if asking whether he understood the message.

I wish we could have stayed with Babs just a few moments longer.

Keoki's hair was making his neck itchy, and his beard was growing in shaggier than ever. He tried to push those thoughts out of his mind.

That doesn't matter right now.

Keoki drew his new stone knife quietly. It felt less comfortable in his hand, but familiar enough to do the job. He gripped it tighter.

Sapphir padded silently to the door, and Keoki followed, trying his hardest not to make any noise. Hushed voices were suddenly audible from inside.

"Matis, you tell him, and you live. We're dead; we're not a threat. That's all you have to say. We're dead, and you live."

The voice was a low grunt. Sapphir's eyes widened, pale blue in the light of the moon. She motioned for Keoki to come closer. The first voice spoke again.

"Good. Now before–"

Keoki's foot snapped a twig. He closed his eyes in frustration, feeling Sapphir's disappointment as the conversation inside ceased.

Suddenly, the door was pulled open, and Sapphir tumbled inside. She rolled sideways as a dagger flashed at her leg. Keoki bowled inside, running headlong into the lithe figure. He grunted in pain as the man's dagger raked across his left arm. The man kicked Keoki to the side and dove at Sapphir, grabbing her roughly by the shoulder and tossing her on top of Keoki.

Sapphir's robe caught in Keoki's sandal. The linen tore as she extracted herself from his bloodied form. On the other side of the room, a man who must have been Matis was tied to a chair and gagged; he had knocked himself and the chair over in an attempt to escape and was writhing on the ground trying to get free.

The sinewy man and Sapphir were squared off. He pushed the door shut to darken the room further. Keoki was in agony. When he touched his forearm lightly, he could feel bone.

GHE CHILDREN OF GHE SEA

In a flash of light, Matis was suddenly free, leaving Sapphir between him and the dagger-wielding fighter.

He's the one. The magician.

Keoki tried to push himself up, but the loss of blood and flesh had left him instantly weary. The three remained in their standoff as Keoki's bleeding slowed.

"Who are you?" the first man said in his harsh whisper.

Keoki could make out the hawkish features of the speaker. He was lean as a wolf. Matis himself was not quite as impressive. His head was shaven, and he was short and plump. His glowing hand revealed why he was so dangerous.

"That's Sapphir of Helike, Daughter of Teremos, and a Child of the Sea," Matis said, grinning.

The dagger-wielder's eyes narrowed. "Another one like yourself, then. Another Fisherman?"

Sapphir looked puzzled. "Fisherman? I know nothing of them."

Matis' hand twitched, and he laughed. "You wouldn't. The Children and the Fisherman are not one and the same, Rizon Atsali. I myself, happen to be both. Being a magician can certainly... be helpful."

Rizon Atsali, the man with the dagger, sneered, "I never needed that kind of help."

His body remained entirely still, with the dagger pointed at the ground. Keoki panted, biting his tongue to try and lessen the pain. Sapphir's left foot rotated around its heel towards Matis.

"But now... now you do need it," Matis said, "Shall I report in that you are alive and well?"

Rizon growled, "I can still kill you with her in the room, Matis."

He flicked his wrist and his dagger leapt towards Matis' shoulder in a flash. Matis tried to dodge it and retaliate, but Sapphir was much quicker.

The dagger dissolved into dust, and Rizon and Matis collapsed to the floor, bound and gagged with rope and cloth. Keoki felt his consciousness ebbing.

"Sapphir," he croaked.

She was already rushing over, falling to her knees beside him.

Is that worry in her eyes?

"Are you always this foolish? Alerting everyone to your presence, racing in without thinking. No wonder you and my girls were captured."

Her tone was less aggressive than her words, as if she were scolding instead of confronting. Keoki groaned, which turned into a yelp when Sapphir picked up his arm to examine it.

"Rizon Atsali is strong," she muttered, "Fractured bone and... oh yes, an artery. Cut right through it."

Keoki closed his eyes, trying to focus on anything but the pain. He heard Sapphir rummaging in the dark for something, then felt a cool liquid splash on his bone and torn muscles. The pain dulled.

How does she do that?

"Just stay here," she instructed.

The two men were squirming in their binding, but it did no good. They were held fast. Sapphir waved a hand and Matis froze on the spot, unblinking and unmoving. She turned her attention to Rizon Atsali and crouched down next to him.

"You. What are you? Not a Child I take it."

Rizon, now ungagged, responded, "You already have my name."

"Not who, *what*?" she snapped. "What is a Fisherman?"

"I'm not one of those," he said, his voice falling.

"Not anymore?" she guessed.

Keoki was already feeling better. He reached for his arm cautiously and was pleased to find that his bone was no longer exposed. He sat up.

"I'm assuming by your silence that I'm correct."

"I was one of them. *Was.*"

"And they are?"

"Whatever you need them to be. Couriers. Fur traders. Assassins."

"What did you mean when you said you needed to be dead?"

Sapphir sat down cross-legged, facing Rizon Atsali, who was still tied and prone on the hard ground. Rizon licked his lips and tried to adjust his position.

"They are looking for me now," he nodded towards Matis.

"I see. And they won't be looking for a dead man. You know nothing of the Children of the Sea?"

"I know who they were. I didn't know they still existed. I didn't know I had worked with any. Not until tonight. The magic... it's all real... it's..."

Keoki scooted towards them, and Sapphir shot him a warning look.

"You told Matis to tell them, *we* are dead. Who else?"

"She's not here," Rizon said simply. "Can you untie me? I've been bound far too many times recently."

Sapphir shook her head. "I've seen you with the knife. Now, I need that man," she pointed at Matis, "If I want to finish my job. But I also can't stand to have anyone alive who knows we were here."

Rizon glanced at Keoki and he waved. Sapphir raised her eyebrows again.

"I'm just trying to protect family," Rizon said softly.

"Unfortunately, so am I."

Sapphir lifted her hand.

"Wait!"

What am I doing? Why should I care?

Sapphir gave him a venomous look.

"Sorry," Keoki started. "Sapphir, what's killing him going to do?"

"Are you forgetting that he nearly cut your arm in half?"

Right. He did do that.

"In his defense, I had a knife of my own. He's being honest with us, and he's not the enemy." Keoki gestured to Matis, who was still frozen and gagged. "*That's* the enemy. The Children."

"Why are you protecting him?" Sapphir asked.

Keoki could have screamed at her then. It wasn't long ago, that she had thought to kill him *for her family.*

How many innocents have to die by her hand before I come to my senses?!

His fist clenched, and a shock of pain leapt to his shoulder. But it didn't seem to be from his arm. That felt mostly healed.

And she did that. She took me prisoner... But she also set me free... she healed me....

"I don't know," Keoki sighed, shrugging his shoulders. "I don't know, Sapphir. But why not just let him live? Spare him; let Matis tell the Fishermen that he's gone, and we'll be on our way. We both win."

Rizon stayed silent and stone-faced. Keoki wondered what was going through his head. It was unnerving, being at the mercy of Sapphir, the Child of the Sea from Helike.

Fire blazed in her blue eyes. She was planning to kill Matis too. Keoki could see this despite the darkness. Now both would need to stay alive so Matis could fulfill his promise to Rizon.

Am I making a mistake?

Keoki knew guilt still weighed heavily on Sapphir. Guilt for imprisoning him, but mostly guilt for her children. Perhaps that would make her see his reasoning.

She lowered her hand, then began untying Rizon.

When she was done, he pushed himself to his feet and helped her up. He looked to Keoki with gratitude. Sapphir pointed at

Matis and he unfroze. She removed the gag.

Matis began to laugh. "Sapphir! Daughter of Teremos! I thought you were dead."

"I hoped you would be."

"Your father longs to have you back. So, what have I missed? Where is your shaggy friend?"

He craned his neck to catch a glimpse of Keoki.

"Ah! Looks a little like the other one, doesn't he?"

Sapphir's nostrils flared.

"You're going to do as I asked," Rizon cut in impatiently. "Tell him, tell all of them, that I'm dead. Me and the girl."

"And you, Sapphir? What do you wish? Information in exchange for my life, I assume."

"Information, yes," Sapphir said coldly.

Uh oh.

"Then travel to Leontium."

"Leontio?"

"All the same. You may want to leave your shaggy boy."

Rizon seemed surprised that Matis had divulged the information so quickly.

"Now you, Rizon Atsali. Wait one moment."

Matis shut his eyes tightly and hummed. He opened them a minute later. When he smiled, his lip curled.

"Is that it?"

"Your friend is saved. And you, too," Matis sneered. "You're dead!"

Rizon shook his head. "How?"

"There are more Children than just me in the Fishermen. They'll spread word to others," he laughed.

They can talk to each other? From here?

Rizon Atsali shrugged in resignation, then asked Sapphir, "Is that true? Can they do that?"

She nodded. "Yes. We can all communicate if we wish. It has... other complications."

Matis smiled. "Everybody wins, yes? Now off with you both, before I change my mind and call in more of my friends."

He laughed again.

"He could be lying Sapphir. Why should we go to Leontio? What if it's a trap?"

"We'll be careful then," Sapphir said slowly. "If it's a trap, we'll just have more leads to follow."

Rizon looked at Keoki and Sapphir with a little confusion. Keoki was glad he had helped Sapphir spare the man.

"I wouldn't betray another one of your shaggy boys, Sapphir," Matis grinned stupidly. "Not again."

He's a fool.

Keoki looked at the bald man with a mixture of disgust and sympathy. Rizon helped Keoki to his feet and began shepherding him to the door. Sapphir leaned down next to Matis, reaching a hand out as if to untie him.

"Your father will be so pleased to s–"

The room fell silent.

Chapter 10

Melani

Melani ran a finger through her hair, still short and stained black. She looked up at the two-story building situated neatly in the center of Patras. Much of the city was farmland and fisherfolk, but there was a growing square of buildings like the one that was so familiar to her. Bottles lined the wall in the window, full of curious mixtures and an amalgam of herbs.

Apothecaries. Father's store is still doing well.

She took a deep breath, her excitement peaking.

I'm home.

She put her hand on the door. The wood was cool against her palm. It was still cloudy and a little foggy in the mid-morning. The light tinkle of bells as she pushed forward almost made her tear up.

Such a familiar sound.

"H-Hello," she said, her voice catching in her throat.

She heard movement from the storeroom – the clinking of glass and shuffling of feet. She knew who it was from the way his sandals sounded against the stone floors. He opened the storeroom door, and froze, his mouth ajar.

"Hi, Father," she whispered.

Time resumed. He threw his arms up and whooped, "Mel! Melani!"

He pushed his way past a table, knocking over a few bottles, which he ignored, and rushed to her. Melani wrapped her arms around him with joy.

"Oh, Melani! Oh! Your mother! Oh, I have to tell your mother! Osanda! OSANDA!"

Her father was tan like Melani, with her same naturally brown hair and brown eyes. He stood only a few inches taller than Melani. He was slight and youthful for his age, though his hair was now flecked with grey.

Footsteps pounded the stairs as another person descended.

"Osanda!" her father called, "Look!"

When her mother rounded the corner, Melani met her with a hug as well.

"Mel! You changed your hair!" she exclaimed with surprise.

"Yes, yes, Mother, I did. How are you?"

Melani pulled herself away. She took in the two people standing before her, relishing in the comfort of her home.

"Oh, my dear. What brings you home? What brings you back to Patras?"

Melani's mother, similarly slight and short, though with darker hair and paler skin, took a seat at the table. Her father followed and motioned for Melani to sit.

"There's so much to tell, I wouldn't know where to start!"

"And your hair! Why did you change it?"

Oh mother... correct priorities, as usual.

"I guess I just wanted it to look more like yours," she joked.

Where do I even begin?

Her father sighed, "Ahh, Melani. So wonderful to have you home. Isn't it, Osanda? I was just saying that we're missing our beautiful artist."

He had an enormous grin on his face and was nodding emphatically to his wife.

"Dear, where is Xander? We'd love to see him."

Melani's smile receded. Her father was chuckling to himself and shaking his head; when he saw Melani's face, however, his fell.

"Is everything okay?"

Melani cleared her throat.

"Um, he... have you heard news of the war between Helike and Boura?"

Her father and mother exchanged a glance, "Rumors, as always. What was it that farmer said yesterday, Osanda? A battle on a beach?"

The beach.

Melani could see the wet sand and mucky brine dappling hundreds of bodies. She could hear groans and dry heaving from injured soldiers before they were taken out of their misery.

And the smell...

Melani could feel herself tensing up. She responded in a hushed tone, "Yes, a battle. On the beaches north and west from Helike."

"And Xander?" Her mother's voice was even quieter than her own.

Suddenly, the familiar scent of herbs and mixtures was nauseating. She wanted to paint in the fresh air with wood ash. She wanted to be in Boura – listening to the sound of Xander's forge.

"Mel, is everything okay? Is Xander... is he?"

"I don't know. I never saw his... I never saw him."

Her mother gasped, "My darling, were you at the beach?"

"Not in time. I was there after."

Her parents' cheerful demeanors had all but disappeared. Her father looked concerned, but her mother was beside herself.

"Dear, Mel! What were you doing there? At a battle site!"

"I went with Xander's brother, Rizon. He," she paused wondering how much to tell them. "He said we were both in danger – that we needed to find Xander."

"What could be more dangerous than a battlefield!"

"Osanda, let her continue," her father nodded to her.

"I'm a healer you know; well, I became a healer for the Bouran army, anyway. So... a few soldiers told me where I could find

Xander at the battle site..."

Behind the fear in her father's eyes, she could see a glint of pride. He always supported her artistry; but a healer for the Bouran army? He would brag of it to anyone who walked into his store.

"...but... by the time I got there... it was over. They were gone."

"Who was gone? The Bourans?"

"Almost everyone. There... there was an explosion. Bourans that didn't die were taken back to Helike."

Her parents sat speechless, staring at their daughter dumbfounded. Melani was surprised to find that her eyes were still dry.

He's alive. Alive, and I'm going to go back for him.

"So, now I'm here. Rizon and I took a ship. Well, we didn't *take* it, but–"

"Melani," her mother interrupted. "Why were you and Xander in danger?"

Melani pushed herself away from the table and stood. "Could I get myself some water, Father?"

"There's wine in the storeroom. Wine and grape juice."

Wine sounded tempting to Melani, but she wondered if indulging was a bad idea.

Should I have wine? With the baby?

It was then that she realized she hadn't told her parents about the child.

One thing at a time. I'll tell Asala when she gets home.

She found the grape juice and wine, selecting the juice to quench her thirst. She took it back to the table.

"Where's Asala?"

"She's with healers today; they're giving her training so she can go to the School of Boura, as you did," her father said, beaming.

"She'll be home soon. Now, Melani, tell us. Are you still in danger?" her mother asked, wringing her hands.

"That's why I'm here, I just–"

"Oh, darling! Oh, Corvi did you hear her? She's in danger!"

Her mother was hitting her father as if trying to get his attention, though he had clearly been listening already.

"Mother! I came to warn you! You and Father. Asala, everyone! Find somewhere else to go. Anywhere!"

"Mel, why? What's happened to you?"

"It's too much to explain! To be quite honest, I'm not even sure. Just get away from the city. For a few weeks."

"I'm not go–"

"Osanda. Listen to Melani. We can leave in a couple days; we could stay with Pani and Joli."

Melani's brother, Pani, had moved inland years ago to grow a vineyard. The wine and grape juice they drank at Melani's old home usually came from him. Her older sister, Joli, had accompanied him two years later. Even Melani couldn't find the vineyard on her own; it seemed a safe option.

"Please, Mother. They'll love your company, anyway. I'm sorry, I... I just...."

Her mother scoffed, and her father looked incredulous. Eventually, however, she conceded.

"It'll take convincing to get Asala out of the city, but if this is what you want, Melani. How much longer will you be in Patras? Ooh, I'm just happy to see you. Too happy to be angry."

Melani smiled, though she felt terrible. She knew both her parents could see this; perhaps they felt it was no use pushing her further. She was clearly upset.

"A couple more days. We can all leave then."

"And you're coming with us to Pani's?" Melani's father asked with hope.

They knew the answer already.

"No... Mother, Father, I'm sorry... we... I need to find Xander. And I can only do that if I know you're safe."

Her mother pointed at her hair. "So that's why you've changed your hair?"

"Yes, Mother. That's why my hair is shorter."

The bells tinkled once more as someone pushed the door open.

"Corvi? Might I come in?"

A woman stood in the doorframe, leaning heavily on a walking cane.

"We'll finish this discussion later, Melani, dear," he said, nodding to his wife, "Yes, do come in madam!"

He welcomed the customer joyfully, pretending as though nothing were amiss. Melani's mother sighed and made for the staircase, then changed her mind and grabbed a bottle of wine before ascending. She beckoned for Melani to follow.

"Come along, dear. I don't want all of our conversations to be dreary while you're here."

****

Two nights passed before Melani returned to her father's shop once again, taking a canteen of wine out of the store closet.

"No, the vintage with purple grapes and elderberry is much better," Asala declared, snatching the canteen of white-grape juice roughly from Melani's hands.

"Sal, I wanted this one! I don't want wine!"

"What, for the baby? Please, Mel, we're both healers. What harm can it do? You'll thank me once you've had this with fresh bread and goat cheese, horse-brain."

Melani rolled her eyes. "Horse-brain? How old are you? Besides, it only works with stupid animals. Horses are smart."

"Well, they aren't as smart as people."

"Maybe some people," Melani retorted, grabbing Asala's prized wine and uncorking the canteen.

A little can't hurt.

She took a sip.

Damn it's delicious.

"See!" Asala laughed, "You know I'm right!"

"You sound like children, girls," their mother said, descending the stairs noisily.

This time both Melani and Asala rolled their eyes, and Melani strangely hoped that her mother hadn't noticed.

How old am I?

"Mother, how are you? You've gathered your things?" she asked.

"Yes. Your father and I both have. Asala, you'll be ready to leave by midday?"

Asala glanced at Melani with sympathy – Melani had been more upfront with her younger sister about the situation. She felt honesty was necessary with Asala; Melani often worried that her baby sister harbored resentment for her since she and Xander had left for Boura.

She may be in Boura soon, too. Her training seems to be going well.

"Yeah. Yeah, I'll be ready whenever you and Father are."

"Great, I hope we won't be a burden on Pani and Joli."

"They'd feel too guilty turning away their little sister. And parents," Asala added, "I don't really care if we're a burden, anyway."

"You're just looking forward to more wine," Melani whispered to Asala who smiled and shrugged.

Their mother shook her head and brushed past them to check that the bolt on the door was working.

"Asala, call Father down. I should be getting on my way."

"Why don't you?"

"I don't like to yell."

"So refined, sister. FATHER! MELANI IS GOING TO LEAVE WITHOUT SAYING GOODBYE IF YOU DON'T COME DOWN!"

"Oh, how you've matured," Melani said, rapping Asala's shoulder with the back of her hand.

Asala danced away, sticking out her tongue playfully. She was four-and-a-half years Melani's junior, approaching sixteen. Melani could tell that she still approached life rather flippantly. She enjoyed the apprenticeship as a healer but hadn't yet committed fully to the craft. Despite her relative youth, Asala stood two inches taller than Melani. She had the same look as the rest of Melani's family.

"Ah, my dear daughter! I do wish you could join us at the vineyard." Her father called as he hopped off the bottom stair and into his shop, "Though, um, I am trying to understand this... situation."

I can't let them know how afraid I am.

"I wish that, too, Father. You'll all be safe and happy with Joli and Pani – that's all I wanted," she said, before quickly adding, "And I'll be fine! We have it under control. Me and Rizon."

"Rizon... he's like Xander, yes? Just as you were saying. You two will be okay."

"Yes," she lied, picturing Rizon's scars and wolfish face. "Quite similar to Xander. We're only trying to... trying to find him. His brother. My Xander."

She could feel herself tensing, and stopped talking, looking to Asala for help.

"I know you'll find him, sister! And you won't have to fear for us."

"Yes, this is very brave of you, dear," her mother said. "Very brave to look out for Xander. He would do the same for you, we know."

Of course, he would.

There was a moment of silence as Melani fiddled with her pack, moving it from one shoulder to another. She looked at the floor, feeling the stares of her concerned family members.

They know this is worse. They know I'm pretending.

Her mother and father had argued with her both nights, pleading for her to come with them to the vineyard.

They wanted me to stop... to just... give up!

"I love you all."

She couldn't say any more than that for fear of breaking down. She knew they didn't want her to leave; and she knew they couldn't stop her.

Even if they tried.

"We love you too, Mel," Asala said. "The next time we see you... we can't wait."

Melani knew Asala didn't want to spoil the news of Melani's baby. It had never seemed like the right time to share with their parents.

They would have made me guilty. Made me feel as if I was

putting the baby in danger.

Melani wondered if she should feel more ashamed.

It's no longer just me at risk…

"It won't be long until then," she said, moving to stand in the doorframe.

But will it?

Her father, mother, and sister all hugged her tightly, whispering words of love and hope to her, ensuring that they would be safe – that she would be in their prayers.

She sniffled as she pushed the door open gently. Her mother embraced her once more, and Asala gave her an encouraging smile. Melani turned, collected herself, and walked towards the harbor.

Her family watched for a moment, before letting the door close behind them. As it swung shut, Melani could hear, perhaps for the last time, the faint singing of the little bells.

Chapter 11

Simon

Simon stood alone in his sparse chambers, gazing at the courtyard. His eyes were transfixed on the statue of a foreign god. Of course, he was rather used to Poseidon at this point. All the Greek gods were like this to him, in fact – foreign, but not unfamiliar. He had been working as an attendant to Euripides for several months now and was learning to like the city of Helike. With all its fame and size, Sparta had always made him feel uneasy. Helike's crisp ocean breezes, regal Council chambers, and eclectic city square made Simon feel much more at home.

If I have ever known what home *is.*

Simon felt strangely closer to the city already. He'd even met with a leader from the Sons of Poseidon that very day. It seemed that this was an oddly important task to leave to an attendant, but

Euripides had been busying himself with concerned citizens in the city square.

The priest was quite kind and cordial, sharing his insight on a cult within the Sons that was becoming more and more troublesome. Simon remembered feeling uncomfortably warm in the priest's presence and very aware of his bald head. The priest's hair was long, dark, and curly, swooping to his muscular shoulders.

He was quite a handsome priest.

Simon curled a finger through the rough curtain.

The priest mentioned... magic. A foolish sentiment, to be sure.

He wanted to tell Euripides. Those so-called "Children of the Sea" needed to be dealt with. A faint knock on Simon's door broke the silence.

Perhaps this is him.

"You may enter," Simon called, straightening his purple robe.

The door opened slowly, and a slender man greeted him with a witty smile. His long, tan fingers ran through perfect brown hair. Simon's pulse jumped.

"Oh, uh, hello. Apologies, Councilor Gaios, I wasn't expecting you."

"May I enter, nonetheless?"

"Yes. Yes, of course."

Simon gave a flourishing gesture, which he immediately regretted.

"How can I help? Rather... is there something you require this evening, Councilor Gaios?"

"You may start by calling me Gaios; I prefer to leave the Councilor in the Court."

"Yes, sorry. Sorry, Gaios."

"You've struck me as quite a bit more eloquent in the past few weeks. Am I mistaken?"

Simon paused, picking at his sleeve, then gave a wry smile. "Perhaps you have erred. I would never strike a councilor."

Gaios tilted his head forward. "Ah, then I must send my apologies now for interrupting your privacy."

"With all there is to think about as an attendant to the valiant Councilor Euripides, I am never fully alone."

This time Gaios actually laughed, though Simon felt his joke had not been very funny.

"If I may ask, Gaios, why have you come tonight?"

Gaios sat on the chamber's small bed, leaving Simon standing awkwardly above him. Gaios was only a couple years older than him. Simon still found that strange. Being a councilor, well-loved by the city, Gaios always seemed considerably more mature.

"I could tell you that I make it my duty to meet with and learn the stories of every servant and attendant in the palace."

"But..." Simon said, moving to lean against the window.

Gaios tapped his fingers against the bed. "But this would be a lie. You, however, have caught my interest."

"With my eloquence..."

Gaios stopped tapping and began to trace one finger across

the linen sheet, as if writing out a message.

"You are from Sparta, yes?"

"Before Helike, I was in Sparta."

"And before Sparta?"

"I came from the East."

"You have that look about you. Forgive me for asking, we do not need to delve into your past today."

Today... implying there will be more conversations?

"It is no trouble. But I don't believe much of my past would interest a councilor of Helike."

And I still don't know why you're here.

"Every man, woman, and child has a story, Simon. An interesting one, in fact. The only matter is whether or not I am interested to know it."

"But why do you want to know mine?"

Gaios scratched his chin with his free hand, as the other continued tracing.

"Because I know what it is like."

What is he talking about? Must he always speak in riddles?

"I'm afraid I don't understand, Gaios. Were you an attendant before you became a councilor?"

"I mean that I prefer the company of people like you – as you prefer the company of those like me."

Simon stopped tugging at his sleeve, holding the end of it tightly between his thumb and forefinger. It was common knowledge across Achaea that many men of stature enjoyed other men of stature. It was seen as a godly right to do so. Most elites Gaios' age were more often seen surrounded by women, however.

"Why are you telling me this?" Simon asked, trying not to let discomfort creep into his voice.

"Simply so you know that you are not alone; you have great potential as a leader of Helike, Simon. Euripides knows this, and the others are learning it. It would be a shame if you did not embrace your gifts. All of them."

Does he truly care? What would he have to gain from this?

"That is kind of you to say, Gaios. Are you–"

"Where do you take your noontime meals?"

Simon shrugged. "The courtyard. Sometimes in the city square if time permits."

"Perhaps tomorrow, I can show you the finest fishmonger the city has to offer. Does this interest you?"

I'm not sure I can say no.

"I enjoy fish."

Why do I say such peculiar things?

Gaios smiled, picking himself up from the bed and extending his long-fingered hand to Simon. Simon accepted it with his own bony hand. Gaios' hand was warm.

"Then tomorrow, we can enjoy fish together."

✳✳✳✳

Simon's midnight mare slowed to a steady trot as he pulled back gently on the reins. He had bought the horse for a crown and a trident, to the delight of its former owner. The mare's name was Athena, but Simon was reluctant to use it. He saw no purpose in speaking to animals. In fact, he often avoided them altogether.

But these days called for special circumstances. The road to Olenus was winding and hilly, too arduous to walk given the urgency of the situation. With the speed of Athena, though, Simon was ten minutes from the city, despite leaving Patras late that morning.

Simon's meeting with Old Patreus had left him worried. He felt powerless knowing that both Gaios and King Basilius shared dreams of controlling Achaea. Simon had hoped to garner support from the most prominent Achaean territories — starting with Patras, Olenus, and Dyme in the West, before he moved to win over the East.

I was foolish for thinking it would be so simple.

The League had begun as a means to protect trade waters from piracy. Today, the League's Guard tended to the few marauders that were left, while each city grew more and more independent. Now, the tenuous alliance between the twelve cities was held together only by fear that any aggression would be met with resistance from a combination of the other territories.

Yet the cities grow less fond of each other with every passing day.

Gaios' vision for an Achaea that was ruled justly from its

124

potential capital, Helike, was becoming less of a fiction to him. Rather, the councilor was certain it was his future.

And now Old Patreus tells me that King Basilius of Olenus lusts for the same glory. How am I to stop them both?

Simon was still trying to formulate a solution. The closer he got to Olenus' walls, the more panicked he became.

Gaios had not always been such a difficult man to work with. He had been one of Simon's mentors and closest friends in the Court, even when Euripides was alive. Euripides had been fatherly in his instruction, while Gaios had led by example and showed him how to navigate political alliances.

And of course, Gaios had been more than that. Simon could vividly remember their first real conversation. He had been wearing a purple robe, watching the courtyard from his attendant's chambers when Gaios knocked on the door.

He was so polite then. Kind and witty.

Simon had not been intimate with anyone in the way he had been with Gaios, though he was certain he was not Gaios' first. However, more than sensuality, Simon had grown to love Gaios' manner. The two were never openly romantic, not wanting to raise questions of their reputations as councilors; but Gaios had been considerate, eager to learn about Simon. He was accepting of his nature. He did not seem to mind that Simon was keener to have a conversation than lie together.

He must have loved me.

Loved. That was what terrified Simon the most.

Is it truly in the past?

Simon had not shared Gaios' bed or even conversed much since Euripides' murder, and Gaios seemed colder to him for it. Simon suspected, and feared he knew, that Gaios was among the facilitators of the assassination carried out by Rizon Atsali.

And now the Golder Spear has perished, too.

Betrayed, saddened, and confused, Simon was unsure he would ever see Gaios the same way.

Something has changed within him.

Simon pulled on the mare's reins once more, and Athena slowed to a stroll. Ahead, Simon could see the walls that bordered the inner city and palace of Olenus. Storefronts, stone houses, and wooden huts surrounded it. The town itself looked very similar to Helike, though there was no central square, as everything radiated from the walled palace.

Basilius hides behind walls, but still wishes to rule beyond the city limits?

Simon knew the next few days could determine the future of the Achaean League. He wished he was as familiar with King Basilius as he was Gaios, though he supposed familiarity had not stopped war from breaking out between Helike and Boura.

I was far too slow... how could I have let him shatter our peace?

Athena stopped, stamping her hooves into the dusty road which lead to a series of inns and taverns. Simon extracted himself from his saddle with care, patting Athena gingerly.

I wonder if one of these inns will let me tether her. She may still be of some use.

Simon tried not to think of the danger that awaited him in the court of King Basilius.

I would be a valuable hostage – leverage over Gaios and the Council of Helike.

Despite this, Simon felt more concern than fear. He had made his choice to protect the League's peace. Athena sighed heavily, kicking up more dust as if trying to tell Simon something.

The horse has no worries, so why should I?

He admired the deep black eyes set in Athena's midnight hide. She was a truly beautiful creature.

If I do not succeed, what will become of you? A warhorse, perhaps.

Simon was suddenly worried for Athena's fate. If war did break out, hundreds of thousands would suffer. Would his mare be among that number?

Is there still hope for Gaios to end this before it begins?

Simon prayed there was. He would do all he could to rally peaceful Achaean support. However, he felt that his hope for Helike lay in the hands of his young attendant, and her Egyptian friend.

If he survived the Battle at the Beach, that is…. If I fail, they're the only ones left who can protect Helike from Gaios. Opi and Nicolaus.

Chapter 12

Sapphir

"You know it could be a trap," Keoki said, perhaps for the tenth time.

"Must we go over this again? What choice do we have? Matis gave us a location... that's all we could ask for."

"And you're willing to trust him? He's already betrayed you before, hasn't he?"

It would not surprise Sapphir if Matis had his hand in Yusef's death. She held many of the Children responsible.

Should I have been so quick to end his life?

Sapphir knew her mercilessness had surprised the former Fisherman, Rizon Atsali; what unsettled her more was how little it had fazed Keoki.

Does he expect brutality from me?

She supposed Keoki had reason enough to feel that way. But Matis deserved his fate. A swift death *had* been merciful.

"Keoki, you must have known finding my father would not be an easy task. If Leontio gets us nowhere, we will simply move to the next territory. Did you expect to be home in a matter of days?"

Perhaps I am being too harsh.

Keoki scowled. "You know that's not what I'm saying. I think we need to be cautious. If he was able to communicate with other Children so quickly for Rizon, what would have stopped him from setting a trap in Leontio?"

He is right, of course.

Sapphir swatted at a fruit fly. "I know, I know... we can be more careful the closer we get to the city."

Sapphir could no longer see the silhouette of Rhium in the starry night. They had parted ways with Rizon Atsali minutes after leaving the shack with the red stone that had belonged to Matis. Sapphir could tell the former Fisherman was wary of her, eager to return to Patras. He had nodded and thanked her, blood trickling from a cut just above his well-trimmed beard.

His eyes held as much darkness as mine.

Leontio was a hard day's walk from Rhium, but with the terrain becoming harsher and their desire to avoid well-traveled roads, Keoki and Sapphir expected to arrive slightly later. She knew little of the city; it was nestled in the mountains, and there were rumors that a cult of Artemis had risen to prominence in recent years.

That wouldn't be terribly surprising.

The wilderness surrounding Leontio probably demanded a healthy relationship with the goddess of the moon and the hunt. Already, the woods were thickening to forest, and Sapphir was reminded of the violent tribes that could be roaming the land.

They remained silent for a few minutes before Keoki decided he could stand it no longer.

Why does he always feel the need to speak?

"If you can communicate with other Children, why not just ask your father where he is?"

Sapphir had wondered when he would come to that conclusion. She exhaled slowly.

If only it were that simple.

"If I contact him, what do you think happens?"

Keoki shrugged. "I don't know how any of this works. The Blood of the Golden Age and all that."

"He has tried to talk to me before, you know. If I respond... he... I'm afraid he can sense where I am – read my thoughts, my chil..."

She let her voice trail off. Would her father be able to use Sapphir's mind as a bridge to her children's?

When he calls to me, I can't see where he is.

But was that by her father's design?

"So, you don't really know either?" Keoki mused.

"I... I guess not. When you're a magician, when you share blood... our blood... it *complicates* things. I can't really explain it."

Keoki opened his mouth as if to retort, then paused. They walked for a few more seconds, and a clearing opened up in the trees.

"Do you want to stop here for the night? We need to rest," Keoki offered.

Sapphir scanned the area, half expecting more Children or outlaws to pour in through the darkness.

I can't sense anyone nearby.

"We can exchange watches, yes?" she said.

"Sure. Sure, let's stop here."

The ground was dry and soft from the leaves and loam. Sapphir sat down, loosening her sandals and setting her pack aside. She stretched her legs out as far as she could. The temperature was pleasant – cool but comfortable.

I hope he drops the conversation.

"Okay, so we can't speak with your father," he said, sighing as he sat down himself, "You really think he can just, kind of, get in your head and see where we are?

You have no idea what he's capable of. Even I don't.

"It seems... I don't know. Risky."

"Riskier than walking into Leontio? Trusting that Matis hasn't already told your father where you are."

Sapphir had to concede that Keoki's grievances were well-founded. In truth, she only feared connecting with Teremos because of what he might say to her.

I'm too vulnerable right now... and he would know it.

Her father knew her too well. He had a way of twisting her thoughts with his honeyed words.

I can't... I can't risk it.

"My children. He would still have no way of knowing where they are unless I let him into my head. Unless I... talk to him."

Right? As long as they stay at the farm. Under my protections.

Keoki sighed. She knew he had a soft spot for her children, especially Ivy and Maya. He would protect their safety.

He cares for my children... but does he have any love for me? Or only fear?

"Okay. Okay, fine. Don't try."

Sapphir closed her eyes, wondering what Ivy, Egan, Cy, Celia, and Maya were doing. With each passing hour, she became more convinced that she was making a mistake. Was it worth it – trying to kill her father when it meant she was separated from them?

He will always plague us. As long as we live. If my children continue to pine for freedom... I must be rid of him.

Yes, ending her father's life would set them free. Ivy, Cy, Egan, Celia, and Maya... they could all see Achaea. She could take them! As long as they kept moving – kept their gifts hidden – they could *live* at last.

And what happens if Teremos ends my life instead?

Sapphir knew he still longed for her to succeed him. But he was well-aware that she had been working against him for years, taking his prizes for her own. Would he forgive such a sin?

And if I die... what becomes of their memories?

Without realizing what she was doing, Sapphir began to sniffle.

"Uh... Sapphir? Is everything okay?" Keoki asked, shifting in the darkness.

"Yes." Sapphir wiped her eyes, thanking Poseidon that he could not see her. "I'm fine. Just thinking."

"You're thinking about them, aren't you? Ivy? Your kids."

She could hear the slightest edge in his voice.

He still can't accept it... that they are my children.

"Yes. I... I miss them. And I worry."

Sapphir had never been this long without seeing them. She could feel the stability of her memory charm wavering ever so slightly.

It will be okay; they just need to stay on the farm.

She couldn't go through that process again – changing their memories.

Never again.

It had been easy the first time. Ivy, Cy, Egan, and Celia had all arrived to her in the same week. In one fell swoop, she had been able to erase prior notions of their past lives, opening them up to happiness under her care; they were safe from the clutches of Teremos and his Children.

He would have found them like he has so many others. Found them and taken them.

She had not planned to find a fifth. She had been in the city one day, wandering Helike to find something special to get for Celia's curly, hazel hair.

I could have just made her something. But I wanted her to know how special it was.

It had been then, while examining a beautiful set of amethyst beads, that Sapphir was struck. Magical energy – beyond anything she had felt before – radiated from a nearby house. Someone was calling to her; they just didn't know it yet.

Against her most sensible impulses, Sapphir had acted. The child, a beautiful baby girl with green eyes, became hers. She had sought a gift for Celia and returned with one for all of them. There was no need to erase Maya's memory. She had none at that age. Modifying the others', however, had proved much more complex than Sapphir anticipated. Something went wrong... and her new child was nearly taken from her in the process.

By the time she finally figured out how to properly work the spell, Sapphir was too terrified of it. She vowed from that day forward not to attempt such a complicated charm.

"I'm sorry, Sapphir. I... I get it."

She could still sense discomfort. She stayed quiet, turned deliberately away from Keoki. Part of her wished he would move closer, but she despised that part more than anything.

He doesn't get it. He still thinks of me as a monster.

Sapphir shut her eyes tighter, trying to catch a glimpse of her children through their minds.

Maybe I can just see that they are safe.

The darkness receded slightly, and she could see her blonde rascal, Cy talking to her. Of course, she was seeing through Ivy's eyes, as they stood in the dusk outside the farmhouse. Cy was kicking a pebble while Ivy spoke sincerely to him.

They are so funny, always playing their games.

The vision skipped a beat, and suddenly, she and Cy were walking through a grassy field.

Perhaps Fil and Agnes' pasture?

But it was sloping down too much; her children were walking somewhere. Ahead, trees lined the edge of the forest.

No... no, no, no! What are they doing!?

Sapphir sat up, snapping back to the dark forest between Rhium and Leontio. She was breathing hard, panic bubbling inside her.

"What? What's going on?" Keoki asked, trying to rouse himself, "Are we in danger?"

"Ivy... Cy... they're leaving the farm."

"Sapphir, what can we do about that?"

"Keoki they can't leave the farm! I'll... I'll..."

"Lose control of their memories."

"No!! I don't care about– Teremos! My father, he'll find them!"

A hand touched her arm gently, and she flinched in surprise, yelping.

"Sorry, I was just–" Keoki started.

"Don't! We... I have to go! They aren't safe!"

THE CHILDREN OF THE SEA

He doesn't understand, he doesn't understand!

"Sapphir, you have to trust them! Egan, your eldest. He's sensible. He'll get them back to the farm; there's no use worrying!"

This time Keoki grabbed both her arms, steadying her back down into a seated position. She didn't resist but shrugged away his hands.

"Are you sure that's what you saw, also? Could it have just been a dream?"

"No... no it was real. I..."

Sapphir felt like a little girl again. Powerless. She felt like she did during that dream – watching Helike drown, unable to save anyone.

"Sapphir, this is about your father. We need to stop him. So, you don't have to be afraid like this ever again!"

He's right, I need to end this. I need to get to Teremos now.

Keoki was sitting very close to her now. She could feel static from his curly hair and the body heat radiating from him.

"I know... uh, I know you might be scared for your children. But this is for them, right? For them and for my parents?"

This journey isn't for him. I should never have brought him along.

"You aren't saying anything, so I'm just going to keep talking. I know you're worried about Ivy and all of them. I know that. I, uh... I do think you care for them. Truly. You do that. You care, I mean." He cleared his throat awkwardly, still very close to Sapphir. "You didn't have to save me. Not really. Back in Rhium. You could have let me bleed or die, or... I don't really know where I'm going with this."

I could let him die. I know I've thought about it. Getting rid of the only person who knows of my children. It would be so easy....

He touched her shoulder lightly, retracting his hand quickly. "I mean... I'm sure I'm not really helping here."

Is he right? Can I trust Egan to protect them?

Almost involuntarily, Sapphir threw her arms around Keoki, burying her face into his long, curly hair, allowing herself to cry. Actually cry. He sat stock still at first, unsure how to react. She could feel his shoulders tense; after a few moments, he relaxed and held her with one arm.

Not since Yusef. I haven't had a man comfort me like this since him.

Sapphir pulled back, wiping away the tears. Keoki's outline looked uncomfortable in the darkness of the forest. Sapphir had no idea what to say.

Should I thank him? Kiss him?

She felt guilty for even considering that, knowing Yusef waited for her in Elysium.

What do I do, Yusef?

"Sapphir, I should tell you something..."

She nodded, encouraging him to continue.

"Felip and Agnes... I shouldn't say anything, but... I owe you. They won't tell anyone... Fil and Agnes, they won't! I told them about Teremos... they understand, they do!" His voice lowered to a whisper, "I'm sorry... they know. I told them. About your children."

Sapphir expected to feel anger. Instead, her sadness deepened even more. Her eyes were already dry. There were no more tears left. So, she simply sat. Keoki's mouth opened and closed.

We should never have left the island. I should have killed him when I had the chance. And now...

This was the danger of anyone knowing my secret.

How could I have trusted him? After I held him prisoner! Am I that big a fool?

She clenched her teeth, though not as tight as usual.

A brother... there was no brother... and I believed him? I believed it was a worthy excuse for Fil and Agnes?

But what could she do now? She could only hope that Fil and Agnes would protect the children's identity. Minutes passed, and Sapphir finally spoke.

"I'll take first watch."

"Sapphir, I... I'm truly sorry. I was angry and..."

"I'll take first watch," she repeated firmly.

"Wake me up when you're ready for sleep," Keoki said, his voice quavering.

He fears what I'll do to him.

He curled up on the ground. She could tell that he was fighting sleep; he was certain that if he closed his eyes, he would never open them again. But the silence, the darkness, and the fatigue proved too powerful.

How long should I wait? Shall I give him until the morning?

Sapphir wished a night of sleep would bring more clarity. She knew, however, that it would not. The decision was already made.

Cy and Ivy are straying from the farm.... And Keoki lied to me. I can't go on with him.

When she heard Keoki's breathing begin to shallow, Sapphir pushed herself quietly to her feet.

She picked up her pack, slinging it over one shoulder. On the ground, Keoki looked like a huge dog, or perhaps a small bear, hibernating peacefully. He was snoring lightly. In the dense wilderness, crickets chirped, and nocturnal creatures rustled through the leaves.

For my children.

Sapphir touched the cold blade of her silver knife.

Chapter 13

Ivy

The statue was made of some sort of smooth rock, maybe marble. Ivy perched on its pedestal, running her fingers along the surface and feeling the warmth of the sun from above. The statue seemed to be at the center of a bunch of shops and stone buildings. Ivy wasn't sure where she was. A temple peaked from behind one of the buildings, made of the same material as the statue.

Who's the statue of?

Ivy craned her neck to get a better look, and saw a looming, bearded figure. He was bare-chested and muscular, holding a trident as a wave collapsed at his feet.

Or is it rising?

A drop of water splashed against Ivy's neck as she gazed up.

Is that rain?

No, the sunny day seemed to suggest otherwise. And she realized rain would not have been able to splash from below. She looked down.

With a gasp, Ivy saw a rush of water flowing quickly around the statue's base. She turned to face the square once more and saw that everything was underwater! It was gushing from the shops, carrying pots and chairs with it. A smaller statue at the edge of the square began to crumble. When it dropped into the water, Ivy could taste the spray.

Salt? It's sea water?

Ivy backed further on the pedestal until she was sheltered beneath the shirtless man. She was helpless and scared.

Mother. I want Mother!

As the water continued to rise, she saw familiar faces begin to bob to the surface.

Cy! Egan, Maya, and Celia! Thank the gods!

But something was wrong... their faces were unmoving, though their eyes were open. Seawater spilled out from their mouths. Ivy opened her own mouth to call out, but no words came to her.

Then three figures emerged from the depths, walking across the sea towards her.

Who are they?

Ivy didn't recognize them. One was huge, dwarfing the other two as he slogged towards her. He wore a breast plate dripping water and blood. Next to him, a pretty, slender woman teetered along, one of her legs dipping into the water curiously with every step. The last figure was a woman, too, older than the first. She waved at Ivy, and it took her a moment to realize that the woman only had one arm. They opened their eyes. All were green.

Where is Mother! I need her!

The water finally reached her own ankles, climbing rapidly until she was entirely submerged. She held her breath.

One... two... three...

Ivy gasped. Her own green eyes snapped open. It was dark in the room shared between her, Cy, and Celia. She could see Cy's shadow moving, and he finally noticed she had sat up.

"I was about to wake you," Cy whispered, pointing outside. "It'll be morning in a few hours. We should go now if you want to, you and me. To find the cow!"

Ivy raised a finger to her lips, glancing sideways at Celia. Cy nodded. They couldn't wake up their little sister, who had insisted on sleeping in the same bed as Ivy. Her hazel curls were a mess, spread across both pillows. She was breathing quietly, blissfully asleep and unaware of her two siblings.

Cy tiptoed to the window pushing the single curtain aside and slipped one leg over, straddling it like a horse. Ivy scooted away from Celia as carefully as she could, praying that her sister was a deep sleeper. Her bird, Blackwing, fluttered its wings in exasperation as Ivy slunk off the mattress.

Shush, Blackwing!

Celia had insisted on bringing the flightless osprey with her, and its big piercing eyes were unnerving in the night. However, the bird seemed more annoyed to be awoken than anything. It clacked its beak at Ivy, and she looked back at the bed, where Celia had rolled over subconsciously.

Still asleep.

Stealthy as a cat, Ivy followed Cy through the window. They landed softly on the grass. Cy picked up the wooden sword he had lain beneath the window the evening prior, and Ivy grabbed her own cloth-wrapped loaf of bread.

It's always good to have bread on an adventure. Cy will learn.

She could see Cy's exuberant grin, even in the pre-dawn. He opened his mouth, ready to exclaim in delight at their successful exit. Ivy lifted a finger once more, gesturing for him to follow her quietly.

We don't want to wake up Egan and Maya in the kitchen!

As they crept along, relishing in their escape, Ivy could hear the light mooing from the cattle; some were still standing, despite being asleep. Ivy almost laughed at the sight, but knew they had to get as far away from the farm as possible before talking.

By the time they reached the hill leading to the edge of the forest, dawn began to break, and Ivy could finally make out Cy's features.

"That was so cool! We made it out," Cy said. "Agnes and Fil are gonna be so happy when we find their bear."

If I can turn it back into a cow, that is.

Ivy was pleased to see Cy so excited. She had hated his gloominess and cold looks.

I knew he just needed to explore with me...

As they continued, Cy would jump over boulders and climb trees, all the while checking to make sure Ivy was watching. He'd taken a liking to spells that made him faster and stronger.

What's the point of that? You can just be fast or strong. Spells are for things you can't already do.

"Do you think Mother will be mad at us?" she asked, the glow of the sunrise beginning to seep through the trees.

Cy consider for a moment, "I don't know... I think we're just helping Fil and Agnes. So..." He shrugged.

"Yeah. Yeah, she would like that."

She wouldn't. She doesn't want us leaving.

She felt reassured by Cy's cheerful demeanor. He was positively skipping, examining colorful leaves and birds.

I'll be careful this time. I know what to watch out for.

"Remember, we have to be cautious. There could be bandits out here."

Cy smiled. "Yeah, but this time, you have me. We don't need to worry like you did with Maya."

Ivy remembered how useless she'd felt, surrounded by the gruff men with their spears and axes. Maya had been the one to protect them, not her. Maya and Keoki had ended three lives.

"Yeah... yeah we'll be fine. I have you, and you have me."

Cy bumped her playfully with his shoulder, "Nothing to worry about! Now, where is this bear going to be?"

Ivy put on a brave face, but she could feel danger looming the further they walked from the farm.

"Um, the bear was pretty close to here last time, I think. Maybe an hour's walk... that way." She pointed, praying it was the right direction.

Somewhere between here and the sea... that's where the cow was. Before it was a bear.

"Cool, come on, then!"

Cy bounced ahead, chopping small branches with his wooden sword.

It will do him no good against a real one.

Ivy knew how much her younger brother lusted for adventure, just as she did. He wanted to see battle and defeat his enemies. After her last journey, fighting no longer appealed to Ivy.

I just want to see the world.

"Do you think we'll be able to see the big city? Or the ocean?" Cy asked as they hiked along.

The ocean...

Ivy was suddenly reminded of her dream. Had she been in the big city? When the sea came? The vision had felt too real.

"Ivy? Do you?" Cy asked again.

"Oh... oh, yeah. Maybe. Depends when we find the bear."

They had been walking for nearly two hours, and Ivy wondered if they were meandering aimlessly.

Was this foolish?

Being reminded of the dream had shaken her. She hadn't told any of her siblings. Strange thoughts kept racing through her mind, worrisome visions of green-eyed people – a large man, a boy, a woman with one arm... She could not figure out who they were.

Ever since her mother departed, they came to her. She was afraid to tell Egan and didn't think Celia or Maya would understand. However, with Cy, she always felt more comfortable. Especially when she was in his good graces.

"Cy..."

"Yes?"

"Have you, um... had any weird dreams? Or seen things?"

"What do you mean?" he asked, looking at her curiously.

"You know... have you *seen* things?"

"I dream all the time! Yesterday, before I was about to wake you up, I was dreaming that I could breathe underwater. It was like I was a fish, swimming around in the ocean. Do you think there's a spell for that?"

"Oh... I don't know. Probably. Egan would know, maybe."

He hasn't seen anything. He would understand what I meant.

The images of the mysterious people danced through her head. Flashes of a house near cobbled stone, somewhere she had never been before. Or had she? A hand grabbed Ivy's shoulder, and she gasped.

"Look, Ivy! A road!"

The sun was finally high enough to indicate morning had arrived, and sure enough, a road curved gently where the trees parted.

We must have gone the wrong way.

"Cy, we should go back. I don't... I don't think the bear will be near a road."

We can't let anyone see us. Mother would hate that!

However, Cy was already sneaking towards the smoothed dirt, crouching as though he could surprise it.

"Cy!" she whispered in alarm.

She quickened her pace, speeding as quietly as she could to catch up to her brother. Cy was not being as careful. Twigs snapped and leaves crunched as he approached the edge of the trees.

He's going to get us in trouble!

Ivy barely had time to grab Cy's shoulder, pulling him back towards her, when a man's voice made her freeze.

"Nice sword, little soldier. Wish I could make such beautiful weapons, myself."

Cy leapt out into the road in response, brandishing his wooden sword menacingly.

No... Cy... Mother will be furious!

Ivy raced out to stand between them, planting herself defiantly in front of Cy. Before her, a bulky man, slightly taller than Keoki, stood smiling. He had a knife stuffed in the belt of a fine leather jerkin. He wore thick boots, and seemed to favor his right leg, leaning most of his weight on it.

He's handsomer than Kiki.

His tan skin was marred by a sunspot on his right hand, and he had light brown hair that looked fairly well-kept.

Cy pointed his sword over Ivy's shoulder at the man. "What do you want? A fight?"

The man laughed, an easy and joyful sound, "I'm afraid I'd be completely outmatched. There are *two* of you after all! And since you asked, I guess I want a nice plate of sausage, or maybe some eggs."

Chapter 14

Nicolaus

"Where are you taking me?" Nic said through his teeth, his voice unusually shrill.

Opi walked next to him, moving in a way that seemed both hurried and natural. They had avoided the main square after passing Krassen's pub, trying not to make eye contact with anyone.

"Just keep walking, Nic. And try to blend in."

How can we blend in? There aren't many Egyptians walking the streets of Helike.

Nic couldn't help but feel happy to see Opi after all this time.

Has it only been a couple weeks?

It had seemed much longer. She looked thinner than he remembered. Under her eyes, lines had appeared that stood out from her smooth face. Nic noticed a cut on her wrist, sealed shut with dried blood. She smelled a little like candle wax.

They turned into an alleyway between a pair of shops Nic didn't recognize. When they emerged back onto a side street, there were no people present. The street became a dirt road, which wound gently uphill. Trees lined both sides of the path. Opi stayed silent throughout the hike, despite the emptiness. After a mile on the dirt road, they came to a particularly large pine. Nic's leather bag with the maps and letters from Elfie were growing heavier by the second.

"We turn here," Opi explained, taking Nic's hand to lead him in the right direction. "Only a few more minutes, I promise."

Nic was beginning to sweat, and he hoped his hands were somewhat dry, but Opi didn't seem to mind either way. Finally, they came to a bush, and Opi stopped

Where are we?

Nic couldn't see Helike anymore, and they had taken too many turns for him to guess. Opi pushed aside a few branches of the bush, revealing a hole wide enough for a thin person in its center.

"You can't be serious," Nic said. "Have you been living underground."

Opi scoffed, "Don't be foolish; Simon said you've used one of them in the castle already."

Nic recalled the damp passageway Rizon Atsali had instructed him to use in Helike's prison.

"This belongs to the Flat-Nose?" Nic asked, incredulous. "One of his tunnels?"

"Simon," Opi corrected. "Call him Simon. He hates the other name."

Why does she care?

Opi lowered herself into the hole slowly. "Come along, Nic!"

She sounded much further away than he had thought.

Can two people fit in there?

Nic stepped towards the bush, pulling branches aside as Opi had done. He peeked down nervously, hating the idea of squeezing into another one of the Flat-Nose's tunnels. However, the area below seemed surprisingly open. He slid both legs in, and pushed himself down, the bush covering most of the sunlight.

"Okay, I'm com– whoa!" Nic yelped.

The drop was further than he expected. He landed in a heap near Opi, who was standing comfortably inside the cavern. It was marginally smaller than Nic's quarters in the palace, with walls of densely packed dirt and clay. There was enough natural light to see, but his eyes still had trouble adjusting to the dimness.

I feel like a rabbit.

"So, um. What now? Do we stay here? Or..."

"I thought you were dead."

Opi's normally calm voice cracked slightly.

"Oh."

"It's, well... I never would have gotten to say goodbye to you if you were."

Nic blushed. He had wondered whether Opi was thinking about him the night before the battle.

I was thinking of her?

"And then, when I heard about Orrin. I just assumed..."

Nic fidgeted, feeling the moist soil climb his sandals.

"I'm happy you're okay," she finished.

"Oh. I am too," Nic responded. "Can you tell me why I couldn't go to Krassen's now?"

Opi nodded, sitting cross-legged on the ground, unbothered by the dirt and grime. Nic followed her lead, though he checked to make sure the ground wasn't too wet first.

"Nic, everyone thinks you're dead. Helike lost hundreds in the battle, and you were Orrin's steward. Since he... passed... nobody expected you to make it out of that explosion alive."

"People saw me after the battle though, I was carrying Xander."

"Who?"

"Xander. He's this Bouran soldier. He was hurt, so I... they were going to kill him, I think. They were killing lots of wounded Bourans."

Opi shook her head. "No, who saw you? After the battle?"

"I don't know. I didn't recognize any of them, not really."

"And you think they recognized you?"

Good point.

Opi indicated the obviousness of this by raising a hand, before continuing, "So, let's say it's discovered that the Golden Spear's steward not only survived the battle, but failed to report back to his post at the castle."

"I didn't fail to report back, I just–"

"What else would you call it? Nic, Simon always tells me that someone must be to blame for these kinds of tragedies. The Council already lost Euripides' murderer... they need justice."

Nic had never heard Opi talk like this. Usually, their interactions never ventured beyond the superficial.

She sounds like the Flat-Nose.

"You think they would... punish me for that? For Orrin! For his..."

"Simon believed Gaios might suspect you for Rizon Atsali's escape. That probably doesn't help your situation."

"He never told me that."

Opi shrugged. "He doesn't tell a lot of things."

Nic put his hands on his head and exhaled slowly. His leather bag was warm against his leg, as if the letters inside had just come off a stove.

Why is it all so complicated?

He felt nearly as confused as when Orrin had asked him to talk to Rizon Atsali, or when the Flat-Nose had told him to observe Gaios.

"Are you okay, Nic?" Opi asked, putting a hand gently on his shin.

"Yeah. Yeah, I'm just trying to understand. To think." He paused for a few moments. "You think Gaios would try to place blame on me... either for Rizon's escape or Orrin's death. But only if they found out I was alive."

Opi nodded encouragingly.

"That's why I can't go to Krassen's. Or let anyone else know I'm alive. That's why I'm in this hole," he gestured at the dirt walls, webbed with roots.

"That's why you're in this hole," Opi confirmed.

"But why are you in this hole?" he asked. "Shouldn't *you* be in the castle?"

Opi smiled, as if she had been waiting for Nic to finally inquire. "I left before the battle began. Simon told me to. He had a plan for the prisoner the Council hoped to execute."

"Have you been living in the hole?"

Opi laughed, pointing at the narrower tunnel behind her. "There is a more, er, livable space in that direction... bigger even than our quarters in the palace. But yes... I've been living in a hole. I go out most days to get food; I didn't expect to run into you."

"Aren't you scared someone will recognize you? You abandoned the palace too, you know."

"I'm good at avoiding people's notice. Simon thinks it's a bit of a gift."

She talks about the Flat-Nose quite a lot.

Nic stretched out one of his legs, flinching when he felt a worm brush past.

"If the Fl– sorry, if Simon told you to leave, why haven't you just... you know... *left?*"

Opi looked down between her legs, poking her finger into the soil. "I thought about it. Definitely, I did. Thought about going home... but Simon is worried about Gaios. And... and I don't think he trusts anyone in this city besides me to watch him."

He told me to watch Gaios too... why would he want both of us doing the same job?

Nic thought about asking, but he didn't want Opi to feel jealous; she clearly liked being the Flat-Nose's only confidant.

"What is he even worried about? With Gaios, I mean."

Hopefully, Opi would continue to trust him if he feigned cluelessness.

"I don't think Gaios has been entirely honest with the Council. Well, Simon doesn't. And I believe him."

"About what?"

"Euripides. The assassin. A lot of things... he wants more than just Helike. More than just his position on the Council, even. And now, with Simon gone and Orrin dead... sorry... with both of them gone, Gaios is the lone power."

Nic didn't need this clarified. He knew Simon had left Helike in dangerous hands by fleeing. Kyros wouldn't care enough to contest Gaios, so long as the man's lusts were fulfilled.

There's no Council anymore. Helike is ruled by a king.

"Why did Simon leave?"

Opi's mouth twitched.

She doesn't know.

"I... I think he was seeking support from other cities. Maybe he couldn't beat Gaios on his own."

What if he simply fled? Leaving us to deal with the

155

repercussions?

"Do you think Simon is right? Did Gaios actually have Euripides killed? And... and what about Orrin? Two councilors dead in a matter of months."

Nic tried to hide his sadness. Whenever he discussed Orrin, his tongue seemed to tie in a knot.

"It would not surprise me in the slightest."

"Could it be proven? If Helike saw Gaios for what he was..."

Opi drummed her hand against her leg. "It would be difficult. If we could get in the castle..." her voice trailed off.

"What? Can we? What would we even be looking for?"

"We can get in. But what we'd be looking for...? I don't really know." She stood, "Maybe if..."

She motioned for Nic to follow her, stepping into the dark passageway that branched off from their comfortable lair.

Maybe if... what?

The light above was dimming rapidly, so Nic knew the sun must have begun to set. Opi's slim figure melted into the black as she continued forward with confidence. Soon thereafter, Nic was forced to crawl, as the walls closed in on him from the sides and above.

"Are you certain you know where we're going?" he called, hoping Opi hadn't made a turn without him seeing.

"There's only one way forward, Nic. Just close your eyes and keep crawling!"

She sounded no more than ten feet away, but in the tight

quarters, Nic could not be sure. Every noise seemed simultaneously muffled and magnified. He could hear his knees and hands padding against the ground, the rumbling of his stomach, and the rustling of papers in his pack, which dragged below him.

It's what I can't hear that I'm worried about.

Spiders unnerved Nic, and he was certain there were many crawling about in the soil. Nic felt like throwing up. He was dizzy and unbalanced without his sight.

My hands will be filthy.

Nic gasped audibly as his head bumped ungently into something in front of him.

"Oh, sorry, Nic! I should have told you we were about to stop."

Finally! Is this the end?

He heard Opi's hands fiddling with a latch of some sort, and suddenly, flittering candlelight filled the tunnel. Opi pulled herself through the small doorway, landing softly against stone. Nic did the same.

"What is this place?"

"Simon has quite a few of them. His secret rooms. He always says they're the safest places in Achaea."

"Wait, we're..."

"In the palace, yes."

Opi collapsed into a chair at a table with old scrolls and tomes. Two candles were nearly spent, but their glow kept the room alight. Both were contained within glass jars, with small holes to let the fires breath.

That's brilliant.

He dropped his bag next to the table, hoping there would be time later that evening for him to study his own scrolls further. A clay bowl was filled with charcoal chunks, and it sat atop blank wooden tablets.

Perfect weapons for a former scribe!

Nic loved writing. Orrin had often asked him to transcribe copies of his letters. His mouth was suddenly dry.

Just focus on Opi.

Nic ran his tongue over the inside of his mouth, trying to moisten it enough to talk again.

Nic took in Simon's work once more. The room was similar to the strange nook hidden behind a tapestry that the councilor had led him to weeks before.

"How many does he have?" he asked, awestruck at the Flat-Nose's resourcefulness.

"I only know of two, though there are definitely more. Simon always said they would no longer be a secret if I was aware of them."

Nic grinned. "Wow, right here! We're already inside the palace! Now we just need to, uh… see if Gaios is as guilty as he seems."

Opi chuckled, "Easier said than done. You should wipe yourself off." She handed him a ragged cloth and a flask. "Here. Drink. Relax. You can take the bed if you want to rest. We'll discuss more tomorrow morning."

Nic looked at the mattress, perhaps made of straw, nestled in the corner of the room. There was space enough for one person, but two would have been tight.

"What about you?" Nic asked. "I don't want to take your spot."

The only other furnishing in the room, aside from the bed, was the table and chair Opi already occupied. There was a rug on the stone floor, soft enough to stand on, but certainly not ideal for sleeping.

Opi waved away the question. "I'm going to read for a while. You sleep first, then we'll switch."

I didn't really know she read.

Nic muttered his thanks, wiping off as much of the mud from his legs as he could manage. He didn't want to sleep in the clothes he wore, which were dirtier than he was and damp with sweat.

But I certainly don't want Opi to see how skinny I am.

He decided the robe would do. Opi's tired eyes fixed on a particularly old looking scroll; Nic concluded that she had much kinder eyes than Rosie. He wanted to offer her the bed to rest. But his body had other ideas. He collapsed on the straw mattress. It was softer than Nic expected.

Gaios... we'll catch him... sleeping, no, killing... or something.

His eyes began to flicker shut.

Chapter 15

Keoki

Keoki's back ached from sleeping on compact earth for yet another night. He groaned.

How long was I asleep?

He hadn't intended to drift off. After sharing with Sapphir that Fil and Agnes knew about her children, Keoki had been certain she would lash out at him. He'd been expecting violence.

Why did I tell her? How could I have been so stupid!

He grasped to find the logic behind this decision. Sapphir had been crying. She looked very different when she cried.

Almost like a regular woman. A normal mother. And I just... told her.

Guilt had plagued Keoki for days; it had seemed right to be honest with Felip and Agnes. They deserved to know the truth.

If I don't come back… I wanted them to understand why I left.

But Sapphir would never forgive him for it. She would do anything… to anyone… to guard her secret. Agnes had fought vigorously to make Keoki stay on the farm.

She can't believe I would side with a woman who rips children from their families.

However, Felip and Agnes eventually realized they could not keep him from leaving. They sympathized with his decision to seek out Teremos. After all, Teremos was the true evil – the one who murdered his parents, the one who had been taking *countless* children across Achaea out of malice.

Sapphir was merely a lonely young woman, whose judgement lapsed from time to time.

Perhaps I framed her in too good a light so Fil and Agnes would accept me leaving. But she isn't… she could have killed me in the cave. Could have let me die at the hands of Rizon Atsali… could have rid herself of me last night.

But she hadn't. Keoki was still alive, still on the ground in the clearing of the forest. The sunlight had woken him up.

She let me sleep through the night.

Keoki wiggled his fingers and toes, spreading warmth to them. He pushed himself into a sitting position, the sleepiness fading. It was a cool morning. Summer was nearing the end of its transition to autumn. The ground was damp from condensation. Keoki's stomach growled.

How long has it been since I last ate?

Finally, he stood, stretching his arms luxuriously and shaking his shaggy hair. He scanned the clearing.

Where is she?

"Sapphir?" he called, his voice carrying until the trees stifled it.

Keoki's mind accelerated. His own pack was alone on the forest floor, and only one canteen remained.

"Sapphir!" he exclaimed. "Sapphir!!!"

She's been taken! A mountain clan... or... or another Child of the Sea!

Keoki snatched his pack and canteen, drawing his stone knife.

I should never have fallen asleep! I should have kept watch!

He had wanted to comfort Sapphir, despite what her anger might have driven her to do.

Stupid! Stupid, stupid.

Keoki was dumbfounded. His instincts told him there was no chance he could find her. He looked down at his own body, completely unscathed. Around his shoulder, his pack was the same weight as before. The stone knife was suddenly uncomfortable in his palm.

She... she couldn't have been taken. Why would they have left me?

A bird landed on the ground in front of him, pecking at the dirt until it extracted a worm. It fluttered with excitement.

They wouldn't have left me. Not unharmed.

"She left, didn't she?"

The bird hopped towards him, then took wing towards the trees.

Keoki threw his canteen, and water began to spill out. He rushed to it and shoved the cork back in place.

Gods, why did I tell her?

Keoki's beard was growing scratchy. He lifted his knife to his face, trying to rid himself of the itch.

A shave. I need to shave.

The stone was cold against his cheek, and Keoki's hand began to shake. He dropped the knife, feeling a drop of blood well up where its point had been. A beetle clambered onto the blade.

"She hates me. I mean... wouldn't you?"

The beetle scuttled to the knife's hilt, its black exoskeleton shining in the morning light.

"I just wanted to be honest. I... I couldn't lie anymore. Not after seeing her like that. Crying. And after she just saved me... my arm..."

Keoki looked at the arm Rizon Atsali had lacerated. It was completely unscathed. The beetle rubbed its forelegs together.

"You aren't as good a listener as Io. She would have mooed or something," he crouched closer to the beetle. "Where would she have gone, do you think? Sapphir, not the cow."

She only had one lead... She must be going to Leontio.

Keoki tried to recall which direction he'd come from. He looked at the sun.

"That way's east. So that way... Leontio is that way."

Keoki reached for his knife and the beetle flew away. He had never much cared for insects. There were far too many of them.

"The gods must favor beetles; else, why would there be so many of them?"

It was typical of his father to find the divinity in such things. Keoki let a drop of water from his canteen fall on his tongue, trying to savor the moisture.

If Sapphir has gone, it must be to Leontio. I can still avenge you, Father. And Mother.

Keoki checked the sun once more, took a deep breath, and walked into the dense forest.

✳✳✳✳

A pair of fluffy white clouds masked the sun just before it reached its zenith. Keoki had been on edge for much of the journey, following a well-traveled path in the direction of Leontio. He had spotted it as the pine trees began to thin and the elevation continued to rise. Though walking on the path may have made him more conspicuous, Keoki noticed strange hunting traps in the trees; he possessed no desire to be captured like some wild boar.

Who will suspect anything from a farm boy strolling into Leontio?

He assumed he could arrive by nightfall, but the winding road made the route much less direct. Keoki had not thought Sapphir's absence would be noticeable; she rarely talked as they traveled, and she was quicker to temper than humor. However, he felt oddly alone.

I'm being stupid, I've always preferred my own company.

"She never even liked my jokes," he muttered.

Several times, Keoki questioned why he didn't simply return home, and hope Sapphir succeeded on her own. She would eventually have to come back to the farm for her children.

But he needed to finish what he started.

The day warmed enough that Keoki began to sweat. He wanted a straw hat – anything to provide a little shade. Ahead, two pine trees were cut down, fastened together to form an archway.

I must be going the right direction.

A stone embedded beneath the tree arch had the face of a goddess engraved in it. She had the outline of a moon on her face and deer antlers.

Artemis.

The goddess of the hunt and the moon certainly seemed appropriate for a city like Leontio. Keoki wondered if they had their own Order of Artemis like the Sons in Helike. He gritted his teeth.

And Children of the Moon perhaps.

There would be cults in the city, that was certain, but Keoki doubted there would really be another filled with magicians. There was only so much Blood of the Golden Age to go around.

The sun began to complete its arc through the sky, shoving its way past the puffy clouds as it neared the horizon. Keoki had been walking uphill most of the day, but he could see the grade steepening ahead. The path changed to rugged stone, narrowing as it climbed. To his left, Keoki could see strange engravings in the few barren rock faces. Along the side facing back into the forest, skeletons hung.

This is the way to Leontio, isn't it?

Keoki pressed on. His legs were burning from the incline, and he had grown hungrier throughout the day.

Why haven't I seen anyone?

As if the gods were answering for him, the shuffling of Keoki's feet was suddenly accompanied by a faint thumping and jumbled voices. The path became wider. The noises grew louder.

The voices were cheering.

Keoki rounded a sharp corner and he found himself on a forested plateau, nestled in between mountain peaks. Buildings made of stone, wood, and clay were at last visible, though they appeared largely empty. The area seemed denser and larger than Rhium or Panormus and was thick with trees. Statues of hunters, deer, and bears were scattered throughout, dwarfed by the grandest of them all – the goddess Artemis, holding a bow and arrow.

Where is everyone?

The noise was almost deafening now; large drums thumped accompanied by pounding feet. Keoki followed the direction of Artemis' arrow.

That's where the noise is coming from.

He stepped confidently behind a row of houses and buildings, wondering what the cheers could be for.

Everyone in the city must be there.

"Oh."

The largest theater Keoki had ever seen lay at the base of a canyon in the mountain. Thousands of people sat in seats carved into the stone, dressed in an odd assortment of furs and pelts. Some wore full bearskins and cheered with rusty spears held aloft. Keoki had never seen anything like it.

This is no play.

In the pit, small figures darted about, wielding weapons and garbed in bearskins like certain audience members. They shrieked and danced about, half in black fur and half in brown. Several lay on the ground, bloodied and gimpy.

Are those... children?

Keoki was frozen in his confusion, when a meaty hand clapped him on the back.

"A strong brood of Leontian children, don't you think?"

Keoki turned to see a barrel-chested, bearded man, wearing a wolf pelt with an axe hanging from his belt.

"Um... they aren't... dying, are they?"

The man laughed, shaking his pelt, "Dying? No! No, rarely does the bear rite take any lives. It's the wolf rite our strong children fear."

"Ah, I see. This is just the bear rite, then."

Some of the children certainly looked like they might succumb to their wounds, until a wave of grown men raced out to pick up the fallen children.

"You must not hail from Leontio! That is of course, why you wear no pelt."

Keoki nodded, trying not to show his confusion. "No pelt for me, yes."

The man threw back his head, howling, "AWOO! You see, my pelt means I have the strength of a wolf. First animal I took in a hunt."

The wits of a wolf, too, maybe.

"That's quite impressive," Keoki offered, noticing that others in the audience had turned to watch the curious exchange. "And when did you kill this animal?"

"Well, I was in my sixth year, of course! The first of the hunt. Then, the rites begin. You must be from a fancy city, not dressed for the cold of the mountain."

Keoki nodded, assuming that any city was considered fancy if it lay outside Leontian borders. The air was growing chillier now that he was no longer moving.

Will the night be cold?

Below, the final child in a black bear suit had been knocked down, smacked in the forehead with the butt of a spear. Cheers echoed through the theater, and Keoki searched the crowd, hoping that Sapphir's red hair would stick out. A group of Leontians were whispering in the ears of the drummers, who had ceased their pounding.

She wouldn't have come to the noise; she would have stuck to the shadows. She has more sense than me.

The man in the wolf pelt turned away from Keoki, jesting about the excellent fight they had all witnessed. Keoki moved to slink away back to the empty city.

She'll be here. Somewhere around the city, searching for another Child of the Sea, another lead to Teremos.

Once again, Keoki wondered why he hadn't simply left to return to his farm. What was drawing him to continue on his mission?

I could leave. I could forget Sapphir and go home to Fil and Agnes. To her children.

Someone would need to be there for Egan, Ivy, Maya, Celia, and Cy if Sapphir met a foe she couldn't beat.

Their memories would return if she were to be killed, right?

And Fil and Agnes would be so happy to see him come home safely; they had allowed him to go only because they saw his determination to bring justice to his parents' murderer.

But truly, they wanted me to stay. They aren't even fully aware how dangerous Sapphir is... so dangerous...

Keoki froze.

What if she didn't leave to find Teremos... to follow the lead to Leontio... what if... what if she knew the only threat remaining to her children's identity besides me were Felip and Agnes?

Keoki clenched his fist.

She wouldn't... Would she? Would she take innocent lives to keep her children safe?

Keoki knew the answer; he knew the lengths Sapphir was willing to go to control her children.

Why did I tell her Fil and Agnes knew! How could I have been. SO. STUPID!

She hadn't killed Keoki.

Only the gods know why.

But he couldn't trust her to give the same mercy to his wonderful family on the farm.

I have to go back to Fil and Agnes, have to make sure she hasn't left to harm them.

Before he could act, the booming voice of the man in the wolf's pelt interrupted his monologue.

"Ah, there he is! Play the drums!"

The drums began to pound once more. Keoki turned to see the huge man, flanked by hundreds of Leontians in skins and furs, holding their spears menacingly.

"It's the man from the fancy city! A trespasser in Leontio! He tried to sneak in while we cheered for our strong Leontian children in the bear rite!"

"I'm not trespassing! Just passing through!"

The men and women didn't seem to hear him over the clattering of spears and *BOOM! BOOM! BOOM!* of the drums.

There's hundreds of them.

"He speaks! But we need not listen. A fancy man? Here?"

Keoki's shoulder twinged.

"Now, let us see his worth. Fancy man! Run! And see if you can evade our guardians until morning."

Keoki dropped his pack as he stumbled backward. He pulled out his knife, believing there must be some kind of strange ritual he had to perform.

No! Not now! I have to go back for Fil and Agnes!

The Leontians parted, cheering, as two men clad in full wolf pelts emerged from the crowd. Each held several chains, bound on one end to grey and white, slavering shapes, with massive paws and vicious teeth.

Wolves.

"Our guardians demand you perform our most daring rite, the rite of the wolf! Why must I tell you again, fancy man? Run!"

Chapter 16

Melani

"Better get belowdecks, then! The rain's only going to come down harder!"

The ship's captain, Lathor, was fighting to keep the vessel on a steady course. Despite the chill from the storm and the ocean spray, he wore no shirt. He was perfectly happy, nonetheless. His ship's wheel tattoo seemed to spin on his bulky arms.

"Yes, down belowdecks then, the Melani," Lathor's brother, Col, instructed as he rushed past, pulling a rope behind him.

Melani wished she could help them in some way, but when yet another wave caused the ship to tilt violently, she decided there was no reason to argue with the deckhand's command. She stumbled across the deck, grasping for the door that would let her descend into the cabin below.

Col and Lathor yelled at each other over the storm, using their native tongue from the land of Nok. Rizon was already inside the cabin, sipping a clear liquid from a glass jar. Melani ran her fingers through her hair to see if the rain had washed the dye away. The floor beneath her feet moved with the waves.

I hate it down here.

She took the chair opposite Rizon, clutching the side tightly. Rizon acknowledged her with a nod.

He's been even less enjoyable since we left Patras. I should've stayed out in the storm.

"Why is it, that it only seems to be raining over the ocean? The weather was lovely in Patras."

They had been on the ship for mere hours, and already the weather had turned sour. She thanked the gods that the voyage would only take a day this time.

Rizon grunted, "Don't know."

"I preferred horseback."

Rizon took another sip of rum. Her stomach rolled as the ship was struck by another wave.

My child isn't fond of the sea.

Melani wished she had Xander to hold her steady against the rocking of the ship. She suppressed a smile.

He gets even more seasick than I do.

Instead, Melani was stuck with Xander's gloomy brother. Rizon studied his glass, as if deciding whether to take another drink.

Lathor and Col made for much better company.

"My family is leaving Patras."

Rizon nodded, turning his intense gaze to her. "Good. They'll be safer."

"You think they'll be okay?"

"I don't know. Yes, probably."

Melani didn't like that answer.

"You did, uh, fix the problem with the Fisherman, yes? We're dead?"

"That's what he told me."

His despondence was growing tiresome to Melani. She took the jar from him and quaffed it liberally.

Gods, that's disgusting.

She spat it out. Rizon's stern eyes glimmered with a hint of mirth.

"What? It's gross. How can you drink this?"

"Practice."

Melani laughed, hoping her enthusiasm would improve his mood.

"This man... the one who declared us dead. Who is he?"

"It doesn't matter much, he's a dead man."

"Dead like us?"

"No."

"Ah," Melani paused. "And, you, uh... made him dead? Killed him."

Made him dead?

"I guess you could say that."

Melani's insides squirmed.

My child isn't fond of killing, either.

Rizon seemed comfortable in his chair, despite the restless ocean and half-finished jar of rum.

"If he's dead – really dead, then how is it he spread the message of *our* deaths?"

"Letters to a courier; it's the best that could be done. He wouldn't be dead if he hadn't given me reason."

To kill him.

"Well... I guess that's good. We're safe to return to Helike. To find..."

Xander. We can find him and save him. Like he would do for me – for both of us.

"...how exactly are we planning to do that?" she asked.

Rizon stretched his arms back and rubbed his eyes. The pounding of the rain on the deck above had reduced to a steady thrum. His movements had changed from canine to feline, calmer and more fluid.

"It's hard to say; last time I was in Helike I didn't see much outside my cell."

"Yes, and Simon was your only ally. Now he's gone – somewhere in Achaea. I guess we can't just... walk into the castle and find the prison."

"There was another – the Golden Spear's boy. You know the Golden Spear?"

"Everybody knows the Golden Spear."

Rizon nodded. "He's got a little servant boy. Came and talked to me. Maybe... maybe he knows some things, or... I don't know."

"So... your whole plan is to *maybe* find a servant of the Golden Spear."

Rizon waved a hand in front of his face, as if dismissing her words. "No. I'm just spitting out ideas. Why's it my job, anyway? To have a plan?"

"You have way more experience with this! At least, I assume you do!" *I hope you do.* "You know Fishermen, like Tarlen and the other guy."

"You're right. Of course, you're right. I know Fishermen." His elbow bumped the jar, and it slid to Melani. "See, here's the thing, Melani. If Xander is alive—"

"He is."

"Right... if he's alive, he'll be in the prison. Surely. It's the only place they could put prisoners of war — at least for the first few weeks until they decide what to do with them. They'll execute some officers, important folk if there are any."

"And the prison... this is the one in the palace?"

"Yes. Below the palace. Like catacombs. Smells like it, too."

Melani put the jar out of reach from Rizon. She needed to keep him talking.

"And what if they know who he is? Xander Atsali, the brother of their escaped prisoner, Rizon Atsali."

"They would have had to identify each of the hundreds of

Bourans locked away in their cells... they almost certainly have not."

But Xander Atsali... people know who he is.

Rizon continued, "And, of course, the Fishermen hopefully believe we're dead, so they won't care for Xander much anymore."

"Is there any way we can get into the palace? Into the prison?"

"There's passages. Secret ones that Simon showed me. When he freed me!"

Rizon hiccupped.

"From the prison, that is. He freed me, and I went through a secret passage. Maybe we can get in there, and then contact the little servant boy – get him to free Xander."

It may be the only way...

"Okay..." Melani said slowly. "Okay, a secret passage into the palace. We'll be out of sight... closer to Xander... you really think you can find one of these passages?"

Rizon straightened with satisfaction, nodding sagely. He reached half-heartedly for the jar, then let his hand fall.

What gave him cause to drink?

"Rizon..."

She'd been wanting to ask for weeks. Before now, the time had never felt right. She felt she needed to know what Xander's brother had done. What crimes had he committed to make the Fisherman so eager to catch him?

"...why were you a prisoner?"

Rizon snorted, shaking his head. "You're trying to get me to talk because I've had some... some drinks... I know... I can tell! But... you don't really want to know. You... you don't."

"If we're going to be in the city that arrested you, I believe it is in both of our best interests that I know."

Melani gave him the most hardened stare she could muster.

"Xander *has* told me it's hard to win an argument with you." Rizon reached for the jar, and Melani moved it slightly further away. "Damn. Okay. For you... for Xander... I'll tell you."

He flexed his fingers, collecting his thoughts. Melani was both excited and scared at what he might reveal. She was thankful that Rizon had saved her from Tarlen, the fur trader. But she was angry that somehow, she and Xander were in danger because of him.

What if he says something I can't forgive?

For much of their time together, Rizon had not been the most pleasant company; however, he was Xander's brother, and Melani felt obligated to love him.

He's nearly my family, too. I need to understand him.

The rain kept its steady beat, droplets beading through into the cabin every now and then. Rizon blinked slowly, trying to will away the effects of the alcohol. Finally, he spoke.

"I'm sure you already suspected this... you're a smart woman.... Sorry, Melani. Would you get some water for me?"

Melani crossed the cabin, her wet sandals squeaking. A stack of jars with clear liquid were crammed atop a few wooden crates.

Hopefully this isn't whatever he was just drinking.

Melani grunted as she struggled to open it. It was caked in

sand and grated as she forcibly twisted it. It didn't smell like anything. She slid the jar to Rizon.

"Thank you," he drank deeply, then splashed his face with it, "Now... where was I?"

"You were pointing out what a smart woman I am."

Rizon's face twitched to something of a smile.

"Of course. Melani, I was a Fisherman... doing whatever I was paid to do. The Fishermen are well-trained; we're taught to learn of the politics in Achaea. And the rest of the world. We learn to use weapons – all types of weapons – and to blend in when we need to stay hidden."

He looked down at his feet.

"We kill.... Eventually, it was... more than I was willing to do. I decided I wanted to leave. But you don't leave them. Once you become one, you are one... until you die. I knew they would hunt me down, but one day... it seemed like my prayers were answered. The gods gave me a chance to leave. A councilor; the handsome one from Helike. He came to me."

Melani wasn't sure to whom Rizon was referring.

The handsome one?

"He said I could complete one last task. One *big* task. And then, my family would be safe. I could leave. I couldn't tell a soul what I'd done, though; I could never share who had sent me to perform the deed – if I did..."

How long have Xander and I been used as blackmail for Rizon's obedience?

She thought about what this important task could have been.

"What kind of job? You don't mean... well... you had to kill someone, I'm sure."

Rizon didn't respond. Melani only had a tenuous grasp on the comings and goings in the city of Helike. The last time she'd discussed them with anyone had been...

"Tarlen... The cult... the councilor who was assassinated..."

Rizon nodded, still looking at his feet. "So... I, uh... I did it. I was able to tell my parents to leave. They're sailing south, probably to Athens or somewhere safe."

"Xander didn't know they left!"

"I was coming to tell Xander. To tell both of you to leave... and then, they caught me. I was arrested. There was nothing to do... I was guilty... I was ready to be executed. I couldn't even confess who had told me to carry out the deed, knowing you and Xander were still in Boura."

"They were going to execute you?" Melani whispered.

And he said nothing... to protect us.

When Rizon's eyes met hers, they looked soft... like Xander's.

"It is more than I deserve, Melani. The things I've done... if we save Xander, if we get the chance... it can truly end."

Melani suspected there were other actions Rizon would take given the opportunity. The handsome councilor of Helike did not know the man he'd betrayed would soon be in the palace. She took Rizon's hand.

"We can get into the palace, Rizon. We'll find the Golden

Spear's servant, and we'll free Xander. He's alive, I know he is!"

Rizon smiled, his eyes unfocused; he pulled his hand away.

"Melani, you're a good woman for Xander. I'm happy he has you."

He pushed himself to his feet, then collapsed onto the mattress in the corner of the cabin. The drink had emerged victorious.

He's not so scary like this... when he's... less intense.

Melani stood herself, noticing that the rain had subsided. After she exited the cabin, she made her way to the bow of the ship. She felt better as soon as she could see that the waves had lessened.

"Yes, the weather is nice now, then! Enjoy our travels as we near the city of Helike!"

Col grinned, raising his fist in triumph as he climbed the mast. Melani waved to him, before sitting in her favorite spot aboard the ship.

Rizon was willing to die for Xander... for me and the baby... and now, he can help me get to Xander.

Melani watched a seagull dive into the sea, emerging with a silver fish. She wondered if she would be able to see the Palace of Helike as they drew closer to the harbor. The seagull soared over her head, darting towards the open ocean.

If only those were the sole fishermen in the world.

She was having a little trouble organizing the information that Rizon had divulged. Rizon Atsali, someone she had to consider family, had murdered the beloved Councilor Euripides.

And why did another councilor wish to see Euripides' demise?

However, Rizon's promised liberation was broken, and he was arrested by the very man who had ordered the assassination. Some councilor of Helike had been the one to offer Rizon this job in exchange for his freedom. Was he somehow in control of the Fishermen? It seemed that way.

And now, if Xander is alive, he sits in the palace cells.

Melani shuddered, her eyes fixed on the horizon, wondering what it would feel like to kill a councilor of Helike.

Chapter 17

Simon

Inside the walls of Olenus, Simon felt more out of place than he ever had in Achaea. The roads were well-manicured stone, cobbled for comfortable foot traffic and wagons.

And it's... clean.

Simon had never been in a large city without noticing food scraps and human waste swarmed with insects. The streets of Olenus, however, were clean enough to walk barefoot.

The inn outside the city was no different from any other he'd stayed in that trip. The bed had been hard and lumpy, the food mediocre. Simon had not expected such a drastic difference inside Olenus' walls. Rows of buildings and homes crowded the streets in an organized manner; most of the people Simon saw seemed well-fed and energetic. Simon looked at his own bony arms, his movements sluggish from a poor night's sleep.

The morning fog hung low in the sky, but Simon could still see the grand temple to Zeus, which clogged the square in front of the palace walls.

Walls for the city, walls for Basilius.

Olenus was named after one of the sons of Zeus, and the city seemed to regard itself as a representation of the Olympian. The temple was twice the size of Helike's own Temple of Poseidon, with hundreds of columns, and statues of gods and goddesses, both minor and major. There was no doubt however, that this was an homage to the God of the Sky.

Marble lightning bolts descended from the ceiling like stalactites, drawing the eye to a frescoed roof, which depicted Zeus' victory over the Titans. As Simon walked through, he saw hundreds of citizens praying and leaving jewels on the statue of a great throne.

There must certainly be a faithful order like the Sons of Poseidon here... perhaps Children of the Sky, too, have terrorized the city.

Simon knew less about Olenus than would serve him in his meeting with King Basilius. He wondered how best to even approach such a man. Surely, he could not simply walk through the gates of the palace wall.

Even if I could, finding court with the King named King would be difficult.

Simon stood between two beautiful columns, gazing at the

royal towers, barely visible over the inner wall.

Why is it, that Dyme is known for its walls, when Olenus is nothing but them.

The city forty stadia west of Olenus, Dyme, was famed for the historic Dymean Wall – one of many grand battle sites from the Peloponnesian Wars. Simon had never seen the place, but he doubted it was more splendid than Olenus' impressive fortifications.

Until he could think of a solution to his current predicament, Simon decided a late morning meal would serve him well. He left the Temple of Zeus, turning to admire its glory one last time; the serpentine fog wound its way through the columns.

Simon touched his flat nose, wiping away a droplet of water that could have been sweat or rain. He stopped at a bakery near the temple, still in sight of the palace. Two women moved about busily, caked in flour and spotted with perspiration. A large window was open, and the scent of fresh bread wafted out. Simon tapped the side of the window.

"A good morning to you both!"

One of the women turned towards him, while the other continued pounding a hunk of dough.

"Ah, a hungry customer! Look at this, Tati – a hungry customer."

Tati did not look up.

"Quite observant, you are. I'd hate to distract Tati from her pounding, though. Do you have a name, as well?"

"Rolal, if you please," she said, wiping her apron and reaching a hand through the window.

Simon took it gently, "Rolal. How lovely! You may call me Simon. Would it be a bother if I were to sit down in your bakery?"

"Not at all," Rolal waved at the door, "Come through and make yourself comfortable."

Simon bowed politely, letting the warmth and even more delicious smells wash over him as he entered. Rolal handed him a pastry, wringing her hands together. Simon placed three bronze mares on the table and took a bite. The sweet roll was delicate and buttery, but firm enough to offset the tenderness of the fruit inside. Involuntarily, Simon let out a quiet moan.

Oh dear.

Rolal clapped her hands once, beaming with pride. She snatched up the mares.

"My dear Rolal... what a delicious morsel!"

"Did you hear, Tati? A delicious morsel!"

Tati continued to pound her dough.

"Oh, I'm just so happy you like it! I just picked the berries myself, didn't I, Tati?"

Tati nodded.

"Last of the season, too!" Rolal continued jovially, "Pickings become slimmer around this time, you know. It seems the chill doesn't agree with them."

"Well, I'm quite lucky, then!"

Rolal blushed, letting the mares plink into a ceramic bowl in the back of the store. Simon took another bite. Tati sighed as she worked on her dough.

What could she be making that requires such effort?

Rolal sauntered back towards Simon and leaned against the table. She smiled.

"Why have I never seen you here before, Simon?"

Simon shoved the last of the pastry into his mouth, considering how much to share with the kind baker and her sullen companion. He was chewing slowly when a rush of air and wisp of fog forestalled his response. Rolal looked at the door and let out a small gasp. Tati stopped pounding her dough.

A gravelly voice broke the silence.

"Why... because he's not from Olenus, of course. He's here to pay me a visit. Come, Simon of Helike. Let us leave these two hardworking women of Olenus be. No sense in disrupting their time with our conversation."

✳✳✳✳

Simon could still taste the pastry. His mouth was uncomfortably dry now, and he wished he could have washed his food down with a cup of water.

"Here will do," the man said, sitting properly at a stone bench, his hands resting in his lap.

Simon sat next to him, leaving a few feet between them. The

187

man had led Simon through the palace gates, into a vast courtyard with flowers, fountains, and statues. Despite the approach of autumn, the garden was exploding with color.

"So, Councilor Simon, did you have a pleasant stay at Lucel's inn last night?"

"Did Lucel have much to say about it when the two of you spoke about my arrival?"

"I'm afraid Lucel was unable to meet with me in the flesh. A letter reached my eyes at dawn."

Simon picked at the fingernail of his thumb with his index finger.

"I see. Inform Lucel in your response that his beds could use extra padding."

"Should not be a difficulty, given the extra padding in his pockets," the man observed as he leaned back. "I have missed being able to quip so freely; my king is not fond of these games."

"A shame. I've been well-practiced by the men at Court in Helike."

The man's lip curled, as if he was aware of *all* the practices Simon had engaged in with a certain man in Helike.

He had a thin mustache, with a completely bald head. His swarthy complexion made his teeth appear prominent. He was as tall as Simon, though of a healthier weight.

"I apologize if I interrupted your morning meal at the bakery. Tati and Rolal do not take kindly to their business being interrupted, but I'm pleased that they made an exception for me.

When King Basilius' advisor comes to your door in Helike, you leave that door open," he laughed with the same gravel quality of his voice. "I trust you know these boasts are simple jests!"

I would be more suspicious if they were.

"Of course. I will admit, the Court of Helike knows little of your role in Olenus, Eté. We only hear of the various triumphs of King Basilius."

Eté chuckled once more, "I have no qualms with my role as an advisor. King Basilius may get credit for the victories…"

As long as he is also blamed for the failures.

Eté reminded Simon a bit of Gaios, though he seemed quicker to a laugh.

Both are quite assured in their own cleverness.

Simon knew Gaios could support his claims of brilliance. He wondered if Eté was equally competent.

"It's no matter who has heard of me. But I have heard of you, Councilor Simon. Tell me – what brings you to Olenus? And as I understand, in the middle of a war between Helike and Boura."

"It is precisely because of this war that I am here."

"You worry that the violence will spread across Achaea?"

"Yes, I worry many will suffer because of the tumult in Helike… there is often a cascading effect when battles begin. I am hoping to quell any conflict before it gains enough momentum to sow discord across the League."

"You speak well for someone who is not using their native tongue."

"How would you know whether I am Achaean by birth?"

"The same way I knew where to find you this morning, Councilor Simon. I make it my business to learn my allies..."

And your adversaries. But which am I?

Simon faced the garden, watching a bee settle down on a nearby aster blossom. He liked bees. They appeared so harmless, with their fuzz and non-threatening hum. Yet their sting was painful.

"Eté, I seek council with your king. There's no need to quibble with our words anymore. Can this be arranged?"

Eté smiled winningly, his thin mustache twitching. "Of course, Councilor Simon. The royal King Basilius could use more contact with other leaders across Achaea. I'm afraid his relationship with Old Patreus and that city to the East has soured of late... a peace accord with Helike would be... prudent."

Do I share that I've spoken to Old Patreus already? I know that his king plans to take the city by force.

Simon was certain Eté knew of Basilius' intentions to claim Patras as his own.

More than likely, he made the arrangements himself.

"If peace is what you seek, you have support from the city of Olenus. This much, I can assure you."

"It pleases me to hear that... I would hate to see the League wounded by the greed of a few."

Eté stood, bidding Simon to follow him as he made his way through the garden. The Nine Muses each had their own fountain in the courtyard, playfully splashing water in harmony. Their faces were dimpled, their hair flowing – but Simon felt that each pair of eyes studied him closely.

"Yes, the welfare of the people is of utmost importance to me," Eté said as he patted Simon lightly. "And I do hope your people are well, despite your absence."

Chapter 18

Sapphir

Sapphir woke, as she often did, abruptly. The shack was warm and comfortable enough, and she was thankful to have slept in a bed for a few hours. She sat up, noticing that the fatigue in her muscles had faded. The strength imbued in her by the Blood of the Golden Age had returned.

Dreams had plagued her as usual. This time, as she stood in the flooding Heliken square, Keoki was the one to approach her; his dark curly hair was dripping and adorned with seaweed, and he opened cracked lips, pleading with her noiselessly. He wore a full bear skin, bleeding from wounds to his chest and neck.

Sapphir said a quick word of prayer to Poseidon that the dream had been nothing more. Keoki was certainly returning to his farm, exasperated at her, but understanding the position she'd been put in.

He was a liability. And he... he betrayed me.

On the ground in the center of the shack, Matis stared at her; his sightless gaze was accusatory. She turned him over, noticing the grisly scar that traced his neck, sealed shut by dried blood.

Perhaps I should have used magic.

The dawn light crept through slats in the decaying walls. She closed her eyes, trying to sense Ivy and Cy. Had the two truly left the farm?

Come on, Ivy. Let me in!

The same vision she'd seen the night before returned, though it was cloudy and choppy, jumping from one location to another. Cy and Ivy were on the move, somewhere just outside the farm.

Where are you, children?

She focused on Maya, Egan, and Celia. Each were sound asleep, still safe at Fil and Agnes' farm. They seemed peaceful.

If Felip and Agnes haven't told them the truth by now, they won't.

Sapphir now understood why Agnes had been so cold to her. She was grateful for the discretion of Keoki's caretakers. They must have recognized the dangers her father posed; it could all end if she stopped him.

Father is the enemy. Keoki knew that... he relayed it to Felip and Agnes.

Sapphir tried to remain calm. She sat on the bed taking long, steady breaths. The fear that had gripped her when Ivy and Maya left on their little boat weeks ago was returning. She had worried then whether she could handle five children on her own. She had searched for them desperately, killed for them in the mountains, and thrown an innocent man in a cave for them.

I should have killed him... I should have rid myself of him and convinced my children to be happy on the island. I should have... why didn't I just take his memories?

Sapphir had vowed never to deal with memory charms, though. After Maya. Her hand sparked as the Blood of the Golden Age circulated rapidly.

I'm making the right choice. I have to kill my father... I have to end the Children of the Sea. It's the only way my children....

She needed them to be safe again. She could make it happen; it had been wise to leave Keoki in the forest. She could move faster without him.

He didn't belong here... with me.

Sapphir wouldn't regret the decision – she was certain. With Ivy and Cy leaving the farm, the urgency to find her father had grown a hundredfold.

Where are you going, Cy and Ivy?

Their whereabouts were still foggy.

My connection with them... it's not fading... it can't be.

She needed to tell Egan. She could trust him. Would she be able to communicate with him? Egan had studied most every spell she knew, but was he prepared for this? Her eyes closed as she pictured her eldest son.

Egan.

Nothing happened. Sapphir put both hands on the bridge of her nose.

Egan!

Matis cackled in her mind.

"Mother?"

Egan! Oh, Egan!

"What is it, Mother?"

Cy, Ivy. Your brother and sister, they've gone! Oh, Egan, where have they gone?

"Mother... I... I'm sorry... I–"

It's not your fault. It's mine... for leaving. Egan, search for them. You know how... tell Felip and Agnes that you need to go. Please...

In her mind, Egan's voice raised an octave.

"Yes... yes, Mother. I'll find them. I promise."

I love you. All of you.

He didn't respond.

"Egan?"

She heard her own voice and opened her eyes. The connection had disappeared. On the ground, Matis' twisted corpse seemed to shake with mirth. Egan would find Ivy and Cy, Sapphir was certain of that. He had to.

"I need to find my Father," Sapphir said to the body. "He's not in Leontio. I know he isn't."

Sapphir believed that she could have found clues in Leontio

that would take her closer to her father. But there was no time for clues. Her brief conversation with Egan replayed in her head.

"It's the only way, isn't it? I should have done it sooner."

Keoki was right.

Her father had tried countless times to speak to Sapphir. He called out to her, pleading with his honey-smooth voice for her to join him. She never answered.

But he never says where he is.

Sapphir had not spoken to him since she fled Helike with Yusef. That time, his voice had rung in her head, drowning out everything else.

And she had talked.

And they came upon the fur trader within minutes.

And Yusef is gone.

Speaking with her father could only be dangerous. But Ivy and Cy were in even greater peril at that very moment. Sapphir threw her silver knife at the wall.

"I need to do this."

She crossed the room, kicking aside Matis' body, and pulled her knife from the wall.

She kept her eyes open this time.

Father?

Suddenly, the shack disappeared, and Sapphir stood in a cold room with marble statues. It was completely empty.

The Temple.

"Daughter," a voice said behind her. "It's been so long since we have spoken. Look at me."

Sapphir's fist clenched. When she turned, she faced a tall man with blonde hair. He had barely aged. His eyes were purple, flecked with yellow. She wanted to draw her knife, plunge it into him and see the life drain from them. But she could not move.

"Violent thoughts, daughter."

"Get out of my head."

He moved freely through the temple. "You invited me. I've been waiting for that."

Sapphir curled her lip, saying nothing.

"I know why you've decided to contact me now. You wish to end my life."

He ran a hand across one of the statues, sighing.

"It will do you no good to pursue such childish desires..."

His hand stopped at the corner of the pedestal. He looked up to admire Poseidon; the crouching figure clutched a trident.

"You already have your doubts. I can see this."

Sapphir's voice came low and menacing, "Then you are blind."

Her father's mouth flashed a tight-lipped smile.

"I will admit you hide more than I expected. I cannot see your children. But this can change."

"Leave my children out of this, Father. You only want me."

"I want all with our blood," he said, opening his arms. "We *all* deserve what we were given. We deserve *everything*. We deserve the peace of the Golden Age – the prosperity."

"Is that what you tell the children? When you steal them from their families?"

"They simply obey. You should know what this is like. Yours are nearly as dutiful as mine."

It's not the same! I'm protecting my children! From you!

"I... You..."

Her father smiled as Sapphir sputtered, ready to explode. "Do not let your emotions control you, daughter."

He stepped towards her, brushing her hair out of her face. He patted her cheek with the same hand he used to strike her years before.

"My Sapphir. Your children will be safe if you see reason and come to me. Killing me will bring you no peace. My Children will always long for a better world. One where we are free to use the gifts we were given."

"You've wiped their memories. The children you've stolen, all of them."

"As have you."

"But... they can remember."

Her father beamed, a full smile she had never seen before.

"They will cherish my legacy, even after death. I sense in you, Sapphir, that you know this. Where has your defiance led you before? Come to me, daughter. I await you. In the catacombs of Olenus."

Sapphir pulled out her knife; she could end it now. She lunged. The Temple of Poseidon faded, and Sapphir landed hard on the floor of Matis' shack. She panted, pushing herself to her feet.

The catacombs of Olenus. He told me...

Sapphir's father never did anything without considering the consequences. He had volunteered his location to her.

There must be some trick involved...

He wouldn't simply give her what she wanted.

My children... he doesn't know where they are. He would have told me. He would have. Just to see me suffer.

If Teremos knew where Cy, Ivy, and the others were, he would have already found them. Sapphir was certain of that. She touched the tip of her knife to her thumb.

He believes I wouldn't follow through with it....

A bead of blood welled on her pale skin.

When I kill him, I'm going to use this. I'm going to make it last.

She stopped over Matis' body as she walked to the door. The memory of him gloating about Yusef's final days made her eyes narrow.

He had asked for the end to come.

And Matis was just another of her father's toys.

The catacombs of Olenus.

Sapphir kicked the door ajar, opening her stride as she made for Rhium's coastline. Her father may not have found her children yet, but the faster she could get to Olenus, the safer they would be.

Egan must find Cy and Ivy... he must get them back to the farm. Under my protection.

She pictured Keoki alone in the forest between Rhium and

Leontio; would he have been useful in the coming days?

It doesn't matter. He betrayed me, and I can't trust him. I can't. Trust. Him.

Keoki was safer this way. He could return to his farm – frustrated? Certainly. But what more could he do? Felip and Agnes were already aware of her children's past lives... and he wouldn't tell her children. He wouldn't risk hurting them with the information.

He knows it would be a death sentence, too...

When she got to the shore, the township of Rhium was just beginning to stir. Fishermen were returning already from a morning on the water, ready to unload their fresh catches. Sapphir waved at them politely, hoping they would ignore her.

The speed of her boat would save Sapphir precious time.

Another thing Keoki was right about.

She tossed a rock at the glassy water and waved her hand. Within minutes, Sapphir's small skiff had left the cove where Rhium's fisherfolk landed each day. The way to Olenus was as simple as following the coastline. Sapphir smiled as a wave splashed her hair.

My children will be safe. I just need to find my father. Quickly.

The boat bounced over another set of waves, speeding along at nearly eight knots. Sapphir turned the silver knife over in her hands. She pricked her finger again and watched a bead of blood trickle down. In the knife, her reflection showed the bold, white scar.

A gift from Father. Soon I shall give him one of my own.

Chapter 19

Ivy

"Put your sword down," Ivy muttered to Cy, before responding, "Sorry, my brother was just making a joke. We're just leaving to go back to our fa– I mean, to get home to our parents."

Mother has warned us about kind strangers... we got lucky Kiki was not bad.

The road was empty aside from the tall man, Ivy, and Cy with his stick. Ivy wondered how far they were from the big city.

"Well," the strong man held his hands up in a placating manner, "I don't mean to get in your way! I'm also heading home."

She gave Cy a look, hoping he would take the meaning, *"Please, just be quiet."*

Cy ignored her.

"How can we be sure you won't try to chase us as soon as we

turn around?" Cy asked, hoping to intimidate the stranger.

"I guess you can never be too careful. But I think a fast, agile man like yourself would surely outrun me." The man tapped his left leg. "Especially now."

"Yeah, I am fast."

"Okay, come on, brother. We should really go back home! Mother and Father will be waiting."

"Did you hurt your leg in a battle?"

Cy was leaning against his wooden sword, trying to appear casual and collected. Sweat made strands of his blonde hair stick to his eyelids. Ivy was still standing between him and the stranger.

"Oh, I'm afraid it's less interesting than that. I try to stay out of battles... as should anyone."

Cy looked disappointed. "But you're so big, you would probably be a good fighter. Ivy, move," he pushed her to one side, so he was standing closer to the man. "This is Ivy, and I'm Cy. We could teach you about fighting, if you wanted."

You shouldn't have told him our names, idiot! Mother would be furious!

Ivy forced a smile, talking through her teeth, "I'm sure he doesn't need our help fighting."

This was a bad idea. Leaving the farm was a bad idea.

"Nice to meet you both... any other day, I would love to have fighting lessons from two experienced warriors like yourselves. But I'm afraid my woman is at home waiting for me... she wouldn't take kindly to me being home so late! Especially, if I returned with fresh battle scars from our training."

He extended his hand with the sunspot on it, shaking Cy's heartily before offering it to Ivy. She accepted with caution, her eyes fixed on Cy. She let go of the man's hand and tugged on her brother's arm.

"Back into the forest, Cy. Let's go home."

Cy wrenched his arm free but began to follow. The stranger smiled and waved at them as they reentered the trees. Cy was about to wave back, when a voice caught their attention.

"Xander Atsali! Is that you?"

Ivy pulled Cy behind a tree, breathing shallowly. She clamped a hand over his mouth, whispering sharply, "Don't move. Stay quiet."

Cy must've heard the sincerity in her tone, because he nodded vigorously. They were out of sight from the road, but she could see the stranger, Xander Atsali, between tree branches.

"Ah, hello there, friends," he called back, leaning on his right leg and squinting. "Sorry, it's hard to tell who you are with the helmets on."

"Why, it's Sir Farlen! One of your best customers. You wouldn't know these seven, but they have heard much about you."

Customers? What does Xander Atsali do?

Eight men approached, all wearing some type of flexible armor and helmets that only covered half of their faces. Sir Farlen stood at the front. He was taller than Xander, but not quite as muscular. In his belt was the largest sword Ivy had ever seen. Cy's eyes widened.

"Xander Atsali made my new broadsword," Sir Farlen continued, patting the hilt. "Expensive... but fantastic steel."

Xander nodded. The other seven stayed quiet. Sir Farlen looked at the trees, and Ivy shrunk back.

Don't see us... don't see us...

"Who is it you were waving at?"

"Just some birds. You know how much we blacksmiths like our birds."

"Hmmm, I was unaware of your collective interest in them," Sir Farlen licked his lips, pointing a gloved hand at Xander's leg. "You were injured, I see. Tales have been spread of your valor in the Battle at the Beach. Is it true that you defeated the Golden Spear yourself?"

A battle... he is a fighter!

Cy tapped Ivy's arm excitedly, nodding at Xander. Ivy glared back.

"An explosion killed the Golden Spear."

"The same explosion that maimed your leg?"

"The very same."

Sir Farlen took a step forward. All seven of his men were armed with swords of their own. Xander stayed rooted in his position, but his grip tightened around his small bag.

Why is Xander so tense?

"It's a shame what happened in that battle, isn't it Xander? Many Bouran lives lost... and few returned to Boura after. The others – they are all imprisoned at the palace of Helike, yes?"

"I... I'm unsure."

"Yet, here you are. Alive and well. Walking freely to Boura. From Helike, no less. I had feared you were dead or captured among the rest. But... here you are."

Xander's eyebrows furrowed. "Here I am. Grateful to be alive and well... as I'm sure all of you who avoided the Battle at the Beach are."

"Are you suggesting that my friends are cowards, Xander?"

Cy let out a quiet gasp. Ivy could not pull herself away from the scene. She knew she and Cy should disappear now. Every minute they stayed off the farm meant more danger. All of Sir Farlen's accomplices dropped their hands to their weapons. Xander smiled without joy. When he spoke, his voice had an edge of irony.

"Of course not, Sir Farlen. I am certain the brave battle plans laid out by Parex the Hammer worked just as designed. Most of us Bourans stayed behind, upriver from Helike, yes? Did our small force at the beach adequately distract the Heliken soldiers? Have we taken the city for our own?"

Two big cities fought each other! A war! Right by the farm! Why didn't Agnes tell us about this?

"Do I sense disrespect? Of the general of our Bouran forces? The Hammer's plan would have worked..."

"But it didn't."

"We have something even better now, Xander Atsali. Peace."

Xander looked at him with confusion. The fact that peace had already been forged between the two cities seemed to disturb him. He tried to put weight on his left leg and winced.

"I see... peace is certainly... better."

"Indeed. Though I believe the terms of the peace included a plan for the upstarts who fought at the beach. The ones left alive, that is."

"Upstarts? You mean the Bouran soldiers *chosen* to fight?"

Sir Farlen took another step forward; this time, his seven friends followed his lead. Cy shifted to get a better look and a leaf crunched. Ivy grabbed him, holding on tight so he couldn't move.

"Cy," she whispered, barely audible. "Don't move."

"This begs the question, Xander Atsali – what are you doing walking the road home from Helike?"

"I merely wished to return home."

"Yes, to the lovely Melani, I'm sure," Sir Farlen sneered and one of his men laughed.

Xander's voice became deadly serious. "The last time I checked, we were on the same side. If you would please, get out of my way."

Sir Farlen raised a hand. "Sides have changed, Xander Atsali. You don't recognize my men here, do you?"

Xander shook his head.

"They used to fight on the *other* side. Now we are allies. Soldiers for the new Helike." Sir Farlen pointed at Xander. "Take him. He belongs with his rebels from the beach."

Ivy's jaw dropped. Cy lunged towards the road, and Ivy barely kept him contained. When he opened his mouth to yell, Ivy stifled it with his own hand.

We can't. We can't help Xander. I can't lose Cy. There's too many.

The first man to reach Xander grabbed at his arm. Xander caught it and threw him to the ground, drawing the man's sword in the same motion. He barely had time to swing his elbow around, catching the second man in the face. He limped away from the other six, leveling his sword at them.

"We don't need to do this."

I can't help him. I'll get captured again... and Mother won't be there!

Cy was struggling with all his might, his body warming as he tried to summon even more strength from his magic. But Ivy was stronger.

Stop! Cy!

Sir Farlen and the other men drew their own weapons now, circling in slowly, "Xander Atsali, it does me no good to kill you. But you belong in the palace."

"The cells below it!" Xander exclaimed with indignation. "Why do I belong there if there's been peace?"

Sir Farlen shook his head and swung his great broadsword at Xander. He leapt sideways, catching a blow from one of the other soldiers and kicking a third.

"Think about your lady, Melani! Would she rather you dead?

Or in a cell? If you kill all of us, what then? A fugitive, Xander Atsali? Is that what you wish?"

Xander took another step back, his wounded leg clearly slowing him. He seemed out of breath, his sword point dipping to the dirt. A teardrop rolled over Ivy's hand.

Oh Cy...

"Put your weapons down, and I'll do the same."

The men Xander had knocked to the ground were back on their feet, though all eight seemed somewhat wary to approach him. Sir Farlen nodded, and the men sheathed their blades. Xander tossed his own on the ground and raised his arms in surrender.

Sir Farlen nodded, and two of the soldiers grabbed Xander roughly, binding his hands together with a thick rope.

Behind the trees, Cy stopped struggling. His muscles went slack.

They're... taking him. Taking him. Wha– why...

Ivy became dizzy. The trees began to spin. She would've fallen if she hadn't steadied herself against Cy.

Taking him. Taking...

The image of the house at the corner of a cobbled street was back in her mind. The huge man and the pretty woman... all with green eyes.

Who... what...?

Ivy forced herself to focus. She took a deep breath and the world became clearer.

Sir Farlen brushed dirt off his armor. The envoy began walking back on the road towards the big city. Xander's hair was matted with sweat and his left leg dragged uselessly. Soon, Ivy and Cy could no longer see them.

Ivy loosened her grip on Cy.

"They... they took him," Cy stammered. "We could have... we could have."

"Done nothing, Cy! What could we have done? I've fought fewer men without swords and armor that strong. With Maya. And... and..."

And we didn't stand a chance.

Cy turned to her, his blue eyes filled with tears. Ivy took a few steps backwards, her head still spinning.

"Cy, we could have been taken right along with Xander! And you saw it! He didn't want to kill them!"

She could barely hear herself over the *BOOM! BOOM! BOOM!* of her pounding heart.

He couldn't resist... and they took him. They...

Cy had his hands on his head. He kicked his wooden sword, stomping on it until it snapped in half.

"What is the point of our *gifts*, Ivy? If we can't help!"

Ivy fell to her knees. Something about Xander's capture was haunting her. She felt like she was grasping for *something*... and it just wouldn't come. Her thoughts, her memories, were blinded.

What's happening to me! I want Mother.

"Ivy? Ivy!" Cy exclaimed, rushing to her side. "Are you okay?"

"Cy..."

She curled up on the soil. Cy sat beside her, laying a hand across her forehead.

"Ivy..." he whispered.

Mother... why am I... why am I so...?

Heavy footfalls caused Cy to leap to his feet and grab for a wooden sword that wasn't there. A strange noise that sounded like the mix between a growl and a yell echoed through the trees.

"Ivy! Cy! You foolish children!"

Out of the corner of her eye, Ivy could see the lumbering form of Egan, moving quicker than she'd ever seen. Her huge brother grabbed Cy by the shoulder. He reached for Ivy next. She didn't resist.

Cy pushed away his brother's hand. "We're not foolish!"

"What were you two thinking? What are you ever thinking! Ivy... why must you cause trouble! Always!"

Ivy said nothing. Her lip quivered. Cy wiped angry tears from his cheek.

"We'll discuss later. Back to the farm, now!"

He pushed them deeper into the woods. Egan was rarely anything but sullen; Ivy preferred that to fury. She slogged next to Cy, staring at the ground wordlessly, while Egan trudged behind.

"Are Fil and Agnes mad?" Cy asked with shame.

Egan grunted.

They just... took Xander. They grabbed him and stole him away.

Ivy noticed nothing as they hiked back to the farm. All of her energy was spent searching for something... some memory.

Chapter 20

Keoki

The wall engravings and bones littering the stone path did not make Keoki feel better. He half-sprinted, half-slipped from Leontio towards the dense forest below.

I have to make it to the trees. It's the only way.

Behind him, the beating of the drums faded. Perhaps the display had only been a tactic to scare away unwelcome travelers – anyone who dared to enter Leontio. Sapphir had never mentioned Leontio's rites.

The cult... it must be new.

Keoki slowed to a jog, watching his feet with each step as he navigated the rugged terrain. He barely avoided stepping on a cracked skull. The drums were now a steady heartbeat. Keoki could see the incline leveling out, as the path became mossier, and dirt covered the rocks.

They were just trying to frighten me. That's all... the wolves were a trick, nothing more.

Something told Keoki that he shouldn't slow down, but he was gasping for breath. He hadn't run such a distance in years. After what felt like miles, he stepped behind a stout pine tree, placing his hand on the trunk. His chest heaved. The forest was dark and quiet – familiar territory for Keoki at this point, though still unnerving.

Just a trick. The wolves... just a trick.

A beetle crawled over Keoki's hand and he flinched. It was black, with a reflective exoskeleton similar to the one he'd conversed with earlier.

"You. Probably aren't. The same beetle. As before. Are you?" he whispered, taking in gulps of air between each word.

The beetle continued to march across his hand, undeterred by Keoki's question. Keoki's heavy breathing and racing heart sang together in harmony.

Ba-boom... ba-boom... Boom. Boom. *BOOM. BOOM!*

Is that...

BOOM! BOOM!

Keoki tore himself away from the stout pine tree, backing further into the forest. A single drum echoed through the night. Keoki moved as quickly as he could without making a sound.

Poseidon... please don't let this be what I think it is.

The trees rustled and leaves crackled as multiple large *things*

214

entered the forest. Keoki was so distracted, he nearly ran into a tall pine tree, with thick branches. He glanced up.

I'll never outrun them.

He jumped, grabbing the lowest bough, which bent under his weight. Keoki pulled himself up, breathing through his nose rapidly. He tried desperately to remain silent. As he climbed, the branches became less sturdy. He was about twenty feet above the ground, surrounded by a thicket of pine needles, when the first handhold snapped. He pressed himself against the trunk, closing his eyes to pray.

Poseidon... or Artemis... whoever...

"The fancy man has the night. And he has the trees. But our wolves will find him, either way!"

Keoki could hear footsteps somewhere to his left, as the man in the wolf pelt from the theater called out into the darkness.

Oh gods, I don't remember how to do this... it's been... too long since I've spoken to you.

"Fast ones can get away while we say our prayers to Artemis," another voice remarked, closer than the man in the wolf pelt. "Perhaps the fancy man has speed to match his bulk."

The second man whistled. The sound of paws on soft earth made Keoki shudder.

If you cared for my father, Poseidon... and my mother. If I was ever a good... servant? To you.

"Call to your sisters."

Then help me. Please.

The wolf howled. Keoki realized how much he needed Sapphir. It was always safer to have the sorceress on his side. He gripped the trunk tighter.

And she left me to the wolves.

Keoki could hear the snarling and low growls of several she-wolves now. The forest was too quiet. He could hear them sniff the air and lick their fur. A shape circled the trunk of the tree, its body lithe and sinewy. The wolf curled into a seated position and let out a quiet howl.

Please don't let it look up... Poseidon... please.

Keoki's stone knife was wedged tight in the belt around his waist, and he wished he could reach it, to hold something that would make him feel protected.

Even with the knife, I would be hopeless against the wolves. And then there's the hunters.

Keoki was confident he could calm the wolves. Well, he was not *confident*, but he trusted his experience with animals. But with the Leontian hunters present...

They're more bloodthirsty than their beasts.

He could still hear the other wolves shifting and padding through the forest. Two forms came to the wolf sitting at the trunk of the tree, nuzzled their companion, and sat down, as well.

Keoki's breath steadied. He would need to get used to the terror if he wanted to survive the night.

How much longer until morning? Hours?

He leaned his head against the tree trunk, his curly hair almost acting as a pillow.

Sapphir... I'd never be in this position with her.

The tree bark was coarse. His hands stuck to the sap. He strained to hear the hunters and wolves, who had seemed to go still.

A faint whistling cut through the night.

THUNK!

An arrow thudded into the tree next to Keoki's head. He gasped, scrambling to gain footing before leaping to another branch. A second arrow breezed past his leg.

"The fancy man! Not so fast, after all!"

Keoki grabbed for another limb. It snapped. He was barely able to catch himself on a sturdier branch below, but the force of the fall caused his shoulder to flare in pain. Below, the wolves were slavering and howling, baring their teeth up at the clumsy farmer.

Why didn't I just go home to Fil and Agnes? Why did I... Sapphir...

A sliver of moonlight illuminated three men, all clad in wolf pelts of different shades. Their bows and arrows pointed at him.

I'm going to die.

Keoki threw himself from his perch towards the tree next to his tall pine. The impact caused Keoki to wheeze in pain. He grappled for a handhold, dizzy from the effort and impossibly fatigued. He hung by one hand from the tree's bough, noticing that an arrow was sprouting from his left ankle.

That's new.

The branch popped quietly, before finally snapping. Keoki fell. He was only ten feet above the ground after his graceless escape through the trees; still, his landing was anything but gentle.

Keoki groaned, drawing his stone knife as he rolled to face the Leontians and their wolves. Each beast could have ended his life on its own at that point. But they were in no rush.

"The fancy man from the fancy city. It does not please me to see that you have failed the wolf rite."

Keoki pushed himself to his feet, holding his knife out shakily. Finally, the fourth Leontian arrived, still pounding her drum. The woman wore a full bear skin.

"We are proud Leontians, fancy man. All of us have pleased the goddess Artemis by succeeding in the rites – men and women alike."

The biggest wolf let out a howl, then looked at Keoki with unmistakable hunger. Keoki was certain his stone knife would do no good. Before meeting Ivy and Maya, the only true pain Keoki could remember was losing his parents, the same day he had broken his foot.

Since then, he had been stabbed and knocked unconscious by mountain clansmen, imprisoned by Sapphir in her cave, and slashed with a dagger by Rizon Atsali in Rhium.

And Sapphir left.

Keoki laughed deliriously.

All because I went looking for a cow.

Before him, the Leontians looked calm, as if this was the

ending they had all expected. A fancy man would never survive the wolf rite. The biggest wolf came a step closer; her nose glistened despite the dim light, and Keoki could see saliva dripping between her yellow teeth.

Mother, Father... I'm not ready yet.

The shadows of his parents flanked the she-wolf on either side; his mother looked like a beautiful mother wolf, with her black hair and sharp jawline. His father stood, strong as always. They blocked his view of the Leontians.

"I know, dear," his mother spoke sweetly. *"We see you, strong and full of life."*

I'm not ready... I want to be with you... but... I'm not ready... not this time.

"And we, still, are not ready for you."

His father nodded, his hand hovering above the alpha wolf's back. Its muscles tensed.

"We love you, dear. We will be with you when it is time."

No... stay with me now! Please...

His parents disappeared. Keoki's hand shook.

And a loud roar caused the big wolf to hesitate. Her sisters yelped, and she slunk back to join them. The Leontians readied their weapons. Keoki turned in time to see a massive shape burst through the trees.

Keoki shuffled sideways, his ankle throbbing. His entire body was in pain. The creature slowed to a stop in front of the Leontians, who backed away in fear. Keoki was close enough to see all the animal's features.

It was nearly twice Keoki's height. Four times his weight. Its dark brown fur was creased with lines of muscle. The animal raised its massive paws, showing off claws the size of daggers. Its teeth were vicious. But its eyes...

I've... seen you before.

The bear's eyes were the shape of large marbles, deeper brown than its fur. Keoki moved towards it slowly, his hand outstretched.

What am I doing?

It lowered itself to all fours and looked at Keoki with curiosity. Its grunts and growls were almost curious.

Questioning.

The girls... they changed you. Ivy and Maya...

Keoki hadn't understood weeks ago, when he saw the beast for the first time. He had been appalled at the sheer size of the bear – disturbed at its friendliness.

How did I not realize it sooner?

The Leontians watched with disbelief as Keoki drew closer to the bear. She growled, but the noise quickly morphed into a questioning grunt.

Keoki spoke, his voice filled with relief and amazement, "They changed you, Io. That's why you chased the girls... why I couldn't find you..."

Keoki lowered his hand to the huge foreleg closest to him. Io's fur was bristly, but soft enough. She turned her head to him, fixing her big, brown eyes on Keoki's.

"This form suits you."

"I do not believe what my eyes are seeing," the large man muttered, shifting his wolf pelt. "The Hunt has chosen you, fancy man."

"The Moonspawn!" the drummer called, beating her drum once.

"The Moonspawn! The Moonspawn!"

Keoki leaned against Io, his body screaming in pain. The arrow in his ankle had been jostled by his fall, sinking the barbs deeper into the flesh. Several ribs were certainly broken, and his shoulder felt as if another spear had been shoved through it.

One of the Leontians whistled, and the wolves scampered into the night. Keoki ran his hand along Io's neck, whispering to the bear.

"Thank you."

The Moonspawn needs a healer.

Io stood back on her hind legs, opened her mouth, and roared.

Chapter 21

Melani

Col and Lathor's ship had already disappeared around the cliffside by the time Melani and Rizon arrived on shore aboard a small dinghy. The beach absorbed Melani's feet as she secured the boat to a thick wooden post. Seawater crept across her toes, suspending the sand for a moment before allowing it to cling her feet again.

Melani looked ordinary with her short black hair and sister's chiton. Next to her, Rizon resembled a large, defiant child. He wore a brown cloak of Lathor's that enveloped him completely. He had rolled the sleeves up, but his hands looked minute in the folds. The brim of a straw sailor's hat dipped over his forehead, barely revealing his feral eyes.

It's only been a few hours since he tried to drink himself to an early death.

"Which way to the, um, room?"

What do I call a secret hideaway known only to the Flat Nose and an assassin?

"Follow me," Rizon muttered.

He blinked in the bright sunlight, certainly regretting his excessive consumption. One of his sleeves unraveled, extending to his knee. Melani suppressed a giggle.

Fisherfolk trudged across the beach, dragging nets filled with silver trout and sea bass. On either side of Melani, the sand gently transitioned to rock, which rose until it became cliffs. The air was heavy and smelled of dead seaweed. Her stomach turned over.

This makes me hate the beach.

Rizon set off at a brisk pace, following in the direction of the returning fisherfolk. A stone path led up from the sea to a line of shops and homes. The streets became more well-kept as they continued, and the density of houses increased.

It looks like Boura. Only bigger.

Melani hadn't been to Helike in almost a year; she had last visited the city to sell a painting of Artemis slaying a stag to a very wealthy buyer. She couldn't remember the woman's name. She never understood why people were willing to pay for extravagant artwork with such abandon, though she was thankful they did.

Traveling to Helike today, however, felt different. She found herself noticing malicious faces and the outlines of concealed blades.

There is rage and violence hidden in every Heliken.

Rizon slowed until he and Melani were walking at each other's side, grunting, "We need to stick to the outskirts of the city."

Melani nodded, trying her best to appear natural. She and Rizon stepped through a side street. Rizon acted quite casual despite his ridiculous outfit. The narrow alleyways were empty for the most part, allowing them to navigate the city with ease. Melani's palms were sweaty.

Nothing to be nervous about. We're simply walking through a city.

With every turn, Melani expected to see Tarlen, the fur-trader and Fisherman. It had been in exposed city streets that he came to kill her, after all. He could do it again.

He's dead; I mustn't be silly.

Melani felt dryness on the roof of her mouth. Inside her stomach, it felt as if the baby were tickling her.

That can't be... the baby isn't even that large yet.

A rat scurried past Melani's foot in a particularly tight alley. She flinched. A shadow appeared on the wall in front of them. He paused for a fraction of a second, then a man in light armor sauntered past.

"Shit," Rizon whispered to himself.

He pulled Melani back to the street from which they had come, then stopped as another guard strolled past the alley. They spun once more and exited the alley, looking away from the first guard as they turned to walk along the larger road.

Melani didn't have to check over her shoulder to know the

man was following them. She could hear the iron of his boots clacking against stone. Rizon adjusted his hat and took Melani's hand, his long sleeve unrolling up to her wrist.

The road led to an open square, with a few shops centered around a fountain. It looked very similar to a Boura. People traversed the street, talking with one another and tossing mares into the fountain. Three more armored men stood at the intersections of other cobbled roads.

"Go through the alley to your left. Don't look at the guards."

Melani banked towards the narrow pass, and Rizon continued in a straight line through the square. She could feel eyes on her. The square was becoming more congested. Melani sifted through crowds of people, bumping into a slight girl with dark skin, who muttered a quick apology.

She ducked below two large men carrying baskets of fruit and dashed into the alley. The space was shady and damp, with a set of stairs ahead. Melani could have touched both walls if she stood in the middle. She glanced over her shoulder and let out a quiet squeak of alarm.

One of the armored men was pointing at her as he pushed through the square. Melani leapt towards the stairs, grabbing at the wall as she stumbled past. She charged up, taking two steps at a time.

Oh gods... oh gods, oh gods.

A man stopped at the top of the stairs, and Melani froze. She looked behind her and saw two other guards approaching slowly.

A sliver of sunlight focused on Melani as if she were staging a play in the Heliken theater.

"That's the girl!" one of the guards at the bottom of the stairs called. "The one who was with the prisoner!"

They were closing in. It would take only seconds for them to trap her from both sides.

Take me to the prison... to Xander... at least I can be with him! Just be gentle...

The guard who had spoken reached his hand out to catch Melani's arm. Her stage light went dark.

"Grab her, Lasur!" the second guard screeched, some instinct telling him to back away.

Lasur didn't have time to look up. A cloaked figure swooped down from one of the buildings that formed the narrow alley. Melani threw her arms over her head; but the figure was not aiming for her.

He landed with a crunch on the armored guard, rolling down the stairs past the second. Melani was so distracted, that she forgot about the third man at the top of the stairs. A rough hand clenched her thin arm, pulling her towards him.

"Rizon!" she yelled.

The baby! The baby's in danger!

The lithe assassin ducked as the guard swung a knife at him. He pinned the man's arm to the wall, pulling his helmet over his eyes. With wolfish ferocity, Rizon bounded past the blinded guard, and kicked him squarely in the back, sending him tumbling down the staircase.

"Rizon Atsali! It *is* him! The assassin!"

Why did I say his name!

"You're to be executed!" the final guard exclaimed, wrapping an arm around Melani's chest and holding a dirk up with the other.

Rizon put his hands up in surrender, picking his way up each step with care.

"Come with me, and the girl lives!"

The guard's voice was shaking.

He's not going to hurt me... he doesn't know what to do.

"Come on!" his voice broke, "Your life! For hers!"

Melani gasped for air, feeling her lungs compress. Rizon kept approaching. He fell to his knees three steps below them and put both hands on top of Lathor's huge sailor hat.

"Yeah, good," the guard said to himself, "I'll recapture the prisoner. Good," he raised his voice, "Stay there!"

Rizon stayed still, his emotions imperceptible. The guard's grip on Melani loosened, and she slipped through his arms.

"No, you stay, too! You stay!" he ordered, pointing for Melani to sit on a stair behind him.

The two guards at the bottom of the stairs began to stir, noticing their companion with both fugitives above them. The nervous guard kept his dirk leveled at Rizon. He felt at his waist for some sort of binding.

"Stand. Stand up, prisoner."

Rizon stood.

"Turn around. And face the bottom of the stairs. Now. Turn now!"

The guard's tone was transparently anxious, but he tried to sound commanding. His back was turned to Melani as he descended the stairs to Rizon.

Now. I have to act now!

"Look out!"

The guard turned to her voice in alarm, and Rizon took the opportunity. He spun, grabbing the man's triceps with one hand and reaching for his leg with the other. The guard grunted in surprise as he was tossed easily over Rizon's shoulder, sprawling onto his back.

"Thanks," Rizon said, pulling Melani to her feet.

They sprinted up the steps, and Rizon tossed Lathor's hat aside. When they reached the top, Rizon directed Melani left. There was no reason to move stealthily now. Within minutes, Rizon and Melani were in a part of the city she didn't recognize.

"This is the road. The dirt one."

Melani stopped running, her chest heaving.

The baby's tired.

"We have to start walking, Rizon... I don't know if I can make it."

"It's not far. If we run, it'll be only ten minutes."

"Rizon..."

"Melani... we can't get caught."

Her feet were aching from the escape. Her sandals had shifted as they ran, causing angry blisters to develop.

I can make it. I have to make it. For Xander.

"We can do it Melani. You can."

"And then we can rest?"

"Yes. And then we can rest."

Melani took a deep breath and ran. Each footfall was more difficult than the one before. The sun was hot, and the air was dry.

I wish it were raining as it had over the ocean.

Melani could barely focus on the trees that blurred past as she struggled up the inclining dirt road. Rizon checked on her every few minutes, though he held his steady pace. Her hair was sticky with sweat.

This will be what actually kills me. Not Fishermen or guards. This. When did I become so weak?

Melani wanted to blame the baby but wasn't sure that she could. She tripped over a loose stone, falling hard into the dirt. Rizon turned to help her up, but Melani was already clambering to her feet.

"No... I can make it."

Rizon looked ahead, "It's that large pine to our right. That's where we're going."

The final stadion was the most challenging, as Melani limped on her blistered feet and followed Rizon past the tall pine tree. He slowed to a walk.

"We've certainly lost them by now."

"Oh, are you sure?" Melani spat. "I think one of those guards was an Olympian."

Rizon smirked. "That wasn't a very good joke."

Melani rolled her eyes, wheezing, "I'm. Tired. It wasn't my best."

"Xander's told me you were funny, though."

Melani glared at him. Rizon didn't look fazed, even though his head must have been pounding from Lathor's drink.

"Ah, don't be mad. We can joke with each other."

Now that I know what you really were? A Fisherman? An assassin?

"Just take me to the place."

"It's right here," Rizon said.

They stood in the middle of the woods away from the dirt road. Melani stood next to a bush and a couple trees.

"Where?"

Rizon pushed aside leaves. "The bush, Melani! See?"

The bush was indeed covering a hole large enough for one person. It appeared to open into nothingness.

It's a relief that I'm not more pregnant.

"You want me... to go inside that hole?"

Rizon put both feet in. "Trust me."

He slid through.

Do I trust him?

Melani put her own legs in the hole, feeling the hollowness below her as she sat down.

"It's a short drop, Melani. Be ready to catch yourself!"

Melani edged into the hole and felt herself begin to fall. She landed on soft ground.

That wasn't so bad.

Around her, Melani could see worms oozing out of the soil. Tree roots sent out thin tendrils, making the walls seem dappled with hair. The hole was more like a room, a cavernous space in the silt and clay.

"And this... leads to the castle?"

Normally, the grime would have bothered Melani, but she was so close to Xander.

He must be close!

"Just through this passage. We're nearly there."

Rizon stooped to a crawl as the tunnel led off from the hole and narrowed. Melani was close behind. Cool soil stuck to her cloth chiton. Her knees felt damp. Black earth caked her palms and wrists.

Xander will *be there!*

Melani couldn't be sure how much time passed as she and Rizon inched along. She was just beginning to worry that perhaps they would be stuck in a dirt tunnel forever, when Rizon stopped.

"Here," he whispered.

Thank the gods.

Rizon shifted, trying to get in position to push open the exit. A latch clanked and twisted with his hand. Candlelight illuminated the tunnel through a crack in the small door, and Rizon paused.

Light footsteps sounded against stone.

We're not alone! He said this place was safe!

Melani took a deep breath.

It must be the Flat-Nose. He's come to hide away... perhaps his business in Achaea was a lie.

When the voice spoke, however, it was not the distinctive nasal tone of the councilor. Instead, the sound was younger, with just a hint of a foreign accent.

"Need a hand, Opi? Here, I'll open it."

The door opened, filling the tunnel with light. Melani blinked. Even though the light was low, her eyes took a second to adjust from pitch black. Rizon was quicker to react.

He pushed himself through the door, springing at the figure inside. Lathor's cloak flapped around, covering them both as Rizon clamped a hand over the boy's mouth. He was small, with dark skin and short, wavy hair. He was a few years younger than Melani and very thin.

"Rizon!" she whispered sharply.

He studied the boy's face, then pulled himself away, shaking off some of the dirt. The boy scrambled to his feet, defiant, before a curious recognition dawned in his eyes.

"Rizon Atsali... I... I thought..."

"Yes. I escaped..."

"But then..."

"I'm back now. With a friend."

Melani slipped through the door, pushing herself to her feet. The room was small with a single bed, desk, and a few candles. It had clearly been lived in for a few days. She stood, brushing herself off.

I'm quite sure I look horrible.

The boy smiled at her, looking her up and down.

"Hi... Rizon's friend, I guess?"

Melani returned the smile. The boy seemed sweet and innocent enough.

"Pleased to meet you. I'm Melani." she extended a dirty hand. "Sorry about the mess... and you are?"

"Yes, of course. No, don't worry about the dirt. Hi, I'm Nicolaus. Well, Nic. You can just call me Nic."

Chapter 22

Simon

Olenus' palace reflected the beauty of its garden. Its opulence made the Palace of Helike resemble a crude hunk of stone. Golden-plated doors were set in an archway that seemed to be composed of more gold, ivory, and bronze. A long, flowing velvet rug, bordered with silver lace, led from the entrance, through an arched hallway, to a grand courtroom. The velvet ended at the foot of a spectacular throne.

Unlike the Heliken Court, which had sparse seating for citizens, rows of manicured ebony benches lined the hall. The seats also happened to be filled.

Another curious difference.

Simon could see hundreds of people – soldiers, guards, bakers, farmers, traders, men, women, and even a few children.

What sort of children yearn to see a political show?

Many were chattering in hushed tones, but their attention was always focused on the man speaking in the front. He knelt, apologizing and pleading rapidly. Before him, King Basilius sat in a golden throne. The throne Simon sometimes occupied in Helike appeared gold but was simply a convincing alloy. This gold was certainly real. Massive jewels crested the top, reflecting King Basilius' own crown playfully.

Another crown... it's a relief I don't have one. It would surely scratch my bald head.

Simon could not deny that Basilius looked the part of a monarch. He was as tall as the Golden Spear, though thinner. His jawline cut through an angular face, intimidating to look upon. He was older than Simon, but his eyes glinted with the ferocity and assurance of a younger man. Long black hair and a thick beard framed his sharp nose well. He wore a silver himation studded with bronze.

And that crown...

When Simon looked closer, he saw that the crown, too, was solid gold and ivory. A single ruby, the biggest Simon had ever seen, was centered above Basilius' forehead like a third eye.

One begins to wonder where all this wealth came from.

Eté beckoned for Simon to follow him to a seat on one of the front benches. It was comfortable, an ergonomic shape that cushioned even Simon's bony frame.

"Most days, I sit there, beside the King," Eté said, keeping his voice low. "But today, I must accompany an honored guest."

How kind.

"Very gracious of you, Eté. And that man there. The one on the other side of your king... is he another advisor?"

Eté smiled, his thin mustache curling. "Yes... Venedictos is a comrade of mine. King Basilius values his council..."

Though not as much as he values yours...

Venedictos slouched in his chair a bit. He was rotund.

A line of servants snaked along the wall to Simon's right. He counted at least fifteen before deciding it was not worth turning his head anymore. There were a lot of servants. They filled cups of water and wine for the citizens and wiped away any spills with haste; a few seemed to be circulating with cheese and olives. An equal number of guards stood at attention in the court, all wearing expensive armor and only the sharpest steel.

Well... the King is safe in his own hall. We can be sure of this.

"Is this man guilty of some crime?" Simon whispered.

Eté leaned towards him. "Sadly, this bard was seen to be forward with some of the King's cooks... both female and male."

"Is it a crime to be intimate with both female and male?"

"It is a crime to consort with one of the King's cooks... when it is the King's own niece."

A dalliance between a cook and a singer? This did not seem to be much of an offense to Simon; perhaps Olenus was a more repressed city than Helike.

"Oh."

Now we shall see how King Basilius deals with disorder in his city.

The singer still knelt with his head bowed, speaking to the floor, "A-a-and I didn't know. It's like I've said. I didn't know she was one of your own blood. Royal blood. King Basilius... please. I didn't know. I-I-I..."

Behind him, Simon could hear two women theorizing what would become of the singer.

"Dead man, he is."

"Dead? For kissing a cook? No... no... chains. A little time to reflect on his lust."

"The King likes his bloodlines clean."

"I-I didn't mean you or your family any disrespect. Honest to the gods! You must believe me."

Finally, King Basilius spoke, "I *must*?"

"Well... er, no... I wouldn't demand that you–"

"Paris, yes? That's your name, singer?"

Even King Basilius' voice was that of a king.

"P-Paris... yes, my king."

"Well, Paris. My *family* knows all too well not to besmirch the royal blood. So... who must be held responsible for this dishonor?"

"I di... I didn't... dishonor her! She... she wan..."

The singer's voice trailed off. Simon believed that the man had not forced anything upon king's niece. He was handsome enough, and his nervous behavior was not that of a seasoned liar.

"Yes... dead this one is," the woman behind Simon giggled.

GHE CHILDREN OF GHE SEA

They seem too unbothered by the prospect.

"Paris, do you believe me to be a just king?" King Basilius asked, leaning forward in his throne.

Paris raised his glistening eyes from the floor. "Of–of course, my king."

"Then, I know you understand the ruling I must make. This was an act of lust. A shameful deed, which the gods abhor. Yet even our mighty Sky Father, Zeus was a victim to this plague at times." King Basilius raised his arms, looking at the sky. "And we forgive and honor Zeus... so shall we forgive you. However, to make it easier for you, Paris, to conquer this lust... take him..."

Two guards rushed forward, grabbing Paris by each arm and dragging him to his feet. Their armor clanked. Paris did not resist, tears streaming down his face in silence.

"...and remove his lustful instruments."

The crowd murmured in approval, some openly cheering. A few gasped. King Basilius rested his hands on his lap in satisfaction. Paris sobbed as he was dragged from the court by the two guards.

"He'll be able to sing higher now, will he not?" Eté said.

Simon forced a laugh, disturbed. The people of Olenus were much too fond of the cruel punishment.

Is Basilius always this unforgiving?

Simon now had little desire to speak with the king.

But I must. For peace in Patras, peace in Helike... peace in Achaea.

238

As the noise died down, Basilius noticed Eté for the first time, sitting in the crowd, rather than at his side. He waved him forward. Eté rushed to his side, and Venedictos looked away. The advisor leaned in to his king's ear and whispered. His skin seemed lighter than Simon had remembered it.

Perhaps it is the glow of the golden throne.

Eté took his seat and winked at Simon. King Basilius raised one hand to quell the audience.

"Citizens, what a day we have! You shall be overjoyed that you chose today to join us at court."

Too late, Simon realized King Basilius would want to have their discussion on the stage of Olenus' Court.

I must sharpen my wits.

"Let us welcome Councilor Simon of Helike! One of the city's *three* great rulers."

Tepid applause echoed throughout the room. Simon pushed himself to his feet and strode forward. He wished he looked more royal. On his bald head he wore only a sheen of sweat. Simon executed a quick bow.

"Welcome, Councilor Simon."

"Many thanks, King Basilius. I have been awestruck at your city's glory. Olenus truly is… beautiful."

"Yes. We seek to be an earthly Olympus."

Simon tried to ignore the whispers from the crowd.

"No doubt your temple to Zeus reflects this. I–"

"We can move past the congratulations, if you don't mind,

councilor."

Right... Eté said he dislikes quips.

"Of course."

"What brings you to my city today? If my information is current, your city is in the midst of a war with its neighbor."

If your information is current... Eté told you seconds ago.

"It is the very war you speak of that brings me to your city. I fear that the conflict may begin to spread across Achaea. The fight between Boura and Helike should have no repercussions in our other great cities."

King Basilius showed no emotion. Venedictos smirked but hid it quickly.

"And you believe the violence would spread without your intervention?"

"Helike does not wish to bring this war to the League. If other cities remain peaceful, firm in their stance against future war..."

Gaios may stand down...

"To be clear, you wish your city to gain power... land... while others in the League stand and watch?"

It does seem like that, doesn't it?

Simon frowned, feeling the eyes of hundreds on him. He didn't want to look away from the King of Olenus. It would show weakness and fear.

"I wish for the League's power to remain strong. We cannot afford Achaea to break apart. There are hungry forces in every direction."

Persia, Athens, Sparta... the League must *remain.*

King Basilius laughed, looking to his citizens for further support. They chuckled as well. Simon felt more exposed than he had in a long time.

Since before Helike.

"Councilor Simon, you must realize how queer this request is. Our city should remain peaceful? While yours is at war with one of the League's own?"

The crowd's mirth grew. Simon had to refrain from touching his nose. He grasped at the inside of his cloak instead.

"Yes, I realize how this might seem. When I was in Patras, Old Patreus seemed to understand my calls for peace... just because there is fighting in Helike... that doesn't mean I support the violence."

Should I have mentioned Patras?

"Ah, so you were able to talk with Old Patreus. Tell me, Councilor Simon... what does he truly think of your proposition? For us to remain peaceful and resilient in the face of a war between Boura and Helike."

"He... he feels Patras is powerless to help... but he doesn't wish for the violence to spread."

King Basilius folded his hands once more, a smug grin on his angular face. Next to him, Eté blinked solemnly at Simon. His thin mustache quivered.

Is he a friend? Or an enemy...

"And did he spread any falsehoods about my city to you?

About my intentions?"

He knows that I know. I shouldn't mince words.

"Old Patreus... he seemed to think that Olenus planned to take Patras by force. That you wish to rule outside the city walls."

"And why would that be!" King Basilius exclaimed, directing his attention to the luxury that surrounded him. "Look at me! Look at all I have in Olenus – at what our citizens have! We are a city of glory, as you so eloquently stated."

And when this glory is not enough? When it could be more glorious?

"Old Patreus is naught but an old man! An old, jealous man, who wishes he held more power in his city than he does. Eté, why have you brought this Heliken? What can the Flat-Nose do in Olenus? Aside from insult his host?"

The crowd jeered, just loud enough to drown out Eté's response. Simon could tell King Basilius was having trouble digesting it. Eventually, he quieted the crowd once more.

Will he take my manhood, as he did Paris the singer? Or perhaps my tongue.

"Ah, Simon! Councilor Simon... I should apologize. My faithful advisor believes I may be misinterpreting your words. Let us change tack. Please, take a room in the palace. Eté will show you the way himself. We... we have much to discuss, I believe. Perhaps I have spoken too quickly; an alliance with Helike would be a benefit to us all."

Simon let go of his robe, the sheen of sweat on his forehead

242

had extended to his palms.

What changed his mind?

"King Basilius... I must thank you. For opening your city to me. Yes... the League could use a cordial friendship between Olenus and Helike."

Simon could sense the disappointment amongst the Olenus citizens; they had wished for their king to embarrass this foreign diplomat even more. However, the guards were already dragging a new raggedy man across the velvet floor. When the benches on either side of the room noticed, they forgot about Simon.

No reason for them to dwell on the Flat-Nose.

King Basilius muttered something to Eté, who nodded as he left the altar. Simon prayed that it didn't pertain to their new *guest*, however he knew this prayer would go unanswered. He met Eté at the side of the room opposite the servants.

"Well, that didn't go as we hoped, did it," Eté said.

As we hoped? When did it become "we?"

"No... no it did not. Your king is a tough man. A... hardened man."

Eté's mustache stretched as his lip curled. "His boldness has made him an effective ruler... you can see how the city adores him."

Do they? Or do they simply seek entertainment?

Eté's skin had returned to the shade that Simon remembered – somewhere between tan and black.

"They do seem to love him."

Simon and Eté turned down a corridor where the noise of the

courtroom was no longer audible. The walls were beautifully painted; the rest of the palace did not pale in comparison to the grand entrance.

"You'll be staying there, my friend," Eté said. "A simple guest room. Though if you ever require anything, servers will always be walking the halls."

"I won't forget your generosity, Eté," Simon said. "I'm sure you will be quite helpful in the days to come as well... I know how much you long for peace in Achaea."

And I won't forget that you advise a cruel king.... So Eté... are you a friend? Or something quite different?

Chapter 23

Nicolaus

Rizon Atsali looked cleaner and healthier than Nic remembered. His beard was neater. He smelled better than he had in the prison cells as well, though the robe he wore was far too large. Despite the bulky outfit, Nic could still see sinew in Rizon's neck.

His eyes are even more hawkish than before.

The woman who accompanied him was a few years older than Nic, past her twentieth year at least. She was thin, tan, and about Nic's height. Her short black hair was streaked brown. She was quite pretty.

"Well, it's a nice place you have here, Nic," Melani said. "Mind if I sit in that chair?"

"No, not at all. Sit down!"

Melani sat and exhaled.

"So, Nicolaus... servant to the Golden Spear. What are you doing in one of the Flat-Nose's secret rooms?" Rizon asked.

He still doesn't know.

"Uh... the Gol... Orrin's dead." Nic cleared his throat. "He, uh... was killed in the explosion. The Battle at the Beach."

Melani put her hand over her chest, mouth slightly open. Rizon's face did not change.

"He was an honorable man. I'm sorry, Nicolaus."

Nic waved away the apology.

"Help them... all of them."

"It's okay. It's..."

If you hadn't murdered Euripides! Maybe he'd...

Nic wanted to say it. He wanted to throw the assassin back in his cell. He wanted to cast all his blame on one man and move on.

But he couldn't.

Rizon continued, "And now you're here. Hiding."

"I never returned to the palace after the battle. Well... I guess I'm here now, but... you know what I mean. I left the beach and... hid... with a friend."

It was better to leave Elfie and the rest of Orrin's family out of it. Rizon didn't press him any further.

"You've been here for weeks?" Melani asked, genuine concern on her face.

"Well, I wasn't *here* the whole time. Just hiding. I was with a wounded Bouran. But he left, so I..."

The sound of a latch clicking made Nic pause. Seconds later,

Opi was nudging the door open, a basket with food clutched in one hand.

"I'm with her," he finished.

Rizon helped Opi through the door, then backed away until he was leaning on the desk near Melani. Opi masked her surprise well; the energy in the room was peaceable.

"Oh... Nic, how did they?"

She set the food down, keeping her eyes on the two new guests. Her jaw dropped.

"Nic that's... you! Simon... why are you...?"

Opi moved closer to Nic, dropping her hand in front of him protectively.

"Yes, I'm the prisoner the Flat-Nose–"

"Simon," Opi interrupted. "His name is Simon."

"–set free," Rizon finished.

"And... how did you..."

"Find this place? This is how the Fl... Simon helped me escape. He took me from my cell to this room. I went through the tunnel."

Opi nodded slowly. She was upset. Coincidental as their discovery had been, Opi had wanted to stay hidden.

He tried to change the subject.

"You got the food?"

"Yes, Nic."

She kicked the basket to him. Nic pulled out an apple, shined it on Simon's chiton, which he had found earlier that day, and took a bite. The skin was crisp, and the noise echoed in the quiet room.

Someone needs to speak.

"Buh wyed comeer?" Nic asked through a mouthful of apple.

He covered his mouth as Melani giggled. He finished swallowing.

"Sorry. But why'd you come here? Melani?"

"Yes, of course," Melani started, smiling sweetly at Opi. "I'm Melani, by the way. You seem to already know of my friend, Rizon Atsali. We didn't meet during his... previous work," she added. "I'm an artist from Boura. Healer... kind of."

The tension in Opi's shoulders relaxed a little. However, she did not sit down.

"I... Rizon and I, are looking for my partner. His brother. We went looking for him after the battle..."

"Oh," Opi said. "And you think he might be at the castle?"

"Prisoners of war *would* be here," Nic confirmed, though he was not entirely certain. "I mean... they *should* be."

Opi and Nic looked at each other. He could still hear the explosion, eyes searing from the light.

If he was in the Battle at the Beach...

"Are you sure he's not..."

"He's alive," she brushed her hand past her stomach. "He has to be."

Rizon grimaced at Nic. The assassin surely knew there was a chance his brother had not survived the battle. He remembered what the man had said to Nic as he sat, defeated in his cell; he had carried out the murder to protect his family. He loved his brother.

He's heartbroken... he won't show it, but he is.

Nic thought of Xander. The Bouran smith who was an impressive fighter. He, too, had claimed he would fight for someone he loved.

And who do I have? My family is far away... would anyone search for me the way these two searched for their lost soldier?

"Did you plan to sneak to the prison somehow?" Opi asked. "To see if your partner was there?"

"I guess... it sounds a bit foolish, doesn't it?" Melani laughed. "But what choice do we have? I'd be lost without him. I am..."

Opi blushed. Nic looked away. How could two people have found each other, cared enough that they would risk their lives trying to find the other? He could hear the sincerity in Melani's voice – the love. She was infatuated.

"I don't think it's foolish," Opi said quietly.

Melani's foot tapped against the stone floor. Nic wanted to help. He looked at Rizon Atsali, his features illuminated by the candle dancing in its glass orb. He wondered if his brother looked like him – lean, with movements as agile as a cat. Had he seen him on the beach?

"What does your Bouran soldier look like?" Nic asked, trying to sift through the gruesome memories of the battle for recognizable faces.

Maybe I'll know if I saw him being taken into the city... or if I saw him die...

"You think you might have seen him?"

Melani seemed reluctantly eager. Rizon's face was stony, as if knew this exercise would lead them nowhere.

"I mean..." he looked at Opi for help, and she shrugged, "Maybe."

Melani stopped tapping her foot.

"Okay... okay. He's about the same height as Rizon, but bigger. You know, like broader. He's tan... kind of the same shade as me. Sandy hair. Oh, he has a sunspot on his hand. It's cute."

Nic fumbled his apple, catching it just before it hit the ground. He looked at Rizon Atsali again.

Why am I so slow!

"Oh gods."

The soldier Nic had taken to Elfie's, *had* looked vaguely familiar to him. Yet, he couldn't place where he'd seen the similarities before.

Xander! And Rizon!

Now it made perfect sense. The familial resemblance was shockingly obvious.

And the woman! Melani!

"Oh gods. Oh, Melani. Rizon! You'll think I'm so foolish!"

Rizon cocked his head. Melani locked her thumbs together, her eyes urging Nic to pull himself together. Nic took a step closer to Rizon, studying his hawkish eyes.

How did I not see it?

"He's a smith! Isn't he? He's... oh wow... Xander."

Melani jumped to her feet. "Yes! You know him... my Xander!

He's a smith! When did you... is he?"

Opi looked completely lost. Nic raised his arm, still clutching his half-eaten apple.

"Melani! He's alive! I hid with him. After the battle. Well, he wouldn't have hidden. But the explosion – it nearly took his leg off. He was hurt. We, uh, stayed low together until he could walk again."

Melani hugged him, then kissed his forehead. She moved to Opi and clasped her hands. Rizon was dumbfounded. He pushed himself from the table and walked up to Nic. His hawkish face still frightened Nic, though it was less disconcerting with the oversized robe. Both of the sleeves had now rolled past his hands. Then, he beamed.

"Nicolaus... Nicolaus! My brother!"

He pulled him into an embrace. It was not as gentle and welcome as Melani's had been. Rizon's body was hard underneath the robe. However, Nic couldn't help but smile. Rizon looked like a gleeful puppy when he pulled away, his sleeves hanging to his knees.

"He's alive! Oh, I knew he was!" Melani exclaimed, quieting when she remembered they were in hiding. "Where did he go? Back to Boura, I'm sure. Oh, I'm such a... an idiot!"

Melani relinquished Opi and went to hug Rizon. He patted her on the back and whispered something only she could hear. When she pulled back, a single tear of joy splotched her cheek.

"Do you know where he went, Nic?"

"He said he was going back to you. He would've gone sooner. Certainly, he would have. He wanted to leave as soon as he woke up the first day. But his leg... he needed to heal."

"How long ago was that? And here I am... and is he..."

Melani turned and mouthed something to Rizon.

In danger?

Rizon shook his head.

"A few days ago. In the morning. With his leg the way it was, he probably got back to Boura around midday."

Nic could see countless emotions on Melani's face. She was ecstatic that Xander was alive, furious at herself for being away from him, worried for his safety...

She really *loves him.*

"I have to go to him... Rizon, are you? I have to go!"

Nic prayed that Xander would still be in the city waiting for Melani. He worried that the smith would have gone searching for her himself, upon realizing that she was no longer in Boura.

And around and around they would go...

"Do you know the way?" Nic asked.

"To Boura? Of course. Yes. I know the way. Rizon, are you coming with me? Every minute..."

Melani looked exhausted as it was. However, she would not rest until she could return to Xander; he was alive, and she meant to find him. They needed to be together. Opi noticed her fatigue, too, and rummaged in the basket for a canteen.

"Water. You need this, Melani. And bread? Or something."

"No, no. I don't want to take anything of yours!"

"We can always go back into town," Nic assured, as Opi pushed the supplies into her hands, "You need this. And Xander needs you. Go to him!"

Rizon nodded, and Melani took the canteen, drinking deeply. She stuffed the bread into her chiton and moved to the door. Her hand paused on the latch.

"Rizon!"

Rizon didn't move; he opened his mouth as if to speak, then closed it.

"Your brother, Rizon! Don't you want to see him?"

Nic and Opi stepped awkwardly to one side, so Melani and Rizon were facing each other. Melani still clutched the latch.

"Melani... those guards?"

"Who cares! We can get past them again!"

Rizon shook his head. He rolled up the sleeves on his oversized robe.

"I have to end it, Melani. *Really* end it. I have to get to him. To Gaios."

"But... but we're supposed to be safe... remember? You said so yourself... we're safe!"

Rizon rubbed his temples and sighed. Nic watched the conversation bounce back and forth. He felt as if he were in a council meeting; or talking with the Flat-Nose; or even with Orrin.

Why am I always two steps behind?

"I'm leaving, Rizon," Melani said. "I can find Xander and... we can go into hiding."

"The Fishermen won't be after you anymore. Not after…"

"After they find you."

Rizon held his palms up, revealing rough hands.

"I'll be safe. Tell… tell Xander that I'll see him soon."

Melani's jaw clenched. She turned the latch, and the door swung open. Before leaving, she hugged Rizon once more, crestfallen.

"Nic, Opi… thank you both. And good luck with… staying hidden."

Rizon Atsali and Melani looked at each other a final time, before she pulled herself into the tunnel and disappeared from view. Nic closed the door behind her.

She'll find Xander. She will!

The three who remained stood in silence in the small room. The candles flickered in their orbs. On the desk, Elfie's map was unrolled. The apple was slick in Nic's hand. After a minute, Opi spoke to Rizon.

"You stayed."

He motioned for Nic and Opi to sit on the bed, moving to the edge of the desk himself.

"I miss my brother. You know that, Nicolaus. You have family. And you, Opi… I believe you aren't from here either."

Opi nodded. She had grown up west of Memphis, Nic knew.

Why have we never really discussed her family?

He wondered if Gabrielle and Ibbie would like her. He

254

believed they would.

She's kind. And smart.

"Yet, here you both are."

Nic was compelled to defend himself. "I'm trying to learn who killed the Golden Spear. Who killed my friend! And Opi..."

"Simon needs someone who understands Gaios in Achaea. He's... we can't let him hold all the power in Helike."

"Do I need to justify why I stayed behind?" Rizon asked, planting his fist on the desk. "Duty and revenge keeps us tethered to this damn castle! And why? Who is the common man in all of this?"

"Help me or stay in this room. I don't care."

Nic looked at Opi. Her mind was working, probably faster than Nic's. They both believed Gaios to be a guilty man in some way; Nic was certain that Orrin's death had been arranged by the councilor... it only made sense. But how would they prove it? And would Rizon's presence help?

"You're not going to just kill him, are you?" Nic asked. "I mean... would that fix anything?"

"No. You can't," Opi said. "Helike needs leadership. You saw the disarray after *one* councilor was murdered. Now another is dead; one is *somewhere* in Achaea. And the other is Kyros. No... we need more. You can't just..."

She made a stabbing motion. Rizon's fierce glare intensified.

"We're not going to kill him. He's a wildfire, and the League is already aflame. We're going to extinguish him."

Chapter 24

Sapphir

A light rain had begun by the time Sapphir could see Olenus from her skiff. High walls and the outline of a palace were etched into the sky. Even from a great distance, the city's magnificence was palpable.

A worthy place for Father to reside.

Sapphir leaned her elbow against the rim of the boat. The water had been calm enough for most of the short voyage, despite the rain. In truth, she did not mind the lack of sun. Her fair skin could not take much more exposure.

The visions of her children were growing cloudier. Sapphir had considered turning back on more than one occasion. For the third time, she closed her eyes, praying to Poseidon that Egan would answer.

Egan! Egan...

Nothing.

EGAN!

She pounded her fist against the boat in frustration. Sapphir had known that it would be more difficult to maintain control the further she strayed from home; she had not, however, anticipated complete silence.

But I'm too close to turn back now.

Sapphir lifted her hand and saw a splinter.

I can't even feel it.

She wished Keoki were in the boat with her. For some reason, it was easier to stay collected when he was around.

She had never felt so uncertain.

Even when I lost Yusef, I knew what I wanted to do. I knew I wanted to find my children... now? Do I continue? Rush back to the farm?

She wondered if they would be safer without her. Of course, she loved them fiercely. But would her father find them? Would they be better off if Keoki brought them to their other families? If he betrayed her?

No... I saved them from him.... They need me.

She prayed once more for Ivy, Maya, Cy, Egan, and Celia. They must be happy together on the farm. It was a new place with so much to do.

So why did Ivy and Cy leave?

Sapphir pulled the splinter from her finger and flicked it off the boat. It disappeared in the calm waters.

Egan would have certainly found his brother and sister by now. He was well-practiced and level-headed. More likely than not, Celia, Ivy, and Cy were helping Felip with the cattle, while Maya read on Egan's lap.

Yet...

Maybe Keoki has already begun the journey home... the children would love that...

Sapphir turned skyward, letting the drizzle speckle her face.

"Yusef," she blurted. "Have I done everything wrong? Why can't I protect anyone I love? My children... you. And... well..."

Her hair stuck to her forehead.

"Have I hurt him?"

A startled water bug flapped away at the sound of her voice. Over the gentle rippling of seawater, it was the only sound. Sheer cliffside loomed to her left.

"Of course, I've hurt him. I left him, didn't I?"

The boat skimmed forward.

"I wish you were here, Yusef. You would have treated the farm boy with more kindness."

You wouldn't have imprisoned or abandoned him.

"I'm sorry... I... I shouldn't be talking about him with you."

Sapphir pulled a strand of red hair from her head. She held it over the water, watching it trace a line across the surface.

"Have I failed you, Yusef? Done wrong to your memory?"

You wouldn't have taken my children. As I did. We could have had our own.

"Father never did like you... at least you can enjoy it when I end his life. Well... maybe not *enjoy...*"

Sapphir pictured Yusef's soft brown eyes. Much gentler than Keoki's. He was kissed by the sun from many days shepherding.

And how he made me laugh at nothing...

A pebble fell from the cliff, its splash resonating in the quiet afternoon.

She sighed, "I miss you."

In the distance, Sapphir could see trade ships weighing anchor outside the busy Olenus port. Another rock splashed into the sea. Sapphir turned to the cliffside.

And gasped.

✳✳✳✳

They were everywhere. Sapphir waved her hand to stop the boat. She was only a stone's throw from the cliff, bobbing with the gentle waves. From there, she could see the ridges and outcrops, cut out from miniature caves to form platforms of sorts. And on those platforms, they stood in silence.

Children.

Over fifty of them. None were older than Egan from the looks of it; each one stared at her with dead eyes. She couldn't find any words. Then, a girl no older than Celia, with choppy blonde hair, giggled. A few of the children around her joined, until they were laughing aloud.

But their eyes...

"Hello, Children!" Sapphir called, as sweetly as she could.

The girl with choppy hair spoke, "Father told us to be silent for his daughter. But you looked so afraid. It was funny."

Father... they called him... "Father."

Sapphir put on a pained smile. The girl's words were familiar – she almost sounded like Ivy. However, her tone was lifeless... as were her eyes. A slender boy with brown curls waved at her.

"We're to take you to Father," he stated. "Will you come with us?"

Like his choppy-haired companion, the slender boy spoke without vitality. The chuckles that echoed from the other Children reflected the same phenomenon.

He's stolen their minds and their souls – they are nothing but bodies now.

Sapphir thought of her own children; surely, they had more free will... more energy and singularity. Yes... yes, they were all unique and lively.

Right? I left them their minds, didn't I? I just... modified... for their own good! Their own safety!

"Well... will you?" the slender boy asked.

"Why do you call him Father?" she responded.

"He's our father, sister. As he is yours! Come to him with us! He wants us to bring you to him!"

Sapphir took the single paddle from her rowboat. The wood was cold in her hands. She rowed towards the cliff. The notion of traveling to her father with dozens of Children didn't appeal to Sapphir. Unfortunately, they had already found her.

Of course, they would have seen me... why did I think I could get to Father unseen?

"Where do I go?"

The choppy-haired blonde girl leaned from one foot to the other. She raised an arm slowly and pointed to a stretch of cliff in front of Sapphir.

"Here. Leave your boat and come to us. Then, we will go to Father."

Sapphir rowed with caution. As she got closer, she could tell that footholds were carved into the cliff leading to a sizeable cave.

When she looked back up for the Children, they were gone.

Poseidon give me strength.

Sapphir steadied herself on the bow; she took a step, her heel hanging off the rocky ledge. After a minute, she had scaled the narrow steps. Sapphir was surprised to see how high the cave was when she arrived.

Even though the day was bright, only the entrance was illuminated. The blood of the Golden Age spread to the extremities of her body. She felt its heat – its energy.

I'm ready.

"Follow us, sister," a disembodied voice called from the cave.

"Come on! We want to show you our home. Father said you

would love it."

Sapphir stepped into the darkness. She was about to summon a flame, anything to reveal her path forward, when a hand took hers. A chill ran up Sapphir's spine, and it took all of her willpower not to flinch.

"Don't be frightened, sister."

A snap echoed in the cave, and Sapphir could see the choppy-haired blonde girl clutching her hand. An athletic boy with green eyes stood beside them.

"It's not far."

Ahead of them, the rest of the children marched slowly. Their steps seemed heavier than a normal child's. Sapphir was thankful they were in the back of the line.

Where are you, Father?

"What's your name?" Sapphir asked the blonde girl.

"I'm Evens. And my brother is Priam. Priam is more fun to play with than my other brothers."

Priam kept walking; he was a couple steps ahead of Sapphir and Evens.

"Well, Evens. I'm so happy to have you leading the way. I'm S–"

"Sapphir! I know. Father misses you so. He was thrilled to talk to you finally. He told us! Right, Priam?"

Priam didn't turn, but his head bobbed forward slightly.

"How many brothers and sisters do you have, Evens?"

"Lots. I haven't counted before. We get so many more from

Father and my older brothers and sisters."

Innocent children.

Sapphir wondered where Evens came from. Her blonde hair was the same shade as her father's. Teremos would claim any child with the blood of the Golden Age as his own. But Sapphir was sure Evens had other parents.

The tunnel reached a fork; one gentle curve banked to the left, and the other made a sharp right. If her sense of direction had not been too distorted, turning right would take her west, towards Olenus. However, the Children continued along the gradual curve.

Where are we going? And why can't I sense him yet?

Monotonous chattering rang in her ears as Sapphir continued to walk. Evens was humming something unrecognizable. Sapphir's palm was beginning to sweat in the girl's tiny hand.

"How much further?" she whispered.

"Oh. Not far," Evens said, looking up at Sapphir with her lifeless eyes. "Not far."

After another few minutes, the procession halted. Sapphir could see a dim haze in front of them. They had arrived at some magical barrier. It would have been invisible to any lesser sorceress.

I... I shouldn't go through.

"Come on, Sapphir! Father's waiting!"

No... no he's not. He's not here. I would feel it by now.

The Children marched through. Sapphir's feet dragged as she approached, and Evens coaxed her forward. The little girl seemed eager to breach the magical wall. As the Children walked through, they became more energetic.

They can't live harmoniously with their suppressed memories outside the wall.

Sapphir was sure Teremos' interpretation of the memory charms was more potent than hers. He was simply more skilled than she was. However, Sapphir was glad her spells had not stolen the personalities of her sweet children.

Priam walked through, finally turning. Something resembling a smile was etched on his face, though it still appeared inauthentic.

Everything was out of order.

I can't go through.... If I do, I won't be able to leave

"Evens, I'm so glad you've taken me here... but–"

"Father misses you, sister!"

Evens leapt through the barrier, yanking Sapphir's arm. She resisted, but the girl's pull was more forceful than expected. Sapphir's forearm passed the barrier, and a shock went through her body.

No! No... what's happening.

Her children's faces sprang into her mind, then disintegrated.

Children! Maya, Celia! Ivy and Cy and Egan!

Sapphir shivered. She fell backwards, wrestling herself from Evens' grip.

"Sister!"

"Get away from me!" Sapphir shrieked, clawing to her feet and sprinting back through the cave.

To Olenus. I need to go to Olenus!

Sapphir couldn't hear the Children anymore. They weren't following her. But she pressed on as fast as she could.

What did they do to me? My children... I saw them...

She lit a flame that danced across her left hand. Her forearm was slightly numb, but there was no pain. Finally, Sapphir stumbled into the forked passage. She dashed through the cave leading west.

Something's wrong!

Sapphir continued running until afternoon sunlight flooded the cave. She squinted, letting her eyes adjust to the brightness. She examined her forearm. It looked normal. There were no marks or discolorations. But *something* had happened when the arm had passed through the magical barrier.

They said were taking me to Father... why was I so desperate to follow? I should have been more careful!

But her father hadn't been in the cave. Sapphir hadn't felt his presence. He was somewhere else.

I can't do what he expects of me. I need to seek HIM out. Not the other way around.

The city walls of Olenus were not far. Sapphir's instincts told her to approach.

Your Children came to me Father, said they were taking me to you. What are you planning?

A paved path snaked between inns, small shops, and a few other huts. Sapphir passed a beautiful black mare, tethered outside one of the shacks. As she grew closer to Olenus, her body began to warm.

You hadn't returned from a day in the city yet, had you? But you didn't want me to find you there... you wanted me trapped in your cave. In your spells.

The walls of Olenus loomed above her. Sapphir felt the numbness in her arm disappear. She still couldn't see her children. However, Sapphir would find the solution to that soon enough.

You're here, Father. The walls won't be able to protect you.

Chapter 25

Ivy

Egan paced the kitchen. He was fuming. The entire walk back to the farm had been silent; Cy had apologized multiple times, but Egan would hear none of it. Now, Maya and Celia sat in the next room, playing some sort of game with sticks. Both were quiet. Ivy and Cy occupied the chairs at the table, dejected. Fil and Agnes were outside somewhere, tending the cows and squishing grapes for wine.

"The one thing Mother told us not to do... the ONE thing! Ivy. Did you learn nothing from your last little adventure? What'll it be next, huh? Will you get on a ship with Celia and head to Ionia? Mother didn't ask much from us!"

"I'm sorry, Egan," Ivy muttered.

Egan balled his fists.

"And Cy? How could you be so reckless!"

"It was Ivy's idea! She wanted to go find Fil and Agnes' old cow! The one she…"

Cy glanced at Ivy, but she continued to stare at the table.

They took Xander… and… and…

"The one she turned into a bear!" he blurted.

Egan stopped pacing. "What cow? What bear!"

"Fil and Agnes used to have this cow, an-and Ivy wanted to try a spell to turn it into a bear. But-but then it started chasing her and Maya."

"Is this true, Ivy? It was your fault they lost that heifer? *And* you thought you could go… what, find it again? Turn it back into a cow? It's a bear, oh Poseidon. A bear! And you went looking for it!"

They took him. And the people with green eyes.

The enormous man, the one-armed woman, and her pretty daughter. They were walking towards her again. Ivy started rocking in her chair, gnawing at the side of her finger.

"What's gotten into her, Cy?" Egan asked. "You do something to her?"

"No… no, I…"

"Gods, I can't believe how foolish you both were. Fil and Agnes would never want you to put yourselves in danger for some cow… even if it was their favorite. And Mother… well, she wanted us to stay on the farm. She put protections around it; I don't know why, but she wanted us to *STAY*."

Maya shuffled into the room, clutching sticks from her game

with Celia. She pointed one at Ivy and gave Egan a puzzled look. Her big brother sighed, his anger fizzling.

"I don't know, Maya. I think she's okay." He glared at Cy. "You realize how stupid you were being, right?"

Cy nodded. "Yeah. Yeah, but Ivy wan−"

"Cy."

"Oh... sorry, Egan. I'm sorry."

Cy covered his face with his hands. Egan looked at Ivy, still shaking in her chair.

The... the green eyes. Like mine... the people.

Egan moved to her side. Maya followed his lead and leaned against him.

"Oh Ivy...."

He rested a hand on her shoulder.

"Ivy? Are you okay? I'm... I'm not mad, if that's what you are worried about. I was... scared."

Ivy flinched at his touch. She jerked her head up from the table.

"They just took him!" she exclaimed.

Maya backed away quickly.

"They took him! The men in the armor! The ones from the big city!"

Ivy's eyes were already flooding. Tears streamed down her cheeks, and saliva filled her mouth.

"Who, Ivy? Took who!"

Cy cut in, "Xander. A warrior from Boura! We saw him on the

road, and I–"

"He was nice to us! Trying to go home... and they took him!"

Maya grabbed Ivy's hand and gasped softly. Her green eyes were too startling for Ivy to look at.

Green. Green eyes. She has green eyes. Like me. Like them. Mother... I want Mother!

Ivy tried to picture her mother. But all she could see was the pretty woman from her dream.

No... no, not you!

"Maya, try to calm her," Egan said. "Who was the man, Cy?"

Maya hugged Ivy's leg, humming softly to her. She climbed up to her lap and placed a finger on her cheek.

"Smile."

She's a little girl. Little girl like me. Green eyes...

"I already said! A warrior! He fought in some big battle and then he was walking home. But he was hurt. His leg. And then, we talked to him and he was pretty nice. But THEN these other soldiers came, and *they* were bad and tried to kill him or take him or something. So, they tied him up and took him away. We were hiding in the trees. Ivy didn't want me to help, but I wanted to help."

"I'm glad Ivy kept you both safe from the fighting... why did it scare her so much? There was no... death, was there?"

Death! Death... I've seen death.

"No. Nobody died," Cy said, a little disappointed, "But Xander did fight some bad men with a sword he took from them. He was a

270

good fighter, Xander. I bet if he didn't have a hurt leg, he would have won."

Maya stroked Ivy's hair, doing the same to her own as she did.

Hair. We have the same hair. Cy and Celia don't. Egan doesn't. But we have the same hair.

"Then why... Ivy, what's wrong? Why are you... are you okay?"

"You don't look like me!"

Egan was taken aback. Maya cocked her head, and Celia finally snuck into the kitchen nervously. She nudged Cy, before hopping onto the same chair as him.

"Ivy, I..."

"And Celia! And Cy! None of you but Maya! Why don't you!"

Egan shrugged. "Wha– we've looked this way all our lives, Ivy... why is this upsetting you so much now?"

"I had a dream!" She pulled on her hair. "I saw people that looked like me. My eyes. My hair. Why! They were dead... and... the big city was full of water... and..."

"It's a dream, Ivy!"

"We all have dreams," Celia said.

"Yeah, I told you about my dream where I could breathe underwater!"

Ivy leapt from her chair, spilling Maya to the ground.

"Hey!" Egan rushed to catch Maya.

"No! No... you don't get it!"

Mother! I want to talk to Mother!

"I need to talk with Mother."

"Mother's gone! With Kiki," Celia explained, looking at Cy in confusion.

Maya pushed herself away from Egan, rubbing her head. He picked her up and set her on the thick windowsill.

"I talked to her," he said. "She's the one who told me you left."

"Show me how!" Ivy demanded.

"Ivy, what is this all about?"

Before she could answer, the door swung open, and Agnes entered alongside Fil. The latter carried a bucket of mashed grapes.

"What is all this commotion, children?" he asked.

"Yes, no need to fight amongst yourselves. We're all happy Cy and Ivy are safe... and they know they were mistaken."

Agnes had not been as calm when Ivy and Cy had first arrived. Fil must have quelled her rage as they worked in the fields.

"Something spooked Ivy," Celia said.

"She's okay, though," Cy assured.

Egan turned to Fil and shook his head.

"She had some dream... and some man they ran into was taken by soldiers.... I don't know; she's never been like this!"

Fil and Agnes shared a curious look.

They're talking about me. All talking about me. I need to speak with Mother.

"Well... dear, maybe we can prepare some food. Perhaps that will make you feel better," Agnes offered.

Fil nodded with enthusiasm, "That sounds wonderful, doesn't

it? Are you children hungry?"

Celia and Cy raised their hands with excitement. Even Maya's ears perked up at the mention of food.

"That would be wonderful," Egan said, "I'm going to take Ivy into the other room, then... she has some questions about... about where our mother is. Thank you, Agnes."

He flicked his head towards the room where Celia and Maya had been playing – where Ivy had danced around Keoki and hit him with her stick sword so long ago. Ivy followed, averting her eyes from the others and scratching her shoulder.

"I'm sorry I raised my voice at you," Egan said quietly.

Her head was spinning.

She responded with something resembling, "It's okay."

His eyebrows furrowed, but his gaze was soft. Ivy hadn't heard Egan talk this much in years – perhaps in her life!

"What do you want to say to Mother?"

Why are my eyes green? Who are those people! The nice man was taken... why'd they take him? Why am I so scared!

"Ah, it doesn't matter. You don't need to tell me."

They sat on the floor across from each other. Egan had one leg out and the other pulled into his body. He was not quite flexible enough to cross them completely, as Ivy did.

Ivy took a deep breath. She was beginning to organize her thoughts. What had been so alarming about Xander's arrest? She found herself unable to justify her outburst.

It was only a dream!

"Okay, I'm ready."

"Alright. So, I've never initiated it myself. But I *have* read the scrolls."

Of course, you've read the scrolls.

"It seems all you have to do is focus entirely on the person you wish to speak with. They have to be one of us of course – someone with our blood. You picture their face, their voice. It helps if you know where they might be. Then, you recite the words. I'll go get the scroll; it's somewhere in my pack."

Egan left Ivy on the ground. She still felt anxious, but sitting on the floor was stabilizing her. There was no reason to fear. Egan returned a few seconds later, unrolling an old papyrus scroll. He handed it to her and pointed at the desired passage.

"Don't say it aloud... I don't want Fil and Agnes knowing anything they shouldn't."

Ivy studied the scroll. There were dozens of incantations scrawled on the papyrus. She admired Egan for being so dedicated to his learning.

Cy and I have never taken it as seriously. I need to become more like Egan.

"Okay... okay, I'll try."

She read the words a few more times, trying to get the correct order and phrasing. After rehearsing under her breath, Ivy closed her eyes.

I can do this. I need you, Mother.

She pictured her mother – stunning red hair, pale skin, and

her jagged scar. She was slender with slim fingers. So beautiful, her mother was. Ivy realized in that moment how deeply she missed her. If only Keoki could have searched for his brother on his own.

Where are you, Mother?

She imagined her deep in the woods, perhaps atop a mountain. Her mother would be smiling with Keoki, making some sort of sweet conversation. She was serious but always playful. She was a wonderful mother. Ivy regretted ever wanting to leave her.

Okay... I just need to recite the words.

Ivy made her way easily through the first two sentences. She kept the image of her mother firmly in her mind. She stumbled through the third sentence, pausing at a few words. But the final one was proclaimed with confidence.

"Reveal yourself to me, you whom I seek – let us look upon each other and speak!"

For a few seconds, nothing happened. Then, she found herself transported. There was a shrine to Poseidon in the center of the room, made of the smoothest marble. The floor, too, was marble, with a soft velvet rug on which one could kneel. Columns formed a doorway behind the statue.

When she looked down, Ivy could see her hands. She was able to walk as she normally would.

Did... did it work?

"Mother!" she called, her voice echoing against the stone.

Can she hear me? Is this where Keoki's brother is?

"Moooother!"

Footsteps rang in the room, and a shadow spilled through the columns.

"Mother! Oh, Mother!"

Ivy began to run forward, past the shrine, then slowed. The figure that stood in the doorway was taller than her mother, though similarly lean. She took a step back. When he came into view, Ivy could see a man with blonde hair and strange purple eyes.

"H-hello? Who are you!"

He spoke with a voice as sweet as honey.

"You must be Ivy. Yes, I can tell by your green eyes. I am sorry for interrupting your incantation... you were doing well. I have no doubt that you could have reached my daughter."

"Your... your daughter?"

Is this man... my grandfather?

She didn't like how he moved, so meticulous and rehearsed. His voice was smooth, but it made her feel... uneasy. Ivy stumbled backwards, tripping over the velvet rug.

The man took a step closer.

"However, the situation is far more complex than you know. It would be too much to explain. No, Ivy... it is time that you know who you truly are."

The tall man raised his hands, and clapped, the sound intensified by the marble room. The shrine disappeared.

Ivy's eyes burst open, and she was back on the floor of Fil and Agnes' farmhouse. Egan looked at her curiously. She was breathing hard.

"Did it work?" Egan asked, standing next to her.

Ivy was about to respond, when a splitting headache made her close her eyes and shriek in pain. She heard a thud as Egan dropped back to the floor. And suddenly, she could remember... everything.

Chapter 26

Nicolaus

It took all of Nic's strength to close the enormous door quietly. He had forgotten how heavy it was. He slid to the floor, his back against the cold ebony and iron. After climbing the stairs and struggling with the door, Nic was quite breathless.

I'm still too damn skinny!

The room was too familiar – the mahogany desk, outlined with gold; the huge bed, big enough for Orrin, with a goose-feather mattress; the wardrobe, which cracked open to reveal flowing himations that would've fit only one man in Helike.

I'm not ready for this...

Opi had insisted that one of them check Orrin's desk for anything – letters, scrolls, Council notes – that would help implicate Gaios. They needed to find concrete evidence that *at least* one of the recent councilor deaths had been arranged by him. Rizon's own testimony would not be enough.

Rizon had confirmed this.

"Who will people believe? The beloved Councilor Gaios, a dedicated servant of Helike? Or the man who already confessed to murdering Euripides."

Furthermore, Gaios only met with Rizon in person or through couriers in the Fishermen. There was no written proof of their agreement.

Risky... but if this is how Euripides was finished, surely it is the same for Orrin. Untraceable.

Opi was wise to consider examining the Golden Spear's quarters; it was unlikely that anyone had sifted through the stacks of papyrus on his desk. Nic felt it was his own duty to do the searching. He had read some of the notes and letters already, after all.

The walk to Orrin's chambers had felt... strange. He had crept through side hallways and untouched corridors to avoid detection. But running up the stairs and throwing all his weight into the damned door...

Normal.

He was simply reminding Orrin that the Council would convene momentarily. The Golden Spear would groan, make a dry complaint about one of his fellow councilors, and don his formal himation.

But it isn't normal... I'm a fugitive. And Orrin...

He looked at the desk, longing to see Orrin seated there. His friend would be focused on some random query from a citizen; Nic would be sifting through the other letters. But all he could see was a room with oversized furniture.

I shouldn't have come. I should've let Opi...

Opi was resting after several hours of her own reconnaissance. Rizon had left in the night, disguised as a guard, in hopes that he could search for orders sent to Hira and Furel.

How he got the guard's uniform... I didn't want ask.

If Gaios had given the two chief officers of the Heliken army direct orders to kill the Golden Spear, or to unleash the weapon that caused the great explosion, there probably would be no record.

But we must be thorough.

There was always Rizon's favorite option if their inquiries proved ineffectual – capture Gaios and force him to confess. Nic would not be opposed.

He picked himself up off the floor and settled in at the desk chair. His feet barely reached the floor. Indeed, there was still a hefty stack of writings. Nic muttered to himself as he scanned each document.

"Citizen note... citizen note... something from Kyros... citizen note..."

He continued for several minutes, shifting the papyrus carefully. If anyone planned on coming to Orrin's room, Nic would surely hear them ascend the staircase, or at least unlatch the door.

"Citizen note... oh... letter to Cerius..."

Nic unrolled the papyrus. His eyes roved the curved writing.

Orrin's writing.

The Golden Spear's tense relationship with his son was no secret. He had opened up about it while Nic was recovering from his run-in with the baker's girl.

Cerius was in the League's Guard, a formerly impressive conglomeration of soldiers from every Achaean city-state, tasked to protect the League from piracy. As noble as it sounded, Orrin resented his son's choice.

He left right after Rosie lost her third child. I... I shouldn't read this.

The letter wouldn't have any information about Gaios, but Nic could not tear his eyes away.

"My son, I am writing to you after an arduous day with the Council, which concluded with my attendant, Nicolaus, being beaten by two rough men. It was in this moment, as I noticed the fragility of life in someone so young, that I felt compelled to write to you.

Cerius, you and your sister have been the greatest joys of my long life. Caring for you and Rosie reminded me why I became the man I am today – to protect the love shared between the people of Helike, and the League as a whole. I was wrong to chastise your decision to leave our family and join the League's Guard. I know you were motivated by the same honorable principles that have guided me in my life. It would be a grave mistake for us to continue this silence.

The bravery Nicolaus showed, which consequently led to his maiming, is something I used to value above all. It is something you have. It is why you stay with the Guard.

However, your mother and I miss you dearly. I will not blame you if you do not respond to this letter, or if you choose to remain in the League's Guard forever. But consider this my open invitation to come home to us – station yourself in Helike; visit us when you are allowed. Your sister, mother, and I love you, and await your return with excitement. I know Rosie has not written either, but she, too, forgives your decision. She wishes only for her brother's happiness and safety. Between your mother, Gerrian, and myself, she will move past her lost children; and I have dedicated myself to finding the man behind these crimes.

Please grant us the same forgiveness, my son. Our family needs you. With love, Your Father."

Nic read the letter once more. His eyes were watery. He rolled the scroll up and resealed it with wax.

If I ever come across Cerius, I will be sure to give him this.

A knocking caused Nic to jump. He dove under the bed, expecting guards to pour through the door at any moment. But it had merely been a bird pecking at the window.

Thank the gods.

He crawled back to the desk. The letter to Cerius was tucked in his waist. The fright reminded him that time was precious.

I've wasted too much time.

He wondered how long he had been in the room. Ten minutes, perhaps twenty. He had to leave; every extra second spent wandering the castle was dangerous. He rifled through the desk for another minute, before finding a tome of some value.

Orrin's notes. This should have been the first thing I picked up.

Who knew how much information could be packed in the thick book? Perhaps it contained his investigations into Euripides' murder.

There would be no time to read it in Orrin's quarters, however. Nic wrapped his arm around the tome and tiptoed to the door. He leaned all of his weight against one of the iron leaves, feeling it begin to inch open.

Nic crept down the marble staircase. A portrait of Euripides now accompanied the other paintings of old, dead councilors. With every turn, he expected to see Heliken guards, or worse, Gaios. But he made it to the bottom without any trouble.

Perhaps the Council is meeting.

The thought of attendants and guards watching as Gaios spoke to himself, and Kyros quaffed casks of wine, was almost funny. He supposed there would be no point to a Council meeting right now.

A narrow corridor with statues and columns led away from the palace entryway, as Opi had outlined. There were plenty of spots for Nic to duck away unseen if he needed. Sweat was building up between Nic's arm and the tome as he moved noiselessly through the castle.

Suddenly, his footsteps began to echo. No, not his footsteps. Someone else was about to pass through the hallway! Nic slipped behind a statue, making himself as small as possible. He covered his face with the tome.

"S-s-so, I t-think there is r-r-reason to trust our n-n-new al-allies from Helike."

The voice that spoke was deep but shaky. A second set of footfalls accompanied the first. One was loud, while the other was muted. Nic retreated further behind the statue.

"Right. You think they'll be good soldiers with us, then? You think we can work with the Helikens. Even though they're sending away our soldiers?"

The second man's voice had a nasal quality that reminded Nic of the Flat-Nose.

"Y-yes. It's l-like I said. T-t-they are only t-taking those who f-fought against them. A-actually fought against them. A-at the beach. A-and those m-men can come h-home once they've p-p-proven themselves."

Work with the Helikens? Proven themselves? Who are these men?

Their steps grew closer and Nic prayed to the gods he didn't truly believe in.

Don't let them see me... don't let them see me...

"More men for us. That's not too bad. Our new army will be far mightier than before. The mightiest in Achaea!"

The speaker laughed. The other man remained silent.

They walked right past Nic's statue, distracted by their own conversation. Nic stifled a gasp when he saw the stuttering speaker. He was broad-shouldered, wearing black chainmail. A massive battle-axe swung at his hip. The crest on his shoulder gave Nic a moment of pause.

He's a Bouran! What are they doing in the castle!

As soon as the men turned into the grand entrance, Nic rushed to his feet, half-sprinting down the corridor. He turned through another narrow hallway, closing in on the tapestry that covered the hidden room.

Just before he reached it, he heard more footsteps.

Shit!

Nic scrambled to the tapestry, pushed aside the stone door and slid into the room. He barely had time to cover the entrance before more men rounded a corner and began walking the hallway.

Nic keeled over. He tried to keep his breathing silent. Opi sat up in her bed, and Nic motioned for her to remain quiet. In the other corner, Rizon stood. The three of them waited for several long minutes before Nic finally whispered.

"Okay… okay, I think they're gone."

"Were you followed?" Rizon asked, fixing his hawkish eyes on Nic.

"No. No, I don't think so. No."

"What do you have there," Opi asked.

She reached for the tome, and Nic handed it to her. She

studied it in the candlelight, flipping through pages.

"This... this could be pretty good. You found this in Orrin's chambers?"

"Yeah. It a book of his personal notes. He was trying to find out who killed Euripides. Maybe there's something there."

"Maybe not," Rizon said, "But it could still help to rule out other suspects Gaios would try to blame."

Rizon sat next to Opi on the bed. Nic followed his lead. His leg was pressed against Opi's. Nic could feel Orrin's letter to Cerius scratching his ribs.

"There's more. Rizon, I don't know what you saw at Hira and Furel's cabins, but I heard people talking... They were Bourans. *In the castle*. What does that mean? Why were there...?"

Rizon opened his mouth to respond, when his muscles tensed.

There was a loud thump against the stone entrance. Opi squeezed Nic's leg uncomfortably tight.

"Who–"

Oh gods... was I followed?

Rizon waved his hand at Nic frantically. Nic understood the message and shut his mouth. Rizon pushed himself to his feet slowly, pointing at the tunnel door. The thump sounded again. Dust fell from the ceiling as the walls shook.

"Now," he mouthed, "Out."

Opi and Nic scrambled up. Their hands met at the latch as Rizon grabbed his knife from the desk. Opi clutched Orrin's tome in one arm. His gaze moved to the scrolls on the desk.

The notes from Elfie...

"No time!" Opi muttered.

Nic let go of the door and took a step towards the desk.

"Nic!"

Opi yanked the latch and pulled herself into the tunnel, a third crash sounded.

The hidden stone doorway began to slide open.

"Go!" Rizon yelled.

Nic dove into the tunnel after Opi, his hands folding against her ankles. They crawled as fast as they could, ignoring the dirt that sprayed into their eyes and the crawling *things* that tickled their skin.

This is my fault! Someone must have seen me!

Nic felt a tug at his leg. He kicked himself free.

No! No!!!

A stronger hand grabbed his foot, and Nic felt himself jerked back.

"No!" he cried out, "Let go!"

A third hand grabbed his other leg and dragged Nic from the tunnel into the light of the enclosed candles. He collapsed to the ground, and a guard leapt on top of him. Rope chafed his arms.

"Nic!" Opi screamed from the tunnel.

No... leave me!

Nic was dazed but conscious enough to see Rizon slam the hilt of his knife into another guard's head. The man fell beside one of his partners, someone else who had clearly underestimated the assassin. Rizon lunged for Nic, throwing off his attacker. The guard rolled and tried to stand, but Rizon's boot met his nose before he could.

"Come on, let's go! There will be more!"

He helped Nic to his feet.

Helpless. Just like the Battle at the Beach.

"Thanks," Nic coughed, "We have to get out! Opi! Keep going!!"

He saw her feet begin to retreat further into the tunnel. Rizon ushered Nic to the tunnel first. Then, a broad figure entered, wearing black chainmail and snarling. Behind him, two guards stood at the doorway.

The man from the hallway!

"Go, Nic," Rizon barked, "Go!"

Nic had his hands on the dirt, ready to follow Opi through the passage. But something made him stall.

"What are you doing Nic? That's Parex the Hammer. Get out now!"

Parex the Hammer. Orrin had almost feared him as a tactician and respected the man's skill above anyone in Achaea.

Brash and bold.

The Hammer said nothing as he approached. He didn't have the axe he'd been carrying earlier, perhaps because the space was too confined to swing it. Rizon shoved Nic towards the passage.

"I always thought I'd die by execution, Parex... they must really want me if you're here. All the way from Boura, no less.

Though I suppose that isn't too far."

Parex stayed silent. Nic realized he carried no weapon. Rizon had the advantage. The Hammer's gloved hands were armored.

Rizon jumped forward, slashing his knife in a deadly arc, before stopping it to bring it stabbing upwards. It was a brilliant feint.

But Parex was faster. He caught Rizon's arm and pinned it against the table. Rizon spun to kick at him, and Parex slid sideways, sweeping Rizon's other leg out from beneath him. Rizon yelled in pain as his arm twisted. Nic couldn't tear himself away. He raced forward, smashing one of the candle bulbs against Parex's half-helm.

The move surprised Parex, and he swatted at the flames; Rizon had just enough time to stand. Then, the other guards came. It was too much in the small room. Rizon and Nic could barely hold off the Hammer alone.

Within seconds, they were dragged from Simon's hideaway. Nic looked back with anguish at the latched door, which had swung shut in the melee. He was grateful that Opi had escaped. Her capture would have only made Nic more furious at himself.

One of the other guards entered the room as they were dragged through the halls.

To search for Opi? For what?

Opi would almost surely have pulled herself up from the hole beneath the bush. With any luck, she would be long gone.

She must be... I need her safe.

Nic noticed nothing of the palace. He and Rizon marched solemnly.

Rizon knows this is the end for him. What about me?

From the sounds of it, at least his brother, Xander, and the pretty woman, Melani, would be safe. It took Nic a moment to realize where they were when the group finally stopped.

The Court!

"Isn't this magnificent," a voice called from the altar.

More people than Nic had ever seen in the Court of Helike were assembled, gazing upon the three men that occupied the five golden thrones. Nic hadn't seen *any* citizens in the Court since Euripides' death... now there were hundreds.

"It has taken us far too long – many months – to find the men responsible for the death of our great Councilor Euripides. But now, as a final peace with our neighbors has been reached... reckoning has come."

Nic looked down at his hands, smeared with dirt. Next to him, Rizon stood firm, his eyes locked on the man in the central throne.

Gaios.

"Dear citizens of Achaea, I give you... Rizon Atsali – the villainous assassin who took his blade to the throat of our beloved leader."

The crowd jeered, delighted that justice would soon be served.

"And beside him... an ally..."

An ally?

"...the former attendant of the Golden Spear himself, may the gods look fondly upon his soul in Elysium. Nicolaus of Egypt!"

Chapter 27

Keoki

"Keep your foot up," the woman said.

She rushed over to the bedside and shifted Keoki's leg back into an elevated position. Keoki tried to get his bearings. He reclined on a soft mattress, his injured ankle wrapped snugly. There were three other beds in the tent, unoccupied; Keoki and the woman were the only two present. His left arm hung uselessly in a sling. There was some sort of numbing agent on his shoulder. Keoki winced when he breathed.

Right... the ribs. Why am I not in more pain?

Keoki could remember pieces of the journey back to Leontio. After Io had lumbered off into the woods, the hunters had fashioned a stretcher with their pelts and pine branches. They had showered Keoki with praise, shocked that he was one of Artemis' chosen "Moonspawn."

Keoki knew that their claim was ridiculous. However, he hadn't wanted to lose their newfound reverence of him. The hunters had carried him up the mountain with ease, despite his bulk. The entire journey, they raved about a man from the fancy city, who somehow caught the attention of Artemis. He would be a hero among men in Leontio.

What a load of shit. If they knew that bear... that cow....

Io's return had warmed Keoki's heart. He had worried about the heifer countless times, praying that she hadn't been ravaged by wolves or mountain clansmen. He had never considered that she was now the top predator herself. She could rove wherever she pleased, without having to fear being dragged back to a farm.

Ivy and Maya's mistake has served Io well.

After scaring away the wolves, Io had nuzzled Keoki's cheek with her coarse snout. He imagined that each growl and grunt was one of her perceptive moos, asking Keoki how he had found her.

Then, she'd sauntered back into the night.

"Let me feel your head," the woman said, resting the back of her hand against his forehead. "Less feverish. That is certain."

Feverish? My head feels funny, not feverish.

Keoki studied her. She had black hair streaked with brown, that curled at the end. She was not thin, but not overly large either – a sturdy height and weight. Her face was round, and she was only slightly less pale than Sapphir.

"I'm still in Leontio then?" Keoki asked.

"Yes. A healing tent in Leontio. You have slept the day away. Perhaps you only wish to see the moon... they are calling you Moonspawn."

"What does that mean? I don't really know."

His voice sounded funny too.

Am I dreaming?

"A person chosen by Artemis, to rule the forest and the animals. They say you tamed a bear with only a look."

Cow. I tamed a cow. A bear-cow; that's funny.

"I don't know how I did that. I don't really like being called Moonspawn."

The woman began crushing purple flowers in a bowl.

"What do I call you?"

"My name is Kiki. I'm a farmer. Keeee-keee. Keoki."

Kiki. That's what Ivy calls me. And Agnes sometimes. Agnes...

She poured oil over the pulped flower, suspending it in the liquid. It smelled quite good.

"Keoki. A sweet name. My own is Asklepia."

"Like that god. Aselpius. Esklipi. The healing one. You're a healer, too, Asklepia."

She laughed, a musical sound Keoki hadn't heard in days.

Sapphir doesn't like to laugh. She never laughed at my jokes, even though I am funny.

"I am, aren't I? My name fits my profession. Though I cannot say it was me who chose this name. Or to be a healer. In Leontio, most children are claimed by Artemis; they become hunters and warriors. They pass the rites and become the next generation of Leontians. Only a few get to follow the path of Apollo."

"Better than killing each other in a pit and being chased by wolves. *I* was chased by wolves."

Agnes... and Fil...

His brain and his mouth were disconnected.

"Yes. My parents followed my path first, and so it became easier for me to." Asklepia poured the mixture over Keoki's ankle and shoulder. The oil was warm, "It is not as respected a craft here. But I am thankful it is mine. Do you mind if I...?"

She pointed at Keoki's ripped clothes. He nodded slowly, his eyes rolling, and she pulled them aside to reveal his midriff. She began to rub the oil and crushed flour on his cracked ribs. Her hands were quite gentle. Keoki could feel some of the pain easing.

"What brought you from your farm to Leontio?"

Keoki sighed, "I'm not sure.... I'm angry."

"What brings you anger?"

My parents... Agnes and Fil. The sorceress.

"A man killed my parents. When I was young. The Sons of Poseidon. You know them?"

Asklepia shook her head.

"They love Poseidon... he killed my parents. I... I..."

His head swam. His mouth twitched, but he wasn't sure if it was from the purple flowers or sadness.

"Someone came for them. He did..."

His voice shook.

"I thought I could find him."

Asklepia put a hand on his chest. She hummed softly until his heartbeat slowed.

"You longed for revenge. That's why you came from the fancy city."

Keoki closed his eyes, leaning his head against the feather pillow. He had felt remorse for so many years. The grief of losing his parents and his home had weighed down on him with each new job. But when he had reached the farm and met Fil and Agnes... he felt as if he could move on – carry their memories with him. He would always miss them and long for them, but at the very least, he could find happiness.

Then he met Sapphir. Her vengefulness, her mysterious powers, her protectiveness for those she loved... children that were not hers.

"I... I don't know. I don't know, Askle-Asklepia."

"And you traveled alone?"

I shouldn't have been alone. Sapphir... left... to... to my farm! Fil and Agnes!

Keoki gasped, "I need to leave!"

He tried to move. His body did not respond.

"Everything needs time. It will be weeks before your ribs and ankle are fully healed. I put your shoulder back in place. But it, too, needs time."

Keoki stifled a giggle. His chest was warm.

I... my farm... I need to go back.

The pain and weariness had distracted Keoki. Perhaps the creams and salves were affecting his mind as well. He needed to get home as fast as possible. If that was where Sapphir was headed... if she truly meant to silence Fil and Agnes for knowing about his children...

"Let me search the town and ask for you. I'll see if I can find a way for you to get home."

Oh good. Oh good, she'll go to the farm for me.

"It will do you no good to worry, Keoki. Lie back and give your bones time to heal."

"Thank you, Asklepia. I... if I..."

His eyelids grew heavy. The scent of the flowers and oil made each inhale pleasing, yet tiresome.

Fil and Agnes... I need to hurry.

But his senses dulled in harmony with the pain. His damaged body would only heal with time. Time and rest.

✳✳✳✳

Keoki's eyes flickered open. He was in the same position as before, his ankle elevated and wrapped, his shoulder supported by a cloth sling. His mind still felt addled, but sleep had refreshed it well enough. The pain had diminished since the previous night in the forest.

I'm in Leontio though... I need to get back to Fil and Agnes. Who knows how far Sapphir has gotten?

Everything in the tent seemed familiar to Keoki, but he couldn't remember much since the hunt.

Did I wake up yet? I must have...

The tent flap opened, and two women entered. The first wore a simple linen robe, while the other was bedecked with wildcat fur. Keoki recognized the woman in the robe.

"Ah, you have awakened, Keoki."

Keoki could tell that it was already dark outside. A full day had passed.

"Um, yes. For the first time?"

The woman giggled. "No... no. Perhaps I should have given you less tonic. The Leontian flowers are quite potent."

Oh, right! The healer! Her name... what's her name?

Keoki recalled vague details from earlier in the evening. He had woken up and talked with the healer. What had they discussed? And what had she given Keoki to make him so forgetful?

"So... okay. This *tonic* you gave me... it was for my injuries?"

"For the pain. The injuries must be treated with rest and support. However, you requested that I find you passage to Helike. This is why I've brought Kalypso. She hunts and trades furs in the fancy cities."

Kalypso raised a hand. She was somewhere between Sapphir and Agnes' age but looked tougher than both. Her head was shaven, and she was almost as muscular as Keoki.

"Oh. Well, thank you... Asklepia!"

I can't believe I remembered her name.

Asklepia beamed at him and performed a little curtsy. She had a very kind face. Keoki felt warm, though he couldn't tell if it was from the strange tonic or something else.

"Thanks for taking me with you, Kalypso."

She nodded. "It is a blessing from Artemis to travel with one of her Moonspawn."

"Can I ask, how are we getting there?" Keoki winced.

"We shall depart at daybreak in my wagon. The horses will pay no mind to the extra weight. If we make no stops, it will not take more than a day and a night."

I'll pray that is fast enough.

Pain began to return as the sleep wore off. Keoki hoped he would be able to walk two mornings from now. At the very least, he could find a cane. Asklepia noticed his grimace as he shifted his weight on the bed.

"You may need more tonic, Keoki. Would that be okay with you?"

Keoki's first instinct was to rebel. He had been tested enough mentally in the past few weeks; he didn't wish for his thoughts to spiral and mix together because of a mountain flower. But the pain...

"Not as strong as before. Just a little."

Asklepia reddened.

She feels like she made a mistake.

"I just want to be able to think, that's all."

She turned away, gathering different liquids, more oil perhaps, and adding them to a canteen. As soon as the canteen was uncorked, Keoki could smell the sweet scent of the tonic. His heart began to race.

"Thank you. Sincerely."

Asklepia's blush became deeper.

"No need to thank me, Keoki. Or Kiki, as you called yourself," she laughed. "Take the tonic with you when you leave tomorrow. You already know to use it sparingly!"

Kiki... is that what I told her my name was?

Keoki gave a tight smile.

"We leave in the morning, Moonspawn," Kalypso said, opening the tent flap. "I shall come by your tent with my wagon. Have him ready please, Asklepia."

Kalypso stepped into the night with confidence, her wildcat pelt melting into the dark. Asklepia poured a few drops of the tonic onto Keoki's ribs and began to massage it gently into his skin. The aches were replaced with warmth.

"That's nice," Keoki said. "The tonic... it's nice."

Asklepia finished applying the mixture, then crept quietly from the tent. Keoki watched her leave, his eyelids closing.

Fil and Agnes, I'm coming to save you. To protect you.

Was Sapphir truly on her way to the farm? If she was, he would beat her there.

But can I stop her?

Whether he could or not, to harm Fil and Agnes, Sapphir would have to go through him.

Chapter 28

Melani

Melani was exhausted by the time she pulled herself up from the hole. She'd barely grabbed ahold of the bush after jumping several times. But she was finally back near the large pine tree that marked the road to Helike.

Xander went home for me. He'll be in Boura... he must be!

She was nervous that Xander would have begun searching for her when he noticed her absence. She could only pray that he was waiting for her in their home, perhaps working the forge as if nothing had gone wrong.

If the gods are listening, please let my Xander be there.

It was much easier to travel down from Simon's tunnel than it had been to climb the hill. Melani stuck to the side of the path, hugging the tree line in case she needed to duck out of sight.

Nobody's looking for me. It's Rizon they want.

However, she could not afford to be careless. Not when she was so close to Xander. The trek to Boura took most people around three hours on the main road, but Melani was certain she could do it faster.

I'll be home soon, my love! Stay where you are!

Melani couldn't tell if her heartbeat was so fast because of the vigorous pace she was setting, or the anticipation of seeing Xander. Even though she had constantly repeated to herself that Xander was alive, deep in her bones she had been unsure if it was true. She had tried desperately to repress the notion that she would never see him again.

I feared it... I feared he was dead. I feared he was far from my reach.

But now he was home. He was in Boura. The skinny attendant Nic had seen him. He was healthy and alive. He had left days ago to find her.

I'm almost there, Xander! We'll be together soon! All of us.

She wished Rizon would have come with her to see his brother. After all they had been through in the recent weeks, it would have been a sweet reunion. She could guiltily admit to herself that time alone with Xander would be more precious, however.

And Rizon will win. He'll get that councilor... and he'll be able to live in peace.

Like the affirmation she had repeated while searching for Xander, however, Melani knew there was a risk that Rizon would not succeed. He was guilty of murdering a councilor of Helike – this was no petty crime. If Rizon was caught, he would be executed.

Melani shivered.

I can't think of this now. He'll be okay. He's smart and trained.

When she reached the base of the dirt road, Melani paused. Would the guards be looking for a short woman with black hair? It was possible. Her escape had been mere hours before.

I need to change my look. Somehow. Anything to help me blend in.

Melani looked at her hands and knees, thick with layers of dirt. Her clothes were unrecognizable.

Could it be that simple?

Swallowing her pride, she lay down on the road. And rolled. The canteen that Opi had provided was already worn enough to pass. Finally, she took a sharp stick and tore into her chiton liberally. Her left breast was slightly exposed, which made Melani bashful, but she decided it would be useful for completing her disguise.

This will do. Guards won't give a beggar a second look.

Opi's bread was smeared with dirt, but Melani nibbled at it anyway. She began walking to the city, giving herself a slight limp. As people passed her by, they averted their eyes, pretending not to notice.

Yes, look away. Please look away.

She picked at her bread crust as she navigated the city center, passing the huge Temple of Poseidon and many statues of the god. She knew the Sons of Poseidon had reigned supreme in the city for countless years – until the Children of the Sea, of course. Everyone had been aware of the cult's existence. Occasionally, Melani wondered if they were still around. There had been rumors of magic surrounding the Children.

Certainly, that can't be true.

Melani wished she had magical capabilities at that moment. Perhaps she could will herself to Boura in an instant, instead of walking through Helike covered in filth. It would have been convenient.

A drunken man stumbled towards her. He hiccupped when he spoke.

"Look, heh, at, heh, you. If it's, heh, money you need, heh... I think, heh, I can spare some, heh, coin for an evening."

Melani wrinkled her nose and covered her chest. He fell closer, putting an arm on her shoulder and leaning in to whisper

"Heh, come on now, heh. A silver even. Maybe two."

Melani slammed her heel in his foot and spat on the ground. The man howled in surprised.

"Don't think about it," she snarled.

For a second, the man looked as if he were about to react. Then he slunk away. Melani felt a strange rush of excitement. She'd love to tell Xander about this.

He'll love that, won't he? A fighter, as well as a healer.

She bit into her bread, then immediately spat out a mouthful of dirt.

Yuck.

Melani chuckled to herself and continued at a brisk trot. Within a quarter hour, she spotted the main road to Boura. People were paying her such little attention, that she decided there was little point to risk getting lost in the forest.

There won't be any drunken fools on the road. Only soldiers and traders. I can make it home to you, Xander!

✳✳✳✳

The hours on the road had been uneventful. Melani saw a few Bouran soldiers, as well as some Heliken. People pushed carts with fruits and cheeses or walked freely toting bundles of scrolls. It was as if there was no war between the two cities.

Things seem... calm.

Taking the main road could have been dangerous if battles were still raging in the territory. However, she supposed that any route would have been equally treacherous. If she kept her head down, there would be no reason to worry.

And what would bandits want with a beggar?

When she arrived in Boura, Melani retreated to the outskirts of the town. In her own city, being recognized was a much greater danger. She couldn't risk being captured.

No... the Fishermen won't be after me. Rizon was only

recognized in Helike because he is a fugitive from the law there. That must be it.

Once again, she was surprised at the town's energy. The shops were open. Kids played in the streets. Soldiers performed light training exercises, though there was no urgency in their movements.

They aren't feeling a threat of battle... what's happened while I've been gone?

Melani dipped into a side street that led straight to the road by her house.

I'm minutes away! Minutes! I'm coming Xander!

Goose pimples crept along Melani's skin as she walked.

I haven't been here since...

She could see Tarlen standing over her, his blade raised. He was going to kill her, going to end her child's life before it began. Then the blood came.

Rizon...

Melani stopped, putting her hand against the side of the house along the alley. She put her hand on her stomach.

He's not here. He's not. Tarlen is dead.

Melani clenched her fist and straightened. She brushed her hand over the filthy, torn chiton. She had run out of water on the walk, and her throat was dry.

Will Xander even recognize me?

At the end of the alley, Melani's heart nearly leapt from her chest. Xander's forge was still, untouched for several days. None of her supplies were strewn across the porch. It was surreal.

I'm home.

Without checking the road, Melani raced across and kicked open the door. She shuddered with happiness.

"Xander!" she called, closing the door behind her. "Xander! My darling, I'm home!"

She moved through the familiar space, her ecstasy fading.

"Xan?"

There was no response. Outside the window, Melani saw Thal dash past, his chubby cheeks jiggling and ginger curls bouncing. She was about to call out to him, when she remembered her ragged appearance.

Loren would flay me alive if I presented myself to her son like this.

The empty house was not what Melani had prayed for. But Nic had seen Xander leave. He had seen a healthy man depart for Boura.

He must *have been here!*

"Oh, Xander. Where've you gone?"

She collapsed onto a kitchen chair, wishing she could be swept into Xander's arms instead.

He wouldn't have cared about the dirt. The grime.

There was no indication that anyone had used the fireplace in recent days. Xander had not been home. She was sure of that now.

He would have made himself some sausage and hen eggs, at the very least.

Melani began to sob. Where was Xander Atsali? Her blacksmith. He was alive... so why hadn't he come home? She buried her face in her hands.

Did he leave to seek me out? When he saw our home empty?

It must have been the case. There was no other explanation. Nicolaus had *seen* Xander. He would have arrived in Boura within hours.

Nicolaus wouldn't lie... would he?

He had no reason to, as far as Melani knew.

She rubbed her eyes. She couldn't feel the baby.

Perhaps she's mourning with me.

Two soldiers walked past the window. Melani prayed they would not peer in and see her. They stopped, and Melani held her breath. There was something strange about their armor. Melani blinked.

What's that... thing on their breastplate?

She squinted.

A trident? These... these aren't Bourans.

What were Heliken soldiers doing in the city? Her crying turned to sniffles. She brushed her stomach absentmindedly.

"That's... that's why everyone was acting so natural. The war..."

The war is over... but Helikens... here?

Had Boura been conquered that quickly? Peace must have been struck with their more powerful foes.

Should I ask the guards?

Something in her mind told her to stay inside.

We've lost... but....

Melani stood. Her thirst was becoming too much to bear. Maybe she would have a bottle of wine somewhere in the cabinet by her bed. As if in a trance, she carried herself to her room.

The baby won't mind if I have a drink.

The bed was just as she'd left it, with blankets crumpled at the foot. She crouched by the cabinet and pulled it open.

Perfect.

She grabbed a bottle of wine made from white grapes. This would be perfect to quench her thirst. She was about to take a sip, when she heard a soft noise.

Is that...

She set the bottle of wine down.

...breathing?

With her dirty hand pressed into the mattress, Melani pushed herself up to peek over the top of the bed... and shrieked in surprise.

Pinned between the bed and the opposite wall, a girl was huddled, her straight black hair hiding her face. Her skin was tanner than Melani's, and she shook like a leaf in the wind.

Melani covered her mouth with one hand and put the other over her heart. She took a step towards the girl, crouching to one knee.

"There's no need to be frightened... I won't hurt you."

Perhaps she'd feel better if I didn't look so disheveled.

"What's your name, dear? Are you lost?"

The girl moved the hair from her eyes; they were strikingly green. She kept her arms wrapped around her knees. She looked to be only a year or two older than Thal.

"I'm Melani. This is my home... but I don't mind that you're here. I don't usually look like this."

The girl's mouth moved, but no sound came out. As Melani studied her more carefully, she saw scratches on her legs and arms, as if she had run through thorny brambles. She wore a linen robe to fit her tiny body and carried no other possessions. The robe was covered in dirt and dust.

How can I get her to talk with me?

"Well, you stay right there, little one. I'll go fetch you some water."

Melani turned to the kitchen, preparing to retrieve a cup for her terrified guest.

And finally, the girl spoke – her voice was quiet and sweet, but her tone was filled with anguish.

"Mother."

Chapter 29

Simon

Even the "simple" guest room was elaborate. The bed was massive and soft, with velvet pillows and satin sheets. Four ebony bedposts held up an artful tapestry, shielding the sleeper from morning sunlight. A plush chair sat at the center of a well-constructed marble desk.

Simon was growing tired of Olenus' magnificence.

Why is it that they have so much, when other Achaean cities have so little?

The wealth was partially a testament to King Basilius' competence. Trade, both within the League and across the seas, had blossomed in the years of Basilius' rule. The city had as many or more dealings with foreign ports than any other city in Greece, even Athens. It was becoming clearer to Simon that the League only remained unconquered because of its two strongest cities, Helike and Olenus.

Without their success, almost any great power could have their pick of Achaean territories.

Simon was sure that the shrewd advisor, Eté, deserved credit as well. The man had left Simon to his room a few hours before, sending a bottle of blackberry wine, along with some kind of fancy cheese.

Both were delicious. At first, Simon worried that Eté may have slipped poison into the gifts; but his hunger overtook his senses. Besides, if Eté wished to see Simon dead, there were several other ways it could have been accomplished.

He is quite *similar to Gaios. Though, perhaps friendlier.*

Despite the luxurious room and tasty indulgences, Simon was not comfortable in his position. There were servants walking the halls, yes. But there were also guards. He was sure that any attempt to leave his room would be monitored. Simon was no less a prisoner than Rizon Atsali had been.

Alone with his thoughts once again, he longed for company. Opi would have been his first choice. He enjoyed her childhood stories, fascinated by her Egyptian culture. And of course, he was curious about whom she fancied around Helike. The girl was kind and innocent but more social and quick-witted than she let on.

Simon had been sure that she and the Golden Spear's attendant, Nicolaus, would have relations at some point, but Opi assured him that this wasn't the case. The boy was too shy and clueless.

I should have met with him earlier. He may be clueless about women, but he is a fast learner in politics.

He wondered if the two of them had begun to conspire together. He hoped so.

There are two Council seats open, after all.

Gaios would never agree to that, of course. Nor would Kyros. The latter would rebel against a female taking a seat; especially a foreign one. And Gaios would feel that he couldn't control either, as one was trained by the Golden Spear, and the other was Simon's confidant.

He would want someone he could lift to power. That way, they would be in his debt.

Reluctantly, Simon wished Gaios were with him. It pained him how they had grown apart after Euripides' assassination, even though he knew it was right.

He would know how to deal with King Basilius.

Simon was quite sure that Gaios could forge an alliance with King Basilius if he desired. Would he have been interested in that? Perhaps not. Peace was not Gaios' specialty.

He would say differently. He would say peace was the objective – his methods didn't need to peaceful.

If Simon were Gaios right now, what would he do? How would he approach the stubborn king?

He would probably have Basilius killed.

It worried Simon that he even considered the idea. Carrying

out the deed would not be so difficult. A few tridents in the right pockets... and Basilius would permanently lose his crown. Then, perhaps Eté's opinion would hold more weight, and the city of Olenus could help quell Gaios' destructive plans.

But he wouldn't do it. Simon knew such a plan could have dire consequences. The benefits were heavily outweighed by the risks.

Simon moved to lie down on the bed. The wine and cheese had made him tired. He pushed aside the curtain and tucked under a puffy blanket. He decided Rizon Atsali may have been slightly worse off in the Heliken prison cell. The bed was large enough for at least three people, so Simon spread himself as wide as possible, delighting in the stretch.

His eyes were flickering shut when two polite knocks sounded on the door.

Naturally. Just when I was about to rest.

"Councilor Simon of Helike," the gravelly voice of Eté said. "Might I have a word?"

Simon groaned and pulled aside the bed curtains.

"It's unlocked, friend."

I wish it weren't.

Eté slipped in, closing the door behind him carefully. A bread crumb hung in his thin mustache. He turned the plush desk chair around and sat down to face Simon.

"I would like to apologize for earlier, Councilor Simon. I did not expect my king to greet you with such hostility. It was unkind of me to allow that."

Eté let the apology settle. Simon scooted himself to the edge of the bed. He wasn't sure Eté's words were sincere.

"Thank you, Eté, but there's no need to apologize," Simon said. "King Basilius is doing what he thinks is best for Olenus."

Eté smiled. "As any good ruler should. However, I have spoken with him about the matter more this evening."

He crossed one leg over the other and placed his hands on his knee. A fly landed on his bald head, and he brushed it away.

"It seems that two of the men from a *certain* group in our military have taken a prisoner of great value today. The man spoke with great malice about Achaea... especially Helike. But there's more, Simon. He had a... peculiar aura about him. And he threatened to kill our men with... magic. He's locked in our most secure cell now – within the walls that separate the palace from the city."

Could it be? One of the fanatics expelled from Helike by Euripides? A Child of the Sea?

"And... you think..."

"I think the League remains a dangerous place. I think there is much to fear and many threats to expunge. The king agrees. He understands that Olenus would be a husk without the other powers in the League."

Simon chewed on these words. The new prisoner must have been quite a terrifying man, if he caused King Basilius to reconsider his position. Simon wondered if the man was really a Child of the Sea. A magician? If so, how many more Children were there with those capabilities? The threat of that particular ilk had seemingly dwindled through Euripides' efforts.

Seemingly.

"What does this mean? Does he still plan on invading your neighbors? Will he support me as I try to put a stop to Gaios' conquests?"

Eté rubbed a hand on his bald head.

"The answers to these questions are complex. He wishes to speak with you again tomorrow in the early evening."

Of course, he does.

"I am glad to hear it... though, I must admit, I have no yearning to be mocked before hundreds of citizens."

"Oh, no. No, King Basilius wishes to hold this meeting in private. It will be you and I in the courtroom, as well as two guards. Even the servers will stay away."

"And Venedictos as well, I presume."

"Yes, of course. My colleague will be there to advise the king, as always."

Simon wanted to know more of the backstory between Eté and his antagonist, Venedictos. Tensions ran high between those two. Simon could understand this.

The Court of Helike is often a competitive environment.

"I accept this proposal. Would you be so kind as to share some of the *complexities* you previously mentioned? I would like to approach tomorrow's conversation with the proper expectations."

Eté laughed. "You and I are similar men, Simon. I would

expect the same courtesies. Remind me of your inquiries."

"Does King Basilius still plan to attack Patras and Dyme? And will he stand against Helike if Gaios refuses to stop his own invasions?"

"Ah yes. You see, to answer these, I must share his newest opinion."

Eté paused. He ran his tongue across his teeth.

"Basilius believes a unification of the League would benefit every city. There are currently... twelve governing bodies? I am sure this is why Gaios wishes to win the League for himself. He would agree that Achaea is too divided at the present. United, we could stand against any empire."

"Are you suggesting..."

"Yes, Simon," Eté said, spreading his arms wide, before bringing his hands together. "Olenus and Helike must form an alliance. A military alliance, if you will. Together, our cities can ensure Achaea becomes one. Perhaps there would still be invasions of Patras and Dyme... however, this would not happen until Olenus and Helike have begun to mutually support one another. Instead of standing against Gaios... what if we stood with him?"

Simon frowned. "I don't want bloodshed, Eté. How would this be different?"

"There would be no grand conflict, of course. There would be no final war between the powers of the East and the West! Two great cities would become one! And you tell me, which Achaean

318

territories would oppose the combination of its two mightiest? None!"

"You think the other cities will simply kneel before this new alliance? And Eté... who would rule? Would Basilius yield his throne?"

I know Gaios will not...

Eté paused before speaking, biting his tongue.

"This... this would be something we can discuss tomorrow," he said. "All the ambitious leaders will have more than they once did... perhaps that will be enough."

We both know that would not be the case.

Simon tried to read the advisor. He still didn't quite understand why the man was so keen to ally with a councilor from Helike. However, Eté had given Simon no reason to question his motives. He seemed to be another power-hungry man, inspired by his own success; these men were often quite predictable. Eté *would* be better off as advisor to some sort of unified Achaean governance.

And with the might of the entire League... who knows how far we can spread?

Eté spoke once more with enthusiasm, "Can you see the greatness that could be, Simon? And all because *you* came here! Without you, there would be no potential... such a bright future wasted. The gods would smile upon a healthy Achaea, don't you believe?"

Simon tried to put on a smile of his own. "Yes, of course.

Nothing could make the gods happier."

Eté's grin turned into a sneer. Simon hoped it was not directed at him.

Perhaps he is a religious type... I would not have expected that from him.

"I am glad we agree," Eté said. "This could be a wonderful arrangement."

He stood from his chair, and Simon followed, reaching his hand out to shake Eté's.

"Of course. And thank you once more, Eté. I truly appreciate your willingness to pursue a positive relationship with Helike."

I may find peace for Achaea, yet!

Eté shook Simon's hand firmly. His grip was much more solid, and it was not ribbed with finger bones. Simon watched as Eté made for the door, opening it with a swift tug.

"Until tomorrow, Councilor Simon."

"Sleep well, Eté."

The door shut, and Simon let out a sigh of relief. He locked it before flopping back onto the soft mattress. The conversation had been informative at least. Simon was unsure whether a military alliance between Olenus and Helike was the right path to take. However, it did seem better than war between the two powerful Achaean cities. Such a conflict would be magnitudes worse than Boura and Helike's squabble.

Simon hoped the battles had ceased in the neighboring cities. Helike would certainly win. How would Gaios handle the defeated

Boura?

Will he be ruthless? Or wise?

Simon hoped Gaios and King Basilius would be able to behave amiably if the two cities were to join their forces. Both were strong leaders, so long as they didn't let their ambition get in the way of the League's best interests.

It so often does, though.

Simon had been tired not long before. Now he was wide awake. He lay on the bed, admiring the painted ceiling above him. Olenus was a truly magnificent city. Perhaps a treaty with its king would be the best decision, after all.

Tomorrow. We shall see how I fare when faced with Basilius. The League needs peace. Is this the only way?

Chapter 30

Sapphir

Her father was close.

She could feel his presence, stronger than she had in years.

He's here. Somewhere in the city.

Olenus itself was quite striking. Sapphir was surprised at how pristine the roads were. Precious metals seemed to adorn almost every building; even the people looked healthy and well-kept. It was, without a doubt, the cleanest city Sapphir had ever seen.

Most of the foot traffic emanated from the center, where high walls surrounded what must have been a palace. Sapphir walked purposefully in that direction.

Come on, Father. Where are you?

The streets were crowded with shops and stores. The grandeur was a stark contrast to what lay outside the city walls. Sapphir couldn't remember any part of Helike being this impressive.

Nobody gave Sapphir a second look as she walked. Several turned their noses away when they saw the stains on her linen robes. It was evidently uncommon to appear so bedraggled in Olenus.

I don't even look as bad as I could, do I?

She had more important things to worry about. Her mind worked on two levels as the city passed her by; one searched for her father, while the other tried to reach her children. Egan still wasn't responding – nor were Ivy, Cy, Maya, or Celia.

Sapphir willed herself not to lose control. She needed to remain stable. She could not solve her problems otherwise. Her children would suffer more if she began to spiral.

The inner walls loomed higher above her head. Sapphir became more certain that she would find her father somewhere inside. The grand entryway was crowded by a massive temple with hundreds of columns. Citizens weaved between the marble pillars or kneeled on the marble floors in prayer.

It's far larger than Helike's own Temple of Poseidon.

The columns were etched with writing that had faded over the years. However, Sapphir could still make out the words – To Zeus Almighty.

Zeus. Of course, this would be a shrine to him.

The Sky Father always attracted the grandest monuments. Sapphir wondered if that bothered Poseidon.

Do the gods quibble as human rulers would?

Something told her that they did. Sapphir moved towards the pillars.

This place would suit you, Father? Reveal yourself if you are here!

His presence did not grow stronger. Her father was not sheltered within another sacred temple. Sapphir looked to the inner walls.

Common folk filed through the gates.

"I heard that Heliken is talking with King Basilius again," a woman said.

Her friend laughed. "Didn't get enough yesterday? If that's how their councilors are, I would hate to live there!"

What's a councilor from Helike doing here?

Two guards were just beginning to close the doors when Sapphir arrived.

"Wait!" She rushed forward, putting her hand on one of the guard's shoulders. "I need to get in there."

"Sorry, miss. Nobody's allowed in until tomorrow. The king has urgent business to attend to."

Through the half-open entrance, Sapphir could see a beautiful courtyard. Thousands of flowers were arranged in neat rows, and trees, both palm and cypress, shaded dozens of garden benches.

"But I... I just dropped my purse in the courtyard... while I was leaving. I don't need to go all the way inside."

The guard looked at Sapphir with suspicion. He glanced at his partner, who shrugged, then shook his head.

"Um… what's it look like, miss? Leather? Burlap? Cloth?"

"It's leather," Sapphir said. "With a red stripe painted on the side. Please, sir, it has all of my silver from this morning's trade."

The guard shifted his helm and scratched his forehead.

"Hmm. I can't let you in, it's what the king wants. But, um… maybe I can go retrieve it. Or better," he looked inside at another guard standing by a fountain in the courtyard, "Ed! Do you see a coin purse in there? Leather! With a red stripe!"

Ed turned to the two guards and Sapphir. "Where'd she drop it?"

"I don't know!" Sapphir called back, trying to use her most sugary tone. "Somewhere on the path, I'm sure!"

Ed marched to the path and began to search the ground for a coin purse that did not exist. Sapphir gulped. This ruse would not be of much use if the guards didn't let her inside.

"Why's the king closing the palace," she asked, moving her hand down the guard's arm.

"Um, it's a… councilor I believe. A man from Helike that the king is meeting with. He would prefer a private conversation."

Sapphir tried to sound coy in her response. "So, he won't even let you in? Important soldiers like you?"

"Well, um, I'm sure I can go in if need be. And I live in the barracks behind the palace, of course, too."

The other guard rolled his eyes. "We all live there."

Sapphir smiled. "I would love to see it. Where you live, I mean."

The guard blushed and puffed his chest, deepening his voice slightly when he responded, "It would be my pleasure to, um... show you."

The second guard hit him with the butt of his spear, so the man quickly added, "Another day, however. The king needs the palace grounds empty."

"You don't want to see where we live," the second guard said, his tone droll. "It's right next to the cells."

The prison is inside the palace walls! A palace... a prison... Father must be nearby.

"Well, I don't think that–"

She was cut off by Ed, "I don't see a coin purse! Are you sure you dropped it here?"

Sapphir was about to respond, when a flash of light blinded her, and she crumpled to the ground.

What... what's happening!

Her heartbeat spiked, and Sapphir felt her spine grow cold. She could see the inside of Felip and Agnes' farm. Her children were strewn across the rooms, catatonic. Then, they began to writhe and scream.

No! Children!

Her thoughts became fractured. She could feel years of magical effort and strain beginning to unravel. The lies she had told her children, their repressed memories... they were leaving her.

No... no! No! The memories! Children!

She gasped, "My children!"

The guards bent over to help her up.

"Are you okay, lady?"

She shrieked and pushed them away, leaping to her feet. Her eyes were ferocious enough to make the guards step back.

How did this... my children. No! My children!!!!

Something had broken. Sapphir had no idea how. She burst past the guards into the courtyard.

How did this happen. I... I had control! They were safe!

Her father's presence intensified.

It's his fault. It must be! I never should have left the island. Or the farm!

"Hey! Lady! Ed! Stop her! Call for the others!"

The guards raced after her and the huge doors closed behind them. Sapphir leapt over a row of flowers, and Ed rushed to cut her off. From elsewhere in the gardens, other men began to close in.

"Out of my way!" Sapphir commanded. "I need to find him!"

"Who? The king! Hey! Get back here, woman!"

Not the king! Not the king, my father! The prison... or the palace... he's here!

The image of her children in the farmhouse was gone, and Sapphir knew she would not be able to see what happened to them next. Memory charms were complicated, and their dissolution was always dangerous.

They won't be able to handle their own memories! My poor children! What have I done?

A hand grabbed her slender arm, and Sapphir felt herself pulled roughly to the ground. The other guards stood around her.

"Do you want to end up in one of the cells, woman!"

"Let go of me. Please."

"We can't let you near the palace. You have to leave the grounds. I won't warn you again!"

Sapphir felt her blood rise. The Blood of the Golden Age coursed through her veins; her body became warm.

It's my father's doing! I can stop this. I know he's here!

The guard holding her loosened his grip.

"She's burning!" he said. "Hey, help me with her, Ed!"

Sapphir was growing furious. She would not be stopped from finding Teremos. Not when she was so close! She had traveled too far – all the way from her island. It could not end now.

Not after I lost Keoki; my children... not after all this time. I must find him!

"Let go! Leave now!"

"What are you planning, woman? It's over," Ed said, securing her free arm.

Her anger exploded. In an instant, the five guards were thrown from her, collapsing to the ground. They clambered to their feet. Each readied his spear, though none looked keen to approach Sapphir.

She hadn't felt so much magical energy in her body in years. She slashed both arms across her body, and two of the guards fell back to the earth, staring in shock at the gashes across their bodies.

Their companions ran to them, cowering in fear away from Sapphir. Ed pointed his spear at her.

"She's evil! What are you!"

Sapphir didn't respond. Instead she closed her fist, and the remaining guards, Ed included, slumped on top of their bloodied compatriots.

The courtyard was silent, aside from the hushed wheezing of the two injured guards. Sapphir turned to the palace, her body working as it hadn't in years.

I'm free. Now... show yourself, Father.

She passed under a cypress tree. When she ran her hands along the trunk, it blackened. She knew her father was inside these walls. She moved along the side of the palace, the heat of his energy dwarfing that of her own blood.

Most everything about the palace and its surroundings were magnificent. Only a few buildings appeared less than regal.

The barracks. The prison.

They still put those of other cities to shame, but they were simple enough. The plainest building of all stood in the center of the guards' housing.

It was multiple stories of sandstone, perhaps larger if it extended underground. She leaned against the palace. Her father's aura was more powerful than ever.

It's over, Father. I'm here. By the palace and the prison.

Sapphir thought of her children, overwhelmed with their memories – the truth. She clenched a fist and felt the cold silver dagger pressed against her leg.

A knife to your neck, Father. This is how it ends.

Chapter 31

Ivy

"Callidora! Calli! Stop biting that, dear."

The woman took a cooking ladle out of her daughter's mouth. She was stout, though still pretty. Her skin was tan, and her hair, black. She had the same green eyes as Ivy. Her daughter, Callidora, couldn't have been older than three. Ivy could see her in the reflection of a bronze plate.

She looks like Maya... only a little younger.

"Rosie dear," a man said. "Your father's coming home today. Elfie told me to pick up a lamb's leg from the market. Do you want to join me? Calli will love a nice walk!"

Callidora clapped her hands jubilantly at the mention of a walk.

Why am I seeing this?

Suddenly, they were walking through the squares of Helike; Ivy recognized a pretty fountain, a big temple, and the castle in the distance.

I know this place... I'm in the big city!

Her mind kept flashing. She saw Callidora's huge grandfather, who carried her around on his shoulders across Helike and attracted the eyes of everyone. Callidora even had a brother, Elias. He looked like Ivy, too.

One day when he was on a walk with their mother, he didn't come back. Callidora and her family had cried about that.

Ivy saw countless meals and strolls along a beachfront. However, she only saw Callidora a few times in reflections.

Callidora had green eyes.

The strangest part to Ivy was that she *recognized* Callidora's mother and her grandparents.

I've seen them in a dream before.

In a distant corner of her mind, Ivy could feel her body, frozen on the floor of Felip and Agnes' farmhouse. Egan was beside her, crumpled in a heap.

But she couldn't leave the memories.

Callidora's memories.

Every time she tried to return to the farm, her headache grew.

One day, Callidora was in her room – a simple space with a bed and cabinet. She was playing with a rock, tossing it in the air, and counting the seconds until it landed back in her hands. Her mother and father were out, and her grandmother, a lady with one arm named Elfie, was cooking in the kitchen. Ivy heard a faint tap outside Callidora's window.

She strained to see the source of the noise… and suddenly, she was on an island – *her* island.

I'm home!

Mother stood before her; or was she standing in front of Callidora? Two boys sat next to Ivy's mother, their eyes closed. The smaller of the two was blonde. In her mother's arms slept a child with sprouts of hazel hair.

"Awaken children," her mother said. "Egan, Cy, Celia."

She said each name at her children pointedly, giving a shoulder shrug for Celia. She turned her icy blue eyes at Callidora.

"Ivy."

****

When she regained control of her body, Ivy found herself gasping on the floor. Egan was sprawled next to her, whispering to himself.

"Egan!" she said, frightened.

He didn't react. Ivy drew herself to her hands and knees.

"Ivyyy!! Help!"

It was Celia, Ivy's little sister. The one with messes of hazel hair.

Like the baby in Mother's arms.

Ivy's head was on fire. In fact, her entire body was warm.

The baby... in Mother's arms. Celia.

From the other room, Ivy heard Agnes and Felip comforting Celia.

"It's okay, dear. You're safe... you're not hurt!"

"Tell us what you saw, again. No need to be afraid..."

Ivy could tell by their voices that they didn't believe their words. She heard Celia sobbing and mumbling incoherently.

No... no, no, no! It's all true... it's all true.

"Ivy!!!"

Ivy stood. Her legs wobbled when she tried to follow Celia's voice. When she came into view, Celia screamed. She was draped over a chair, shaking. Her face was almost red enough to drain away her freckles.

"No! You're not my sister! Ivy..." she choked out a sob and her voice turned to a whisper, "Ivy... you're not...."

Fil knelt at her side, and Agnes stroked her head. Behind them, Maya cried silently. Cy was still catatonic.

"Celia... what did you see?"

"That's not my name! Ivy..."

Not her name... it's not my name. It's... Ivy's not....

Fil grimaced. "Oh dear, I think we just need to take a deep breath now."

"Shut your mouth, Felip," Agnes snapped. "They know! Something must have happened to that *sorceress*, and now... they know!"

Fil wilted, shaking his head sadly.

"You knew!?" Ivy shouted in disbelief. "You knew that she... that Mother..."

"She's not our mother!" Celia interjected. "She took me! She took you!"

She... from my room. Callidora's room... where I... she was throwing the rock. Up and down.

Cy was screeching before his eyes even opened, "Ivy!! What's... what's happening!?"

Ivy reached towards him, her movements jerky.

"No! Don't touch me! I... Ivy... I don't know you!"

Yes, you do!

It all made sense now – why they couldn't leave the island; why they didn't look like each other; why Sapphir never left their side.

That was her name after all – Sapphir. She wasn't Ivy's mother; Ivy's mother's name was Rosie.

But at the same time, Ivy *felt* like they were her kin. Her brothers and sisters... she still loved Egan and Celia, Cy and Maya... even the pale woman who used to be her mother.

Everything I've known... it's all been a story! A made-up game like Cy and I used to play!

Cy banged his head against the cabinets; Maya hugged the wall, her lip quivering; Celia wailed uncontrollably; Egan was still in the side room, unmoving.

And in the middle of it all, Ivy felt broken.

I'm... Calli... Callidora. So who is Ivy?

She wanted to call for her mother, but she didn't know which one.

What's become of Rosie? And Elfie? My parents and my grandparents? What of my real *brother? Elias....*

She ran her hands through her hair, clenching her teeth.

"Fil... what do we...?"

How many lies have I been told?

"I don't know, love. We didn't... we couldn't have..."

"You see now what you are?"

No... not you... not again!

The honeyed voice drowned out all other noise

"A granddaughter of Achaean royalty... and still a Child of the Sea."

What's a Child of the Sea?! Get out of my head!

"I will do as you wish, Ivy. Or would you prefer Callidora? It matters not... soon, we can speak of this face to face."

Ivy opened her mouth to scream, but the voice was gone.

Callidora. It's... true.

Celia and Cy were still manic. Ivy rushed to help Fil and Agnes calm them down.

"Soon we can speak of this face to face."

She scanned the fields visible from the kitchen window.

The tall blonde man... is he coming here?

She squinted at the tree line.

No!

Her blood reached a full boil.

Two men and two women made their way leisurely towards the house. They wore linen, just as Sapphir did. One woman had her hair wrapped in a bun, while the other let dark curls fall down her shoulders. Both men were a normal height – identical – with no other exceptional features.

Where's the blonde man?

"Young man, give the cabinets a rest. You're going to hurt yourself," the gentle voice of Fil said.

They don't see the four people.

"Fil... Agnes," Ivy said.

Linen... like us... like Mother.

"Magicians," she whispered.

Her suspicions were confirmed when the woman with the bun conjured fire from thin air, casting it towards the house. She was hundreds of yards away, but somehow, the fire continued to fly.

"Look out!" Ivy yelled.

It was too late. The roof was already ablaze.

"What... what was that?" Agnes yelped, grabbing Felip's arm.

The old couple peered out the window. And saw them.

"Oh, Fil!" Agnes wept, "Fil, do something! Get your bow!"

Felip moved faster than Ivy expected, dashing to a cupboard and taking out his bow and a quiver of arrows. Cy stopped pounding his head and collapsed to the floor. Celia cowered away from the window in fear.

"Agnes, take the girls out back," Fil said calmly, drawing his bow back and gazing down the shaft of the arrow.

"Celia, Maya. Behind me... stay with Agnes," Ivy ordered.

I need to be brave. I need to be their sister.

She turned to face the two girls. Celia, formerly red from crying, was now flush with fear. Maya looked at Ivy quizzically, with those familiar green eyes.

"You both need to listen to Agnes. Protect each other... like sisters...."

Because you are...

"You understand? Celia?"

Celia nodded, shrinking back behind her hands and whimpering.

"Maya?"

Maya shook her head. She reached for Ivy, her face resolute. Ivy pushed her hand away gently.

"No, Maya. Celia needs you... and Cy. I can't..."

I can't put you in danger again – not like I did when we left the island.

Maya rushed forward and hugged Ivy's leg, then moved to Agnes, tugging Celia's smock as she went.

"Agnes! The girls!" Fil repeated, more forcefully this time.

"My dear–"

"Do it!"

This is our fault! My fault.... For leaving with Cy. I can't let them get hurt!

Agnes grabbed Celia and Maya's hands and made for the door

leading to the cow pasture. She looked at Ivy expectantly.

"No, I'm staying. I can help Fil until Egan wakes up!" Ivy exclaimed. "Put Cy in the wagon and take him out with you. Fil needs me!"

Agnes was about to retort, but Fil nodded.

"You're brave, child. If it gets... messy... you run. You run, and you leave me. Your big brother... I'll make sure he gets out safely. Ag..."

He lowered his bow and crossed the room, leaning in to whisper something to his wife. Agnes blushed, her eyes watering. Then she straightened.

"Outside, girls. Let's go."

Maya and Celia shuffled through the door, holding it open for Agnes as she plopped Cy into her cheese wagon and followed. The four strange figures in their linen robes drew closer, never deviating from their straight path to the farmhouse.

"Who are they?" Ivy asked.

"Oh... don't ask me, child... I fear I don't know for certain. But they won't hurt you."

They were a stone's throw away now, though they made no moves to inflict more damage to the house. The blaze on the roof fizzled to smoke.

Perhaps the fire was just a warning.

"What's your business here?"

Fil's voice boomed across the field. The woman with the curls responded. Her voice was melodious.

"I believe you already know! We are here for the children. All five, please. You'll want to put your bow down, old man."

The other woman snapped, and another ball of fire sprang into her hand. Fil licked his lips.

"The children aren't yours to take! If you would kindly leave my farm, we can all go on with our lives."

The two men and two women stopped, less than fifty feet from the window. The twins began to chant softly; their words were inaudible.

Get as far away as you can, Agnes!

"For the sake of the gods," Fil muttered, "I'm going to have to use this bow, aren't I?"

Ivy tried to remember a spell – any spell – that could help the kind old man defend his home.

Why couldn't I have paid more attention to Mot... to Sapphir!

"If this is the decision you've chosen, old man! So be it!"

The twins continued to chant, and the sorceresses lobbed huge swaths of fire at the farmhouse. Ivy screamed, and Fil released his arrow at one of the twins, drawing another with incredible speed and aiming at the second twin.

Everything seemed to slow. The arrows dissolved as they came within inches of the two men. The fire landed, surrounding the entire house.

But nothing burned. The flames dissipated.

How...

Then she saw the burly figure standing between the intruders and the house.

"Egan!" Ivy yelled, diving through the window to join him.

He looked at Ivy, his face dark.

He's seen... he knows what I know... that we used to be someone else.

But even in his unrelenting stoicism, Ivy could see affection in his eyes.

"Get to the others, Ivy. Get everyone out safely... they don't want to kill us... they *want* us."

What does he mean?

She didn't have time to try to puzzle it together. The twins rushed at Egan, arms flailing as they summoned a whirlwind of rope and bindings. The woman with curly hair thrust out her arms and Ivy was knocked backwards.

She landed next to a small black beetle, and an incantation finally came to her.

As she rolled away, Ivy focused on the insect. Her arms grew warm, and it expanded unnaturally until it was the size of Ivy. The beetle charged the woman, its mandibles clicking.

That's even scarier than the bear.

But the sorceress with the bun merely flicked her hand, and the beetle was reduced to ash. Ivy backed up, trying the spell on everything around her. Countless insects expanded and disappeared.

Ivy tried desperately to remember any other useful trick. Her foot hit the side of the house, and Ivy knew she could retreat no further. She would need to fight or flee.

I can't flee. I can't reveal Agnes and the others!

Egan's form blurred as he battled with both twins. Ivy couldn't tell who had the upper hand. She saw Fil burst through the side door, yelling madly and releasing arrows at all of the invaders, to no avail.

He knows he can't kill them... what's he doing?

"Fil!" she screamed, as he charged forward. "No!"

However, the men were so focused on Egan, they hadn't noticed the farmer. Felip fired an arrow at one of the twins.

It found its mark. The old man grimaced.

Blood spattered Egan's face as the arrow buried itself in the man's neck. Ivy tried to look away.

The other twin shrieked in fury as his brother collapsed. Egan was knocked to the ground, and the curly-haired woman fell upon him, securing him tightly in a magical binding. The living twin flew at Felip, grasping him by the neck. Ivy lunged to protect the old farmer, but the second woman blocked her path.

No! Fil!

She tried to roll sideways but found herself tangled in the grass. It snaked around her, the blades stronger than they should have been. Within seconds, Ivy was completely inert. When she opened her mouth to speak, she found it gagged with soil.

The curly-haired woman waved a hand, and Ivy was dragged across the ground until she sat, back-to-back with Egan. She tried to invoke a spell – any spell – but her energy felt stagnant.

"Find the other three," the woman commanded.

Her two remaining magicians stalked away; the man brushed his hands on his linen robe as he went. In the dirt, less than ten feet away, Felip groaned, his breath ragged.

Fil!! Who are these people! What do they want with us!?

The curly-haired woman paced through the yard. She stopped by Fil and cocked her head, then continued pacing. Fil's breath was a faint wheezing now. Long minutes passed. The sun dipped behind the hills.

The curly-haired sorceress stopped.

"Where is the other?"

Ivy craned her neck and saw the man and woman return, the paralyzed bodies of Celia and Cy suspended in front of them. The man dragged a wagon behind him, dumping its contents next to Fil. He gasped and pulled himself to the shape, cloaking it with his body.

Agnes!

Ivy couldn't tell if she was breathing.

No. What did I do? What did I do!! It's... it's all my fault.

The male magician grunted, "She slipped through our fingers."

"How!? She's the youngest one! How could you let a mute get away?"

The man shrugged, dropping the other two children next to Ivy and Egan.

"He'll be furious. She's who he wanted most. The most

malleable."

Maya... she made it out. She got away!

"Search for her. Both of you," the curly-haired woman demanded. "I'll take the others."

Ivy gave one final effort to break her bindings, but there was no point trying. She was helpless. She looked at Fil and Agnes, lying in a heap in their field.

I'm sorry... I'm so sorry.

She prayed they would live to see another day together. She prayed they knew how sorry she was.

The woman waved her hand, and Ivy felt herself go limp.

Chapter 32

Nicolaus

An ally...

The crowd of Helikens gathered in the Court cheered. He could hear a smattering of words from the crowd.

"Traitor!"

"Egyptian scum!"

Some were much more vulgar.

Rizon did not look away from Gaios. Kyros sat to the councilor's left. His blonde tuft of hair looked especially sweaty, and it was clear that he had not lost any weight, despite the stress of war. The man on Gaios' other side was short and bald, wearing regal robes.

Ucalegon. It must be him. That's why Parex the Hammer is here.

Gaios let the cheers die down before continuing.

"Rizon Atsali has already confessed to his crimes – he was taken prisoner weeks ago. However, with the help of this man... this *boy*," Gaios pointed a spindly finger at Nic, "He escaped his cell. Today he was recaptured *in* the palace. What schemes had he devised? On a day that meant the unification of our two cities! Thankfully, we needn't worry. The valiant Parex stopped him before any nefarious deeds could be executed."

Parex nodded curtly. He had one hand on the collar of Rizon's oversized robes.

"And speaking of executions! Councilor Euripides' soul will not rest until justice is brought to his killer. Parex!"

Not here... he wouldn't. They can't execute him here!

"Take him to his cell. There will be no escape this time. When the sun is at its highest tomorrow, Rizon Atsali will meet the judgement of Hades."

Parex pulled Rizon roughly. The assassin's hawkish eyes bored into the councilor. He remained rooted to the spot. Nicolaus wondered if Gaios felt any fear.

One of the most dangerous men in Achaea wishes him dead.

"Nicolaus," he said loudly. "Tell them. Tell them how Councilor Gaios ordered the assassination! How he used the Fishermen to threaten my family as blackmail. Tell them!"

It seems like you've already told them.

Silence fell over the crowded Court. People murmured to each other, and some chuckled nervously.

Parex struck Rizon with a mailed hand. Given the force of the blow, Nic expected him to buckle. However, he did not move. He looked Parex directly in the eye and spat. A tooth bounced off the Hammer's cheek, along with bloody saliva. Parex clenched his fist, fire in his eyes.

"Enough!" Gaios demanded. "Enough. There is no need to punish a desperate man for desperate allegations."

The crowd was still restless.

Do they believe Rizon?

Kyros cut in, quaffing his wine first, "Trust me, if Gaios were cruel enough to rid the Court of any councilors, he would have started with me."

Kyros' blotchy features shook as he erupted with laughter. Ucalegon joined politely, and soon, the citizens were all sharing in the merriment. How hysterical, that an assassin would blame their loyal councilor for the death of one of his own!

I have to defend him.

"It's true!" Nic shouted, trying to drown out the frenzied men and women. "Rizon is guilty... but he's not the only one!"

Kyros snorted, "You're right, little servant. What should we do with you?"

"Execute him, too!" a voice called.

"Throw him in a cell!"

"Castration!"

Castration?

The laughter in the Court became deafening, and Gaios had to

347

wait once more before answering Kyros. Nic felt hundreds of eyes on him; he couldn't turn and indulge them. He kept his gaze on the thrones.

Is Elfie in the crowd? Are Rosie and Krassen?

He hoped not.

"The boy's role is still not fully understood. We'll hold him captive for questioning until a worthy punishment is decided. Certainly, he was not one of the minds behind this operation."

He gave Nic a knowing smile, as if the two of them were sharing in a secret. He gestured to Parex, and the Hammer redoubled his efforts to drag Rizon from the Court, this time with the help of two other guards.

Nic wanted to chase after them, demand that they ease the sentence. But he couldn't. He was still wrapped in chains, tethered to another guard like an anchored ship. He looked at Rizon, who passively resisted against the men.

"I'm sorry," Nic mouthed.

Rizon shook his head, grimacing. The lithe man was seasoned enough to know there would be no second escape. This would be the last time Nic saw Rizon Atsali. He gave Nic a half-smile and glanced at Gaios. The message was clear.

"Get rid of him for me."

Rizon Atsali disappeared from the Court, marched to what would certainly be his last night. The crowd watched him go, ignorant to the truth of his crimes.

They would make the same choices he did. Each one of them.

Nic glared at Gaios. In the corner of his eye, he could see Kyros washing down a wedge of cheese with more wine. Ucalegon appeared formal, yet uncomfortable and nervous. Gaios, however, seemed completely at ease. His hair remained perfect, not a strand out of place.

"I shall escort the accomplice, Nicolaus, to his own cell myself. Before we conclude this assembly, we in the Court wish to express our gratitude to the citizens of the new Helike. You have all shown great dignity in the beginnings of this transition, as people of the greatest city on this Earth. In celebration of this peace, the Council shall sponsor a performance in the Helike theater in a moon's turn… Olympian athletes and only the best actors!"

Cheers erupted in the Court; many of the people stood as they applauded.

Wrong… this is all wrong… what peace!?

"Until then, the Court will convene daily to hear the pleas and concerns of our people. May Poseidon bless your evening!"

Gaios clapped twice, and the doors opened. Guards, both Bouran and Heliken, began to escort the joyous citizens from the Court.

✳✳✳✳

The sound of a bird chirping woke Nic from a fitful sleep. Nic felt small on the massive bed. He had never slept on such a comfortable mattress. However, he couldn't seem to relax. The bird was a swallow. Perched on the windowsill, it flitted from stone to stone.

It still hasn't happened yet, has it?

Nic could see the city clearly from the window and had witnessed no public display of Rizon Atsali's execution. He wondered what was causing the delay.

Could he have escaped again?

The bird took flight.

Nic had not understood why Gaios had chosen Orrin's bedchambers as his prison at first. It took several days of tortured sleep – moving from the bed to the mahogany desk, then back to the bed – before he realized the motivation. The room reminded Nic constantly of the futility of his position.

It didn't matter how immaculate his accommodations were. It didn't matter how many times he could read through the Golden Spear's old letters.

Nic would never properly avenge his friend.

It's a taunt.

Gaios had not come to question him yet. Each day, Nic waited, somewhat eagerly, for the councilor to walk through the door. Surely, he was curious about how Rizon had escaped. He couldn't truly know.

He'll come…. He has to.

The day Gaios had walked Nic from the Court, he'd spoken cordially. He told Nic how impressed he was at his progress and how thankful he was to have found peace with King Ucalegon. Nic had expected Gaios to berate him, goad him, or punish him in some way.

But Gaios simply talked.

"You'll be curious about the peace treaty, of course. It was a simple accord with the Bouran. He knew fully well that they would lose a war with Helike. However–"

"Why are you telling me this?" Nic interrupted.

Gaios smiled. "Because... you have to listen."

Nic grunted.

"As I was saying... it took a battle to prove to the world that Helike would best Boura without question... we performed that battle. The Battle at the Beach was a ruse. A performance to solidify Boura's surrender."

Gaios let that hang.

A ruse!? Orrin died... for a ruse!?

Nic wanted to shove the man down the stairs. Could he do it without falling himself?

"You see, all I needed to do was promise Ucalegon a seat on the Council. And he knew that his power would be greater than ever before... even greater than you could imagine!"

"I don't care," Nic said. "I don't want to know. I've lost. I *know* I've lost."

"Precisely, Nicolaus. *You've* lost! But... Helike has won! You see, I've struck a deal with Ionia. The Persian Empire will be on our side as we absorb Eastern Achaea... all of it! Who knows where such conquest could lead our city? We could become the greatest city the world has ever known!"

Nic tugged at his chain. Gaios held it firmly.

"Why... why would you share all this with me?"

"Because it doesn't matter, boy! I grow tired of being the only man who *knows*. And who will you tell? The walls? With the Flat-Nose gone... well, my position has never been more secure."

Nic had tried to figure out how he could use the information. But Gaios was a careful man. Nic had absolutely no evidence against him, aside from his words.

And he is right... Boura and Helike are at peace...

Gaios had created a war, and immediately ended it. As much as he hated to admit it, Nic was impressed. Simon had been correct that Gaios' war with Boura was inevitable. But the Flat-Nose had never suspected that Gaios had arranged its ending before the battles even occurred.

He orchestrated an entire war. And it worked... just as he desired.

Helike was stronger than ever and Nic was powerless. All he could do now was witness its conquest... and the suffering that would accompany it.

If the violence spreads to Egypt... to Memphis... if only I could warn Gabbi and Ibbie! My family!

Nic looked at the mahogany desk, wondering if he could send a letter to them. The creak of the heavy ebony doors caused Nic to sit up. He drew the blankets up to his neck, covering his naked body.

"Good morning, Nicolaus," Gaios said.

"What do you want?" Nic asked menacingly.

Should I ask him about Rizon?

"Oh my," Gaios chuckled. "Intimidation doesn't suit you. It seems to me that you could use some company in this large cell you occupy."

Perhaps not... if it already happened... and I missed it... I don't want to know.

"I don't mean myself, of course. That would be... No..."

Gaios pushed the door open wider, revealing a second person. He coaxed the girl into the room. She was bound with a thin rope, which Gaios untied. Her caramel skin was still splashed with mud, though it had grown crusted and dry.

"Opi!"

He wanted to rush forward and hug her, but his clothes sat at the foot of the bed.

"How tender. Two friends – confined to this room together. I trust you'll keep each other entertained."

"How did they catch you?" Nic asked, ignoring Gaios.

"I don't know. I thought I could get away... I made it all the way to Boura..."

"And they caught you there."

"Heliken guards... in Boura... I don't understand–"

"Well, I'll allow you two to catch up," Gaios said. "Don't try to escape, and perhaps we can find something of value for you two in the coming months... we shall be... dealing... with your kind soon. Until we speak again!"

Gaios shut the door, the heavy iron leaves clicking together. Nic heard the sound of a bar lowering into place. There would be no purpose in trying to escape.

"What does he mean?"

Opi rubbed her wrists where the rope had been and moved to sit at the foot of the bed. Nic pulled the blanket up further.

"I don't know. It has something to do with the Persians... I don't know. It's all one city now. Boura and Helike. Gaios, Ucalegon, and Kyros... they control the entire territory."

"That was his plan? All along?"

Opi looked distraught. He knew she was thinking about Simon, wondering if he had been aware of these schemes.

He must have known more than he told us.

"That was his plan."

Opi exhaled heavily and shook her head. "That's brilliant. Nic, he beat us. All of us. And your home... your family... will they be in danger?"

"I don't know."

Nic covered his face. Orrin had given him one task – to help as many people as he could. Nic had known he would fail... the job was too large even for a hundred people; however, he had not expected to fail so spectacularly.

Every person I've touched... I've let down.

Everyone he cared about was worse off for knowing him.

Orrin, his friend and mentor, was dead; Orrin's family was without the vengeance Nic had promised. Even Opi was now a prisoner.

And my family....

Opi sighed. She stood from the bed, stretched, and walked to the window. The swallow had flown away, so Opi was able to lean against the sill and look at the city below.

"Have we really lost, Nic? Will we be in this room forever?"

Nic tugged on the sheets until he could reach his dirty robe. He put it on under the covers while Opi was turned away.

"Forever? No. Gaios will tire of us eventually; maybe he'll have us killed. Or find some *use* for us."

Nic edged off the bed and went to join Opi by the window. The city of Helike looked peaceful from such a high tower on the castle hill. Nic could see waves breaking against the shore and people as small as mice crawling along the streets.

At least my cell has a view.

"What happened to the book, Opi?"

"She has it," Opi confirmed. "They don't know I saw her."

Nic let himself smile for the first time in days. He put his hand on Opi's.

"Then who knows what'll happen? We aren't the only people seeking to uncover the truth."

Chapter 33

Melani

The girl was shaking harder than before; tears flowed from her green eyes and dripped to the floor.

Mother?

Melani took a step towards her, kneeling once more to face the child. For the millionth time, Melani wished Xander were with her.

He's so gentle with children.

"Aw, don't cry, sweet girl. Here, do you need a hug?"

Melani crossed her legs and motioned for the girl to approach. She did, slowly. Her legs quaked as she got close, and she collapsed into Melani's lap, sobbing in silence. Melani touched her hair lightly.

"What's upsetting you? There's nothing to fear!"

Where did she come from?

356

For a few minutes, nothing was said. Melani let the girl cry. She looked up at Melani, chewing on the neck of her robe. She hoped her own child would be as cute.

"You're a precious little thing, aren't you?"

The girl didn't respond. Instead, she moved her hand next to Melani's, admiring the difference in sizes. Melani laughed, holding her palm up.

"Yes, I've got big monster hands, don't I?"

The girl giggled, sniffling, and placed her tiny hand on Melani's.

Will this be what it's like? To have one of my own?

Melani's palm began to warm.

A rush went through her suddenly. It felt as if a cold wind had entered her bloodstream. She gasped, instinctively pulling away from the child. But the girl followed her movement, keeping her hand pressed against Melani's palm.

"What... what are you—"

The room disappeared. Melani yelped, but her voice was silent. She looked down at her body, expecting to see the torn clothes, exposed skin, and dirt that she currently wore. Instead, there was nothing.

Am I dreaming? Has any of this been real? No... I must have fallen asleep... or... something's hit me in the head...

A wave splashed against a rocky shore. Melani examined her surroundings. She was by the ocean – that much was clear. She could see water in three directions. Small cliffs, dotted with caves and outcrops, jutted from the sea. Above her head, seagulls circled in a cloudless sky.

Where am I?

She floated upwards, summiting one of the cliffs. A flat, dusty expanse greeted her. The rock was barren, aside from a few shrubs and spiky grasses. Four children stood in a circle, playing a game with sticks and a hoop. The oldest had a face that looked to be eight or nine years of age, but he was tall and bulky enough to be several years older. He monitored a toddling girl with hazel curls, who chased the two middle children.

"Careful! Hey, watch her, you two!"

The two in question were a few years younger than the tall boy. They were quite engaged in their game, though the rules were completely unclear. One was a wiry girl who looked nearly identical to the child in Melani's house. She whacked the other, an equally thin blonde boy. As Melani floated closer, the children began to look up.

Can they see me? I can't even see myself!

"Mother!" The girl dropped her stick. "I win, Cy. Mother's home now."

A slender woman walked past Melani, holding a tiny bundle in her pale arms. Her long red hair fluttered in the wind.

"She brought something home! What is it, Mother?" the blonde child asked, rushing forward to get a better look at the form beneath the pile of blankets.

The scene dissipated, and Melani was transported to a cave,

where the same four children dined with their mother, the woman with red hair. This time, however, they were joined by a fifth child.

The girl!

She was slightly younger, but it was undoubtedly the same girl. They ate merrily, the two middle children jostling for a position next to their mother.

"Just sit next to Maya, Ivy," the oldest boy said, pointing to the open chair next to the fifth child.

The little girl beamed at the sound of her name, and the wiry girl, Ivy, sat next to her.

Maya... her name is Maya.

The cave dissolved, and suddenly, Melani was in the woods, face to face with a bear. Maya and her sister, Ivy, trembled. A shaggy-haired man leapt between them.

Then, she was inside a farmhouse. The same man sat with Maya on his knee, talking to an old man and woman. The room darkened, and Melani saw all five children sprawled on the ground, while the old man and woman scrambled around, trying to wake them.

What's happened to them? Are they okay?

The scene shifted one last time. Melani saw Maya racing across a pasture, while the farmhouse burned behind her. A woman with a tight bun was subduing the blonde boy and hazel-haired girl. The old woman was draped over a wagon like a dirty rag.

"Run, Maya! Run!" the girl with hazel hair screeched.

Maya wore the same linen robe, smeared with dirt. She panted and cried, looking back at her siblings as if she longed to go back for them. But a man was hard on her heels, his eyes filled with rage.

He's going to catch her!

Just as the assailant was about to catch Maya, a small pop sounded, and the little girl disappeared.

✳✳✳✳

When Melani's room returned, she was breathless, but strangely calm. Maya took her hand away and looked at Melani expectantly. The residue of her tears blotted her cheeks.

"Maya... that's your name, right? Maya?"

She nodded. In Melani's lap, Maya looked like any other child. There was nothing abnormal about her eyes or hair – any of her features.

But she's not normal, is she...?

"How did you do that, Maya? That was *your* life, wasn't it? How did you..."

Her voice trailed off. She was frightened. But Maya didn't seem malevolent. She was just a sweet young girl.

They're real... like the ones in Helike...

"You're a magician. A little sorceress... I thought–"

I thought your kind didn't exist.

Melani knew she should have been more disconcerted. A

magician was in her house. She had shown her pieces of her own memory. And the first vision... the one of her as a bundle in her mother's arms... that couldn't have even been her *own* memory. It should have frightened Melani more than it did – that would have been the logical response.

But how can I be scared of someone so innocent?

Maya studied Melani's face, trying to mimic her facial expressions.

"You're frightened, aren't you? Of those two people... the two you showed me. The ones at the farm. That's why you came here. You had to run away."

Maya nodded solemnly.

"Oh, sweet thing... your family! Those people took them. Who are they? Where did they take them... oh..."

Melani remembered how Tarlen had described the Children of the Sea. He had joked that they may have even practiced magic – a crazy thought, to be sure. But they had also been violent.

What could they have done with Maya's family? Her brothers and sisters?

Maya shook her head, covering her eyes with her tiny hands.

I'm going to be a great parent, aren't I?

Oh, no. Maya, I shouldn't have... I can help you find them! Would you want that?"

Maya shook her head again, more vigorously this time. She pointed at Melani, then tapped her head.

What does she want?

"What do you mean? Do you need my help?"

I can't leave here again... not if Xander is nearby. I'm so close to him. I can't lose him now!

Melani heard her front door creak. Maya flinched, startled by the noise. She shrunk back into the corner.

She's scared. The man and woman from the farm – they must be looking for her!

Melani drew herself to her feet, grabbing the wine. If anyone tried to take to the girl, they could expect a bottle shattered against their head.

Heavy footsteps pounded into the house. Melani slunk through the kitchen, ready to strike. The person rounded the corner.

"Thal!" a harsh whisper called. "Get out of their house!"

The chubby kid leapt into the kitchen, arms outstretched.

"Melani! Mellll-ah-neeeee!!"

Melani lowered the bottle. She couldn't hide the smile that broke across her face. She pulled her chiton over her exposed breast quickly, wishing she had changed clothes.

"Thal! She's not here!"

The voice of Loren came closer, and bony arms sprang to catch Thal. Loren froze. Her long healer's robe swept in behind her, covering Thal. He burst forth and raced to Melani.

"Oh," Loren said in surprise. She noticed the dirt that coated Melani before adding contemptuously, "You're home."

Wonderful.

Melani ruffled Thal's ginger curls.

"Yes, Loren. I'm home."

"And what is with your... uncouth appearance."

"I thought it looked good."

Thal beamed at his mother, pointing at Melani as if Loren hadn't noticed the only other person in the room.

Loren huffed, "Well. We shouldn't have barged into your home like this, without any warning for you to... clean up. We should leave you to your painting. There must be more work to do now that Xander is... away."

"Thal! I lost my favorite paintbrush under the couch in the other room! Would you look for it? I could use it to paint a little warrior!"

The boy bobbed his head and sprinted back to the entrance, searching desperately for the prized possession. Melani glared at Loren once they were alone.

"What do you know about Xander? I swear to the gods, Loren, I've been through more in the last two weeks than you have in your entire life. If you're just playing petty games to get under my skin...." She lifted the wine bottle. "I've had enough of your shit."

Loren blinked, "Melani... what has become of you?"

"Loren!" she snapped.

"He was taken by Sir Farlen, Melani! I thought you knew! Helike... they took over the city – well, Boura surrendered. Honestly, Melani... I thought you knew. Xander... he's one of the soldiers from the beach."

"So! What does that have to do with anything? It's over, isn't it? There's peace, then! If we surrendered!"

Loren's face was flush with embarrassment. When she spoke, it was full of worry, as it had been before their quarrel began.

"It was one of the conditions, Melani. Of Boura's surrender. The soldiers from the beach – the prisoners – they're getting sent somewhere... to win their freedom... or... oh, I forget, I'm so sorry! I thought..."

"Get out," Melani growled.

Loren lifted the hem of her robe and hurried out, grabbing Thal's arm as she went.

"But I haven't found the paintbrush! Melani!!" he protested.

Loren didn't respond. She pulled her son through the door and let it slam shut behind her.

Melani stumbled to the water basin and threw up. She dropped to one knee.

No. Prisoner! When I was just there... and he's being sent somewhere! Oh, Xander... I've failed. I've failed you.

She pulled herself up to throw up again and began to sob, leaning against the basin for support.

What will I do? How can I raise this child without you, Xander!

Melani was light-headed. The thought of Xander in the cells below Helike, about to be sent off to fight a battle in the name of a new alliance, was making her sick. Or was it the baby? She fell to the ground, wiping vomit from her mouth and uncorking the bottle of wine.

Maya shuffled through the door. Melani realized she'd almost forgotten about the little girl. She took a drink of the wine, wetting her dry throat.

This girl's gone through just as much as me. More.

"I'm sorry, Maya. I promise you that I don't usually act like this."

The girl kneeled in front of Melani, patting her thigh gently.

"We need to get you to your family, don't we?"

How will I do that and save Xander? How can I possibly do both when I couldn't even do one?

Maya blinked, then pointed at Melani.

"Xander."

"What? How do you…"

She must have overheard my conversation with Loren.

"Xander," Maya repeated, letting her hand rest on Melani's leg.

Once again, Melani watched her kitchen disappear, until all she could see were dark walls and thick iron bars.

A cell!

Next to her, a broad-shouldered man with sandy hair shifted. There were two others in the small cell, making the space extremely cramped. The man turned his head away from his cellmates, seeking some sort of comfortable sleeping position. And she was able to see his face for the first time.

It had only been a few weeks, but Melani's heart leapt from

her chest at the sight of his kind eyes and the sunspot on his hand.

Xander! My love!

The cells brightened until Melani was on the deck of a massive trireme, standing in the middle of hundreds of oarsmen. She recognized Xander's muscular back, hard at work as he rowed alongside the other soldiers.

They're already on their way... where are they going? Where can I find them!?

Seconds later, Melani was back on the floor of her kitchen, clutching a bottle of wine and covered with dirt and vomit. Maya smiled at her and nodded.

How does she do that?

"He's already gone, isn't he, Maya? What can I do? I don't even know where he's going!"

Maya trundled away, searching for something in Melani's bedroom. After a moment, she returned, holding a scroll that Xander kept by his bedside. She unraveled it, revealing a map of Achaea and all the surrounding territories. The sea extended all the way to Egypt and Persia. Maya pointed to a small island. Melani squinted to read the small text.

"Thera?" Melani asked.

That's the middle of the sea!

Maya nodded with excitement. Melani opened her mouth to respond once again. There was no way the little girl could know where Xander was being taken. Then again...

"I can't go to Thera, Maya."

I want to... but I would just fail him once more.

"We need to get you to your family."

Maya shook her head, faster than ever before. Her eyes filled with fear.

"Oh.... They're looking for you. That man and that woman."

Maya nodded sadly. She balled her tiny fists, then released them in resignation. The girl wanted to pursue her siblings just as much as Melani wanted to find Xander. Something was giving her pause, however. Certainly, she was cautious about the two magicians who were searching for her. But there was more.

"What do you want me to do, Maya? How can I help you?"

Maya looked at Melani.

Such pretty green eyes.

She lifted her tiny index finger... and pointed to the island of Thera.

Chapter 34

Simon

The Great Hall of Olenus was eerie in its emptiness. Simon felt miniscule in the vast atrium, standing before rows of vacant pews. There were only two guards present, though Simon knew more were at the ready. Before him, King Basilius sat in his regal throne, adorned by his crown with its ruby eye. His himation was bronze today, rather than silver, inlaid with onyx. Venedictos and Eté sat on either side of him.

Must we keep these formalities?

Simon had waited for hours in his guest room. He'd enjoyed a small meal early in the day but found his appetite scant. Basilius had entertained hundreds of citizens before Eté retrieved Simon.

Splendid murals decorated the wall. Simon hadn't focused on them the day prior.

Directly behind the throne, a depiction of Lethaea and her husband, Olenus, showed the couple petrified atop Mount Ida. The story was vaguely familiar to Simon – Lethaea had declared herself more beautiful than some goddess, and for that, she was turned to stone. He couldn't recall why Olenus had been likewise doomed.

"Councilor Simon," King Basilius began. "I believe my faithful Eté has given you an idea of why I wished to meet with you today."

The king stroked his thick beard. His hair matched the onyx on his himation.

"That is correct, your majesty. It would seem you have devised a plan for our two cities to unite."

I must be careful in my approach today.

"Yes, after thorough discussion with Eté, I see the value of an alliance between our two cities."

"It would be in both of our best interests," Eté added, nodding at Simon with encouragement.

"Yes. Olenus alone could conquer all the western cities of Achaea…"

And planned to.

"…as Helike could do in the East. But together – together, we can bring the League more glory than even the Athenians had. A power to rival that of the Persians, the Spartans… anyone that could stand in our way!"

Eté's thin mustache curved as he smiled.

"That is correct, my king. And I believe our wise councilor understands this."

Simon picked at his fingernails.

I understand the power you desire. But will you be able to share it with others?

"Of course... the joined might of Helike and Olenus would be... significant. With your city's wealth and Helike's population, the League would be ours."

Ours... not yours.

"However, I worry about resistance from our brothers and sisters across Achaea. It could become violent."

Basilius rolled his eyes. Venedictos opened his mouth to respond, but Eté cut in. The former's face darkened.

"Yes, there will always be destruction during shifts in a regime. However, you know the alternative could be much bloodier. You told me yourself that Gaios would have his wars if it meant a unified Achaea. An accord would be prudent. No... it would be necessary."

Simon could see that Basilius was convinced. Venedictos would not speak against his king's wishes, either. The deal was as good as done.

Why am I so reluctant to finalize it? This is what I sought when I left Helike! A peaceable solution.

Eté's dark skin seemed to shimmer as his smile widened.

"Necessary... yes, perhaps you are correct. I believe the League *will* be more harmonious with a more central power."

Simon began to pace.

"Our twelve territories could find unprecedented peace. There is no need for war. I'll bring this to my fellow councilors... I'm sure some agreement could be reached."

King Basilius clapped, and Venedictos readied his hands to do the same. But Eté spoke, and the applause ceased before he could begin.

Is Eté always so purposefully cruel to the other advisor?

"Yes, war is always a tragedy. Though, I hear the war involving your city has ended."

"It has?" Simon asked, astonished.

Eté nodded. "Indeed. So, you may have to convince the old Bouran King of this idea, as well as your councilors."

What sort of treaty was arranged?

Venedictos sneered, "When did you receive this news!? Why is this the first my king and I are hearing about it?"

Eté chuckled at Venedictos' annoyance.

"It doesn't change any of the plans that King Basilius and *I* have generated. Helike and Olenus could still–"

"Don't act as if this was some sort of mistake, Eté!" Venedictos' chin wobbled as he interrupted. "I know you withhold information from me... from our king! This is not–"

"Silence, Venedictos!" Basilius snapped. "I'll have none of this squabbling in front of a guest! Especially one with whom a deal has been reached!"

Eté grinned. He had known this fresh bit of information would perturb Venedictos.

The two hate each other. How many countless offenses has

Été committed against Venedictos in the years they've worked together?

"I do apologize if anything I've said has upset you, dear advisor."

"You quiet yourself, too, Été! You know that Venedictos..."

"That I what? Am left out of decisions that could benefit our city!" Venedictos stood, wagging his finger to the other two men.

He paused, then quickly sat down. There was shock in his eyes, as if he had acted against his own best judgement. He looked down at his swollen hands.

"Apologies, my king... I don't know what came over me. My partner... well sometimes he can..."

The king's nostrils flared. Simon backed away from the altar, not sure why the discussion had soured so rapidly. Été wore a mask of false concern.

I can't leave this room with the king in a rage! He'll turn to violence if we don't make peace now... I need this!

"My friends," Simon said shyly, before raising his voice. "My friends! Might we... finish? I–"

"*You* should stay out of this conversation, Flat-Nose," Basilius said. "It does not concern you."

Simon shrunk back to one of the pews. The king turned his attention to Venedictos, whose face was a mixture of rage and embarrassment. The advisor looked at the floor in resignation.

The empty court seemed to magnify the silence. Simon stared at the frescoed wall, clutching the inside of his robe.

"My king, I should have you know that I never wished to cause any problems. Especially today, with such an honored guest in our midst," Eté said.

Basilius didn't respond. He continued to glower at Venedictos.

"But, don't judge my dear Venedictos too harshly. I know his mind has been distracted by other matters of late... the closure of his favorite brothel, for instance."

Venedictos leapt to his feet, slavering, "You... you *minute* man! Yyyyou *CRAVEN!*"

Basilius lifted his arm to stop his enraged advisor, but the man plowed past. Eté didn't move; instead he clapped once. The two guards rushed forward. Venedictos slid to a stop, his hands raised.

"Guards, please. This is a mis—"

It happened before Simon could react. The first guard reached the altar and plunged his spear into Venedictos' belly without pause. Eté laughed and rose from his chair, stepping sideways while the second drew a dagger.

"What have you done!" King Basilius roared.

He made to jump from his throne but found himself face-to-face with the second guard.

"Eté! What have—"

King Basilius looked to be somewhat of a warrior. He would have towered above the guard if he had been standing, and he certainly had the body of a man who could handle a weapon.

However, slouched in his throne, he was defenseless. The dagger raked across the king's neck. Simon could only watch as the king and his advisor slumped. Their blood pooled together in a horrifying medley on the altar.

Simon covered his mouth with his hands and fell into the walkway between the benches. He backed away hastily.

"Where do you think you're going, friend?" Eté said, pointing at the guards that had joined at both entrances to the hall.

"Eté... wha– why? What did you do!?"

Eté strode to the front of the benches, where Simon had previously stood. Behind him, the bodies of King Basilius and Venedictos gave the regal hall a ghastly appearance.

"*I* did nothing. These loyal soldiers," he indicated the men that surrounded him, "Seem to have ended our king's life! Or... perhaps it was Venedictos. Yes, it appears that Venedictos flew into a rage and stabbed the king with a hidden blade. He was about to provide me with the same grisly fate, when our brave guards put an end to his bloodlust."

He walked closer to Simon. "Or, even more terrible... a foreign councilor paid two guards to carry out the deed. Perhaps he even did it himself."

Simon sidestepped into one of the bench rows. He shuffled through, trying to put as much distance between himself and the advisor. Eté's dark skin seemed to be glowing.

A trick of the light... it must be.

"Eté... you don't have to... you're the lone power in Olenus now. Join with me and Helike! We can bring the League together... you said it yourself... we can conquer the whole region. Peacefully!"

Eté stopped. He closed his eyes and inhaled deeply.

"Peacefully... you see, Simon... it's not the League that I want. Power is not what I yearn for in this world... I–"

The sound of a body falling made Eté's head snap to the grand entryway. The guard was facedown, his spear clattered to the floor. Simon tensed.

I need to get out... I need to leave now.

The two guards leveled their spears at the entrance. Eté squinted.

He doesn't know who it is either... this isn't part of his plan.

Simon slipped quietly from the pew as the distraction continued. Seconds passed. He slowed his breathing.

If I can just...

Out of the hallway, a woman approached. Her red hair looked to be aflame, as the torches glowed behind her.

Who...?

She was pale. Even from afar, Simon could see a strange white scar on her upper lip. In her right hand, she clutched a bloodstained knife.

Eté's eyes widened. Rope leapt up his calves, and the advisor fell to his knees.

Where did those come from!?

"Father!" the woman yelled.

She charged towards Eté, her linen robe flowing. She closed her fist and his hands were suddenly bound.

A huge smile broke over Eté's face. His skin was definitely

shimmering now, lightening and oscillating until it was as pale as the woman's. In his bonds, the man laughed, growing taller and blonder. His eyes turned a piercing shade of purple, flecked with yellow spots.

Simon tiptoed backwards in a trance. He felt a rough hand as another guard rushed in from a side hallway. Simon dodged out of reach and began to run towards the entryway. However, he couldn't take his eyes off the scene. Eté had *changed*. His skin, his hair... his mustache....

He was an entirely different man.

When he responded, his voice was no longer rough. Instead, it was sweet and smooth.

"Daughter. It seems my Children let you out of their sight... what a surprise."

The ropes that bound Eté caught flame and disappeared.

No. It can't be... they're doing... their kind is gone....

Simon was transfixed. But he knew that if he stayed any longer, it would certainly be the end of him. He dashed from the guard to the open entrance, ignoring the temptation to look back as the two pale magicians spoke.

He tried to wrap his head around the past few minutes. Eté... or *whoever* he was, had stood, laughing as King Basilius and Venedictos were murdered. The red-haired sorceress had come... his own daughter, if that could be believed.

Are they Children of the Sea? Was I talking and dealing with one this whole time?

Simon almost tripped over the body of a castle guardsmen, who groaned softly. His stomach turned over, and he burst into the courtyard. More guards were flopped in the yard, shaded by cypress trees and flowering plants.

The woman... she must have done this. She must have.

Nobody stopped him as he raced through the city. He picked up a hat as he went to cover his face. He'd forgotten how it felt to run like this.

It's been years since I fled the scene of a brutal murder.

He slowed to a walk as he approached the city gates, falling in line with merchants and farmers who were leaving for the evening, blissfully unaware of the chaos that would surely ensue in the coming days.

Simon did not check to see if he was being followed; he did not turn around. He passed Lucel's inn, and finally found her. Athena – the pure black mare.

It's a miracle she remains here.

He mounted the horse, ignoring everything in his surroundings. There was too much to think about; he couldn't stop moving. He couldn't start considering the truth of what he had just seen.

It can't be real... it can't.

As the city walls faded from view, Simon pressed Athena harder into the dusk. He could still see the two magicians, facing each other, their bodies emitting the most mysterious energy.

I have to go back. I have to return to Helike and warn them of what I've seen! They're back. They're real.

He tried to erase the image of Basilius and Venedictos, draped across the altar in a bloody argument. He focused on the mural behind them, of Lethaea and Olenus, frozen in stone.

He almost laughed, as he finally recalled the story.

He insisted on sharing the blame for her hubris. He couldn't leave her to perish... and he was punished for eternity.

Simon looked at the road ahead, feeling Athena's legs working furiously onward. How long would it take him to reach Helike? What would await him when he returned?

And here I am. Like Olenus atop Mount Ida... unable to relinquish myself from Lethaea.

Chapter 35

Keoki

The trade road was a winding dirt path, snaking past small villages from Leontio. Most of the region was wooded and hilly. They traveled along the outskirts of Ceryneia, a large city, though not one of the major Achaean territories.

Keoki had always wanted to go to Ceryneia to see the magnificent statue of the Ceryneian Hind – a huge, antlered creature that Heracles defeated during his labors.

Father must have told me that story hundreds of times... it was my favorite.

Kalypso had taken their wagon past the monument. It was nothing special.

"The Moonspawn would have been gentle with the Golden Hind, I'm sure. Unlike that barbarian, Heracles... he knew nothing of our woodlands."

Keoki had taken the compliment. He was growing more comfortable with his new, strange title. The Moonspawn in Leontio could come and go from the city as they pleased. In return, they maintained a peace between Leontians and the vast wilderness.

They walk the forest all day... and the Leontians revere them.

Moonspawn could always find rooms, food, and wine in Leontio. They were never expected to pay. The sustained peace between their city and Artemis' realm was enough for the Leontians. Of course, he had only learned this from Kalypso *after* they'd left the city.

I would have been tempted to stay.

However, the safety of Fil and Agnes was paramount. Kalypso drove her mules at a fast clip; Keoki was fairly confident he could beat Sapphir to the farm. At least, it would be close.

Especially if she traveled on foot.

His leg, ribs, and shoulder ached ceaselessly from the hunt, but Asklepia's healing draught dulled the pain well. He was careful to apply just enough to ease his discomfort. Relief could not come at the expense of his wits.

"See, Moonspawn? The city of Helike is not far. Where shall I direct the mules?"

Keoki recognized the surroundings. The morning dew clung to the grass that surrounded them. If they continued along the road for another stadion, his farm would be at the crest of the hills to their right.

"Stay on the road. I'll let you know when to stop."

Kalypso nodded her shaven head and kept their pace. Keoki enjoyed the trader's company. She was stoic, commenting only to describe their surroundings. The men and women she dealt with seemed to respect her; it was clear that nobody shortchanged Kalypso.

The healing draught kept Keoki relatively quiet as well. He wondered if his ramblings would have bothered Kalypso.

Sapphir hates them.

"This will do," Keoki said, minutes later when they reached a patch of wildflowers that marked Fil and Agnes' farm.

Kalypso pulled on the reins. "An easy ride, was it not, Moonspawn?"

"Very easy. Thanks, Kalypso. It would've been tough to walk all this way on my ankle."

"There is no reason to thank a Leontian for assisting the Moonspawn. It is an honor we give to Artemis!"

Well then... thank you, Artemis!

The mules slowed to a stop, huffing in exhaustion. They needed the break that awaited them in Helike. Keoki grunted as he shifted his weight, pushing himself from the seat beside Kalypso. Asklepia had fashioned a solid oak cane, which supported his weight nicely.

Keoki took a few steps, leaning heavily on his cane. He was pleased to find that his wounds didn't pain him too much.

Thank the gods for Asklepia.

"Well... good luck in Helike," Keoki said.

Kalypso held her hand out to Keoki stiffly. He shook it.

"Leontio will wait eagerly for your return, Moonspawn."

She flicked the reins, and the mules' hooves clopped onward. Keoki watched as the muscular woman disappeared behind a curve in the road, her supply of furs dwindled from a day of trading.

She's a capable woman. Probably makes good coin in Helike.

Had Agnes ever dealt with Kalypso? Perhaps she gave her cheese and wine in exchange for a warm winter's coat. He'd be sure to ask. Agnes would certainly remember Kalypso; the Leontian had a very memorable look.

Keoki hobbled past the wildflowers.

Io would like these.

The hill was steeper than he would have preferred. But this was the fastest way. Keoki would emerge behind the farmhouse.

The early autumn morning was cool and comfortable. He couldn't wait to enjoy a breakfast made by Agnes. Perhaps it would be fruit and porridge. That sounded best to Keoki. His cane sunk slightly into the fertile ground as he approached the purple grapes.

I'll steal a couple to whet my appetite a little.

When Keoki knelt to pick a particularly juicy one, his ankle stung. He reached for Asklepia's mixture, then paused.

I need my mind functioning properly.

He clenched his teeth, trying to ignore the ailing ankle. The farm seemed peaceful enough. But Sapphir could have already arrived; or maybe she was only minutes away. He needed to prepare for a fight. He prayed it would not come to that.

I can calm her down... before she does anything foolish. Or cruel.

He made his way past the grapes, listening for distant moos, or the sound of the children playing in the field. A breeze rustled the vines. Keoki's hand was warm and slick against his cane.

I have to be ready.

At last, the farmhouse came into view. Keoki sighed in relief. He was home. He could find Fil and Agnes – make sure they were okay.

But something was wrong.

The roof... why does it look like that?

Keoki limped quicker. He squinted, trying to make sure his eyes were not playing a trick on him.

No... was I too late? How could I have been too late!

The roof was blackened and burned. Keoki noticed matted grass where the cattle had been.

No... no, what did she do?

The hoofprints told Keoki that the cows had been running.

Something scared them.

Keoki broke into a run, ignoring the screams from his wounded ankle. He reached the back of the burned house. The door was ajar. He was nearly blind from pain.

Only one thing was still clear.

Kalypso traveled fast... but the sorceress was faster.

ΤΗΕ CΗILDREN OF ΤΗΕ SEA

****

They were lying in the field on the opposite side of the farmhouse.

Keoki stood inside. It was empty, save for a few ants that marched across the countertops. They held breadcrumbs triumphantly.

The children were gone.

Something had burned holes in the roof, causing it to cave in above the kitchen. Chairs were knocked over, and some of the cupboards were askew. A clay dish lay in shards by the table.

And in the soft grass visible from the kitchen window, they lay, side-by-side.

No...

Keoki walked in a trance through the open door. He held his cane tightly in both hands, putting all his weight on both feet. The pain in his ankle was meaningless.

What did she do!

Keoki reached them in seconds. He fell to his knees, his shaggy hair hanging over his face. He brushed it to one side.

It can't be them. It can't be.

But their faces were too familiar. The old man's arm was draped over his wife, shielding her from some unknown threat. Agnes' jet-black hair was disheveled.

She'd never allow that.

Keoki straightened it. Their eyes were closed peacefully. Keoki knew then, that Felip must have outlived his wife.

She wouldn't have closed her eyes. She would've glared at her killer... right until the end.

His jaw began to quiver. He slumped over the two bodies, longing for the warmth that usually radiated from Felip and the ferocity that made Agnes so dear to him.

There was only cold.

It couldn't have been Sapphir! She wouldn't... she would have taken their memories... or... she wouldn't have–

Keoki couldn't convince himself. He'd seen Sapphir deal with those she regarded as her enemies. Remorseless.

But Fil and Agnes... they weren't her enemies! The children loved them! Just like they loved me!

"It's my fault. I told them... why did I tell them?"

She must have snapped. All the hatred and evil she'd brought to the world must have finally caught up to her. She'd run from it for too long.

Now she's accepted it. She's embraced it.

After several minutes, Keoki pushed himself to his feet. His shoulder and ribs throbbed, and his ankle hurt more than either. Keoki looked at the sky and growled.

"Why, Poseidon? Why is it... that every time..."

He snapped his cane in half, screaming at the pain – all the pain. He wished his foot would fall off.

"I should never have gone with that witch! One of your *Children!*"

The god of the sea gave no response. Keoki threw his cane aside and uncorked Asklepia's potion. The scent of the strange mountain flower was nauseating. Keoki ripped his tunic until his ribs and shoulder were both visible. He upended the bottle, feeling the warm oil and crushed flower ooze over him. He gritted his teeth as the formula soaked into the wrapping on his ankle.

When the potion was nearly spent, he opened his mouth and poured the remains down his throat. It clung to the roof of his mouth and numbed his esophagus.

"Is that it, then?" he yelled at the sky, coughing, "Is that all I can do!?"

Fire swept through his body as the healing draught overcame him. Keoki staggered, staring at Fil and Agnes in disbelief.

"She did this, didn't she?"

His head spun, and he fell to a seated position. He reached out to rest his hand on them.

Mother? Hello, Mother? Father? Shouldn't you come talk to me now? I'm ready for both of you.

For some reason, he was unable to conjure them. Were they merely a product of his addled imagination?

I need you both now! Please.

Fil and Agnes sprawled at his side, as his parents had so many years before. He tried flicking his wounded ankle. Nothing happened. No pain.

He felt nothing.

"It was the Children once; it was the Children again. One Child this time," he mused, almost laughing at the tragic irony. "But I trusted this one, didn't I?"

He coughed, keeling over. His throat still buzzed from swallowing the mysterious flower. He pressed his face against the damp grass. A ladybug strutted past his glazed eyes.

It didn't have any spots. It was only red.

"Red, red, red. I hate red."

His heartbeat was too slow.

"Where'd you take your children? Back to your island. Back to the sea... that's where the Children go."

He reached for Asklepia's draught, before remembering that the bottle was already empty. He closed his eyes – maybe if he awoke from this dream, he could go tend to the cattle in the morning. Fil would have him help with the grapes, and Agnes would bring some fresh cow's milk into Helike. She would return later with rumors from Philomena.

Had she ever traded with Kalypso?

"What rumors do you have today?" Keoki asked Agnes.

She kept her eyes closed, tranquil in the arms of her loving husband. Keoki cried.

"No rumors anymore. No wine. No cows."

The rising sun made the clouds shimmer, forming dozens of rainbows in the morning sky. Keoki stared up at them. His eyes burned.

He closed them. His head spun. In the days to come, he would have to endure the agony without anything to satiate it.

It will heal with time. My body will heal.

Keoki's mind drifted further from consciousness. He knew his ribs, shoulder, and ankle would recover. Sapphir would have been able to fix it with a flick of her wrist. But he could manage it on his own.

The ladybug stopped in front of Keoki. Then it fluttered away.

Red. Red hair. She has red hair.

His body would heal. It would just take time.

As for his heart and mind, Keoki needed Sapphir. He pictured himself on the island, facing the sorceress.

She was once so enchanting.

He was facing her. And she was facing him.

Her red hair mingled with his wild curls.

He could picture it so clearly.

And in that image, they were both dead.

Chapter 36

Sapphir

Sapphir knew she was in the wrong place as soon she entered the sandstone prison.

He diverted me... somehow.

Gripping her silver knife tighter, she raced back outside. Her chest heaved as she sprinted past the grisly bodies of the fallen guards.

The doors to the palace were plated with gold, surrounded by an archway with gold and ivory. Sapphir pushed them open.

I should have known... Father wouldn't deprive himself of such luxuries.

Soldiers stood on either side of a fine velvet carpet. They both tensed, readying their spears. Looks of surprise were stamped beneath their half-helms.

"The palace is–"

Sapphir didn't let the man finish. She waved three fingers, and the men collapsed, their faces pressed against the royal carpet.

The rug led through a dim hallway with three torches on each wall and revealed a spectacular courtroom. Sapphir's head pounded; she knew her father was here – inside the palace. The Great Hall was blocked by another guard. As Sapphir crept forward, however, she could tell he faced the same direction as her. His eyes were focused on something inside the courtroom. She strained to listen.

"Eté... you don't have to... you're the lone power in Olenus now. Join with me and Helike! We can bring the League together... You said it yourself... we can conquer the whole region. Peacefully!"

The voice had a nasal quality. It was vaguely familiar to Sapphir.

Helike... this man is from Helike! What does he mean? Conquer the League?

A second voice, presumably Eté's, responded.

"Peacefully... You see Simon... it's not the League that I want."

The speaker had a graveled tone. But Sapphir knew she had found him.

It's not sweet like your old voice... but I know your inflection – the way you hold your words... the way you drizzle them over people.

The silver knife in Sapphir's hand was nearly glowing from the heat coursing through her body. The Blood of the Golden Age had never flooded through her as intensely as it did in that moment. The only thing standing between Sapphir and her revenge was a single soldier.

Sapphir clenched her jaw, picturing her five children suffering and confused. She jabbed the blade in the guard's exposed waist.

"Power is not what I yearn for in this world... I–"

The guard grunted and fell. His spear clattered against the floor, echoing around the courtroom. Sapphir leapt over him and raised her hand.

"Father!"

Ropes lashed around his legs and hands. Sapphir nearly lost focus when she finally noticed his appearance. His skin was dark, rather than pale; his eyes were not their usual shade of purple.

This must be Eté.

Recognition dawned over Teremos' face, and his false mustache twisted into a smile. His form began to shimmer, and he rose in height. His eyes brightened until they were a deep purple, with yellow flecks. Eté's bald head sprouted blonde hair.

"Daughter. It seems my Children let you out of their sight... what a surprise."

His voice had recaptured its normal sweet quality. The binding Sapphir had conjured turned to flames and disappeared. Sapphir was so intent on reaching her father, that she barely noticed the rest of the court.

Rows of benches were positioned before an altar, which

contained a regal throne. Two men lay sprawled at the foot of the throne, their blood mingling. A bald man with a rather flat nose dashed from one of the pews, making for the entrance with haste.

The man from Helike.

"Ah, Daughter, now my guest has left."

Sapphir snarled, lifting her hands so the benches beside her father rose from the ground. Their wooden legs snapped, and Sapphir flung them at the blonde man.

He didn't even seem to react. His smile twitched, and the benches disintegrated.

"You have grown into a capable sorceress. Come with me, Daughter. End these foolish games."

Sapphir screamed in frustration, and fire erupted from her hands. The flames washed over her father, but he simply closed his eyes and inhaled.

When the blaze dissipated, he was unhurt.

"Speak with me, Sapphir. There is no need for these pointless spells. Everything you know..."

I've learned from you.

"I'm not here to talk, Father," she spat.

Teremos took a step towards her, curling his hand into a fist. Sapphir felt cold iron clamp around her slender arms. When she looked, there was nothing there. But soon her ankles and wrists were held fast.

"Ah, yes. You are here to kill me, is that it?"

Sapphir closed her eyes, trying to focus on breaking free from the chains. All she could see were the faces of her children.

"What did you do to them?"

Teremos stopped approaching.

"Your children? I merely... reminded them of who they are."

Sapphir felt like crying. No spells came to her mind – no ideas. She was a red-haired girl again, standing before her father... her face stinging from yet another slap.

"See for yourself."

No! I don't... I don't want to. I don't want to see what I've done to them.

The court of Olenus disappeared, and her children were sprawled on the floor of Felip and Agnes' farmhouse. She saw them awaken, cry for her, scream for each other... she could see the anguish in each of their faces... the realization that their mother had taken them from their homes.

"No... Father, no. How–"

"Did I find them? You should have never left your little island, Daughter. The further you moved from them, the easier it was for me to slip past your protective enchantments, and into their little minds... as soon as you made it to Olenus... into my cave."

I... I failed them.

"And..." she choked, "And if you've found them..."

"They are Children now, Sapphir. True Children. You can be with them again..."

Sapphir was almost tempted. She could live with them in the caves and catacombs of Olenus. She could restore the memory charms... convince them that she had only wished to protect them.

Can I even convince myself of that?

She looked at her father, tears welling in her blue eyes. The contorted smile remained on his angular face. It was an unfamiliar expression.

He never wore it with me... even when I could have been happy, when I was with Yusef...

...before I became broken.

"They will never be your Children, Father."

"And they were never yours."

Sapphir screamed once more, this time allowing the Blood of the Golden Age to curdle at her fury. She didn't think of an incantation, didn't try to recall any words.

The invisible chains responded to her emotions, melting away. She flung herself at her father, her silver dagger still glued to her right hand. Teremos cried out in surprise, catching her arms as he fell backwards to the floor.

Sapphir plunged the knife directly at his heart. Her father had just enough agility to twist his body. Instead of piercing his chest, Sapphir's dagger buried itself between his collarbone and shoulder.

Her father's earsplitting wail was the sweetest sound Sapphir had ever heard. She tried to extract the knife in order to deliver a second blow, but his pain turned to rage. She found herself thrown into the benches. Her back cracked against the wood.

"Enough!" he yelled, his honeyed voice now ragged. "That's

enough. I *have* your children. And I could have you, too. But if this is how you plan to treat me..."

"Then kill me, Father!"

He won't... he can't bring himself to do it. He needs me to see him fulfill the vision of Poseidon.

The blood stood out from Teremos' pale skin. His wound looked exceedingly painful. The silver knife was twisted from its original position but still stuck in his body. She had never seen him so unnerved.

He expected only magic from me... he doesn't know what I've become.

"Kill me!" Sapphir yelled, staggering to her feet.

Teremos' eyes appeared more yellow than usual. He sneered. The court of Olenus swirled into nothingness.

✳✳✳✳

Sapphir came to her senses on her hands and knees. She clambered to her feet, brushing the dust off her robe. The air was clean and tasted of salt. The sky was clear blue – the sound of the ocean, omnipresent.

I know this place.

She began to walk, taking care to recognize everything about the island. It was all the same. The three caves that made up her abode; the flat, dusty expanse where her children trained; the azure sea, only a short walk away.

I'm home.

Sapphir descended to the ocean. There was no sense in searching for her children in their caves. Teremos had them.

Sapphir wondered if this were simply a vision – some sort of dream forced upon her by her father. But the ground felt too real beneath her feet. The misty sea spray clung to her hair.

I'm here... I know I am.

She reached the rocky shore that Cy and Ivy loved so much. This was where they had taken Keoki fishing ages ago. This was where Celia had found Blackwing, her fishing osprey with the broken wing.

She adores it so.

Maya swam from here to other small beaches, ever searching for wildflowers to bring home to her mother.

Though... I'm not her mother, am I?

Saltwater tears melded with the sea. Sapphir wished, more than anything, that she could have her old life back – the one where her children played, and she took care of them... as any good mother would.

Sapphir leaned towards the water. She swirled her forefinger in the cool ocean, then removed it. She wanted to see the water dance.

Nothing happened.

She tried again, willing the sea to obey her, for the droplets to curl around her hand.

Come on!

The water remained as it was.

Sapphir kicked at it, splashing a spider crab in the process. It scuttled away in surprise. Sapphir focused on the creature; she could turn it into something prettier – perhaps a baby bird.

Once again, her blood did not awaken. She could feel no magical energy.

I'm... powerless.

Sapphir studied the horizon. It was closer than it should have been. The sky had a certain hazy quality that was quite unnatural.

Sapphir sat cross-legged. There was nothing more she could do. For some reason, known only to the gods and Teremos himself, Sapphir's life had been spared.

In return, her father had marooned her on her own island.

I've never come across such a spell before... all the way from Olenus.

He had enclosed her in an open prison.

And I will not be able to leave.

Sapphir watched the spider crab disappear into a hole.

"Now I understand why Keoki talked to your kind. To the animals. When nobody else is around... when there is no future to be had..."

Sapphir wondered where Keoki was. She hoped he had found his way home. Then again, what had become of the simple farmhouse on the outskirts of Helike? Would Keoki be safe there?

She assumed not. More than likely, Agnes and Felip had been

driven from their home by Teremos' Children.

Or worse...

She prayed it was not worse.

"Poseidon... please. Let Felip, Agnes, and Keoki be safe. Let them be at peace in their city."

She guessed Keoki had not reunited with his beloved farm family yet.

I pray they find each other.

As concerned as she was for Keoki, Felip, and Agnes, it was nothing compared to the worry she felt about her children. If she could have walked to Mount Olympus and spoken with the gods to ensure their safety, she would have.

I would even fight them for it.

"If my children have been harmed, Poseidon, there is no place you could hide where I would not find you."

She wished she could only blame the gods.

I shouldn't have left my children... no matter how much I wished to be rid of Father. I should never have let them from my sight.

Was it all her fault? Would her children have been better off without her?

Should I have just let them live their lives?

The thought of Ivy, Maya, Celia, Egan, and Cy, wandering the tunnels by Olenus made Sapphir sick.

Is that what they are now? Mindless Children, like Evens and Priam?

Sapphir gazed at the indistinct horizon. Her children were still alive; Sapphir was sure of that. Her father wouldn't give up such valuable prizes.

At the very least, that was a consolation.

What must they think of me? My sweet children.... Will they ever love me again?

She didn't know if Egan, Celia, Maya, Ivy, and Cy would ever call her their mother again. But that would not stop her from loving them.

Wherever you are, children... whatever you've become... I will find you. I'll get off this island... and I will finally set you free.

Chapter 37

Ivy

Ivy couldn't see anything but the back of a rough wool blindfold. It made her eyeballs itchy. She didn't know how long she'd been asleep. The last thing she could remember was... was...

They took me! Like Mother did.

The magicians had taken her and her siblings – all except Maya.

At least she escaped... at least she's safe.

Ivy closed her eyes; there was no use keeping them open. It was too dim for light to even sneak past the wool. She could tell from the way the air smelled that she was not outside. It was damp and stagnant.

Where have they taken me?

She could hear some sort of distant chanting. It was muffled, perhaps by walls. She tried to move her legs and found that they were restrained. So were her arms. Ivy wanted to cry.

I need Mother.

That confused her even more. Sapphir was not her mother. She was a sorceress who had taken her children and erased their memories. But she *had* cared for them.

She took me from my home. From my real parents... how could she have done that to us!

Yet, she knew Sapphir would have saved her from the magicians that had come to Fil and Agnes' farm, just as she had rescued her in the mountains.

The chanting stopped.

"Egan? Cy, Celia?" she whispered.

Am I alone?

Nobody responded. She heard a shifting from somewhere. It sounded like feet dragging across cold stone.

"H-hello..."

This time, a voice answered. It was the same smooth tone that had spoken to her in the strange temple.

"Callidora. I am so pleased to see that you have found your way home."

"Th-this isn't my home. I-I..."

I don't want to be Callidora... I want to be Ivy.

"Don't stutter, child. You should never show your fear."

This is Mother's father... my grandfather. Well... not really.

Ivy had to force herself not to stumble over her words.

"Where. Are. My. Brothers and sister."

"Your brothers? They're here with you. As is *one* of your sisters. The other... I fear she eludes us."

"What are you going to do to them?"

Warm hands touched her face, and Ivy flinched. She felt the blindfold slide off her eyes. He was taller than she remembered. Everything else was the same – purple eyes, blonde hair, lean. They were in a cave. Stalactites and stalagmites made it look like a mouth with jagged teeth. There was nobody else in the cave. Light filled the space beneath a door.

That must lead somewhere.

Ivy wore no physical restraints, but she was still unable to move.

"What am I going to do to *them*? The same thing that I'm going to do to *you*. I am going to help you reunite with your real Brothers and Sisters. My Children."

No... my real... Callidora's brother used to be in the big city! But Cy... and Celia....

"I... you're not my..."

"No, child. *We* are your family. My Children are your blood. The Blood of the Golden Age. You know this."

Ivy had no idea what to think. Her head still ached from the new memories. She couldn't decide whether to feel saddened, betrayed, or enraged – perhaps all three. And she didn't *know* her true family, even though she could now remember them.

She wanted to be with Celia and Cy, Maya and Egan. They

were the only ones who could understand her frustration.

"Take me to them, then! Show me the others are unharmed."

"You have a boldness to you, Callidora. I enjoy this. I cannot wait to help you find your way with the Children of the Sea."

Ivy struggled against the restraints. She remembered the bodies of Fil and Agnes; were they alive? She had no way of knowing. She recalled how the magicians had attacked her and Egan.

"I won't! I don't belong here! I want... I want to go home!"

"Ah, child. You will come to understand the path. You will grow to love a world in which we can use our gifts – gifts given to us by the gods. We can share a harmonious world."

Ivy tried to scream, but the blonde man silenced her with a wave of his hand.

"Listen now, child." He walked to the door and opened it. "I shall return for you in a moment."

For a second, Ivy could see a corridor leading to a larger cavern, well-lit by torches. The door closed, and Ivy was alone again with her dark thoughts.

I need Mother. Either one. I need someone... I can't be alone.

She thought of her island – of the morning she saw the sunrise with Sapphir. She'd been kicking a rock, ignoring the beauty.

I was hungry... I think I wanted figs. Or I was waiting for Cy to wake up.

Sapphir had asked her if she was happy.

I was. Why did I ever want to leave?

Suddenly, the honeyed voice echoed into her small cave. It was curiously magnified, so Ivy couldn't tell where it originated.

"Children, which of you would like to awaken your newest brother? He came to us today, all the way from Helike."

Rustling chairs and strange voices overlapped. The children that spoke had little excitement in their voices, though their words were jubilant.

"Oh, Father! I would be honored."

"Father let me. I can't wait to meet our new brother!"

The speaking subsided, and footsteps rang against stone. The man must have chosen someone. Nearly a minute passed before a girl began to recite.

"Brother, for far too long you have lived in darkness. Now, you will be shown the true light of the Golden Age. You will be born into this ocean, a Child of the Sea, a chosen Son of Poseidon."

Ivy heard a clap.

Then a final voice spoke – one she recognized, though it sounded monotonous. It was joyless.

"Thank you, sister."

Cy!

Ivy struggled harder with her binding. The cave spun. Cy was *here*. He was close. She could find him if she could just. Get. Free. Ivy felt all of her magical energy shoot through her fingers and toes. A faint *CRACK* sounded, and she stopped, breathing hard.

She rose slowly. The restraints had vanished.

Cy, I'm coming!

Ivy pushed on the door gently. It was unlocked. She crept through the tunnel, silent as a fish in water.

It didn't matter that Cy wasn't her real brother; she loved him as if he were. She would not lose him when she knew he was so close.

I'll be there, Cy! Trust me!

The huge cavern was marked by a ring of torches. Silvery moonlight seeped through cracks between the stalactites. She could tell that smaller caves radiated from this central room.

It was empty.

Where did the man go? Where is everyone else?

Ivy inched along, staying close to the wall and the shadows. She had to stop herself from gasping when she saw a bony man, whose grey hair glinted in the moonlight. He looked like a skeleton, withered and ancient. He stood inside one of the cozier caves.

That must be it!

Ivy could hear muffled whispers and the shuffling of scrolls. She closed her eyes. There was one spell that could help her sneak through unnoticed, though she had never tried it on her own.

She racked her brains, sifting through old memories. Somewhere in there, she had the words to the spell.

Just like Mother... Sapphir... did in the mountains... I can do it! I have to... for Cy!

She was less than ten feet from the old man; she could now hear the children's voices clearly.

I can!

"How did you come to find Father, Damien?"

No!! That's Cy! Not Damien!

"I had been living on a farm. Father found me there."

The sound of his vacant tone almost made Ivy cry once more.

No, he took you, Cy! Don't you realize that!

"I'm very thankful for Father. And excited to meet you all."

I need to save him. I need to get to him!

Ivy focused all her energy on finding the words to that spell. She clenched her fists, scrunched her forehead, and...

A cold breeze moved through her. Ivy looked down at her hands. They weren't there. She slipped past the old man. He seemed to notice the faintest movement of the air.

But he made no indication that he could see her.

I can do it. I can grab Cy and go find the others. I need them.

She stuck to the side of the room. She could see that desks were fit snugly in the comfortable cave. The room was filled with children, whose eyes stared blankly at the boy sitting in the front of them. A scroll was unraveled at each desk.

They're magicians... all of them... like me.

Cy perched on a stool. The room was dim, but she could see his wiry frame and blonde hair.

The tall man stood beside him. He almost looked like he could be Cy's father, with the same blonde hair and slender frame. But she knew he was not. He was cruel – and his eyes told a different story than Cy's.

And Mother is not Cy's real mother.

"Very good, Damien. I am so pleased that you are eager to be one of us. Were you raised with any brothers and sisters of your own?"

He knows the answer! He knows Cy grew up with me and Celia and Maya and Egan! Even if we aren't his real siblings!

"No."

The response was a stab in the heart to Ivy. Did Cy believe that she wasn't family to him – perhaps not by blood... but did they not share a bond?

"A sad, sad tale. Well, now here you are! One of many Children. Look upon your brothers and sisters! And there are more like them! Many more."

Ivy was close enough now that she could see Cy's blue eyes. The light was dim, but even so, Ivy could tell that they weren't the same. There was no life in them. They saw, but they did not perceive.

Oh... Cy... what did they do to you?

She reached for him, prepared to fight off any of the children in the cave if it meant she and Cy could escape.

I shouldn't have left the island... explored with Maya... gone looking for that bear with... This is all my fault... but I can fix it!

"And look at this!" the man exclaimed, startling Ivy. "Another one of our new talents! See Children... this sort of young ability is exactly what we must all strive for."

Ivy backed away quickly. It was too late. She felt the bony ribs of the old man as he grasped her. His grip was shockingly strong, despite his apparent frailty.

"Bring her here, Gerros."

Wordlessly, the old man walked Ivy to the front of the room. She couldn't find her voice to cry out. The invisibility charm wore off completely by the time the old man passed her to his blonde leader.

"Thank you. You do remind me of my own daughter, child. You have the same bravery."

"Cy," Ivy whispered, "Cy, it's me. It's Ivy."

The boy turned to her; his blue eyes were blank. There was no recognition.

"Damien only remembers his true brothers and sisters now," the old man, Gerros, said. "The poisons of his past have been remedied."

"Cy..."

"Now, Callidora. Look at me, Callidora."

No... I'm Ivy! He called me Ivy before!

Ivy looked at the blonde man, glaring fiercely into his purple eyes. Golden flakes danced within the purple.

"Good." He turned to the room. "Children! Here is your new sister! Callidora. She, too, has joined us from Helike. Give her a warm greeting."

"Callidora!"

"Sister!"

Similar greetings resonated in the small cave. Ivy's bones

turned to water. The blonde man looked back at her – the father of her false mother.

He's going to make me forget... just like he made Cy forget me!

"Callidora, for far too long you have lived in darkness."

I can't forget. I don't want to forget. I don't want to be Callidora.

"Now, you will be shown the true light of the Golden Age."

Ivy couldn't open her mouth to protest; she couldn't run.

"You will be born into this ocean..."

Mother...

"...a child of the Sea..."

The blonde man smiled.

"...a chosen Daughter of Poseidon."

Epilogue

The rank odor of shit and urine was oddly comforting in the cells below the Palace of Helike.

At least it's consistent.

A little over a week prior, Xander had thought himself free of the war. He had fought bravely at the Battle at the Beach. He had nearly died for his city. What more could they ask of him?

The city, apparently, did not feel that he'd done enough. As soon as he sought freedom – as soon as he was prepared to return to his normal life as a smith and be with Melani again – Boura responded.

I always hated Sir Farlen.

Xander had cursed his leg dozens of times. If his wound hadn't been so profound, he could have fended off all of Sir Farlen's men. It wouldn't have been easy, but Xander preferred it that way.

Damn my leg!

Instead, Xander found himself tucked in the farthest corner of the Heliken prison, with an empty cell to his left. He shared his own cell with two other men, and constantly admired the vacant one. There was scarcely room for a single person to sit comfortably – or even sit at all. Three full-grown soldiers of the Bouran army? That was laughable.

Xander was keenly aware of every body part that pressed against him.

A few torches kept the prison dimly lit. Occasionally, rats scurried through the iron bars, scratching their way over Xander's legs and arms. It was always the exact same amount of unsettling.

"Move your arm, Jace," his cellmate, Bryon said. "It's too damn close to my pecker."

"Who says pecker, anyway?"

"I dunno, Jace, just move it."

"Say it like a normal person. Then maybe I'll–"

"Do as he says," Xander snapped.

Jace grumbled and shifted his arm. Bryon grunted a thank you. The two were not the worst company Xander could have asked for. Jace was farmer, whose plucky attitude outsized his short stature. The other, Bryon, was a rugged man who harvested timber. Strangely, both were missing a finger on their left hands.

Bryon's missing finger was the result of an old axe wound, while Jace's had been lost during the Battle at the Beach. Jace had boasted about this briefly, before finally sharing that he'd cut it off on his own while drawing his blade.

"They don't warn you about that, but they should. It's wickedly sharp coming out of the scabbard."

Xander wished they'd met under different circumstances. He found them both mildly entertaining. Like most men who'd fought at the beach, Jace and Bryon were not trained fighters – merely recruited to fight Ucalegon's war.

This fact had not bothered Xander as much until he was on the beach, covered in blood that was both his own and others'. He had even crossed blades with the Golden Spear. Rather, he had taken a few stabs at him while the great hero batted him away with his famous weapon.

Xander had long admired the Golden Spear. He had been pained to hear of the man's death and felt monstrously guilty. Spending several days with the councilor's family made it worse. If he could have reversed the course of time and fought again, he would have steered well-clear of the Golden Spear.

I would've tried not to harm anyone, in fact... it was not my place to kill another man... just for living in another city.

All the stories that Xander had learned as a boy revolved around heroic warriors. Achilles and Hector, Jason and Perseus... all of them had been willing to battle monsters and other men without remorse.

Was Achilles mournful after defeating Hector?

Xander couldn't remember just then. Either way, he had been compelled to fight for his city, simply because it was *his* city. He had not considered why the war was being fought, and which injustices he rebelled against.

It was a rich person's war – for power that would only be enjoyed by a few men and women.

After Sir Farlen had plucked him from the road Xander had learned the truth of it all. The Battle at the Beach had been a facsimile. Only a few thousand Bouran soldiers had been sent to fight a platoon of Helikens three times its size.

Xander had found this disconcerting at the time; but once again, he did not rebel. They were merely a diversion to allow Parex the Hammer the chance to defeat a fractured Heliken force... it was logical.

This reasoning was far from accurate.

We were puppets, moved about on the largest, bloodiest stage in the world.

The Helikens triumphed at the beach, though they lost their greatest commander. Days later, the Bourans and Helikens were at peace; Ucalegon sat on the Council, with more territory and power than ever.

And the soldiers from the beach... the men, brave and cowardly, who'd been coerced into fighting a war? They rotted in the prison alongside Xander.

We were somehow painted as the only enemies of Helike... the only ones who have to prove our value and loyalty.

The sound of soldiers descending the staircase made each prisoner stir.

"S-s-soldiers of Boura!" the familiar stuttering call of Parex the Hammer drew everyone's attention, "S-s-stand at attention!"

Jace and Bryon muttered curses as they stumbled over each other to stand, hoisting Xander up along with them. A row of soldiers, both Bouran and Heliken, stood to Parex's right. Three more broke off from his left, dragging a tattered man in an oversized robe towards the empty cell near Xander.

"It is our p-p-pleasure to share that y-you will have the ch-chance to redeem yourselves to our n-new city."

Shouts of anger arose from some of the defeated prisoners.

"We were following orders, Hammer! *Your* orders!"

"What do we have to prove!? Soldiers that fought for our city... we've already shown loyalty!"

They're right, Parex. But not enough are willing to speak up about it.

"S-s-silence!" Parex demanded.

The Hammer preferred for his battle-axe to do the talking.

An axe that I *created.*

"H-Hira. Explain the r-r-rest."

A smattering of heckles jabbed at the Hammer as the dungeon quieted. A thin man stepped forward. It was hard to make out his features in the gloom. Meanwhile, the ragged man in the oversized robe was thrown roughly into the cell beside Xander.

"Filthy assassin," the Heliken spat at him.

Hira spoke. "Brave soldiers from the beach. I saw you battle; I saw you fight valiantly for your people. However, we are a *new* Helike now. And our peace is reliant on total compliance from both cities. Both militaries."

He waited for protests to die down.

"Now! Thankfully, you all have the chance to prove your loyalty to this new Helike... this new *vision* for Achaea."

The tattered prisoner breathed quietly. He emanated fury.

"A united force... 2,500 Bourans... and 2,500 Helikens. Led by myself and Boura's own Sir Farlen, will join the mighty Persians on the field of battle against Egypt! Imagine the glory! Imagine the stories told of you and your fellow man! *We* shall take down an EMPIRE! *We* shall be among those that topple the most ancient society known to this world. Then... *we* shall conquer Achaea... alongside our Persian allies."

I just want to go home to Melani. Have a nice plate of eggs. Fall asleep beside her.

"And YOU hundreds from the Beach shall lead this charge!"

Xander could tell that the tension in the dungeon was waning. It was human nature to thirst for glory, and these Bouran prisoners were no exception. They longed to redeem themselves after the humiliation on the beach.

Fools... it is still the same war! The same! It is ALL the same!

"Bourans! It is time... to fight! It is time to WIN the League and bring peace and unity to our home!"

Some cheers came as a response; other men, mostly those who were injured or sick, griped at the prospect of more violence. Still more, like Xander, who knew the choice was out of their hands, simply remained silent. They would fight for the Council and risk their lives... or there would be no life to live in their prison beneath the palace.

"There it is, Jace. We're dead now. What do ya say, Xander?"

Xander chuckled at the merciless irony, "I say you might be right."

The oversized robes shook as the man beside them leapt to his feet.

"Xander?"

Xander must have been imagining it. He blinked and pushed Jace aside until he was pressed against the iron bars.

It can't be!

He squinted in the dim light. He would have recognized his older brother's lithe shape and hawkish face anywhere.

How could I have missed it?

"Riz... Rizon?"

"Melani's going to be furious," Rizon Atsali said, pulling Xander towards him, until both were poised in an awkward hug around the metal bars.

"Who is it Xander?" Jace asked.

Xander ignored him.

"How... why are you..."

"I think it's his friend," Bryon postulated.

"Shut it, you two," Xander snarled, before looking back at Rizon. "What do you mean about Melani? Have you seen her? Is she okay?"

The memory of her face was so deeply imprinted in his mind.

It was all he saw when he closed his eyes – the shape of her nose; the exact distance between her eyes; the way strands of her hair escaped their companions.

And our child... I need to get home to my daughter. Or son... whatever it may be. I need to be a proper father to our child.

Rizon laughed, "Yes, brother... yes, I saw her. I like that one, Xander. I really do."

"It's his brother," Bryon amended.

"Ah, smart!" Jace exclaimed.

Both quailed under the look Xander shot at them.

"Tell me when. What happened?"

"It's quite a long story, brother." He pointed towards the soldiers unlocking cells, and binding prisoners to a series of ropes. "And I'm afraid, we don't have much time."

No! They can't be taking us now!

"Well, shorten it, then! Why are you here? In this prison? I mean... you know why *I* am."

Jace and Bryon muttered to themselves, but they knew not to interrupt.

"No reason to hide the truth from you any longer," he sighed. "I was a Fisherman, Xander. Being a regular soldier... it wasn't enough for me... I don't know why..."

"You always were the better fighter. And smarter."

"I don't know about that." Rizon shook his head. "If I were smart, I would've stayed well away from them."

The sound of iron locks opening made Xander tense.

How much time do I have with him?

"I did bad things, Xan. I stole. I spied... I killed"

"I have too," Xander murmured.

"No. Not like me. And it finally caught up to me. The last one..."

Xander could hear the shame in his brother's voice. What had compelled him to pursue that life? Xander wouldn't have even known how to find his way into an elite organization like the Fishermen.

That's how talented Rizon is.

"They're going to execute me, brother. I thought you should know before you leave."

Jace and Bryon gasped. Xander was speechless.

"Melani and I. We searched for you. We went to Boura and to Patras. Then back here, to Helike. We thought we'd find you in the prison," he laughed. "Then an old friend, Nicolaus, told me he saw you. Going back to Boura."

"Nic... yeah, he took care of me. Kind of. He saved me from the battle."

"That little guy? Oh, Xander... you must be even worse a fighter than I remember."

"Oh, go to Hades, Rizon."

He paused. The innocent quip hung in the air.

"And here I am. And here you are. Melani went back to Boura, as Nicolaus suggested. That was before they caught me."

"How did they find you? When did you see Nic? An old

friend?"

Two soldiers, armed with short swords, stood outside Xander's cell.

"No time, brother."

"No! Rizon, come with us! Come fight…"

"That there's the assassin of Councilor Euripides. Don't speak with him," one of the soldiers commanded.

He looped a section of the long rope around Jace's wrists, then Bryon's. They were connected to a long line of the other hundreds of Bouran men from the Battle at the Beach.

Assassin… of that councilor!

Xander looked at his brother. Rizon held his head down, like a sick puppy. He didn't see a villainous assassin. He only saw his brother.

"Rizon… no…"

"Let me go, Xander. Do it for Melani, not me. Fight for your freedom. For her."

Xander pulled his hands away from the soldier, who barged into the cell.

"Come on, Bouran. We have to get you on these ships. There's no time for this. No use resisting."

Rizon… is this really the last time I'll see him? After so long… after worrying… and wondering.

"Rizon, I can't just leave you. My brother."

"Get out, don't be stupid. My fate is sealed… I deserve this. Xan… I do."

Xander didn't have the strength to stop the two soldiers as they grabbed his broad shoulders and pulled him from the cell. They tied his hands together roughly. He felt himself tugged towards the stairs behind the line of bound soldiers.

"Rizon!"

"Oh... Mother and Father are well, brother. Safe. I made sure of that... before...."

"Rizon..." Xander's voice cracked as it turned to a whisper.

Rizon bared his teeth... a wolfish grin.

"Live happily with your woman, Xan. Tell Melani... tell her I got my final chance to say goodbye."

A Preview of:

The Fall of

Helike

Book Three of The Secrets of Achaea

Coming soon...

Prologue

Clouds threatened the small township of Rhium. Rainy nights didn't usually frequent the area this early in the Fall. Such weather was reserved for winter. A single drop fell.

Father always said Zeus refuses to cooperate when you need him most.

Cerius drew up his hood. The red stone marked the rugged shack, just as Icaria had claimed. Cerius wished she could have joined him tonight. It was lonely to range without a companion.

Lonely and dangerous.

However, this sort of work was not uncommon in the League's Guard. Though its fame may have waned long before the Peloponnesian Wars, Guardians were still tasked with protecting Achaea.

Even when it doesn't know it needs protecting.

Cerius' family had not appreciated his rushed departure from Helike. Of course, they all assumed he was motivated by some dream of glory and heroism – another young boy longing to be Perseus or Achilles.

Except for Mother... she understands.

Not even his father – not even the famed Golden Spear – forgave him. Perhaps he should have written to Rosie. But it was no use. He could never truly explain that Helike was no longer safe for him – that her children were still alive, and only he could find them.

A raindrop landed on his boot. How long had he been standing by the red stone?

I should have written Father.

Cerius pushed lightly on the door. It swung open. He ducked his head to enter. Even in the dusky room, he could see the dried blood that swallowed the figure on the ground. He clicked his tongue.

Not cleanly done.

There was nothing remarkable about the man. His head was shaven, and he looked rotund; if his skin had once held any color, it was now entirely gaunt. But it was certainly him.

Everything is familiar.

Well, most everything. A dark scar ran the length of the man's neck, cut just shallow enough to bring about a slow death. A painful death.

Not even a Fisherman deserves this.

The League's Guard and the Fishermen crossed paths more often than Cerius wished. For a group that boasted complete secrecy, cracks had begun to form well before the botched assassination of Euripides.

He took two paces back, taking in every detail of the scene. The room was simple enough; an overturned chair, a bed... there was nothing extravagant to suggest that it was a haven for important people. He ran his hand over a gouge in the wall.

A blade?

Someone had buried a knife deep opposite the bed – recently judging by the keen edge of the splintered wood. The dead man was contorted in an odd fashion.

He either collapsed this way or was moved after death.

Unfortunately, there was not much else to be learned. Their contact was indeed, dead. Whether he'd been discovered by the Fishermen, or finished off by an old client, the Guardians would need a new man amongst the fish.

Icaria will not be pleased.

Just as Cerius was preparing to leave, he paused. Crouching, he slipped a hand to his waist, feeling the light leather scabbard.

Were those footsteps?

He waited.

Outside, the rain had stopped completely. Cool air made its way through the cracks in the wall, and the sky had finished its transition to darkness.

After minutes that seemed much longer, Cerius shifted. He drew himself to his full height, stooping once more to pass through the doorway.

If the rain had continued, he would not have heard the gentle *WHOOSH* of the first arrow. As it was, he had just enough time to twist in the narrow doorframe.

It took all his effort not to scream. The hooked arrowhead buried itself in his abdomen, below his right arm. Cerius toppled backwards into the room, collapsing in a heap next to Matis. Breathing laboriously, he kicked the door shut and tore off his hood.

It doesn't matter if they see my face now...

It took him a moment to realize that a second arrow had thudded in wall behind him. Gritting his teeth, Cerius crawled to the door, crouching beside it. The room offered no true cover.

I should have never come alone.

Creaking in its rusty hinge, the door inched open. From the light footsteps, Cerius guessed that his attackers numbered two.

Is this how he went?

His breath rattled. The door was half open. Cerius could feel the barbs in the arrow pressing against his lungs.

Father. Is this...?

His leather was soaked.

I should have written Father.

A large boot stepped through. Cerius pressed himself against the wall, urging his mind not to lose focus. He could still fight. He could still stand a chance if he could just think of the words....

I should have written, Father.

Cerius closed his eyes. His body began to grow warmer. The

pain was constant, but it was slowing. In the distance, he could still hear the two figures. They stood above him, admiring their kill.

Soon, I'll be able to explain.

Then they fell. In the shadows, he saw a third form... a more *familiar* form. She reached down with her one arm.

"You'll never stop needing your mother, will you, Cerius?"

Acknowledgements

Here are my thank yous for this book. There is a recurring pattern with the last one.

My editor, Francie Futterman, for being very timely and fixing some grammatical errors that I will probably never stop making.

My illustrator, Aven Jones, for illustrating – which is something I still cannot do. She is talented.

My readers: Elise Vincent, Allie Schneider, and Will Cytron for reading this and giving me only positive feedback (who needs criticism!?).

About the Author

Theodore Jacob "Teddy" Vincent is currently a Knowledge Engineer (this title means nothing to most people) working at Amazon. *The Children of the Sea* is the second installment of *The Secrets of Achaea* book series, documenting a fictional (probably) history of the First Achaean League, a largely forgotten part of Ancient Greek History. Theodore is from St. Louis, Missouri, and currently lives in New York City in his tiny apartment. He misses his dog.

Printed in Great Britain
by Amazon